Killin

Killing for Klimt

A Megan Crespi Mystery Series Novel

Alessandra Comini

SUNSTONE
PRESS

SANTA FE

Sunstone books may be purchased for educational, business, or sales promotional use. For information please write: Special Markets Department, Sunstone Press, P.O. Box 2321, Santa Fe, New Mexico 87504-2321.

Book and Cover design › Vicki Ahl
Body typeface › Bernard Modern
Printed on acid-free paper
∞
eBook 978-1-61139-281-4

Library of Congress Cataloging-in-Publication Data

Comini, Alessandra, author.
  Killing for Klimt : a Megan Crespi mystery series novel / by Alessandra Comini.
    pages cm. -- (Megan Crespi mystery series)
  ISBN 978-1-63293-006-4 (softcover : alk. paper)
  1. Murder--Investigation--Fiction. 2. Art thefts--Investigation--Fiction. 3. Mystery fiction. I. Title.
  PS3603.O477K55 2014
  813'.6--dc23
                        2014019840

WWW.SUNSTONEPRESS.COM
SUNSTONE PRESS / POST OFFICE BOX 2321 / SANTA FE, NM 87504-2321 /USA
(505) 988-4418 / ORDERS ONLY (800) 243-5644 / FAX (505) 988-1025

To Charlotte,
Jim, and Carl
for believing in this book

1

"Damn!"

An agile seventy-seven, Megan Crespi managed not to fall directly on the corpse blocking the dark doorway to her best friend's remote house outside Santa Fe.

Letting her roller bag go and scrambling to get up and switch on the porch light, she shouted to her hostess who was still unloading the back of the Subaru, "Claire! There's something blocking the door! I think it's a body!"

"A *body*?" Claire Chandler asked in disbelief. "Animal or human?"

"No," cried Megan, "I'm serious! It's bulky. I almost fell right on it. And it smells to high heaven. Come look."

It was nine o'clock on an early May night, cool, and very dark despite the now illuminated entryway. The electronic dog motion detector just inside the front door had been activated by Megan's arrival and its deep barks and staccato yelps filled the air.

"For heaven's sake," breathed Claire, as she made a rapid advance toward the front porch, now bathed in a ghoulish electric light that magnified the dark shadows on either side. "It *is* a body! A *human* body!"

The two women froze as they stared with disbelief at the rotting corpse of what looked to be an elderly woman. She was lying face down. Next to her was an upturned plastic watering can.

"My god, let's get inside and call the police," urged Megan, pulling her friend back from the body. Nodding silent assent and beginning to shiver from revulsion and shock, Claire followed Megan around to the back door.

Once inside, Megan ran to the dog alarm and turned it off, then hurried to the land line telephone in the kitchen. There was a panic button on the phone marked with a red cross. She knew about it because once Claire had inadvertently touched it and within minutes a police car had appeared in the driveway, a record response out in this Las Dos section of high desert. Now Megan hit the panic button on purpose and, speaking crisply to the voice that answered, she reported their find.

"Don't touch anything," the voice on the other end of the line calmly instructed. "We won't," Megan replied, "just please get someone out here as fast as you can."

She found she was becoming calmer as the minutes passed, whereas Claire was beginning to buckle under the horrific specter of their discovery at her own home, Still Point, the vacation home she and her husband had built together thirty years earlier.

"Sit down, dear," urged Megan, alarmed on behalf of her agitated friend.

Claire did so, then asked in a hushed voice, *"Do you think this could have anything to do with the Klimt?"*

2

"But no one knows about the Klimt except *us*," mused Megan.

Although arriving in New Mexico a few days later than they had originally planned, due to an air-conditioning breakdown at Megan's Dallas home, she had eagerly agreed to come out to Claire's calming, T. S. Eliot-inspired "still point of the turning world."

Megan needed a quiet place to sort things out about the startling discovery she had made just one week earlier in Vienna. It was a discovery she felt she could not reveal to any of her colleagues at the international art symposium there, as one of them might plausibly have been involved in a decades-old cover-up.

But *who*, she wondered, once again mentally picturing the guests. They included fellow art historians, museum directors, art dealers, gallery owners, and former students, all present at the closing ceremony honoring Megan's life work.

Megan had been in Austria only a week this time, hardly long enough to have become involved in yet another imbroglio concerning the main subjects of her work, Vienna's master of Art Nouveau, Gustav Klimt, and his Expressionist protégé, Egon Schiele.

Klimt's elegant oil portraits, enigmatic allegories, and beautiful landscapes were proud possessions of a legion of museums and dedicated private collectors. And they were only rarely on the market. When they were, the bidding prices began in the millions of dollars. Klimt's gold, busily byzantine 1907 portrait of Adele Bloch-Bauer was a famous example. Now in New York's exquisite Moderne Galerie Museum of German and Austrian Art, it had fetched a stunning $135 million dollar figure in 2006. At that time it was the highest price ever paid for a painting.

What Megan had chanced upon in Vienna was a horrendous secret involving theft, fraud, and deception. The story was blurted out to her by a grandnephew of Klimt, Hans Ernst Klimt. She had known him for many decades and had just visited him in the Vienna General Hospital a few days before his death.

"It haunts me, *ach*, how it haunts me!" he had cried out to her suddenly.

"What are you talking about?" murmured Megan apprehensively, alarmed by the old man's palpable dread.

"*Ach*, what they did to cover up the shame!" he wailed in response.

"What shame, what do you mean?" pressed Megan.

"The robbery!" he rasped, "the robbery!"

Megan instantly remembered how she had begun her 1975 monograph on Klimt with just such an event: "On a chilly thirteenth of January in the year nineteen eighteen, in Vienna, burglars broke into a painter's studio while its owner was away and helped themselves to its contents."

Supplying a photograph of the two large unfinished canvases in place at Klimt's Hietzing studio at the time of his death in February of 1918, Megan's text continued:

> One thing they did not take, but at the sight of which they must have paused in amazement, was a large, unfinished canvas on an easel next to the studio windows. For here, even to the uninitiated, was an extraordinary revelation of what might be called a "dirty old master"

technique. In opposition to the floating knot of figures covering the left side of the canvas, the splayed-out nude body of a young girl dominated the other half. Her face was averted in a profile turn to the right, and a mufflerlike wrap at the throat seemed to separate the head from its glimmering white torso, creating a startling effect of mutilation. The knees were bent and the legs spread apart to expose a carefully detailed pubic area upon which the artist had leisurely begun to paint an overlay "dress" of suggestive and symbolic orna-mental shapes.

Megan's text offered further details:

The painting was called *The Bride*, and the absent owner of the studio was Gustav Klimt, who two days before had been felled by a stroke as he was dressing for his morning stroll to the Tivoli gardens for breakfast. Paralyzed on his right side, he was hospitalized and kept alive for a few weeks, but pneumonia set in and he died on the sixth day of February at the age of fifty-five. The unfinished paint-ing, by the mere fact that it was unfinished, contained the clue to the erotic premise of Klimt's great allegories involving female figures. The unknown ransackers of the studio had, by sheer accident, caught the artist in the secret and revelatory act of flagrant voyeurism.

"Unknown ransackers?" Did Klimt's grandnephew know *who* had been the ransackers of almost a century ago? Gently, Megan queried the dying man: "Hans Ernst, are you, are you talking about the robbery of Klimt's atelier?"

"Yes!" he moaned, "yes! They were hired to remove the *secret* panel— the Secretum."

"What secret panel?" Megan asked, astonished at the idea there could be an unaccounted-for major work of art in the artist's well-documented oeuvre. But the fatally ill man had no more breath to talk. He merely lay jabbing with one hand at the unsettling vision that held his wild-eyed, silent stare.

* * *

On the long flight back to the States from Austria, Megan had racked her brains as to what subject a panel by Klimt could have addressed, when it might have been painted, early or later in his career, and why it was "secret." No answers were forthcoming. If the panel had been stolen in order to be sold, where was there any record or evidence of such a transaction? It might have been a surreptitious arrangement, a secret kept over decades. Could one of Klimt's siblings or perhaps one of his wealthy collectors or even one of his fellow artists have known about and coveted the mystery panel?

If the artwork had been taken merely for the private delectation of a relative or collector, what was the subject matter that made it desirable enough to hire burglars to abscond with it? Was it a portrait? Was it an erotic motif? Or could one of Klimt's densely populated, palpitating land-scapes have been the target? Another possible candidate could be one of the artist's riveting allegories, possibly with autobiographical content.

But why "secret panel"? Could the subject matter reveal such a secret that someone would have wanted to suppress any knowledge of the panel's existence as Klimt lay dying?

Perhaps, if the panel were, presumably, a portrait, it might have been an image of the very person who commissioned the burglary. Or that person's husband? Klimt was known for his iconic, flattering portraiture of women, but not of men.

Fräulein Friedericke ("Fritzi") Maria Beer was one of the women Klimt had famously celebrated in paint. She had been portrayed first by Schiele in 1914, shown suspended vertically in an existential void. Back in the early 1960s she had told Megan that when she approached Klimt in 1916 to have him paint her as well, the artist's brusque response was: "Why do you want another portrait when you've already been painted by a very good artist?"

"Because you will immortalize me," was Fritzi's nimble answer.

And immortalize Klimt's portraits did: witness the enduring fame of his Adele Bloch-Bauer portraits. And he painted yet a second one of her in 1912.

So the subject of any stolen or "suppressed" portrait would most likely have been a woman. And unlike Schiele's prolific self-portrayals, Klimt was not known ever to have depicted himself.

In a rare statement entitled "Commentary on a Non-Existent Self-Portrait," Klimt himself had in fact said: "I have never painted a self-portrait. I am less interested in myself as a subject for a painting than I am in other people, above all women. Whoever wants to know something about me...ought to look carefully at my pictures."

There was one exception, however, one which Megan had in fact first published at the end of her monograph on the artist: a small self-caricature of a web-footed scrotum topped by the artist's bearded and tufted balding head. In this humorous drawing Klimt's Eros-centered conception of the world was deftly and humorously encapsulated.

What about Klimt's longtime "platonic" companion and unmarried sister-in-law, the fashion dress designer Emilie Flöge of the once famous Flöge Sisters Salon? Had she been involved in the theft? Hardly likely, as she had the keys to his studio and in fact was the one trusted by Klimt's heirs to dispose of his belongings.

But was Emilie perhaps the subject represented in the secret panel? Shown in the nude, possibly? Klimt's 1902 elegantly garbed portrait of his "eternal love," presenting a body-filling swell of repeated decorative and symbolic motifs, was a tour de force of exterior environment posited as interior definition. It was closely akin to Freud's contemporaneous exploration of subconscious feelings made manifest in dream symbolism.

And, a "panel" was unusual for Klimt, except for his University allegories. He ordinarily worked on stretched canvases of portrait dimensions. If it had been stolen only in order to keep it from public knowledge, then its subject matter might well have been erotically scandalous. That would have been a good reason for Emilie to suppress it, if indeed it was of her. But then why the burglars, since she had free access to Klimt's studio? Emilie was in a position simply to remove an offending image herself.

Or could the stolen secret panel not have been a portrait at all, but indeed an allegory? An allegory like the artist's ceiling panels (actually oils on canvas) created for the auditorium of the University of Vienna at the turn of the last century. Commonly known as the University panels, they represented the realms of Philosophy, Medicine, and Jurisprudence. But outraged critics complained that the "pornographic" female nudes floating overhead throughout the allegories were, to say the least, distracting. Klimt ultimately bought back the panels in the face of such heated indignation.

Perhaps such a panel had survived destruction when, in May of 1945, in the face of advancing Russian soldiers, retreating German troops in Lower Austria near the Czech border had purposefully set fire to Schloss Immendorf.

This was the castle where at least thirteen known Klimt paintings had been hidden. They belonged to one of the artist's major Jewish patrons, the Wilhelm and Sara Leatherer family. Included were five magnificent "mosaicked" landscapes, allegories, a few portraits including a fantasy one, *Schubert at the Piano*, and the three infamous University panels.

Could it possibly be, then, that a panel related perhaps to those magnificent, brooding allegories was also at Schloss Immendorf and that somehow it had *not* burned up in the conflagration? Was that the secret about the secret panel? There was, after all, the fact that a few of the major Klimt works stored there and thought destroyed, had indeed miraculously shown up in the art market in the 1970s.

It was against all odds that the panels had survived. But an art loving former British MI 5 agent had tracked them down early in 1970 to where they had been secretly removed to an adjacent vineyard cellar prior to the Schloss fire.

The art world was still hopeful that others of the thirteen known Klimt works had been saved as well. Certainly every single nearby and distant vineyard had been thoroughly searched by Austrian government officials eager to turn up missing national treasures since the startling discovery of the preserved University panels. But so far, nothing.

Megan's meditations were interrupted by the sound of a siren coming up the winding gravel driveway of Claire's Las Dos home.

3

Claire hurried to the back door to meet the police van that was just pulling up to the house. Megan caught up with her and together they greeted their old friend and neighbor, a retired veterinarian turned local county sheriff, Terry Wright. His tall, strapping figure was a comfort to see.

"What's happened to you two gals?" he shouted across the drive, jumping out of his vehicle.

"There's either been an accident or a murder," blurted out Megan, while at the same time Claire cried, "A dead woman is lying across my front doorway."

Full of disbelief but cautious, Terry crossed over to the front entry, now bathed in additional light from his van's headlights. "What in god's name?" Terry breathed, squatting next to the corpse but touching nothing.

"Oh my god," cried Claire suddenly, "is that, could that be *Jayne!*"

A recent divorcee, Jayne Box was her nearest next door neighbor, although out at Las Dos that meant several acres distant.

"Aren't those the walking shoes and lavender sweats she often wears?" pressed Claire. Terry nodded slowly in dawning assent as they studied the rotting body lying next to an upturned green watering can.

"She must have come over to water the geraniums, as she does once a week when I'm away," explained Claire agitatedly.

"The question is, did she fall and hit her head," said Terry, "or did someone *hit* her?"

"Yes! And what was she doing at the front door?" pressed Claire. "She always enters through the back garage door, so as not to set off the dog alarm."

"Someone must have tried to follow her indoors or maybe they were already inside when she entered the house," mused Terry, looking around searchingly.

"But this must have happened days ago," whispered Claire to Megan, sickened by the thought that Jayne might not have been missed by anyone for several days in a row. Neighbors kept friendly track of one another out at Las Dos, although not necessarily by daily phone calls back and forth.

The Las Dosians were an independent lot on the whole. They continued the tradition of the two plucky pioneer women who in the 1920s homesteaded the acreage that made up the community of widely spaced private homes. Nowadays, Las Dosians kept track of each other simply by waving at a passing car recognized on the main road or bumping into a neighbor while out walking the hilly terrain searching for Indian artifacts.

The only neighbor who was likely to be really abreast of goings on at Las Dos was Paloma Sanchez, Claire's nearest neighbor to the west, toward the Jemez Mountains and Los Alamos. She and her beautiful German Shepherd dog Hazel roamed the neighborhood most mornings and afternoons, and often dropped in on Claire, when she was in residence.

After Terry placed a call to the Santa Fe police department to send out the crime scene investigation unit, he turned toward the two women.

"Claire? Megan? You two have had a quite a scare. I'm going to ask you to go back into the house now. You've had a frightening experience and you need to sit down. This front area is a crime scene now. I'll need to close things off," he commanded, moving purposefully ahead of the women through the garage where the back door stood open.

They entered the house through the spotless utility room, then into the narrow kitchen and banco-benched breakfast room. Nothing out of place, pronounced Claire provisionally. They proceeded carefully into the dining and living rooms with their high clerestory windows. Everything was as it had always been: the blond upright electric piano behind the inviting white sectional sofa facing the fireplace, and a large flat screen TV. The spacious front windows framed a view of the Sangre de Cristo mountains, still snow capped even at this time of the year, early May.

Then they stepped out into the long many-windowed, multi-glass-door corridor, justly called the solarium. In contrast to the bloody sight outdoors, eight pots of extravagantly blooming geraniums in various hues held sway. There was no sign of anyone having entered the house so far.

Terry thoroughly checked all the bedrooms while the women waited apprehensively. Nothing had been disturbed. He had the women confirm his finding. Then they gathered solemnly in the breakfast room to await the crime scene investigators. Terry looked concernedly and affectionately at his old friends. Dignified Claire, eighty-seven, mother of two, grandmother of five, author of two books on notable Santa Fe women, had nursed her Alzheimer's-afflicted husband for some seventeen years before becoming a widow. She often told Terry and others about the great joy Megan had brought into her life.

And Megan, ten years younger, petite and physically fit, had long been married to her teaching, lecturing, and publishing careers. Back in the 1960s she had helped raise the two adorable children of a colleague, Isabelle Emerson. And earlier, in 1956 as a graduate student at Vienna University, she had helped refugees of the Hungarian Revolution find new homes. And now, via e-mail, she continued to advise two generations of students. Jerry smiled at the fact that Megan still dyed her hair brown. For the benefit of her lecture audiences, she maintained.

After a long silence the three friends began to discuss how Jayne could have fallen. Yes, she had bad knees, two replacements in fact. But still a fall smack down onto her face like that? Could that have been fatal? Perhaps someone had approached the front door, setting off the electronic dog. Alerted that someone or something was outside, had Jayne opened the front door to check? Had she tripped and fallen while doing so? But surely if that were the case, the person at the door would have summoned help.

Not wanting to move the body, Terry had not checked to see whether the front door was locked or not. He did so, casting a glance at the now unplugged electric dog as he strode past it. The front door was unlocked. Terry thought long and hard. Suddenly he asked the women: "Weren't you two supposed to have been here three days ago?"

"Yes," confirmed Claire, "but Megan was delayed by an air-condition-er disaster so we only just now arrived. I haven't even brought in my suitcase yet."

Terry glanced at them both thoughtfully. "If Jayne wasn't killed by her own fall, one of *you* may have been an intended victim, not Jayne."

Claire was nonplussed. "What? One of *us*? But *why*?" Automatically, Terry and Claire both looked at Megan, the world traveler. An expression of shocked comprehension began slowly to spread over Megan's features and she gasped a bit, her hands in the air in front of her, warding off a dawning thought.

"Um, I think I need a strong drink," she said, rising to go to the kitchen. They all crowded into the little room and Claire opened a bottle of red wine, for she knew Megan considered a strong drink either Bailey's Irish Cream or sweet red wine. She herself settled for Scotch whiskey. Terry, on duty, drank nothing. When they were seated back in the breakfast room, Megan sipped her wine silently, deep in thought.

Finally she began to speak haltingly. "Um, Terry, I learned something unexpected in Vienna last month, something that apparently no one in the art world knows about. Because of that I discussed it with someone I probably shouldn't have talked to. It was in regard to an extremely rare work of art by Gustav Klimt and the possibility that it had been hidden in a private Swiss collection for decades."

"For decades?" Terry interrupted.

"Yes, And the plot thickens. I heard from my confidant that an unidentified art dealer had been given access to that Swiss collection upon the recent death of the last known member of the Leatherer family."

"Who was that?" asked Terry.

"The heiress was a retired flight attendant, totally uninterested in her great uncle's art. She was only too happy to receive the dealer's surprise offer to buy, sight unseen and at a very handsome price, the art contents of the Leatherer's bank vault. Gossip had it that the acquisitions were even more than had been hoped for, and that one of the major acquisitions was being shipped surreptitiously that very week to a collector in the U.S."

Megan took a deep breath. "And now, because my contact knew when I left him that I would be in hot pursuit of any Klimt that might have surfaced in the Leatherer collection sale-off, and because I'd mentioned to him that I was coming to Santa Fe, it is possible, as you suggest, Terry, that Jayne wasn't killed by a burglar at all.

"It was perhaps a case of mistaken identity."

4

Forty-nine years earlier, in the summer of 1963, Megan arrived in Vienna as a graduate student from Berkeley. She was the same age, twenty-eight, that Egon Schiele had been in 1918 when he died of the influenza epidemic at the end of World War I. She had discovered his riveting work at an exhibition held in the small Berkeley campus museum. It was a show organized by Professor Herschel Chipp of the University of California's art history department. Until that life-changing moment in the museum, Megan had only been interested in medieval art. In fact she was well on her way to writing a master's thesis on the beard of Christ as it appeared in early art.

But then, one look at an agonized Schiele Self-Portrait in which the young artist flailed out at the angst-filled void surrounding him, and Megan experienced an epiphany. Egon Schiele would be her scholarly life from now on, and she would simply have to get herself to Vienna as quickly as possible. With an Italian father who was only too pleased to fund his daughter's European odyssey, Megan was able to travel that very summer to Vienna.

Megan's first lucky discovery however was not about Schiele, but about Gustav Klimt. Curious to see if Schiele as a student had done any copy work at the famed Kunsthistorisches Museum, Megan was granted access to the museum's permission-to-copy records. Flipping back a few pages before Schiele's years at the Academy, she suddenly came upon the signature "Gustav Klimt" next to a request, dated 28 April 1885, to copy Titian's lustrous *Portrait of Isabella d'Este* of 1536.

Apparently no one had thought of consulting the Kunsthistorisches Museum's records for such a find, and Megan was only too happy to report it to Christian Nebehay, a friend whose acquaintance she had recently made. Owner of a respected Antiquariat book store and gallery on the nearby Annagasse, Christian was writing a Klimt Dokumentation book and so had taken a special and avuncular interest in Megan's own work. He provided her with suggestions and resources from his own private library as well as access to his rich collection of art, a collection which contained superb drawings by both Schiele and Klimt.

Soon Klimt became as much an object of interest for Megan as was Schiele. Eleven years later, after her dissertation-turned-book on Schiele's portraits was published and nominated for a National Book Award, one of the collector families whom she had come to know and love well, the Viktor and Dollie Fogarassy family of Graz, gave Megan an extraordinary congratulatory gift. It was a 1913 work in pencil and watercolor by Schiele showing him drawing Klimt.

Entitled *Erinnerung—Remembrance*, it addressed the rarified, monastic world into which both Klimt and Schiele often wished themselves vis-à-vis public life in a conniving, quarrelsome, gossip-prone Viennese society.

What a research reward! Later Megan would give the two-sided drawing (the verso contained a view of a rowboat, seen from above, and drawn without a single lift of the black chalk) to her own home-based Dallas Museum of Art. She wanted it to be shared with many more people than just students and friends.

The coupling of Schiele with Klimt in not only the Fogarassy drawing but in Megan's own continuing research placed the older artist firmly at the magnetic North point of her scholarly compass. In contrast to Schiele's many erotic drawings of nudes, often repellant in their angular gymnastics and staring, vacant eyes, Klimt's nude studies of women Megan found more sensuous with their fluid contours and controlled sense of self.

Christian Nebehay, whose father Gustav had been Klimt's dealer in Vienna, initiated Megan into the fascinating world of intrigue and underhanded goings-on that took place exponentially following Klimt's death. The artist's closest and most constant female confidant for the last twenty years of his life, Emilie Flöge, had presumably acted honorably, disposing of Klimt's household and painterly legacy according to the terms of his will. But there were other players in the artist's circle who had claims on Klimt's estate.

For example, no fewer than three of the artist's female models came forward to claim that they had had children by the artist. One son was identified: Gustav Ucicky, born to one of Klimt's longtime models. Born in 1898, this son lived until 1961, dying of a heart attack at the age of sixty-three. Years before that, his long-suffering wife had left him, taking with her their infant son Peter Ucicky.

Klimt's namesake had become very successful as a movie director, contributing to a number of films during World War II. He was known to have doggedly acquired a number of his father's works from Nazi-looted collections after the German invasion of Austria in 1938—the *Anschluss*—right up to the end of the war in 1945.

And he appears to have bought some of these gems from de-accessioned Jewish collections with an absolutely clear conscience.

5

Megan had been musing, staring unseeingly at Terry and Claire. Well, if Ucicky was involved with loot from the Klimt robbery he could only have been nine years old. Not much of a suspect. But what about his Prague-born mother, Maria? A possibility. She might have slipped into the artist's studio, or hired burglars. But how could that relate to the present? Quite a jump from an imperial Austria of 1918 to an unknown large Klimt artwork now in all likelihood on its way to the New World.

Megan had learned about this surprising possibility while in Vienna during the hasty conversation she had had with a private collector she had known for two years, Günther Winter. An attractive and fascinating man, he had recently opened an art gallery in downtown Vienna. And it was to him that Megan had, perhaps ill advisedly, discussed the secret panel affair revealed to her by Klimt's dying grandnephew.

Vastly wealthy, Günther was a most successful entrepreneur and private investor, with offices and employees spread out on two continents in multiple countries. He was also perhaps the world's most single-minded collector of art by the late Austrian artist Friedrich Hundertwasser. His whimsical, decoration-studded canvases of fanciful buildings and people were greatly indebted to Klimt's mosaic fills of decoration as content. Indeed Megan had once remarked upon this to an enthusiastically agreeing Hundertwasser upon their first meeting in Vienna, back in 1963. There had been a spirited, wide-ranging conversation in English about art, in which she sweetly but firmly corrected his addressing her as "Miss" to "Ms."

Now it suddenly occurred to her that along with all the Hundertwasser artworks Günther may have managed to snap up from the artist's estate, there might also have been a Klimt, since Hundertwasser was also a collector of the artist's works. Possibly the lost portrait of Sara Leatherer's mother. Or, oh! Could the secret panel Hans Ernst Klimt had talked about be among those works? This would not have been public knowledge since Hundertwasser kept his own collection absolutely private.

* * *

Just then the CSI unit arrived at Still Point and organized bedlam broke out as photographs and dustings for prints were meticulously taken all around the house, a still point no longer. Jayne's body was carefully removed to the ambulance after photographs had been taken of its position.

"I'm afraid you'll have to spend the night in town until the crime scene has been thoroughly gone over tomorrow in the daylight," Terry informed Megan and Claire. "The coroner will determine the time and cause of death and whether it was accidental or if it was inflicted by someone. And you know, considering the burglaries in this neighborhood last year, Jayne might well have caught someone in an attempted burglary," he added.

As per Terry's mandate, the two women settled into the Bishop's Lodge Hotel for the night. Megan voiced her most recent thoughts to Claire. "What I learned in Vienna about the secret panel doesn't seem to have anything directly to do with Gustav Ucicky, but it's possible his mother might have commissioned the robbery.

However, even if this were so, wouldn't whatever she got from the burglars have been passed on to her son when she died? The works Ucicky had acquired as an adult were all known and accounted for now by scholars. Nothing like a panel had ever been owned by him, only canvases and drawings."

Claire mulled this over, then asked: "And why would Klimt's grand-nephew have told you he was haunted by what they did to cover up what he called the 'shame?'"

"Yes," agreed Megan, "*what* was the shame? *Who* wanted to cover it up? And, regardless of all that ancient history, how does it add up to the here and now?"

"Well," quizzed Claire, "how come you've told me *what* the dying man said to you so dramatically in Vienna, but haven't identified *whom* you told about it when you were in Vienna for the symposium?"

"Because, Claire, I didn't think it was important until now, until just this evening," answered Megan somewhat shame-facedly, embarrassed by the fact she had indeed blurted out to Günther Winter about having learned of the possibility of a long missing, possibly unknown, artwork by Klimt.

"So, whom did you tell?" pressed Claire, warming to the subject.

"I'm ashamed to say it wasn't to a fellow art historian but to the Viennese man you and I met on our Antarctic cruise year before last, the man we found so simpatico, Günther Winter. You know, the hedge fund genius and big Hundertwasser collector. Now he's started up an art gallery and I wanted to encourage him, since he intends to handle Viennese art—Jugendstil, Expressionism, and contemporary."

"Oh, yes, of course I remember that very attentive and good looking man. What's the name of his gallery and where is it?"

"It's called *Kunst Vienna: Damals und Heute*, which means 'Art Vienna: Then and Now', and it's across the street from Christian Nebehay's Antiquariat on the Annagasse. It's in a prime location right in the middle of downtown Vienna."

"So do you think you can trust Günther Winter?"

"Well, I certainly *thought* he was trustworthy."

"Hmmm, *he* may be trustworthy, but what sort of people does he run around with. Who are *his* art connections?"

"Um, concerning that I *can* tell you something. Günther told me all about an extremely helpful American contact, an elderly art dealer who's lived in Vienna for decades, and who actually gave him the idea for opening the gallery. He was a GI during World War II and saw action in Europe.

"Seems that at the end of the war in 1945, he was detailed first to Germany, to Leipzig, I think. And then he was sent to Austria as part of the Allied occupation's attempt to restore lost works of art to their rightful owners. He fell in love with Vienna and never went back to the States. Now he's in his eighties. He married late in life, is a widower, but has a daughter and son who both also live in Vienna.

"I may even have caught sight of the daughter, as she now works at Christian Nebehay's Antiquariat, where I dropped in for old time's sake. Günther said the American ex-GI's name was Herring, something like Jeremy Herring. He…"

"Ha!" interrupted Claire with a twinkle in her wise blue eyes, "are you sure Günther wasn't feeding you a *red* herring?"

Megan moaned.

6

That same mild May day in Vienna, Günther Winter sat luxuriating in the large white bathtub that had once been Hundertwasser's.

It was situated outdoors on the roof of Otto Wagner's justly famous 1895 Ankerhaus, with its two-level glassed-in penthouse apartment overlooking downtown Vienna's Graben with its Pest Monument. A grassy corridor from the roof exit door led past a forest of television antennas to the far end of the roof where the outdoor bathtub stood.

There, just past the ribbed cupola of the building next door on the

Spiegelgasse, towered the steep, chevron-tiled roof and tall spire of Vienna's great cathedral, the Stefansdom, every tile clearly visible in sparkling detail.

Hundertwasser had enjoyed this view for many years, whenever he returned to Austria from his travels abroad to exotic locales, and now he, Günther Winter, owned it. In a bold and deft business deal, he had purchased the Ankerhaus right after the artist's death, keeping Hundertwasser's penthouse studio intact and visitors out, much to the complaint of local newspapers. Now he sat in blissful solitude on his—*their*—rooftop, surveying the city he so loved and so hated.

Hated, because so many Vienna museums seemed to conspire against him at every turn, bidding for the same artworks he wanted. Loved, because the city had produced not only a Friedrich Hundertwasser but also a Gustav Klimt. Günther had gone back to Hundertwasser's source—Klimt's decorative, symbolic mosaic fills of nature and people.

And now Klimt was his secret passion. When the Leatherer bank vault art contents were sold sight unseen by his last heir, it had been bought by a middleman, his American agent Jeremy Herring. Herring had been absolutely sure that the Leatherer collection would yield the suspected results, and he had been right.

There were not one, but two large Klimt artworks, both encased in individual liners. This was beyond their wildest dreams. The outside world must never know what they had found. The Klimts would be shipped out of Europe immediately. Thank god they were in Switzerland and not Austria. The Austrian government had severe restrictions concerning the export of national treasures abroad. And this trove was indeed, from the looks of it, a national treasure.

Of course, extreme measures had to be taken when the retired flight attendant, the Leatherer heir, was stirred up by sensationalist, speculative newspaper reports concerning the recent sale. She asked Jeremy Herring to see her great uncle's collection, even if it were not hers to view anymore. There was talk of instigating a lawsuit. Friends were urging her to annul the sale she had just authorized.

But then there was that fatal automobile accident. Klara Hubner had been killed by a hit and run driver while crossing an intersection in downtown Geneva. He must congratulate Jeremy Herring again.

A timely and well-executed death, thought Günther to himself as he gazed contentedly out over the Stefansdom to the far hills beyond. Life was good.

Then Günther moved with a jerk, splashing the water which had turned cold. Life *would* be good again once that Crespi woman had been taken care of, he brooded morosely. Why, oh why had he lost his cool and mentioned to her that something "colossal" was being shipped to America?

He knew that with her immense scholarly curiosity and dogged determination, Crespi would not stop until she found out by whom the colossal work was and if it might be the "shameful" Klimt about which she had told him the dying Hans Ernst Klimt had spoken so agitatedly. She had confided to Günther, and he, in a stupid, proud moment, had told her about a large *Sendung* to the States.

Well, Herring's son Thad should have taken care of the problem by now, even if he had to rush down from Alaska to Santa Fe.

1

In indifferent disobedience to the no smoking sign posted on his bedroom wall, Jeremy Herring's son Thad sat dragging on his fifth cigarette at the El Rey Motel on Cerrillos Road in Santa Fe.

Thad was a tall, thin, clean-shaven man in his early fifties with pale complexion and a beak nose. His long unkempt locks of black hair curled about the nape of his neck, defying an increasing baldness at the top of his head. He was studying the local newspaper attentively. So far there had been no mention of the murder about which he knew only too well.

Jeez, maybe it hadn't been Megan Crespi after all whom he had put out of commission. When the woman yelled curses at him, telling him to clear out, he had punched her square in the face, knocking her to the ground. After that she hadn't moved. A dog had begun barking the moment he had approached the front door of the house, but the critter just kept barking. Only the woman had come out of the house. The dog had not.

Maybe it wasn't Crespi's house after all? But no, there she was, obviously in the midst of watering her geraniums, when she suddenly opened the front door and confronted him, watering can in hand. Over the dog's incessant barking, she demanded to know who the hell he was and what the hell he wanted. That was when he felled her with one vigorous blow.

Well, give it another day and if there was still nothing confirming the corpse as that of Megan Crespi, he would simply fly back to Alaska. He would fabricate some sort of explanation for his dad to relay to Herr Winter.

Last week in Vienna, at Günther Winter's urgent command to get two crates out of Switzerland at once, Jeremy Herring had dispatched his son to take care of the matter. Thad in turn had Federal Expressed the crates from Geneva eight days ago. The cargo was addressed to himself at Herr Winter's private annex building behind the sprawling hotel he owned in Girdwood, Alaska.

The next morning, news of the killing, along with a few details but no photographs, was emblazoned on the front page of the *Santa Fe New Mexican*. The victim had not yet been officially identified. Not identified! Of course they should know who she was. Fuck, didn't she *own* the place?

And so Thad waited. And while he waited, he put in a second call to Southern Methodist University in Dallas, again pretending to be a former student and inquiring as to how best to reach retired professor of art history Megan Crespi.

The friendly departmental administrative assistant, Joy Dickinson, answered chattily: "Dr. Crespi? Oh, yes, I just talked to her this morning. She's at the summer house in Santa Fe. Uh, actually it's the home of her friend Mrs. Chandler, but they go up there together every few months or so." Trying to hide his dismay and anger, Thad thanked the helpful informant curtly and hung up.

8

So Thad Herring had made a mistake!

Damn it to hell! Crespi was still alive. He had been startled, then irritated by the large-sounding dog that kept howling at the front door after he had killed the old woman. Thinking the continued loud woofs were bound to attract attention as they echoed across the valley, he had run across the low rise of piñon trees shielding the house from the main road turnoff where his car was parked. He could still hear the incessant barking he had triggered. He was well out of there, he thought, as he hurried back to his motel.

Whom had he encountered at the Las Dos house then, if Megan Crespi was still alive and making calls back to her university? Had he killed her friend Mrs. Chandler? It must have been she, the owner of the house, methodically watering the goddamn geraniums. Hell! An unnecessary killing.

Not that Thad had not chalked up a few necessary ones already, but this was the first time he had miscalculated. He would have to get to Crespi before she became suspicious. Before she realized the link between her art collector buddy Günther Winter in Vienna and the two Klimt crates Winter had shipped to America.

The conceited man, his dad had told him contemptuously, had actually boasted to Crespi that his Hundertwasser collection and a few other choice pieces were housed in the west annex building of the five-star resort hotel he owned in Girdwood, Alaska.

A mere thirty-nine miles southwest of Anchorage, the Hotel Alpenglow was a majestic eight-story modern structure that fanned out from a central hub into four long arms punctuated by four towers, and containing thirty-eight rooms per floor. The sub-basement of one of the easternmost arms housed a capacious indoor pool and a large, rectangular hot tub.

Günther Winter had expressly told Jeremy to have his son ship the Klimt crates to himself at the Alpenglow annex and then dispatch Megan

Crespi at her summer home in Santa Fe. Too bad about the need for hurry. Thad had looked forward to examining the Klimt artworks secretly to his heart's content before they entered oblivion in one eccentric billionaire's private collection up in godforsaken Alaska.

9

Claire's iPhone rang the next morning after the *Santa Fe New Mexican* had at last officially identified Jayne Box as the victim of a killing at Las Dos. It was an agitated Wyatt Box, Jayne's divorced husband, on the line.

"I can't *believe* it," he kept repeating, full of genuine, bewildered grief. Claire consoled him as best she could. After all, their divorce had not been acrimonious, merely a sensible parting of the ways.

Their interests had become widely disparate, what with Wyatt's concentrating totally on his magnum opus about planet warming's changing the migratory pattern of birds, and Jayne's museum work with American Indian pottery. Wyatt had moved back to California, but he wanted to come to Santa Fe for the memorial service. Did Claire know when her nephew would be holding it? Yes, that very weekend, she confirmed. It would be held in the Basilica Cathedral Saint Francis downtown. Considering how active Jayne had been in the museum and music world, there would most likely be lots of mourners in attendance.

Lucas Labra and Nadia André, Jayne's closest neighbor to the north, had flown back from South America in time to attend. Regrouping at Claire's house after the moving memorial service, were her closest Las Dos friends: Paloma Sanchez, Terry Wright and his veterinarian wife, Alberta;, retired physician Reggie Gallet and his wife Bella, the tomato growers Berta and Buddy Gribban, the French artists Caterina and Gerome Vachet, and Megan Crespi.

Wise Paloma summed up what the group had been heatedly discussing. "So Jayne was probably the unintended victim of a botched burglary."

How much should Megan tell them? Her eyes met Claire's and they silently agreed, nada. The neighbors were ready to chalk up the killing to a misfired burglary attempt by a bunch of kids revved up on coke or worse. After all, five empty homes had been broken into last summer.

Those robberies had been solved when the police discovered a Dickensian Fagin character was driving a trio of young street kids into high desert residential areas around Santa Fe, such as Las Dos and Las Campanas. He would drop them off by obviously empty houses, picking them and their loot up a few minutes later. But the whole gang had been caught and they were all, including Fagin, still in prison.

Was this the beginning of a new spate of break-ins then, in which the first one had simply gone wrong and murder was the result? They all knew how feisty Jayne was, Wyatt reminded them, shaking his head sadly.

The sun had set several hours earlier, revealing an unbroken expanse of star spangled sky with a couple of shooting stars. "In honor of Jayne," Paloma had observed solemnly before they all decided to go home.

After cleaning up in the kitchen, Megan and Claire retired to their rooms for the night, both reflecting sadly on the fact that they had sensed it was better not to bring in the Klimt connection, if indeed there was a connection.

10

"What do you *mean* you didn't get Crespi?" demanded Jeremy Herring when his son finally got him on the phone. Thad explained about thinking their intended victim was the logical owner of a house in which a woman was watering geraniums. That only later had he learned from Crespi's university the house belonged to someone else. And yet the police report, finally published in the day's paper, referred to the dead woman as being one Jayne Box, a nearby neighbor. Whoever she was, it sure as hell wasn't Crespi. And not the owner of the house either.

"We've got to get Crespi before she figures out about the Klimts being in America," insisted Jeremy angrily. As an afterthought, and considering how unpredictable and headstrong his son was, he added, "They *are* in America, aren't they, Thad?"

"Yeah, Dad, I signed for them myself the day before you gave me the Crespi assignment. Brought the two crates down into Winter's annex basement, just as instructed."

"And when do you think you might be completing the Crespi caper?" urged Jeremy working himself up to angry sarcasm.

"Tomorrow," lied Thad.

"So, how are you going to eliminate her?"

"I don't know yet. She's still here in Santa Fe. I spotted her from the photo you emailed me while I was at the memorial downtown for the neighbor. I don't know how much longer she'll be staying though." He was tempted to tell his father about the dog that had so spooked him, but thought better of it, especially since the old man was obviously straining to grasp his every word.

"You've got to get rid of Crespi, that's final," thundered the older Herring.

"Um, Dad, do you think Herr Winter could invite her to Alaska to see his Hundertwasser collection or something?" spurted out Thad, grasping at the first idea that came to his scheming mind. Silence on the other end of the line.

"That is not a bad idea," admitted Jeremy after a moment, suddenly serene at the idea of an elimination in remote Alaska. "Not bad at all."

After another moment's silence he said "I'll talk to Günther about it right now. It's probably best that you go on back to Alaska anyhow."

After they hung up Thad, feeling suddenly drained, stripped down to his shorts and went to bed. After a last cigarette, he fell into a sound, untroubled sleep.

11

The cell phone call came in at eight-thirty-three am. Fumbling with the phone, Megan answered sleepily, and after a man's heavily accented voice inquired authoritatively for Megan Crespi, she answered guardedly, "Yes?"

"*Ach, ja, gut!* Megan! It's Günther, Günther Winter."

"Oh! Günther! How nice to hear your voice. Sorry I didn't recognize you."

"No offense taken. Now look here, Megan, darling. It turns out zat I haf to fly to Alaska day after tomorrow on business und, as I discovered from your university zat you und Claire are in hot Santa Fe.

"So, I tought to myself, since you seem to be traveling around zee States, vhy not come up to Alaska, cool off, und let me show you vat vee have talked about in Wien—all my Hundertwassers und a couple of ozer items, you especially, liebe Megan, vould find near und dear to your heart.

"I'll reserve a two bedroom tower suite for you at my hotel. *Wie wäre das?*"

"Well, it's certainly a *sudden* invitation, Günther. But things have sort of fallen apart here in New Mexico. So, well, well, *yes*, Günther, it would be wonderful fun to come visit you in Alaska."

"*Ach*, zat ist prima!"

"But Günther, I can only come for a few days as I have a museum board of directors meeting in New York in two weeks. Claire and I were in Alaska just last year on a cruise and fell in love with the place. It's the next best thing to 'our' Antarctica, except it has lots of green!"

Antarctica had been where Megan and Claire had first met the handsome blond Günther. Two years ago they found themselves in adjacent cabins on the lurching top level of the *Clelia II*, a handsomely appointed small cruise ship commanded by a Russian captain. The genial captain let all three of them stand in the glass-paneled bridge next to him with the caveat that none of them talk out loud while he was at the control monitors.

Embarking from Ushuaia down at the tip of South America, the ship had first skirted around South Georgia Island where Ernest Shackleton had commenced his ill-fated voyage on the *Endurance* so many decades ago, in 1914.

When they began cruising around the actual Antarctic peninsula, Günther had thoughtfully been on hand to help Megan and Claire into the bouncing Zodiacs. Twice daily the Zodiacs made excursions to shore so the passengers could sit or walk among the wide-eyed baby seals while hoards of plodding penguins resolutely made their way to and from the water.

Claire had closely studied the penguins' determined manner of strutting with outspread wings and she began to imitate their distinctive waddle, claiming it helped her balance. Ever since suffering a ruptured disc in her lower back, Claire's walking had been painful and compromised. Standing too long or walking too far was hard on her.

Megan was more impressed by the varying blues reflected on the giant icebergs that floated majestically by, some of them with caves bathed in dark blue light, others tall and thin with ice blue tints.

In the evenings on shipboard she and Günther talked art, while Claire played Scrabble with Whitney Darien, a remarkably bright and darling twelve-year-old boy she had befriended. How really remarkable,

Megan and Günther enthusiastically agreed, that they were both *Kenners*, experts, on Klimt and Schiele.

And it was truly amazing that Megan had spent a number of years in Günther's Vienna, Günther's Wien. In fact she was first there in the fall of 1956, which was the very year Günther had been born. Megan, freshly graduated from Barnard College that spring with a major in art history, had begun classes at the University of Vienna. But like so many of the other students, she had stopped going to the University when in October of that year the Hungarian Revolution broke out.

With thousands of Hungarians pouring over the border into impromptu refugee camps set up at Triaskirchen and other towns, classes on ancient Greek and Roman art seemed totally out of touch with reality. Megan became one of many students who spent their days at refugee centers, handing out clothing. She had learned some phrases in Hungarian which she still remembered to this day: *túl kicsi*? for too small? and the ubiquitous "*Dohányzás tilos*" for no smoking.

In addition, Megan was one of the few students who owned a car, a spacious Opel Caravan station wagon. It was large enough to transport four people at a time from the border crossing to Vienna. They communicated in English, German, Italian, Spanish, or French, in that descending order, since Megan spoke no Hungarian.

Because the refugees could leave for America if they had relatives there, Megan's parents had gamely volunteered to be "relatives." "Krespi" sounded Hungarian to Austrian officials, and several Hungarian nationals had ended up in Megan's home town of Dallas because of this.

Claire was not a bit surprised, having heard Megan's end of the conversation, to receive the excited announcement that they were off to Alaska for a breath of fresh air. What a serendipitous invitation to get us out of this dismal situation. Fine with her. Staying any longer at Still Point so soon after Jayne's death was certainly not on the agenda.

What would her late husband Gerald have thought of this despoilment of his beloved summer escape home? Despite his advanced stage of Alzheimer's, Gerald would have been genuinely upset by the premature death of one of his neighbors in peaceful Las Dos. A retired oil man from small Nocona, Texas, he had completely taken to the relaxed Las Dosian way of life and had been very fond of Jayne Box and her husband.

Even more eager to clear out than Megan, Claire proposed that they leave as soon as possible if they could get on connecting flights from Albuquerque to Seattle to Anchorage. They could take with them some of the warm winter clothes they kept out at Las Dos.

Megan got on line and within minutes was able to book the desired flights for the very next day in convenient segments, with only a two-hour wait in Seattle before the three and a half-hour flight to Anchorage, where they would rent a car to drive down to Girdwood.

Although they would not arrive until nine o'clock that evening, it would still be light, as the sun did not set in Alaska until ten-thirty or so at that time of the year. And so the intrepid travelers were game to undertake this spur of the moment "art" trip that would help distract them from brooding over recent events.

On an impulse Megan telephoned her younger sister Tina. She proposed that Tina and her best friend, Ellie Carruth, join them at their double suite in the Alpenglow Hotel whenever they could get a flight up from Dallas. They could both use Megan's Advantage miles, as her constant travel had chalked up a significant surplus. American Airlines did not yet have its direct flight in operation, but the Seattle connection was nice and the layover for an Alaska Airlines flight included time to shop at one of the airport's most amusing stores, called Tourist Trap Seattle.

After a quick conference, Tina and Ellie, also single professional women, leapt at the impromptu invitation. Within fifteen minutes they already called back. Their flights had been booked for the next day and they would link up with Megan and Claire in Anchorage, arriving an hour and thirty minutes before them at the airport. They would tend to the car rental.

By nine the next morning Claire and Megan had closed up the Santa Fe house and were on their way to the Albuquerque airport in the car Claire kept year round at one of the nearby parking lots, On Time Parking.

The Crespi quartet was on its way.

***

After his plane set down in Anchorage, Thad Herring arrived at Günther Winter's Girdwood complex at eight that evening. He got there just half an hour after Tina and Ellie's flight landed, and precisely one hour before the Alaska Airlines Boeing 747 carrying Megan and Claire touched smartly down on the rainy runway.

12

Günther Winter's face was a study. Usually animated, his even features took on a look of rigid self-control when his hotel manager cheerfully informed him that his four guests had arrived safely and were already installed in their suites on the top floor of Wing Three.

Four guests? Günther knew he should have expected that Megan would come with her Santa Fe hostess—witness the Antarctica adventure—but *two* more people? *Verdammt!* Who could they be? Things were becoming more *kompliziert* by the moment. Just like that old Viennese saying, *Warum einfach wenn es komplizierter geht?* ("Why simple when it could be more complicated?") Turning away from his beaming employee, he realized he was so angry that his hands had become clenched fists, the nails digging into his flesh.

And he had good reason to be angry. That idiot son of Jeremy's had only reported in a couple of hours ago. They had met in the Alpenglow annex, Günther's residence and private museum with a view, as he liked to say, of the Alaskan Austrian Alps.

He had listened to Thad's account of the killing gone wrong at Santa Fe with growing anger. Curtly, he had instructed Thad to retire to one of the staff sleeping rooms in the hotel. He would confer with him tomorrow, probably after lunch. Thad would have to wait until Günther had sized up the situation before a time plan could be established.

That was okay with Thad. He was dead beat. And for what? To be cursed out for knocking off the wrong woman. He had no plausible answer for that charge and found himself accepting the chastisement in sullen silence.

Well, all would become clear in the morning, Günther thought resignedly to himself as he slammed the door after the rapidly retreating figure of Thad Herring. Two more persons in the picture would certainly compound the problem of getting Megan alone and in position for Thad. At least that idiot had no qualms about getting rid of Megan. But it would now have to look like an accident.

And first, before Megan's demise, he would take enormous pleasure in disabusing her of the idea that a lost panel by Klimt could possibly be in his private collection. That was *his* secret and must remain so. Instead, he would reveal to Megan another secret, one so grand that her mind would be taken entirely off the Klimt possibility.

And he would have to determine whether or not Megan had taken Claire into her confidence, as that would necessitate a double accident, not just one. This could be difficult. Perhaps it would be best to invite them both to see his collection. No, no, only Megan had the background and knowledge to appreciate fully what he had so cunningly masterminded. He would find out from *her* if she had shared her thoughts about a missing Klimt work with Claire or anyone else.

As for the other two guests, well the morning would reveal all. But for now the Klimts were under his roof and he could sleep well tonight. Switching off lights, he strode to his master bathroom on the second floor and soaked for a long time in a hot tub. He went to bed feeling physically relaxed but mentally on edge.

13

The early morning brought whoops of joy from Tina and Ellie as they ran across the common sitting room and into the connecting bedroom where Megan and Claire were savoring their freshly brewed Folger's Classic Roast morning coffee. The Starbucks' packets provided by Alpenglow were far too strong for them.

They were looking out at the snow-covered panorama of Mount Alyeska with its aerial tram route spread out before their four large picture windows.

"You didn't *tell* us it's so *beautiful* here!" reproached Tina cheerfully. Ellie, the quiet, efficient techie of the group and a graphic artist always open to natural beauty, immediately set about snapping photographs, alternating between her iPhone camera, with its new tripod and telephoto attachment, and her trusty old Canon SureShot.

"If you don't mind, we'd like to take a little hike before breakfast, since it's not raining yet," said Tina, the most athletic-minded of the group. Fifteen and a half years younger than Megan, she had not followed her sister's scholarly path into academia. Instead, she had devoted her energy and professional life to working with lost and found animals, setting up and running several rescue groups as well as a chain of dog day-care and boarding services.

Megan had always been slightly amused by her sister's dismissive positioning of her in an ivory tower, as goodness knows, she had done quite well in the outside world, particularly in the stock market. She had bought shares in Ms. Magazine when it first opened, and more recently she acquired some 500 shares of Apple stock. Ivory tower indeed! But on the whole she got along well with her baby sister, probably just because they *were* so different in their tastes and occupations.

"Of course, take your hike," agreed Megan good-naturedly, "we'll catch up with you later." Fondly she watched them leave, knowing that their little hike could well last several hours.

A few minutes after Megan had downed the last of the several mandatory morning pills that being a septuagenarian entailed, there was a knock on the door. Claire, who was closer, opened it and a young hotel employee stood just outside with a colorful bouquet of tulips in a magnificent vase. A wide smile was on his face.

"Good morning from Mr. Winter," he said, handing Claire the flowers and an envelope addressed to Megan. After the boy left and while the flowers were being artistically rearranged by Claire, Megan opened the envelope and read out loud: "Greetings and welcome, dear ladies, to Girdwood and Hotel Alpenglow. May I have the pleasure of your company for lunch at our Ski Lift Restaurant at one o'clock this afternoon? Here's my phone number. Looking forward so much to seeing you, Günther."

"Oh, that's nice," Megan said. "We can have a quiet breakfast and then take the morning to look around the hotel and Girdwood a bit before meeting Günther for lunch."

She was pleased to have some free time before getting down to what she presumed would be the business of art. Looking at private collections could be quite demanding, since proud owners usually had a legion of clever-me acquisition stories to relate, leaving scant chance really to *look* at their collections.

One exception had been the wonderful Fogarassy family of Graz, in 1963. Viktor had placed seven heavy portfolio boxes containing individually matted drawings by Klimt and Schiele before her on the wide dining room table, then left her alone for the day, with pencil, paper, and camera at hand. No boring stories about how he had shrewdly obtained this or that drawing, no need to expend energy in oohing and aahing. Certainly there was plenty of occasion to do so privately, as Megan carefully removed each drawing, some twenty to a box.

Taking a cue from the early twentieth-century American art historian and connoisseur Bernard Berenson, she carefully made a sketch in her notebook of each artwork, so as to develop a greater feeling for each artist's particular way of wielding the black crayon.

Although she did not realize it at the time, this procedure proved to be excellent preparation for her later expertise in determining Klimt and Schiele forgeries. Capturing an artwork through sketching—that eye through brain to hand connection—worked better than any computer so far as indelibly imprinting images on the mind was concerned. As the years passed she had developed an invaluable memory bank of works by Klimt and Schiele.

It was about to come in handy once again and sooner than she thought.

14

Günther, dressed all in black corduroy with his hotel logo discreetly displayed on the left pocket of his sport jacket, was waiting for Megan by the elevator bank at the entrance to the Ski Lift Restaurant when she arrived promptly at one o'clock. She was alone.

"*Ach*! Darling! So *good* to see you!" They embraced. "But zis is bad! Vere is Claire?" he asked. Günther's English was near perfect, but uttered with a thick accent, as he declined to articulate all those "w" and "th" sounds. *He* did not lisp! Except in Spanish, as he had spent several summers as a boy in Madrid.

"She sends her hellos and is so sorry to miss lunch with you, but she woke up this morning feeling queasy and a little unsteady so she thought it would be better to rest right now," explained Megan.

Claire had indeed felt a little weak as the morning progressed. It was what she called her "mystery malaise," as no physician had been able to diagnose specifically just why she occasionally woke up feeling this way. Yes, her blood pressure was sometimes abnormally high in the mornings, but that was all the doctors could confirm. There had been no actual diagnosis, although she was on blood pressure pills just in case.

"Vell, I'm sorry to miss her for now, but vee can get togezer later in zee day or tomorrow, I hope," said Günther solicitously, secretly pleased that he and Megan would have a chance to talk alone before he showed her his Hundertwassers as promised.

And what about the other two uninvited guests he was putting up? Who were they? After ordering lunch—wild Alaskan salmon salad for both, as it turned out—Günther asked with false geniality, "Und *who* are your two ozer travel companions, my dear?"

"Oh, Günther, I do hope you don't mind, but I looked up your hotel on the Internet, and since the second double bedroom in those huge tower suites you so kindly reserved for us would have stood empty, I invited my sister Tina and her best friend Ellie to come join us. They both love being out in the wilds of nature."

"But of course, I do not mind at all," lied Günther, inwardly exasperated and furious. Having a phalanx of friends and relatives surrounding Megan would present major difficulties for Thad Herring as he closed in on his target. "Vere are zey now?" he smiled inquiringly.

"Oh, Tina and Ellie went out hiking this morning and they're probably still at it, as they weren't back yet when I left to come meet you."

"Vell, I do hope to have zee pleasure of meeting zem, zat's for sure," lied Günther again serenely.

More pleasantries were exchanged and Megan reminded Günther teasingly that toward the end of their Antarctica trip he had to be flown out by helicopter. He had ignored the captain's warning for all passengers to stay in their cabins as they crossed the turbulent Drake Passage, and he had foolishly gone down the stairs to dinner. At an especially strong lurch of the ship, he had tumbled down two flights, breaking his collarbone and several ribs. Günther flushed with embarrassment and immediately changed the subject to what he was impatiently waiting to discuss.

"Megan, in Wien you told me zat you had heard from an unimpeachable source zat a lost vork by Klimt may have emerged decades after it vas stolen from zee artist's atelier."

"Yes," said Megan evenly, no longer in the first flush of excitement at having learned about the existence of a secret panel, and greatly sobered by the killing/accident in Santa Fe. And she was now more aware than ever that Günther had boasted about "a few ozer items" in his collection. She proceeded cautiously. After all, how well did she really know the charming, daredevil Günther of Antarctic days? The fabulously wealthy collector who seemingly would stop at nothing to acquire Hundertwasser works?

"Yes, that is so, but I have no idea where or what it might be." A brief silence fell. "Do you?" she hazarded pointedly.

"Certainly not!" exclaimed Günther, feeling that he must be even more on guard than usual, now that he was face to face with the Crespi woman. Old she might be, but senile she certainly was not. In fact she looked and acted like a spunky woman in her mid-fifties, not mid-seventies.

"But vere do you imagine it might be, zis stolen lost panel you told me about in Wien?"

"Well, I suppose it must be somewhere in Europe, wouldn't you think?" responded Megan innocently.

"Could still be in Switzerland," answered Günther, equally innocently.

"The last direct Leatherer heir, that former air line hostess, died in a traffic accident in Geneva a few months ago. We talked about that in Vienna, don't you remember?" quizzed Megan.

"*Ach, ja*, so ve did," admitted Günther unwillingly. He was feeling increasingly certain that Megan could already have found out what had happened to the Leatherer art collection that had been stored in a Geneva bank vault ever since the death of Sara Leatherer's last surviving son, Fritz.

Although Günther had bought the trove through his go-between Jeremy Herring, Crespi might have figured out that a middleman could have been acting on his behalf, since the collection did contain a few Hundertwassers. He had been right, he thought, nodding in solemn agreement with himself, to put Thad Herring on her trail when she went back to the States.

Although Thad had botched the job in Santa Fe, Günther would make sure it did not happen again. All he had to do was get Megan to take the scenic aerial tram up the 2,300 feet to the restaurant and gift shop on top of Mount Alyeska. Thad could take care of the rest. But first he would show Megan his legitimate Hundertwasser holdings.

In remote, easy-going Girdwood there was space and time enough for everything.

15

"Vell, are you in zee mood for looking at a few Hundertwassers?" Günther said after lunch. "Do you tink Claire ist vell enough to join us?" he added with a feigned solicitude.

"Well, let me go upstairs for a few minutes and check on her," Megan answered.

"All right. Meet me in zee lobby and I'll valk you over to zee annex where zee Hundertwassers reside."

"Good, Günther, I'll see you downstairs."

Megan was concerned about Claire, who was in fact still feeling wimpy after yesterday's long flight. She was relieved to see that she was up and dressed.

"It's probably better anyhow that I see Günther alone. He might possibly reveal something if it's just the two of us," she consoled her friend.

"And you really think he could have honed in on a Klimt and that it might have been brought to America?" ventured Claire.

"Well," Megan hypothesized, "after what Günther blurted out in Vienna to me, in spite of his protestations of ignorance in the matter, I think it's extremely likely. If a Klimt were in the Swiss vault trove, he would have gotten to the heir through a middleman, and then gotten it out of Europe as fast as possible.

"After all, if the major part of his Hundertwasser collection is based out here in Alaska, why not also make Alaska home for the Klimt, thus out of reach from Austrian officialdom in general and possible litigation in particular?"

"Steady, now," urged Claire gently, as she watched Megan whirl around the multi-windowed, clerestoried tower room, picking up her pen, notebook, and camera.

"Don't volunteer anything," Claire admonished. "And I see no need to bring up what happened in Santa Fe, do you?"

"You're quite right to rein me in," laughed Megan appreciatively, "and, no, I'm definitely not going to bring up Santa Fe."

She put on her brimmed black and red hat, her artificial brown and black fur jacket with matching fur-trimmed hood, stuffed a pair of red leather gloves in the pockets, and was off down the hall to the elevator bank.

When the elevator door opened on the first floor, there was Günther waiting in the lobby, also dressed for the outdoors in a dashing green parka. They smiled at each other genially. Was it really possible that Günther could be involved in something underhanded? They exited from a rear door off the lobby, heading for the three-story annex which stood in the back of and apart from the main hotel.

"Hey! Megan!" shouted Tina, just appearing around the corner, Ellie bringing up the rear. "*Verdammt!*" cursed Günther to himself as Megan invited them with a wave to join her. Within seconds she was introducing them to Günther, who had recovered his benevolent manner. To his relief he heard Megan say "I'll catch up with you two later at the tower suite. Right now Günther and I are off to talk art."

"Sure thing," said Tina, happy not to be invited along, as she and Ellie still had the nearby Bake Shop to explore and perhaps patronize. They said goodbye and were off a second later.

"Please to enter," said Günther courteously, as he carefully unlocked the double doors to the ground floor entrance of the annex and stood back to let Megan enter. He helped her off with her coat. The many windowed interior was framed in two kinds of wood, the main panels in dark mahogany, the trim, a handsome light pine lined with ever varying knotholes. The carpeting was dark green with red, brown, and beige giant leaf patterns curling throughout. Comfortable dark leather chairs and a matching couch were grouped around a massive fireplace, with gas flames gaily dancing from the artificial logs.

"Oh, how cozy!" exclaimed Megan, genuinely impressed by the simple elegance, and by the fact that the great den contained not only legions of crammed bookshelves, but also a grand piano. She went over to see what make it was. Ah yes, quite so, a Hamburg Steinway—the very best. How could she have expected less from Günther?

"Oh! May I try it?" she asked, never able to suppress the urge to try out a piano. Although she could only play by ear, she loved rendering one of the Italian songs her father had taught her so long ago. She didn't really read the bass clef well, only the treble, as she was a moderately accomplished flutist.

"But of course," said Günther, remembering how Megan had enjoyed playing Italian songs on the *Clelia II*'s piano.

Megan sat on the piano bench and, in Günther's honor, played not something Italian, but something extremely Viennese: the old Heurige song "My Mother Was A Viennese" ("*Mei' Muartterl War A Wienerin*"), singing it in almost flawless Viennese dialect.

As Megan serenaded a surprised and delighted Günther, he began to have regrets about eliminating her. Perhaps it was not necessary after all? Still, he had to find out what she knew and what she suspected.

Megan ended with a flourish of chords, then stood up from the piano bench and said, "Well, enough music for now. Your Hundertwassers are waiting."

"Quite so," agreed Günther, "vee go now on zee lift to zee zird floor, which is my museum avay from home."

As they took the elevator up, Megan glanced at their reflections in the polished copper sides and ceiling. Günther, now fifty-seven years old, cut a handsome figure with his curly blond hair, graying just slightly at the temples, and his ruddy complexion. Megan was glad she had on her favorite cap which kept her hair in place.

They exited into a very large area with a high ceiling. The space was subdivided into nine-foot high partitions, with paintings three and four deep on each partition wall. Each artwork had its own ceiling spot light, as the rooms themselves were quite dark. Thus one could, was even compelled to, concentrate on the artworks themselves without distraction. Günther joined her silently in looking at the colorful images on the wall.

"Yes, yes!" approved Megan genuinely every now and then as they slowly advanced down one wall, then up the next. There were some eighteen small, black-framed Hundertwasser oils on each wall, all of them excellent examples of the artist's singular manner of combining bobbing heads, see-through houses, and quaintly invasive nature. Very much like the fanciful apartment house complex that had been built after the artist's plans in Vienna's Second District—a great tourist Mecca.

Megan turned to Günther after they traversed the next two corridors, both also lined with Hundertwasser oils, and said with genuine fervor: "You've assembled a superb collection of Hundertwasser's best efforts, Günther, just superb."

"A compliment from you means everyzing to me," cooed the fanatic Hundertwasser collector. He wondered whether now might be the moment to reveal his further treasures to her.

"Günther," said Megan, plunging into the rapids, "you said in Wien that you had a couple of 'other' choice works, some of which could be of special interest to me. Are any of them here in Girdwood as well?"

"*Ach, ja,* zey are in my den. Follow me." They returned to the first floor and entered yet another dark room, illuminated only by discreet ceiling spots as they lit up some sixty framed drawings and watercolors. They were all by Klimt and Schiele.

"Oh, my god, what a treasure trove!" exploded Megan with admiration and keen interest. She was gratified to see that she knew almost all the works, some of them from the former Fogarassy collection, but what a treat to see them all together in a single room.

There was a fly in the ointment, however.

One of the Schiele watercolors depicting two little street urchin girls was a forgery—a composite of two different drawings by the artist, both of which were in Vienna's Albertina Museum. Should she express her thoughts to Günther? Perhaps *he* was testing *her.*

She spoke up gently, placing her hand soothingly on Günther's shoulder. "Um, Günther, the works are all first class, but there is one doubtful Schiele in the group, I have to say."

"*Mein Gott!* Vich one? Please do tell me, Megan, if you vill!" cried Günther in instant alarm.

"This one here, the two little girls. One, this one, is from the front side of a drawing by Schiele and the other, that one, is from the verso of the drawing. Decades ago, I reproduced both images in my *Egon Schiele's Portraits* book."

"I have all your books on Schiele right here. Let me take a look immediately," responded Günther excitedly.

They looked up the two drawings and he was instantly convinced. "Off it comes from zee wall *right now!*" he cried, taking the framed work down and leaning it with its front against the wall.

"At least you weren't duped by a fantasy Schiele, Günther; you actually recognized two Schiele models, so you can feel good about that. Just bad about the price you paid, I suppose."

"*Ach*, vell, I got it so long ago, years ago, so it vas not all zat pricey. A *gut* lesson for me," Günther lied bravely.

Immensely impressed by Megan's acumen, Günther poured them both a glass of sweet red wine, one of the few alcoholic beverages he knew from shipboard in Antarctica that Megan liked.

After taking a few sips Günther decided now was the time to show her the so-called *Sendung* from Wien. He guided Megan into an adjoining small room in which only one artwork was displayed. A very large triptych, its wings open and extended, and probably measuring some eight feet wide and six feet in height filled the entire wall. The center panel, showing peasants going about their daily business, was flanked by its two eye-catching wings.

"I doubt that even you knew Hundertwasser had painted this," murmured Günther with obvious pleasure and pride.

"Heavens no! I certainly did not," breathed Megan, looking with wonder at the wry depictions on the wing panels of hell and heaven. They were replete with quotations of bumbling Bruegelesque figures and quaint houses, demons and cherubs spilling out over two landscapes that situated them either in hell or heaven.

"This is truly, truly remarkable," breathed Megan, impressed at the scope of Hundertwasser's medieval-turned-modern vision. All was apocalyptic in hell with eager monsters tumbling everywhere. On the contrary, things were engagingly sublime in heaven as reincarnated trees shared the sapphire sky with exotic birds and flying fish, humans and beasts, all happily going their own way or coupling in celestial harmony.

"What a pity people don't know Hundertwasser did something like this. Will you ever lend it to an exhibition, Günther?"

"Certainly not!" exclaimed Günther with a vigorous and dismissive wave of his hand. "Zis is a masterpiece to be enjoyed only by Kenners, not zee common crowd—*odi profanum vulgus!*"

"Now, now Günther, quoting Horace isn't going to excuse you from an obligation to share. Aren't you at all motivated by the desire to bring pleasure to other people who admire Hundertwasser?"

"*Ach!* Zey admire his colors und bulging onion domes, but zey do not understand zee *meaning* behind his deceptively simple art. I do."

Megan stared at Günther quietly. He really means it, she thought. Better change the subject.

"Do the side wings have anything on their backs?" she inquired.

Günther's face flushed with pleasure.

Walking to the depiction of hell on the left, he swung the wing halfway across the central panel. An amazing depiction practically jumped out at Megan. It was a self-portrait! There stood a very young and quite naked Hundertwasser, suggesting the days when he was still just Fritz Stowasser. He looked out at the viewer, his hands held up with palms facing outward, as though warding off something or someone. The only thing he wore was an agonized expression on his face. But why agonized?

Megan remembered the early years of the artist's career in the 1950s and beyond, when, in homage to Schiele's shocking nude self-portraits from 1910, he would, while delivering a public lecture, suddenly disrobe, calmly continuing the lecture *pudelnackt*—stark naked. Only after his speech had been delivered, did Hundertwasser put on his clothes again.

All this was familiar to Megan, but still she was puzzled by the angst in his demeanor, his hands almost pushing out at the beholder and a look of terror in his eyes.

"Yes, I know exactly vat you are tinking, Megan. I too vondered why he looked so frightened. Are you ready to see zee matching ving?"

"You bet I am," declared Megan, totally intrigued by what the verso on the right panel might hold.

She was not prepared for what she saw.

Instead of what she suspected might be another self-portrait with Hundertwasser showing himself older and calmly in possession of the fantasy world he had created, three figures in black uniforms bolted across the panel toward the centerpiece. They held machine guns in their hands and wore Nazi swastika bands on their arms.

Megan remembered something she had forgotten about Hundert-wasser: that he was part Jewish and that during World War II he and his mother had posed as Catholics, his father's religion, to avoid detection. He had even enrolled in the Hitler Youth.

Sixty-nine of his mother's relatives were killed by the Nazis. Stowas-ser emerged unscathed physically from the war, but with a dark legacy of persecution and fear. Heroically, he had turned these pent up emotions into the positive feelings that emerged from his imaginative, beguiling images. With his commitment to worldwide ecology, he had populated his fantasy planet not only with winsome human beings and composite animals, but also with rich forests, blooming plants, and clear seas.

Seen closed in together, side by side, the two wings completely covered that middle section of the triptych which depicted life on earth.

Megan asked to see the center panel again and Günther obliged. Now she began to notice that the everyday tasks people were involved in could be read as potentially sinister: a farmer was beating his pigs with a long pole, a woman was throwing shellfish away on the ground, and a man with dreadlocks was busy sewing small armbands with the word *Jude* on them.

What a scene! It was much more than just Hieronymus Bosch done over lightly. This was the sinister world that was coming into being under Hitler. And sure enough, when she looked more closely Megan saw figures crowded around two distant hilltops. The one on the left showed Moses with his tablets, the one on the right showed a very recognizable Hitler mesmerizing an excited crowd.

"What an ensemble!" Megan cried out, overwhelmed by the whole and its dramatic placement.

She walked around the room quietly, studying the triptych from a distance, noting its large size and narrow black framing. Günther watched her closely with an expression of supreme satisfaction on his face.

"Might I make a few sketches of some of the details?" she asked finally?

"I vould prefer zat you do not," answered Günther coldly and immediately.

"Oh, so sorry, Günther. It's just my old art history training kicking in, I guess. Sorry!"

Damn it, Megan thought, that was really stupid of me. Why did I do that? Why am I so impetuous after all these years?

Günther refilled her wine glass, then went over to a CD player on the shelf above a small desk. He plunked down a disk and started it up.

"Remember zis?" he smiled, fast forwarding to the ninth track. An orchestra began the winsome preamble to Robert Stolz's operetta song *Du, Du, Du sollst der Kaiser meiner Seele sein* ("You, You, You shall be the Emperor of my Soul"). He held his arms out to Megan as the soprano began to sing the words. They had danced to this once before, in his stateroom on board the *Clelia II*, after Megan had presented him with a CD entitled *Klimt Musik*.

She had been commissioned to select the tracks and write the liner notes for "music from Klimt's time" by the Moderne Galerie for its extensive Klimt exhibition a few years earlier. The *Klimt Musik* CD made a marvelous gift and she always carried a few copies with her, even to Antarctica.

What pleased her most about the CD's track selection and sequence was that she had been able to include music by a *woman* composer—Alma Mahler.

Always the feminist, if engagingly charming about it rather than angrily aggressive, Megan had found a fine ally in the Moderne Galerie's director, Renata Teuer. Renata was a scholar born in Vienna but who, like Megan, had also attended Barnard College. Gentle feminists, they believed in fair dealing in both language use (i.e. chairperson) and action, going out of their way to engage and encompass women artists in their work.

And now this veteran feminist of seventy-seven found herself cheerfully waltzing to Robert Stolz in Girdwood, Alaska. She wondered again why her attractive dance partner had never married, never had children. He must be as committed to his passions as she was to hers.

Actually, although she did not now trust Günther, she still could not help liking him immensely. He was so passionate about his convictions concerning art and music. And they liked so many of the same things: Klimt and Mahler, Schiele and early Schönberg, Rothko and Rock and Roll, Edith Piaf and Carly Simon. And especially Elvis Presley's "Heartbreak Hotel." Both she and Günther had taught themselves guitar and been folk singers in their youth.

And Megan the art historian was endlessly intrigued by Günther's expressive body language. When he spoke in German he frequently steepled, clasping the tips of his fingers together at chin level and exuding a justifiable air of authority. As he was missing the distal phalanx of his left index finger, this presented a memorable sight, guaranteeing the listener's full attention.

When Günther spoke English, however, his body language was markedly different. He often hugged his own chest with arms crossed and hands clasping his elbows. A self-protective but also assertive stance that had quite amused Megan.

Now she was in Günther's arms and slowly revolving around a room in Alaska. Although he maintained a proper distance and held her extended left hand quite lightly in his, she thought she should at least be a bit frightened and certainly on her guard. She remained the latter but actually felt quite comfortable in Günther's arms. Perhaps her suspicions about him were unjustified.

She decided to test the waters. "*Güntherchen*," she said lightly and she hoped beguilingly, "was the Hundertwasser triptych the 'colossal' *Sendung* you said you'd shipped to America two weeks ago?"

"*Exactement, ma chère amie*," lied Günther easily. "It vas installed just a few days ago by my curator. How do you like zee placement?"

"It is absolutely compelling, Günther. A total experience. The lighting is so subtle. And the drawing room? How long have you had those formidable Klimts and Schieles?"

"Ah, zey go back many years, before I discovered Hundertwasser."

Megan gauged his answer and deemed it possibly legitimate. She decided to take a bold chance: "Well, you know, Günther, back there in Vienna I thought for a moment, when you mentioned shipping something 'colossal' to the States, that you might be talking about another Klimt."

"*Ja!* Vould zat I vere! What did you tink it could be? Zee lost portrait of Sara Leatherer perchance? But zat vould have been too small; und I did tell you I vas shipping a colossal *Sendung.* Remember?"

"Oh, yes, that's right," Megan feigned sudden recollection. "But one can always hope, can't one?"

"*Ach, ja*, to locate the Sara Leatherer portrait has alvays been a dream of mine."

"Well, yeah! You and several hundred other Klimt *Kenners*, to say nothing of museums."

Abruptly changing the subject, Günther daringly accused Megan with a triumphant laugh: "Is *zat* vat you und Claire tought I had!?"

Megan could hear Claire's calm voice urging her to proceed steadily. "Oh no, I never mentioned my suspicions to *Claire*, Günther. Remember, she only likes Santa Fe artists, like Fritz Scholder."

"Junk!" declared Günther instantly and vehemently. "Pure junk," he repeated.

Megan refrained from telling him that some connoisseurs considered *Hundertwasser* as populist, playing to the masses. She liked the artist well enough, but certainly did not rank him with the likes of the great Vienna trio of Gustav Klimt, Oskar Kokoschka, and Egon Schiele. Although the triptych she had just been treated to certainly elevated Hundertwasser in her mind now.

And she was happy to have had the opportunity to clear Claire of any suspicion of knowing about a long lost Klimt having emerged on the

European art scene. It was good that she'd come alone to view Günther's extraordinary collection.

The Hundertwasser triptych was quite a prize, she had to admit. *But the installation did not strike her as having just taken place. She had noticed a telltale layer of dust on the narrow rims of the three frames.*
Hm. Well, she'd think about that later.

The CD had gone on to the next track and they had stopped waltzing in the heat of their animated conversation. It was time to get back to the hotel room and check on Claire. Also to see whether or not Tina and Ellie had returned from their trek to the bakery.

"Ven do I haf zee pleasure actually to talk to your sister und her friend," asked Günther with an engaging smile on his face. He had to make sure neither of *them* knew anything about the Klimt find.

"How about dinner together this evening, our treat?" responded Megan.

"Deal! Shall vee meet in zee lobby at eight o'clock?" Because the sun did not set until 10:30 pm or so, people tended to eat dinner quite late on a May evening in Girdwood.

"Here. I'll fetch your tings und valk you back to zee hotel," offered Günther, hoping fervently that Megan's sister and her friend would not have to be on his kill list.

It was really a shame that Megan would have to be done away with. He was genuinely fond of her.

16

Thad Herring was becoming impatient. He had slept his fill, some ten hours, and had yet to hear from Günther about the target. It was way past the lunch hour. Should he call Günther? Better not. He might be in the middle of chatting with his four guests or discussing business with the hotel manager.

Just then his own cell phone rang and it was Günther. "Hallo, Tad. I have just dropped zee target off at zee hotel. I've proposed zat tomorrow morning ven zee sun is out, Megan und her group take zee cable tram up to zee top. I'll ring you ven zey leaf, und you can take zee next tram up. From zen on, it's up to you to choose zee exact timing, okay?"

"Is the mission on for both targets, or just the one," asked Thad, determined not to mess up again.

"Just zee one, Megan Crespi. It absolutely has to look like an accident."

"Right-O," affirmed Thad, but Günther had already hung up. Good. He had the whole late afternoon and evening to scout around. Perhaps he should take the aerial tram up now, since he had only ridden it once and that was over five years ago. That had been the first time he'd been sent to Günther's hotel on an errand from Vienna.

Leaving the Alpenglow Hotel he walked to the adjacent aerial tram station out back and took the next cable car up the mountain. It was three-thirty in the afternoon.

11

The icy white behemoths surrounding Mount Alyeska had trapped the clouds just above the tree line. When the Crespi quartet reunited that afternoon, they had on an impulse decided to take the aerial tram to the top of Mount Alyeska immediately, rather than wait for morning. But after they arrived at the top, a few minutes after four o'clock, visibility was very poor. A few snow swirls gusted round the tram as they disembarked, and walking on the icy platform was precarious, especially for Claire. They consoled themselves over welcome cups of hot chocolate in the Glacier Café, deciding to return first thing in the morning.

"What's that round house over there?" asked Ellie, pointing toward a small circular hut at the end of the boardwalk that projected a short way beyond the café. "Looks like a good place to take photos if the weather clears."

"Oooooh!" exclaimed Tina, "That's a *gift* shop! Let's go! Never mind about no view right now. I wanna see if they sell those cute little gold nuggets suspended in glass globes, like the ones we saw at the airport. Maybe they're a better price here and I could get a whole lot of them for gifts."

"Or they might be more expensive here at the top of Mount Alyeska," cautioned a no-nonsense Ellie, restraining her generous, always gift-minded friend.

The four of them walked gingerly in the fresh snow, as yet unaddressed by a shovel, to the ornately carved wooden door of the gift store. Tina held open the heavy door for Claire, who was lagging behind, doing her penguin walk on the snow, and they all entered the shop. Historic photographs from pioneer days in old Girdwood lined the circular walls, and souvenirs, books, and maps were on attractive, tempting display.

Eyeing the group casually as they fanned out around the store was the only other customer—a man in his early fifties, slender, tall, and pale of complexion. He was wearing jeans, a dark blue parka, and a reversible two-color white and gray woolen cap that only partially covered the long black curls that fell at the back of his neck.

When he heard one of the group address the older woman bundled up in a red parka as "Megan," Thad quickly replaced the small ulu knife he had been testing. Casually, he sauntered past the friendly cashier, who was still laying out goods for the opening of the summer season next week. He went out the door, keeping his back to the group. Then he hastened to the nearby men's restroom, took a leak, washed his hands carefully, and sighed in relief.

That was a close call! Coming upon his target when he was not prepared. Why hadn't Günther called to warn him she would be taking the tram car up top? Maybe he didn't know. Should he attempt something now? How was he going to separate the target from her group? Risky. But this might be his big chance.

The Crespi quartet cheered unanimously when the snow stopped while they were still paying for their purchases in the shop. The sun suddenly came out, lighting in miniscule detail the slender green pine trees below now flocked with new fallen snow.

"Let's go back to the outdoor observation deck and see if we can spot our hotel," urged Tina, herding the others toward the exit. Claire, though lagging behind, was game and so eventually they all lined up along the wire railing. They began pointing excitedly to their majestic hotel with its four sweeping arms and corner towers, now looking like a miniature toy, so far below was the structure.

They could just see the annex on the west side of the hotel where Megan had been earlier to examine Günther's Hundertwasser hoard. Her report of the tour was enthusiastic enough, but none of the others really minded missing it. Alaska outdoors was more to their liking and brave Claire was still not in top form.

Thad stood inside the partially full café watching the four women from a window booth. How on earth was he going to break up the group and isolate Megan? They were huddling together now for warmth as the wind began blowing snow crystals in short blasts. Then, to Thad's astonished delight, the two younger females miraculously peeled off to return to the gift shop and the older two began to approach the entrance to the café.

Thad became smaller in his high-backed booth, but no need, because at that moment the older of the two women, dressed in a green parka, headed straight for the restroom, leaving Megan standing at the bakery display counter looking momentarily undecided. All of a sudden she gave a determined jerk to her hood and, pulling her camera from her parka pocket, she headed back to the observation deck.

If Thad were going to make his move, he should do it now. Silently he followed Megan out the door.

She was already near the end of the deck, passing by some construction barriers in front of a damaged section of railing. Spotting a sight she knew her sister would just love, a bear warning, she pressed against the compromised rail and leaned precariously out over it. Then she raised her iPhone to photograph a government sign warning hikers to watch out for bears below the tree line. No one else was on the deck.

How perfect, thought Thad. A sudden hard push would do it. Looking around quickly, he began inching toward Megan through the ice and snow. A last look around and he lunged straight at his target.

Just as he reached her, Megan straightened up abruptly and turned around. Her elbow hit Thad hard, knocking them both off balance, and sending him hurtling through the gap in the damaged deck railing and onto the slope below. Megan watched in horror as the man in a dark blue parka slid down the incline, coming to a stop just above the tree line. His body hit a brushy thicket at the base of a cluster of pine tree trunks. Dazed, Thad looked around him, not knowing which side of the incline was up or down.

A startled brown bear who had been feeding nearby with her young cub in the alder bushes where Thad had landed, was loping directly toward him.

He tried to get up, cursing the bear at the top of his voice. Seeing the bear charge, Thad panicked, stumbled to his feet and began to run, even though he knew that one is supposed to hold one's ground in a bear attack. Within moments the bear was on top of him, clawing his back right through the parka. Just before losing consciousness, Thad instinctively assumed a protective fetal position. Some seconds later, inexplicably, the bear suddenly turned and trotted off, leaving Thad curled in on himself and unconscious in the snow.

"Help! A man is hurt! Bear attack! Bear attack! Get help!" yelled Megan. Hearing Megan's shouts, Claire, Tina, Ellie, and a few other tourists came out on the observation deck to see what was happening. Seeing the plight of the poor man curled up on the snow below, cool-minded Ellie ran inside the café and informed the waiter, who immediately telephoned down to the hotel. Help was on the way he reassured her. Other tourists in the café gathered on the outside deck, each with a concerned question or opinion.

One young woman spotted a large snowmobile coming up the South Edge Run. "The medics are coming!" she shouted.

Claire said, tiredly, "Let's go indoors, there's nothing we can do here except be gawking bystanders. And I need to sit down."

Reluctantly Megan, Tina, and Ellie followed Claire into the café, wondering if that unfortunate man had also intended to photograph the bear warning sign.

"To think! I am responsible for his toppling down the slope," fretted Megan for the tenth time.

"No, Megan, you mustn't think that way. He had just gotten too close to you and the damaged rail," consoled Claire. No one realized the man in the dark blue parka had sinister intentions. Least of all Megan. Not in this halcyon Alaskan setting so many miles from Santa Fe.

"Okay, we're on our way down," one of the triage team barked into his cell phone, as they expertly lifted the badly mauled Thad up onto a stretcher. Within minutes the three medics had their patient loaded in the snowmobile and were on their way down to Wade's Way and the First Aid Center at the base of Chair Lift No. 4.

The throng of concerned tourists was asked to wait for the next aerial tram, which would be there in fifteen minutes. Some ten minutes later the sound of an ambulance siren wafted up to Mount Alyeska and the Crespi quartet looked eagerly down toward the Alpenglow Hotel Day Lodge. The poor man was "near relief," as Claire liked to say, an expression her Irish grandmother used to use when fixing her dinner.

18

Thad, with puncture wounds in his back and a scraped skull, woke up in the Girdwood Clinic on Lindblad Avenue at six thirty in the evening to find himself staring into Günther Winter's narrowed and furiously glaring eyes. "You *idiot*," he hissed, "you complete, total, inept idiot!"

"It wasn't my fault..." began Thad weakly.

"Shut up, just *shut up!*" commanded Günther. "Your father und I both vant you out of here, out of Alaska and back to Wien *now*. It's bad enough zat you missed her, it's zat she's *seen* you. Now she knows your goddamn face."

"But," interjected Thad weakly, suddenly aware of his throbbing scalp and back wounds, " but..."

"No buts about it," interrupted Günther, seething with anger. "I've booked your flight back to New York and then on to Wien and you're leaving this afternoon at four, regardless of how you feel.

"Und, incidentally, you're *fired*."

* * *

Günther was still irate when he returned to the annex after seeing fumbling Thad. An hour earlier he had telephoned Jeremy Herring in Vienna, furiously describing Thad's botched job. Now they would have to act precipitously. He hadn't planned for the Moderne Galerie caper to take place yet. "Now you must send your daughter over to New York right away, zee very next flight.

"Give Rita her instructions and tell her she *must not fail!*."

19

The Crespi quartet regrouped in their suite after the bear incident. Michael Brown, the hotel manager, informed them that the man who had been mauled by a bear earlier that afternoon had regained consciousness, was not seriously hurt, and would be released tomorrow morning. They pondered the deceptive feeling of well-being and safety they had enjoyed at the top of Mount Alyeska. All Megan could really remember about the bear victim's looks as he catapulted past her, was that he had a hawkish nose and dirty long hair. His bloody wool cap had lain a few yards away from him on the snow, a lonely reminder of something gone awry in nature.

After the girls retired to their room to change clothes for dinner with Günther at eight, Claire and Megan exchanged urgent views on whether or not the mauled man could possibly have been stalking them. A distinct reality, they concluded. But if the mangled man were involved, could Günther be as well? It would be highly interesting to observe Günther's demeanor at dinner this evening.

In the meantime Megan would ask her sister, who could charm birds out of trees, to pal around with the hotel's security officer to see if he knew anything about the bear victim's identity.

"Oh, yes, I've already seen him and gotten his whole life story," boasted Tina proudly, when Megan talked to her a few minutes later.

"He's twenty-seven, has been here at the hotel six years and had what's called 'gigantism' as a young boy. He just kept growing taller and taller till, when he was thirteen, he already reached six feet, five inches. Then a school nurse looked up what she considered his phenomenal growth rate and discovered that he had the abnormal growth commonly called gigantism. He was successfully operated on for a tumor on the pituitary gland at the base of his brain. That's what caused the disease. They found out afterward that if he had waited any longer, his internal organs would have continued to grow and he'd most likely be dead within ten years."

"Golly, that's some story!" exclaimed Claire, who had commented to

Megan on the exceedingly tall security guard with the bulldog-like face.

"Okay, well, Tina, little Sis, your new assignment is to quiz this Colossus of Rhodes, Mr. Tall, about today's bear victim and find out what you can."

"If we can locate him, betcha I'll have an answer for you by dinner time," responded her sister optimistically rising to the challenge. With a conspiratorial smile back toward Megan and Claire, Ellie gamely followed Tina's purposeful stride down the dark wood paneled hall toward the elegant bank of three elevators. Their gleaming metal doors, layered with thin overlapping plates of gold and silver, suggested silhouetted scenes of the mountain panorama outside.

Down in the lobby the duo was in luck. There stood the affable slim giant, Eddie Hoch, talking to the concierge at her computer desk. They approached him, and after a few good- natured spars, Tina asked concernedly about the man who had been attacked by a bear today: how was he "bearing" up?

"He'll be in the clinic overnight, but they'll probably release him tomorrow morning. His wounds weren't as bad as they first seemed," answered Eddie.

"I heard he was from New Jersey," declared Tina innocently.

"Nope. He had a foreign passport on him, think it was from Austria or was it Australia? Lots of them foreign folks come here this time of the year."

Tina and Ellie lingered a little while longer, making more small talk with friendly Eddie, then peeled off to rush back to the eighth floor suite. They had a morsel of potentially interesting news for Megan and Claire.

20

When they had all comfortably assembled in the Vista Bistro on the top floor of the hotel, and Günther had ordered champagne, an increasingly lively conversation centered on the colorful, friendly inhabitants of Girdwood, both human and animal.

Günther told them about the many excursions possible in his "new Austria." The small local airport featured helicopter flights over the glaciers, landing upon various glacial lakes for photographs.

Or one could drive through the longest tunnel in North America to nearby Whittier and take the twenty-six glacier cruise with the local travel company.

And, farther afield for instance, one could drive down the Kenai peninsula to the port town of Seward or, a bit farther in a parallel direction, all the way down to the busy port of Homer, the "halibut capital of the world." There was plenty to do. The women really should plan to stay for a few days.

Over dessert Ellie brought up the unfortunate accident that had happened that afternoon. Günther feigned ignorance: "My manager keeps bad news hush hush from me," he explained, pushing his hands vigorously away from his chest.

"I heard he was a foreigner, not an American," ventured Megan, looking directly at Günther. Without flinching he said petulantly, "*Gott!* How many languages do zose bear varnings have to be in anyhow?"

"But that's not the point," Megan persevered. "Just before the man plunged over the railing he passed right by me. In fact, if I hadn't just straightened up he would have run smack into me. As it was, my elbow hit him, he collided with the guard rail, and catapulted right over it."

"Vell, zat's most unfortunate und of course very upsetting, but tourists sometimes go crazy when zey get to zee top of zee mountain. Zey do all sorts of insane tings, like climbing over zee guard rail to make snow angels or have snow ball fights. May I suggest an itinerary for you ladies for tomorrow," Günther said, abruptly changing the subject.

"Oh, yes," they all chimed in.

"Vell, it is important to get acclimated, so after you've explored zee rest of Girdwood tomorrow, und it's very, very small, as you've already ascertained, you might consider taking a short drive, just about sixty miles, to see zee old mining settlement called Hope. It faces zee Turnagain Arm und snow mountains beyond, und zere ist a dramatic forest zat sweeps right down to zee sea. Zere is a small restaurant and bar, a very modern school, und even a museum und library, all quite interesting."

"Wonderful suggestion. I love it," said Tina happily. She and Ellie thought nothing of driving long distances. Sixty miles was no challenge and they could watch for moose on the highway both coming and going. More amused than enthusiastic, Claire agreed and Megan opined that they could all get some good photographs. With thoughts of Klimt and killings temporarily consigned to the background, she finished her dessert and the group adjourned for the evening, thanking Günther again for his generous hospitality. Even though she had tried to pick up the check, he insisted on paying.

Back in her room, after a quick hot shower, Megan fell asleep thinking of the extraordinary Hundertwasser triptych she had seen earlier that day.

But what about that dust? she suddenly heard herself ask, awaking with a jerk. Yes, what about that? How could an artwork installed just a few days ago already have a layer of dust lining the frame?

She got up and took half a sleeping pill, then, calling to mind Scarlet O'Hara in *Gone With the Wind*, said to herself calmly, "I'll think about that tomorrow." She fell asleep instantly.

21

Megan's iPhone rang at exactly six o'clock the next morning, the melodious strains of Massenet's *Méditation* from *Thaïs* waking her gently. Checking the caller ID, she saw that it was Renata Teuer calling from New York. This was one of the few calls she would have answered at that time of day, but it was the director of the Moderne Galerie on the other end.

"Well, hello there, Renatachen," she answered, sleepily. "Do you realize you've just woken me up in *Alaska* of all places?" she asked merrily, referring to the four-hour time difference. She was always happy to hear from her Viennese "daughter" who, like Günther, had been born the same year Megan had begun graduate studies in Vienna. Renata's voice sounded strained.

"Megan," she began, "something terrible has happened here at the Moderne Galerie."

"What? What do you mean, Renata?"

"I can't tell you over the phone, it's too complicated. But would you consider flying here immediately? We need to consult with you. Our board of directors meeting is weekend after next week, as you know. But could you leave today so we can talk in person right away?"

"Well, of course, I'll do it if you need me. But I won't be able to fly out until this afternoon at the earliest. There's only one flight a day out of here that could possibly connect to New York. I'll see what I can book and call you back."

"Thank you, Megan, thank you. Of course we'll reimburse you and you can stay in the usual hotel on Madison Avenue. But it's truly urgent."

"Okay, Renata, let me get started contacting the airlines and informing my companions here that they'll have to explore Alaska without me."

"Oh! *So* sorry to break up your trip. But it would be really helpful if you came, believe me. And, please, Megan, don't tell anyone *why* you're coming. If you have to tell people, just say it's to prepare for the directors meeting."

"All right," Megan reassured her, indeed convinced by the tone of Renata's voice that something of major importance was wrong. Something that had to be kept out of the public eye for now at least.

After some ten minutes on her MacBook Air, Megan was able to secure a four o'clock flight that afternoon for New York with a layover at Seattle that would get her into La Guardia at midnight.

Hastily she explained to her three friends that she had to tend to an emergency situation concerning the Moderne Galerie's board of directors meeting in New York. She would try to rejoin them as soon as possible. They would have time though for lunch in town as they had planned. Then they would return to the hotel for Megan's luggage and she would take the shuttle to the Anchorage airport.

She made a call of explanation and thanks to a startled Günther.

* * *

Thad had boarded the same New York bound flight some fifteen minutes earlier than Megan. His seat was far back in the plane's main cabin, just a row away from the toilets. Megan had had to buy a first class ticket in order to get the last remaining seat on the aircraft, so she did not see Thad, nor did he see her. At La Guardia they went their separate ways into town. Megan took a taxi to her Madison Avenue hotel and went right to bed. Thad importuned a friend who lived in the Bowery to pick him up and let him spend the night before his flight back to Vienna the next evening.

Like the Alaska mountains, the New York skyscrapers were majestically indifferent to the presence of two additional mortals in their midst.

22

After bolting down a hearty breakfast at her cozy Hotel Wales the next morning, Megan walked down the few blocks to 86th Street and Fifth Avenue, arriving at eight o'clock sharp just a few seconds after Renata Teuer. They entered the beautiful mansion-turned-museum through the basement, briefly alarming the guard who had just gotten off night duty. Silently they took the elevator up to Renata's private office on the fourth floor, where they sat in two magnificent Wiener Werkstätte-designed chairs facing one another.

"What is that strange onion-like odor?" Megan asked, wrinkling up her nose and looking around inquiringly.

"That's part of what happened here," moaned Renata. "Early yesterday morning, just before the shift change, someone with a mask over his face managed to get inside the museum from the roof over our private bathroom and our glassed-in courtyard. Our security cameras show that he first entered my office briefly, placed a paper on my desk, then ran downstairs to the 'Adele' room and *spray-painted* the portrait up and down. He then added an obscenity with a final flourish.

"When the guard downstairs finally noticed him in the Adele room on one of the security cameras, he sounded the alarm and came running up the stairs to apprehend him. But the intruder downed him with pepper spray. It's all on our surveillance cameras. Then he immediately ran back upstairs to the roof, continuing to blast pepper spray all the way. That's what you're smelling."

"So he escaped! What about the obscenity scrawled on the portrait? What does it say?" Megan asked with growing alarm, imagining the damage that could have taken place to Klimt's famed portrait of Adele Bloch-Bauer. Damage that she knew, thank goodness, would have instantly been deflected and contained by the nonreflective, bullet proof glass in place over the painting.

"I'll show you in a minute. It is terrible to behold, Megan. The destruction that was intended. But first I must ask you if, when you were in Wien week before last, you heard anything about the recent Swiss sell-off of the Leatherer bank vault collection?"

"Well, yes, of course, I heard exactly what we all must have heard, that someone bought the entire collection from Leatherer's last heir, that flight attendant. And sight unseen, apparently."

"I suppose you have surmised who that buyer was?" asked Renata carefully.

"Yes, I have an educated guess, Renata, but it's only a guess, well, a suspicion rather."

"A *suspicion*?"

"Yes, and I imagine you are thinking of the same person I am."

"Maybe yes, and maybe no," answered Renata quixotically.

" Well, Renata, we are old and dear friends and I won't play guessing games with you. Tell me who you think it might be and I'll probably be able to confirm it."

"We think it must be that eccentric Danish collector of Klimt who bids through a middleman at all the major auctions. Asta Holm-Ditlevsen. That reclusive widow of the founder of Selandia Shipping."

"Yes, I know about her. She's reputed to be a real hermit. But why do you say eccentric?"

"Because she assigned her entire Klimt collection on long-term loan to the Aarhus Museum in Denmark with the stipulation that it only be open to the public on weekdays."

"But why?"

"Because every now and then she likes to spend a weekend viewing it privately at the museum. They did a wonderful job of hanging the collection, which had become far too large for her home in Switzerland, but she insists on savoring it alone, in silence, without the distraction of crowds or even guards. Now I'd call that eccentric."

"Well, even with that restriction, I think the Aarhus Museum got a good deal. Isn't that the museum which bid unsuccessfully for Klimt's three University ceiling panels, after they were discovered not to have been destroyed in the Schloss Immendorf conflagration?"

"Exactly," confirmed Renata. "Originally those enormous panels were bought from Otto Leatherer by Asta Holm-Ditlevsen's husband, just a few weeks after being miraculously recovered from their vineyard cellar hiding place back in nineteen seventy."

Megan speculated, "So, Asta Holm-Ditlevsen's husband got to Otto even before the auction houses or gallery owners or Austrian government could contact him?"

"Yes," replied Renata, "and even before Günther Winter, that other bizarre, sometime collector of Klimt, could. After all, he was only fourteen when this happened.

"Oh! The look on your face, Megan! Is Winter the one you suspect?"

"Quite right. When I was in Wien, I talked to him about the possibility of a Klimt find, a secret panel, that I had just learned existed, and he then as much as told me he had something big and was shipping it to the States."

"And when I called you in Alaska, weren't you visiting him at that private museum of his out there?"

"Yes, he got hold of me in Santa Fe at Claire's house. He found out from my university where I was and called to invite us up to his hotel in Girdwood, since he had suddenly been called there on business."

"Well, did you find out if he had a large Klimt, a giant panel?"

"Yes and no. He certainly had a very big work of art on hand, and very recently installed, or at least so he said."

"Was it a Klimt?

"No, that's the frustrating thing. I had expected to see a Klimt, possibly the artist's redoing of that fourth University ceiling panel which was originally painted by his partner Franz Matsch. You know, the one on Theology, the one that Klimt did not allow the Leatherers or anyone else to acquire. He kept it in the basement room of his Feldmühlgasse atelier in Hietzing till the day he died."

"If it wasn't the *Theology* panel you saw in Alaska, then what was it, for heavens sake?"

"It wasn't by Klimt at all. It is a totally unknown, very large, late work by Hundertwasser, a fantastic and significantly personal triptych."

Megan described the artwork to Renata, whose limpid brown eyes widened with growing interest. They had both momentarily forgotten the Klimt desecration downstairs.

But Renata soon came to herself and, after pronouncing that it would be exciting to imagine what Matsch's *Theology*, reinterpreted by Klimt, might look like, said, "It's good to think about pleasant things, but now let's go downstairs and let me show you what almost happened to our poor Adele."

They walked down the two flights to the now closed-off second floor, the "Adele floor," as the guards referred to it, and entered the main room. There, on her own wall was the white and gold framed life-size Adele portrait. Large loops of bright red spray paint methodically fanned out on the protective glass overlay, running from her chest across her dress, and up and down her body in all directions, almost as far as the rims of the frame. On the nonreflective glass the hands were covered with paint as well.

Only the face had escaped the spray can. At the bottom left patch of green carpet the single word "HURE" (WHORE) had been sprayed across the glass in capital letters.

Underneath the glass the painting still glowed with its gold mosaic intact and unharmed.

"Oh, my god!" exclaimed Megan. "How terrible! How insane! How could *anybody* do that to her, even symbolically on the glass? And *why*?"

"Well, of course that's the one-hundred-thirty-five million-dollar question," commented Renata, angrily, visibly perturbed at seeing the violated Adele again.

"The vandal got out via the roof just moments after he'd sprayed the guard. And he left a cardboard note in my private office in the middle of my desk. I didn't dare touch it in case of fingerprints, but it was easy enough to read. It was comprised of just nine words scrawled in large *Kurrentschrift*, you know, the old German script Klimt and Schiele used to write in. It says: *Wollen Sie Ihre Klimt Hure für das Secretum einhandeln?* In translation it reads: '*Want to trade your Klimt whore for the Secretum?*'"

"'*For the Secretum?*'" Megan's ears picked up. That was the very word Hans Ernst Klimt had used to Megan as he lay dying. "Do you know what that is supposed to mean, other than being the Latin for *secret*?"

"We don't have a clue. Why would anyone try to attack a painting like that if they really had something they wanted to trade it for? Why didn't they simply approach me and propose the idea? And, as you say, to what could the word Secretum refer? Could the Adele portrait perhaps have been part of a larger canvas and then cut down? Might a larger canvas have included other figures? Like, say, Klimt's *Portrait of Schubert at the Piano* in which the piano playing figure of Schubert is surrounded by one male and three female singers?"

Megan speculated in tandem with her distressed colleague. Following the tack of Renata's last remark, she asked, "If there were another figure in the painting could it have been Adele's sugar baron husband Ferdinand? Or a group portrait of the whole family?"

"But surely we would all know about such an humongous undertaking," marveled Renata.

"And how could the pepper spraying intruder possibly think a legitimate museum like the Moderne Galerie would trade anything with a criminal who had targeted such a world famous work of art?" mused Megan out loud.

"All these are questions that will have to be answered at the board of directors meeting next weekend," sighed Renata wearily. "With the exception of the police, only I, the Moderne Galerie's president Lyonel Retter, the pepper-sprayed guard, and now you, have seen the damage.

"I've had the floor closed off to the public, and even to the guards and staff ever since our discovery. The newspapers have learned about the closed floor and are getting inquisitive. We didn't want to close the museum completely. Visitors know something is up, now that the whole second floor is closed off.

"The police are taking an awfully long time with their fingerprinting and forensics. They are going through all the security cameras' video feed. And they've scoured every inch of Adele's room as well as the side rooms and the stairs leading up to the fourth floor, my office, the conference room, the bathroom, the interior patio, and the roof above. So far, though, nothing to go on."

"So how can I be of help?" murmured Megan, deciding not to tell

Renata yet that Hans Ernst Klimt had used the word 'Secretum' on his deathbed. Megan didn't want to burden her just then. She felt desperately sorry for her friend and the huge responsibility she was bearing so well.

"Let's go back to my office and pick up our things. We're meeting Lyonel for lunch. And he'll tell you what we have in mind."

23

One of the many visitors to the Moderne Galerie late that morning was a strikingly tall man with a flat nose and a protruding jaw. In fact he looked like a bulldog. He took a quick tour of the open floors, including the basement. Returning to the ground floor, he noted that the popular Café Zigeuner was already in full swing.

Retiring to the museum's gift shop, he spent an inordinate amount of time at the rear of the store, hunching over various books. He quickly paged through some of them, specifically those by Megan Crespi on Klimt and Schiele, and also her memoir, *In Passionate Pursuit*, while keeping a wary eye on the entryway to the museum.

An hour passed.

Edie Hoch's vigilance paid off at last. Abruptly at the noon hour there appeared in the lobby the figures of the Moderne Galerie director, Renata Teuer, and his quarry, Megan Crespi. They were met at the base of the stairway by a man whose dignified mien and sense of relaxed ownership could only identify him as the museum's president and cofounder, Lyonel Retter. Tossing an obviously amusing aside to the guard at the front door, he grandly escorted the women from the museum. The group turned right and made for Madison Avenue.

Eddie followed at a discreet distance. He was in no hurry. If Crespi had time, he had time.

24

Asta Holm-Ditlevsen sat in her panoramic Swiss breakfast room overlooking the waterfront shops and moored bobbing boats on the curving inlet of the town Ascona just over the Italian-Swiss border on Lago Maggiore. Her late husband Rikard had bought this hillside Swiss getaway house decades ago, before the Swiss had become more stringent about foreigners owning Swiss property. As a Dane, he had loved the phenomenon of pines and palms holding sway together.

Even though she was in her mid-eighties, keeping her tall figure still slender and her hair still blonde, Asta now felt more at home here than she did in Denmark. Things in Aarhus, in Jutland in general, were changing so fast.

Even the Danish language was altering. For example people no longer said *farvel* (goodbye), they said *hej, hej*. And when she entered shops in Aarhus, clerks now greeted her with the informal *du* instead of the time-honored formal *"De."* She sighed.

"Av for Søren!" (*"Ouch!"*) she suddenly muttered, cutting her finger as she sliced a hunk of Danish Fontina cheese to go with her black bread. Rikard would have been indignant at having been addressed in the *du* form. But then so much of his world was no more since his death in 1974. As majority shareholder in Selandia Shipping, he had made sure that the shares were kept in the family.

But the death of their son in a car accident on New Year's Day of 1980, left Asta with no heirs. In addition to supporting several Scandinavian charities, she had channeled her considerable fortune into modern art. Well, modern by the standards of turn-of-the-last century Impressionism and Art Nouveau.

Wanting to keep her Ascona house light and airy, so different from the dark condo she kept in Denmark facing Aarhus's new opera house, she had furnished it with all white, original Gustavian Swedish furniture. The white walls of her dining room were graced with white-framed works by several Scandinavian Impressionist artists of the 1880s: Denmark's Anna Ancher and Berthe Wegman, Norway's Asta Nørregaard, Harriet Backer, and Kitty Kielland, Sweden's Jeanna Bauck, and the philanthropist/painter Eva Bonnier, who suffered from major depression disorder and took her own life at the age of fifty-one in 1909.

Asta's bedroom walls were entirely devoted to the extraordinary Helena Schjerfbeck of Finland, whose old-age self-portraits, she hotly maintained, equaled in intensity Picasso's gaunt self-renderings at a similar age.

One other artist held sway in Asta's Swiss home: the Swedish playwright and gifted amateur artist August Strindberg. Painted directly on canvas with a loaded palette knife, his swirling landscapes and seascapes illuminated the large office-den of Asta's house, making her home indeed light and airy.

This handsome plethora of Scandinavian works, however, had left no space for Asta's Klimt drawings and paintings. No space, that is, except for one, the large oil-on-canvas panel by Klimt on the wall of her two-story living room. It rose up the full height of the tall room, with its long outdoor balcony and sliding doors that looked out over the comings and goings of boats in the bay of Ascona.

Klimt's reworking of his colleague's original version of *Theology*, the panel he had kept to the end of his life, had departed completely from Matsch's concept. Continuing the floating human towers that spiraled upward in his previous panels—*Philosophy*, *Medicine*, and *Jurisprudence*—Klimt had created a swirling continuum of upward striving human forms in his dark version of religion.

Some images were recognizable, such as the small, morose figures of Christ and Buddha at eye level. Other forms were enigmatic, with grinning skeletons and floundering women and men at the top of a hurricane of hurtling human and animal shapes.

Asta realized how fortunate she had been to persuade the Vienna-based American art dealer Jeremy Herring to intervene with Otto Leatherer and procure for her this Klimt panel, thus completing her ownership of all four ceiling works. *How* Herring had acquired it, he would not tell her, but he had adroitly shielded it from nosy scholars who importuned him, hoping to make an accounting of all works by the artist.

Especially annoying, Herring confessed to Asta, had been the persistent preparer of a new oeuvre catalogue of Klimt, one Janette Killar, co-director with Helene Blumenstock of the venerable Galerie St. Sebastian—the gallery that introduced Klimt, Schiele, and Grandma Moses to America.

Her new comprehensive catalogue of Klimt works would supersede the old, reliable, but incomplete one issued by the Hungarian Johannes Dobai in the mid-sixties and updated in 1975, too long ago for hungry modern scholarship. Apparently Janette Killar was on to something concerning the Klimt University ceiling panel. Did she suspect that the Matsch one, supposedly redone by Klimt, still existed? From the way she had talked to Jeremy, it sounded that way.

Well, thought Asta, gingerly doling out three drops of cream in her coffee and attacking her four-minute egg, that was his problem, and now it's mine. I certainly don't want that busybody scholar visiting me in my beloved Ascona.

Glancing at *Theology*, the mysterious large panel mounted on the tall wall opposite her balcony, she once again tried to fathom its obviously complex meaning. All she could make out was that Klimt's painting seemed remarkably anti-theology, consigning revered religious leaders of the past to the lowest level of the panel, and showing at the top a confused, grasping humankind, figures, including animals, trying to outpace one another.

All seemed threatened with their own inevitable mortality, as symbolized by the smiling skeletons surrounding them. No place really for the comforts of religion. Certainly no rebirth or immortality here.

"Don't look at it," she advised her adored little white Maltese dog, Minne, who had just strolled into the living room with a questioning look.

Asta would love to talk over the *Theology* panel with an art historian knowledgeable about Klimt, but not Janette Killar. Once again she thought of contacting the Klimt/Schiele expert, Megan Crespi, who lived in Texas of all places. Some years ago, Crespi had contributed a long chapter on Scandinavian artists that included her painters in a handsomely illustrated book entitled *World Impressionism*. Her letter asking for permission to reproduce was a model of politeness, appreciation, and enthusiasm, she remembered.

Ja! She made up her mind. Asta would ask her secretary to locate Crespi that very day.

25

The courtly Lyonel Retter escorted Renata Teuer and Megan Crespi into his favorite nearby vegetarian restaurant, Candle 79, between Lexington and Third Avenue on East 79th Street. They took the booth reserved for him at the back, away from the noisy din at the front.

"We're waiting for one other person to join us before we talk business," Lyonel announced.

"Oh, and who might that be?" questioned Megan.

"In fact you know him," Renata answered quickly. "It's Erich Knadel, the Nobel Prize Laureate neuro-psychiatrist who has lectured for us at the Moderne Galerie,.

"Oh!" Megan's face lit up with pleasure. "That would be so nice to see him again. I haven't talked to Erich, except for email, since his book on Viennese art and medicine, *The Age of Insight*, came out earlier this year. It's doing quite well, I hear. The critics loved it and the Adele Bloch-Bauer portrait detail on the cover is certainly compelling, even for people who aren't necessarily pulled toward a dialogue between art and science."

"Hello, hello all!" exclaimed the dapper, bow-tie wearing Erich Knadel cordially, as he came up to the group a few minutes later. His body language said it all, thought Megan to herself, fondly observing Erich's self-confident demeanor and somatic integrity, with hands lightly clasped together. Standing up to greet the white-haired celebrity, Lyonel made room for him on his side of the booth.

After the niceties were exchanged, first asking for complete confidentiality, Renata explained to Erich what had happened at the Moderne Galerie: the strange symbolic violation of the Bloch-Bauer portrait and the note left behind on her desk with its enigmatic question about swapping the "whore" for the "Secretum."

"But this is awful! Even if the canvas itself was not damaged, the *idea* behind desecrating it, was, well, it was pathological," pronounced Erich solemnly.

"That is exactly why we've asked you to join us today," Lyonel said quietly. "The police are working with us to find out the identity of the vandal, of course, but they are slow and what we need is something like a psychological profile *now* so we can figure out who, amongst a bevy of art fanatics, the criminal might be. Would you be willing to do this for us?"

"Of course, I'll do whatever I can, based on the few facts and items you have. Could I see the note? Did you bring it?" asked Erich thoughtfully. "And did the pepper-sprayed guard see anything more of the intruder's face or do you only have the video feed of the masked figure as captured on your security cameras?"

"Yes, here's a photocopy of the note left on my desk, Erich," answered Renata, handing it over, "and, no, unfortunately we don't have video frames that show any details of the man's face. But here are a few choice and clear printouts, just to save you time."

"Aha! I see the note is in *Kurrentschrift*. I still had to learn that as a nine-year-old boy in Vienna. But what could the writer mean: 'Want to trade your Klimt whore for the Secretum?'"

"That's what none of us can figure out," sighed Renata sadly. "What could the word Secretum possibly refer to?"

Erich silently studied the *Kurrentschrift*. "The funny thing is," he said at last," it's written by someone who doesn't ordinarily write in it. I can tell by the mistakes in the number of loops for 'e's and 'n's. They all look like over-extended 'm's, he said, reading the cursive script easily.

"Well, I suppose that's some sort of clue right there," offered Megan. She got up and crossed over to Erich and Lyonel the better to see the video feed printouts they now began to examine.

Abruptly Erich exclaimed :"Hey! Look at *this* photo. See right there. How tall would you say the intruder is?"

"Well, not very tall. Perhaps five foot, four or so?" guessed Lyonel.

"And quite slender, as well," mused Erich, reaching for the other printouts. Suddenly he exclaimed: "Oh, but don't you see? That's not a man at all. It's a young boy, no, wait, it's a *woman*!"

26

Rita Herring said goodbye to her father and put down her cell phone. He was pleased. She had gotten in and out of the Moderne Galerie without being stopped, and she had left the cardboard note, just as Jeremy directed, nicely centered and in plain view on the museum director's desk. She had also sprayed with extreme care red paint all over the glass covering of Adele's figure and her clothing, leaving only the face free from paint. Lastly she had printed the word *HURE* over the bit of green in the lower left of the painting. Just then she heard an alarm and the sound of someone galloping up the grand stairway.

Sprinting from the Adele room, she pepper-sprayed the advancing guard directly in the face, then bolted up the third and fourth floor stairs, wriggling through the bathroom window overlooking the interior courtyard, and hoisting herself back up onto the roof. She heaved a long sigh of relief, then laughed triumphantly to herself. She was safely out and the job was done.

Two roofs over, toward 85th Street and Fifth, she descended the same way she had ascended, on an interior courtyard fire escape. She reached the ground of the inner courtyard that gave access to the apartment building she had managed to enter by merely sliding in behind a mother and two noisy brats. No doorman had been in sight. Now she pulled off her mask, untangling her long dark hair from the Velcro binder band, and entered the back hall that connected to the courtyard. She traversed it to the front lobby, and nodded cheerfully to the doorman as he held the door open for her to exit into the street.

Her mission had been accomplished. She could return to Vienna and her job at Nebehay's Antiquariat from which she had abruptly taken a few days off without explanation. Her boss, Dr. Hanskarl Klug, Nebehay's devoted and capable successor, had been surprised but agreeable to the time off, as Rita was his newest but best worker. And, Rita smirked, it would probably take weeks before Thad would speak to his older sister who had succeeded where he had failed. She smiled to herself: "Now good old dad will finally see that *I'm* the capable one in the family, not that lily-livered, clumsy brother of mine."

21

The lunch at Candle 79 was well under way. Two desserts for four people were ordered, as both Renata and Megan maintained a careful watch over their diets. After close study of the assembled sequential photographs, all had agreed that the slender masked figure security cameras had caught had to be a woman. Indeed one printout showed the vandal brushing her hand quickly against her hair. Why hadn't they noticed that before? What about the police? Had they come to the same conclusion? The detectives were excruciatingly slow in sharing information on how the case was progressing.

"Well," said Erich, "I have an appointment in another twenty minutes, so I'm going to have to leave this delightful company. But I shall work hard to draw you a profile that might help identify what type of individual the vandal is, and what her habits are likely to be." Looking inquisitively at

Megan, he asked "And what is *your* part in all this, Megan, darling?"

"I haven't been informed yet," smiled Megan, looking questioningly at Lyonel and Renata. The latter two looked at each other, then Lyonel spoke.

"Megan, if you are agreeable, we have a travel assignment for you. One we hope you can take on and get back in time for the board of directors meeting at the end of next week."

"Well, of course I'm willing to do anything to help, and my Alaska trip has already been interrupted," Megan said gamely, if a tad accusingly.

"What we have in mind," continued Renata, "is your meeting with, on some irresistible pretext, the person we believe is responsible for the break-in at the Moderne and the only person we can think of who might have the secret panel.

"And that would be whom?"

"We think it is Asta Holm-Ditlevsen."

"And not Günther Winter?" Megan asked incredulously.

"Not Günther, we don't think," said Lyonel firmly, picking up where Renata had left off. "He is the world's most fanatical Hundertwasser collector. He was his main patron for all those decades before Hundertwasser died. When was that, some ten years ago, right?

"He even visited the artist in his New Zealand studio, and tried to buy it after Hundertwasser died. He *did* buy his Vienna studio, as you well know. And this Winter character, he secretes his art hoard not in Vienna where he lives, but in Alaska, as you well know."

"But he does have a sizeable collection of Klimt drawings," remonstrated Megan. "He might well have an interest in acquiring something really big by Klimt. And I did tell him in Vienna about the existence of a lost Klimt which had just come to my attention.

"Incidentally, Renata and Lyonel, my source referred to it as the 'Secretum.'

"Winter in turn told *me* that he was shipping something really 'colossal' to himself in the States. And of course he did show me something really large—a Hundertwasser triptych which had just been installed, or at least that's what he maintained..." Megan broke off, thinking of the dust she had spotted on the frame.

"Look," said Renata earnestly, "we think it really has to be the Holm-Ditlevsen woman. She and her husband stopped at nothing to get the Otto Leatherer's Klimt University panels after they had been discovered intact from the Schloss Immendorf fire. Remember? Leatherer told Janette Killar and Helene Blumenstock at the Galerie St. Sebastian that an unnamed buyer working through Jeremy Herring insisted on buying the three panels from him, as they "belonged" with another Klimt which the prospective buyer owned."

"How long ago was that?" asked Megan, suddenly realizing an entirely different scenario might indeed be possible.

"Well, as close as the Galerie St. Sebastian people could gauge it, it was quite soon after Gustav Ucicky's death, in the early nineteen sixties. You know, the illegitimate son of Klimt who became a film director," declared Lyonel.

"Hm. So that gets Günther Winter off the hook then," Megan said slowly, almost unwillingly. "He would have only been a child in the early nineteen sixties. I know because he was born the year I was doing graduate work in Vienna, nineteen fifty-six, one year before *you*, dear Renatachen, were born.

"Let's see," Megan said rubbing her palms together in a rush of inspiration, "Asta Holm-Ditlevsen would have been how old in nineteen sixty-two? Let's say around thirty-four or thirty-five? Golly, I haven't thought of her since I once asked permission to reproduce some of her works by Scandinavian women artists."

"Yes," mused Renata. "She would have been in her mid-thirties then. Seems she began collecting Klimts when she married that shipping magnate Ditlevsen as a young girl. Helene Blumenstock told us that. And Helene would know. She's ninety-two herself and still going strong. She's been at the Galerie St. Sebastian for over seventy years."

"Yes," reminisced Erich, "we were all there at her seventieth anniversary celebration, and you brought your charming friend Claire."

"Let's do a Google on Asta just to make sure," suggested Megan, picking up her iPhone. Before anyone could comment, Megan had entered Asta Holm-Ditlevsen on the Google website. Sure enough, not only was there a long Wikipedia entry on her, but her birth date was given as 1927.

"Okay, that settles that!" announced an enthusiastic Erich, as he regretfully rose to leave the animated group. "God speed, Megan, and come back with the goods!" he said, waving an amiable goodbye.

* * *

Renata, Lyonel, and Megan bent toward each other over the table in concentration. "How, may I ask," queried Megan concernedly, "can we present Asta Holm-Ditlevsen with an 'irresistible pretext' to visit her?"

"We've thought of that," answered Lyonel with a smug look on his face. "You will visit her with a confidential, and of course totally fictitious, offer from the Moderne Galerie to swap our Adele portrait for her presumed Klimt whatever, call it a panel if you like. If she is behind the break-in, she will know we're responding to her 'swap' note. If not, or if she has no fourth Klimt panel, then she won't be interested."

"That must be what Secretum means!" interjected Renata. "See, it all makes sense."

"Well, it's certainly a distinct possibility now that we've done the age math. Winter is out, Holm-Ditlevsen is in. It's that simple," mulled Megan.

"When can you leave?" asked Lyonel.

"Where am I going? Denmark or Switzerland?"

Lyonel proffered: "We've done some checking. It seems the H-D woman just visited Aarhus where her Klimts are, so it's most likely that she's back in Switzerland if she's not traveling. Which isn't likely at her age."

"Wait a minute! Hold on there," said Megan heatedly, thinking of eighty-seven-year-old Claire's active travel agenda with her over the past ten years. "People can still travel when they're older, you know." She shot an indignant glance at Lyonel. "That's pure ageism."

"Look, I'm not all that young myself, Megan. Sorry, I simply misspoke," proffered Lyonel apologetically.

"All right, apology accepted. But *where* is the Danish damsel?"

"We propose to find out for sure by telephoning her and telling her we'd like to send our representative, you, to confer with her on a confidential matter."

"You think that would do it?" asked Megan, not convinced.

"We'll let you know right now if we're lucky," Renata answered, rising from the booth. "Let's get back to the office and call her."

As the trio walked back to the Moderne Galerie, the figure of a tall, pugnacious-looking man merged with the river of pedestrians coursing up 79th Street. He followed them, some twenty feet behind, all the way back to the Moderne.

28

No sooner were Megan, Lyonel, and Renata re-ensconced in the latter's Wiener Werkstätte office when Megan's iPhone vibrated. An expression of pure astonishment crossed her face as she checked the caller ID. Waving her hand to attract Lyonel and Renata's attention, she silently mouthed, pointing to her phone, "It's Asta Holm-Ditlevsen! She's calling *me!*"

"Hello. Yes, this is Megan Crespi," she confirmed into the mouthpiece, being extra careful not to disconnect the call with her chin.

"Professor Crespi?" repeated Asta Holm-Ditlevsen. "Ah, good!" Asta spoke with a slight British accent. "Your university gave my secretary your cell phone number. I hope this is a good time to call you?"

"A *very* good time," responded Megan, nodding at Renata and Lyonel meaningfully.

"Well, let me explain why I am calling. I have long admired your work on women Scandinavian artists ever since I read your chapter on Nordic Luminism in that book on World Impressionism."

"Oh, that impossibly heavy volume," sympathized Megan with a chuckle, adding, in some of the limited Danish she knew, "*Mange, mange tak, Fru Holm-Ditlevsen.*"

"And I was wondering," continued Asta ignoring Megan's Danish, "do you have, by any chance, plans to come to Europe in the next few months?"

"Well, no, not really," fibbed Megan.

"Well, I should like to invite you to fly over to Switzerland and visit me in Ascona to see my collection, if you have a space in what I know must be a very busy schedule."

"To see your Scandinavian women artists collection? And in Ascona? I would come to Ascona even if you didn't have that important collection, Fru Holm-Ditlevsen. I *love* Ascona," responded Megan, quite truthfully.

She had in fact stayed at the town's beautiful Hotel Castello del Sole for several summers back in the 1990s. The hotel had its own private farm acreage, complete with friendly donkeys, that ended at the sandy white lakeshore. The small town of Ascona had long been a point of interest for Megan for many reasons: the works of Russian painter Marianne von Werefkin, compatriot and lover of Alexei Jawlensky, were in the local Ascona museum. And the great German dancer Mary Wigman had worked with Rudolf von Laban there on the shores of Lago Maggiore. Even Isadora Duncan had visited there.

The nearby Monte Verità had attracted, since the beginning of the twentieth century, an equal number of vegetarians and anarchists to its nudist colony atop the hill. And finally, her Italian grandmother was buried just a few miles across the Italian/Swiss border in Pallanza. She'd located the tombstone on her last visit to Switzerland, in 2003.

"Does that mean I might tempt you to fly over, all expenses paid of course?" asked Asta, encouraged at the turn the conversation had taken. What a surprise to learn that Dr. Crespi had visited and loved *her* Ascona. She laughed to herself. So had Paul Klee and Carl Jung become charmed by Ascona.

"Yes, you could tempt me, indeed you could," answered Megan, giving Renata and Lyonel a silent V-for-victory sign.

"When might be a good time for you to fly over?" asked Asta.

"Well, this might sound odd, but sooner rather than later. I have to attend a board of directors meeting in New York at the end of next week and after that I have several publishing deadlines."

"I don't suppose you could come this week?" hazarded Asta hopefully.

"Well, yes, I could and would, if I can get a flight reservation. Um, I'd be leaving from New York rather than from Dallas."

"I'll instruct my secretary to secure a round trip flight immediately. And would you want to return to New York, instead of Texas?"

"Yes, I'd have to be back in nine days for that board meeting."

"Excellent, Professor Crespi. I am so very pleased. May I put you up at the Castello del Sole?"

"I should love that, yes, thank you. It's my favorite hotel in all Ascona," answered Megan with an excited intake of breath.

"All right, then. You'll be hearing from my secretary, Karl Hansen, directly, and probably within the hour."

"Wonderful! Is there anything I could bring you from America, Fru Holm-Ditlevsen?"

"Well, how about a Klimt drawing, ha, ha! One from, say, the Moderne Galerie, since you are there in New York?"

"I'm no Klimtomaniac. Can't oblige, I'm afraid."

Both women were laughing delightedly as they rang off. Megan told Renata and Lyonel the details of the conversation and they rejoiced at the fortuitous events that had led to the Holm-Ditlevsen invitation.

"Let's not get the Moderne Galerie involved at all," said Renata. Don't go as our representative. Go as yourself, the art historian, part of whose expertise is Scandinavian artists."

Lyonel Retter, who had been silent through the entire exchange, spoke up with a droll expression on his long face: "We would have paid for you to go regardless. But we know an investigative bargain when we see it."

Megan gave him an affectionate gentle punch on his belt buckle.

After Lyonel left, the two women ironed out details of how Megan might go about gleaning information concerning what had happened at the Moderne Galerie. Supposing, of course, that Asta Holm-Ditlevsen were indeed involved, as Renata definitely thought she was. At least Megan might be allowed to see that putative fourth Klimt panel that had not been loaned to the Aarhus museum, and which Klimt scholars like herself and Janette Killar believed to be in her private collection.

After a long afternoon, Renata and Megan parted company. Renata had several TV interviews to prepare for, as a new Klimt show had just opened at the Moderne Galerie, and Megan was just plain tired.

29

Instead of walking back to the Hotel Wales, Megan turned off abruptly and entered a forty-story apartment building on the east side of Madison Avenue at 89th Street. By the time the exceedingly tall man following her could react and enter the building's lobby himself, Megan had disappeared. Eddie Hoch cursed under his breath, then sized up his chances of where to keep watch without attracting attention. He could not wait in the lobby. The man at the service desk was already looking over at him inquiringly. Pretending he had just realized he was in the wrong building, he shook his head in feigned exasperation, then exited quickly.

For a moment he sat on one of the stone stanchions that fronted the building corner of East 89th and Madison. He would simply wait. There was enough pedestrian hustle and bustle to shield his lanky tall figure, at least through the rush hour. He eyed the buildings opposite the condo scraper. Perhaps one of the stores across the street would be a better waiting place. The surging herds of noisy children on their way home from school were beginning to annoy him.

"Wish I was back in Alaska," he muttered out loud.

30

Upstairs, at the north end of the narrow hall on the twentieth floor, Megan's Barnard college classmate, Betsy Barr, opened the door of her condo with a flourish. "Megan, darling! What are you doing in New York?" The doorman had just called up to say a Dr. Crespi was downstairs in the lobby, so Betsy had been advised of the surprise a few minutes in advance.

"Hi, dearie!" They embraced and entered Betsy's spacious condo, heading for the living room that overlooked Madison Avenue. "I'm here early for a Moderne Galerie's board meeting that's coming up. Had a lot of conferring to do with Renata Teuer concerning a Schiele exhibition I'll be curating for her." She had told the truth. Megan had been asked to curate a future show, but the theme, Egon Schiele's portraits and self-portraits, had yet to be announced publically.

"Well, lucky, lucky me, to get a chance to see you!"

The two friends caught up on their respective lives and news, Betsy's two daughters and their children in particular. "I was just going to drive up to Riverdale to see Alessandra and the kids," Betsy said. "Would you like to go with me and have dinner with us?"

"Great idea," responded Megan, truly happy at the idea of relaxing with her old friend and her daughter and grandchildren this evening after such a day of Klimt duress. Also, she loved and was especially good at playing with children, since as her friends often pointed out, she had really never grown up herself. And Alessandra had two darling children: Lucy, age seven, and Molly, age three. If Asta Holm-Ditlevsen's secretary had been able to secure flight reservations for tomorrow, she could always be reached on her cell phone.

"Wonderful! Let's go. I'm all ready," interjected Betsy. Megan followed her around the rooms as she gathered all the things she needed for exiting her domain—purse, scarf, night glasses, medications, keys, and... "Oh, yes, I have something for the kiddos," Betsy exclaimed, starting out of the condo for the third time.

Finally they were off down the corridor and made their way to the elevators. "No, no, follow me," Betsy commanded as they reached the lobby and Megan started to head for the front door.

"We'll take the service entrance. It's closer to the garage." Making their way across the back of the lobby, they exited on 90th Street between Madison and Park, and immediately entered the building's vast parking garage to their right. Within another few minutes they were safety-belted into Betsy's new Toyota Prius, and were driving up Park Avenue and then on to West Side Highway in the direction of Riverdale.

* * *

As he continued sipping his drink, Eddie glanced in boredom at his watch one more time. He had been sitting, pretending to read a newspaper, at the Three Guys Restaurant on Madison. The Greek diner, located almost cattycorner to the building under surveillance, offered a perfect view of all comings and goings. What was Megan Crespi doing that was taking so long? Perhaps she was having dinner with friends in the building? She simply could not have left the building unobserved by him. But it was getting late. And surely she had to return to her hotel.

What to do? Eddie pondered angrily. He was not going to spend all evening either in front of this apartment building or in front of Hotel Wales just to report to Günther Winter the comings and goings of Megan Crespi, when she was obviously just visiting friends. Why would he even be interested in what places his former guest at Hotel Alpenglow was frequenting anyhow? Let's call it a night's work and be done with it. Giving a long evaluative look at the building across the street, Eddie rose from the table and, leaving a generous tip, he exited the restaurant, walked toward the Lexington Avenue subway stop on 86th Street, and disappeared down the stairs.

31

Megan's cell phone rang during the jolly dinner she was sharing at Betsy's daughter's home in Riverdale. The caller ID again showed the name Asta Holm-Ditlevsen. She excused herself from the dinner table and took the call in the deserted playroom.

"Professor Crespi?" asked Asta eagerly, almost joyfully.

"Yes, yes! Hello!"

"My secretary has been able to get you on tomorrow's flight from New York to Zürich, first class, with a connecting flight to Lugano, where my chauffeur will pick you up at the airport. Is that all right for you?"

"That sounds perfect. I'll be in black slacks, wearing a black vest, red shirt, and a black hat."

"Excellent! I'll convey that information. The chauffeur will drive you straight to Castello del Sole and you can rest up that afternoon. He could bring you over to my house for dinner in the evening. Does that suit you?"

"It's perfect. A wonderful plan. Thank you for being so thoughtful about letting me catch up on jet lag," answered Megan.

"Well, I think you might be closer to my age than not, and I know how one needs one's rest after an international flight."

"All right, then," concluded Megan, "I shall see you in two days and I look forward to it immensely."

Back in the dining room she told Betsy about the astonishing turn of events. That one of the primary collectors of Scandinavian women artists was financing a visit to view her collection. She did not mention that she hoped to ascertain whether or not the collector also owned a certain Klimt panel and whether or not she might have had anything to do with recent horrific events in New York at the Moderne Galerie.

Watching Betsy's grandchildren at play, Megan began thinking about how her colleague Renata had managed to keep the reason for closing off of the second floor of the Moderne Galerie a secret. In fact, she had even thrown out the rumor, backed by what could be actual fact, that a special exhibit of the Flöge Sisters fashion designs—dresses that Adele Bloch-Bauer might have bought and worn—was being installed to complement the present Klimt exhibition.

Megan shook her head in silent admiration. Give Renata two more days and by golly she'll have a Flöge exhibition set up in the Adele room. And why not? There was always keen interest in the art world for anything having to do with Klimt, and certainly Emilie Flöge, as the artist's trusted companion had garnered public awareness and immense curiosity. Was their relationship platonic or sexual? Would that question ever be answered? A British researcher, Peter Simpson, had spent years investigating the true nature of Gustav's relationship with Emilie and many people were awaiting what was expected to be his illuminating book on the subject.

After the children had been put to bed and the grownups had talked politics and art, Betsy drove back to Manhattan and dropped Megan off at her hotel. They said an affectionate goodbye. Once in her pajamas and comfortably in bed, Megan placed a call to her sister. The abandoned trio must be back from their day's activities by now.

"Hi, Tina! This is the sister who left you to the wilds of Alaska."

"Well," exploded Tina. "It's about time we heard *something* from you. What's going on?"

"Oh, a lot, but I don't really need to talk about it now. I want to know what the three of *you* have been up to. How much of Alaska have you managed to see without me?"

"Quite a lot actually," replied Tina enthusiastically, filling Megan in on two days' worth of activities.

"And how was the little town of Hope? Was there too much walking for Claire? How is she holding up?"

"Oh, she's fine! We saw the founder's cabin and a gold-panning site and we had a delicious dinner up at the Summit Café. There was the most adorable dog there named Henry. We all wanted to take him home with us."

"A dog! Well that's one reason I called. It looks as though I'm not gong to be able to get back to Alaska before your return flight to Dallas. Tomorrow I have to fly to Switzerland for the Moderne Galerie, and then I have to be back for the board meeting in New York. So I'm not even going to be able to pick up my own dog in Dallas from my former student Evelyn, who's keeping him."

"Ah hah," interjected Tina savantly. "So you want *me* to pick up Button for you?"

"You've got it, right on the button," confessed Megan apologetically.

"Sure, Big Sis, I'll be glad to keep Button for you until you get back to Dallas. You know how he loves playing with my pooches." Tina was the devoted mother of two feral cats and four Japanese Spaniels, and Megan's stalwart little Maltese fit right in with the ménage.

"Oh, thank you, really, thank you, Tina. And say hi to everyone there for me, won't you? I'm pretty much pooped right now, so forgive me if I don't bring you all up to date on my news. I've really got to turn in and get some sleep. But just tell me one thing. Are you all still going to take the helicopter ride we reserved for tomorrow?"

"You bettcha!" replied Tina playfully, imitating the bouncy voice of Sarah Palin, whose humble town of Wasilla they had been planning to check out. This tipped both sisters into singing the ditty their little niece had taught them: "My country 'tis of thee, from my front porch I see, Russia and such."

"Good night, and sleep tight," they wished each other and hung up. Suddenly feeling extremely tired, Megan dropped off to sleep almost instantly, with visions of Ascona's beautiful waterfront promenade in her dreams.

32

Renata's call came in while Megan was having a leisurely breakfast at the hotel and observing the other guests.

"Erich Knadel has come through with a bit of psychological profile for us. It's based more on the *Kurrentschrift* than on the camera footage," she reported. "Seems the pen pressures and spacing of the cursive script indicates an extremely controlled and probably highly controlling personality, while the body language of the video exhibits great calmness under stress and a meticulousness bordering on obsessive compulsive behavior."

"That's it?" Megan asked, disappointedly.

"Yes, that's it," affirmed Renata, equally disappointed.

"I suppose we can at least conclude that the vandal was merely a hired accomplice, perhaps a New York local, and that the employer was the controlling force initiating the act either from here or from, possibly, abroad."

"Yes," Renata said again. "Are your flight arrangements all set then?" Megan told her what had transpired the previous night and that Asta Holm-Ditlevsen's chauffeur would be picking her up in Lugano.

"Not bad!" whistled Renata, suitably impressed.

"And guess what I'm going to look for if I have a chance to stop by a certain music store I know about there in Lugano?" Megan asked.

Before Renata could answer, Megan pulled out her tiny four-hole harmonica from her purse and blew *Camptown Races* into the iPhone to the amusement of the other hotel guests having breakfast.

At the end of the fanfare, Megan confirmed: "A really good quality, sixteen-hole Hohner chromatic harmonica. I've misplaced my old one, and Hohner makes them much better nowadays anyway."

The prospect of this acquisition did not thrill Renata as much as it did Megan, and the two friends soon concluded their conversation, promising to stay in daily touch while Megan was in Switzerland. Megan's flight that day did not leave until 5:50 pm from Kennedy to Zürich, where she would arrive at 7:55 the next morning, just in time to catch a 9:20 flight down to Lugano.

Arranging to pick up her suitcase later, Megan checked out of the Hotel Wales and walked over to the Guggenheim to pay homage once again to Schiele's simpatico 1916 portrait of his father-in-law, Johann Harms, a partial gift of Janette Killar's grandfather to the museum. Well, dear brooding philosopher, she thought, wish me luck on my European travels. Megan then took a cab to the Galerie St. Sebastian and dropped in on her old friends Helene Blumenstock and Janette Killar.

It was high time she had a conference with them about things Klimtonian in general and Asta Holm-Ditlevsen in particular. Knowing how busy they were, she telephoned ahead to let them know she was dropping by. She was heartily encouraged to do so by a very surprised Helene, who had no idea Megan was in New York when she was supposed to be in Alaska. She had in fact just received a wooden postcard from Megan with a romantic Alaskan mountain scene. Within another few minutes Megan had paid off the cab and was in the Galerie St. Sebastian. The trio went into Janette's inner office, after her dog, Gary, had sniffed at and okayed the new intruder.

"So, what is your mission?" asked Janette after Megan had told them she was leaving for Switzerland early that evening. "Surely not just to look at a collection of Scandinavian women artists in Ascona?" she added astutely, knowing that Megan always had several irons in the fire whenever she went to Europe.

"No, of course not, although you know how interested I am in them," smiled Megan. "I hope to manage to see the presumptive fourth Klimt panel, the redo of Matsch's *Theology* allegory. We all know, if Asta Holm-Ditlevsen has it, the panel must be either in Ascona or some other hideaway."

"Actually," uttered Janette with exasperation, "I hope you have better luck than I did. Even though I was doing a complete catalogue of Klimt's works, that darn Danish lady would not receive me. Nor would she admit to owning the Klimt panel, much as I skirted around the probability."

"Perhaps because you are a gallery owner she was fearful that you might want to buy the Klimt?" asked Megan, a bit naively.

"Oh, no, that wouldn't have scared her," interjected Helene adamantly. "She's just a recluse. We know the type. Think of that Mr. Herrly in Vermont. He wouldn't let Janette see his Schieles when she was doing the catalogue raisonné of the artist's complete works. It was only after the catalogue came out that he allowed her to visit his collection in Brattleborough. And then he was furious that the catalogue included asterisks next to the titles of works he owned, indicating that they had not been seen and verified by the author. Ha! Served him right."

The ninety-two-year-old veteran of the arts was working up a perfect fit of indignation and both Janette and Megan sought to calm her down. The past is the past, they consoled her.

"No, on the contrary," objected wise Helene strenuously. "The past never rests. It has too many secrets begging to be discovered."

Megan and Janette regarded Helene with fond respect. She certainly knew what she was talking about. How many ownership mysteries had *she* solved in the ever changing world of provenance during her seven decades plus at the Galerie?

Wolfing down one of the substantial deli sandwiches they had ordered in for lunch, Megan told them in piecemeal sentences about the amazing encounter she had had in Vienna with the dying grandnephew of Klimt. Trusting the two co-directors of the Galerie St. Sebastian completely, she confided what Hans Ernst Klimt had said about the robbery of a secret panel, the Secretum, and the so-called shame of it. Neither Janette nor Helene could shed any light on what work it might have been. Klimt had kept his reworking of *Theology* all his life, but certainly that was not a secret.

They promised to ponder the matter as Megan took her leave. Another taxi brought her back to the Hotel Wales where, leaving it for a minute, she picked up her suitcase at the front desk, then instructed the driver to take her to Kennedy Airport.

It was two o'clock in the afternoon, still plenty of time to check in comfortably for her flight to Zurich. She felt her heart sing: *Andiamo a Ascona, andiamo a Ascona!*

As she did so often, Megan blessed the amazing profession of art history that had taken her so many places around the world—from tracking Gauguin in Tahiti to admiring Akseli Gallen-Kallela's two-story A-frame log house, his "wilderness studio" on Lake Ruovesi in the middle of Finland.

Gallen-Kallela's grandson, John Gilbert von Galen, had heard her lecture at New York's Institute of Fine Arts once. Excited that she had shown his grandfather's work in her presentation, he invited her to visit his grandfather's studio in Ruovesi. It was an art and nature experience she would never forget.

She was given free access to the artist's riveting works and meticulously designed studio with a balcony above and massive fireplace below. Also, the family introduced her to the steam sauna routine which included a mandatory after-dip in cold lake Ruovesi just as the sun came up over the horizon. Ah, Finland!

"Others bring you cocktails. I bring you clear, cold water," Jean Sibelius had once said of his music and therefore of his country. How right he was.

33

Megan was just settling comfortably into her window seat in first class on the Swiss Air flight to Zurich. She was wearing her favorite travel duds: black, easy-to-slip-off Merrell shoes, black slacks and matching multi-pocketed black vest, with a long-sleeved red fleece shirt that had a high zippered neck. On her head was a small, short-brimmed black wool cap, so not to feel any draft from overhead, one of her perennial pet worries.

All had gone well through security and the plane was filling up quickly. The two aisle seats in her row were empty so far. She began her favorite boarding game: sizing up the passengers coming down the aisle and *willing* them either to pass right on by, or be the ones assigned to the seats next to her.

She willed well. An attractive older man with a pleasant-looking young woman paused at Megan's row, eying the two vacant aisle seats and checking their tickets. "Yes," she said, smiling and beckoning to the seats, "I've saved them just for you."

This broke the ice nicely and after hoisting their overhead bags into the luggage rack above, the two sat down and introduced themselves. "I'm Theresa Laird and this is my father, Harvey Laird," said the young woman, leaning across the aisle toward her father who had chosen the aisle seat next to Megan. After introductions were made, Megan learned that their trip to Switzerland was a present for Theresa, who had just graduated from Vassar College. Both she and her father were avid skiers and they were headed for the slopes at Zermatt.

As they talked easily for a few more minutes, Megan asked Theresa what her plans were for after college.

"Well, I majored in anthropology. I thought I might pursue a graduate degree in forensic anthropology." Theresa was obviously a serious young person and deeply engaged with her subject.

After the plane had taken off, Megan settled down with her Mac and began working on the fictional "Krimi" murder mystery she had begun in Dallas before flying to Vienna. It was about Gustav Mahler. She was calling her book *Murder for Mahler* and had gotten a good start on it before all hell had broken loose in Vienna, then Santa Fe, and now New York. Writing fiction was so much easier and just plain more fun than all the scholarly books she had laboriously researched and written over the years. Why hadn't she discovered this sooner?

Dinner was served early, and afterward Megan began to assemble what she considered her must-have equipment for night on a plane. She exchanged her Merrells for a pair of soft slipper sox, blew up her little travel pillow, placed her Bose earphones over her ears, applied some moisturizer to her lips, pulled a flannel circle scarf she'd bought in Antarctica up over her chin and mouth (she had a horror of falling to sleep with her mouth open), put on a large, soft eye mask, and drew her black woolen cap down over her headphones and low onto her forehead.

She was now in what Tina had once quipped was her "black-out acoustic tent," and set for a good night's sleep without distractions. She pulled out her beloved iPod, into which she had transferred well over 17,000 "songs" (a symphony, an opera, a concerto were, apparently, all "songs"), and tried to decide between falling to sleep to Bach's B minor Mass or the Brahms Requiem. She chose the latter and was soon off to a dreamless, peaceful sleep.

Some five and a half hours later Megan woke up to the sounds of breakfast being served in the rows ahead of her. She put away her tent items, downed her mandatory morning senior pills plus a melatonin capsule, and smiled up at Harvey Laird, who was just returning to his seat from the toilets. She embarked on her almost motionless "in-seat" foot, leg, hip, stomach, back, shoulder, and neck exercises. Theresa woke up just as breakfast was being served to their row, and over more conversation Megan learned that Harvey was a physician and that he was writing a book on medicine and musicians.

"That's why Dad is so happy with my being interested in forensics," Theresa said happily

But a book on medicine and musicians?

Instantly the conversation became animated, as an engaged Megan happily threw out names of composers she presumed would have to be in such an interesting volume.

"Of course you're including Robert Schuman, with his mood swings," she said, "but to what do you attribute his constantly hearing the note A in his head during his last years and when he was at the asylum in Endenich?"

"Well, until recently many scholars have attributed that symptom plus his demonic visions to the use of mercury to treat the syphilis he might have contracted as a young man. In other words, his symptoms were supposedly the result of mercury poisoning. But now we tend to think that Schumann may have suffered from a severe bipolar disorder. Remember he tried to commit suicide by jumping off a bridge into the Rhine."

"Oh, yes, and he was saved by some boatmen and taken home to Clara. That's when he asked to be placed in a sanatorium. I've visited the building at Endenich, as a matter of fact," declared Megan proudly. She had also photographed Clara and Robert's elaborately sculpted gravesite in the cemetery at Bonn.

"Is that what you think then, mercury poisoning?" she asked.

"No. You may know that an autopsy indicated he had a tumor at the base of his brain. If it was a chordoid meningloma, that would make sense, as they are known to cause auditory hallucinations."

"Oh, gosh!" exclaimed Megan. "That certainly sounds likely, since he heard the A4 note for most of his adulthood and complained about it frequently.

"Who else is in your book," she inquired, thinking about her own long book on Beethoven's portraits and the various theories for the cause of his death, the most consistent one being failure of the liver. "Beethoven?"

"Yes, I go over all the possible causes, as well as the informative autopsy report. Beethoven is, of course, a must, but my book also treats Franz Schubert, who did not die of typhoid fever but rather from syphilis. And of course I address Tchaikovsky, who officially was supposed to have died of cholera from drinking unboiled water, but whom we now know..."

"Oh, yes!" interrupted Megan enthusiastically. "It's pretty much accepted now that because of the increasing boldness of his homosexual activity within imperial circles, the tsar himself sent a commission offering him the 'honorable' outlet of suicide by taking arsenic."

"Quite right," agreed Harvey Laird. "And since his brother Modeste was also gay, he had a special interest in collaborating with the elaborate cover-up by the doctors who tended his brother."

Time had passed so quickly that neither Megan nor the Lairds noticed they were banking for a landing until a man's voice over the loud speaker announced that they were about to set down and to please return seat backs to an upright position.

At the baggage claim they exchanged business cards and promised to keep in touch. Theresa gave Megan a hug and then father and daughter were out of the security area. Megan picked up her easily recognizable Eagle Creek roller bag, which she had decorated long ago with white circles painted on front and back, then checked in at the local Darwin Airlines desk for her flight to Lugano. She had a pleasant hour and forty minutes to wait, time to catch up on email. And time to ponder what, oh what she might be permitted to see of Asta Holm-Ditlevsen's very private collection in Ascona.

34

Paul Czermack, private chauffeur to Asta Holm-Ditlevsen, stood holding a discreet white sign with Megan's name on it at the Lugano airport exit. They smiled at each other and the pleasant young man immediately took possession of her roller bag. Megan hung on to her multi-pocketed, lightweight shoulder bag, made up of different black squares, as she entered the gold Lancia Delta HF at the curb. Lugano was still a small airport and one could park conveniently close to the exit where rental cars were kept.

She had recently received an invitation from President Warren Griggio to speak at his private American school in Lugano, Franklin College, and she asked Signor Czermack to drive by the Grace Library on the Kaletsch Campus so she could get an idea of where she would be speaking the following fall.

He circled round the campus, taking a look at the grotto terrace with its mixture of firs and palm trees where the students hung out. Then Czermack returned to the downtown area and Megan made one more request of the patient driver: would he be so kind as to stop at the music store Cuzzocrea on the via Trevano? *"Ma certo, Signora!"*

Czermack quickly found the shop and waited in front while Megan dashed inside with her shoulder bag. Perhaps fewer than five minutes later she reappeared, a wide grin on her face. She was brandishing a Hohner Super Chromaica harmonica in her right hand.

"And now we can go to Ascona!" she informed an amused Czermack, who deftly turned onto the main road out of town in the direction of Ascona. Megan sat back and drank in the beautiful mountain landscape as the chauffeur expertly drove the fourteen winding miles to Ascona. In half an hour, shortly after one o'clock, they pulled up at the palatial entrance to Megan's beloved hotel, the Castello del Sole.

After she had checked into a second floor room in the original part of the hotel, Megan sat out on her private balcony and absorbed the sights and sounds of this idyllic spot with its great green lawns, charming donkey compound, flower beds, and seating areas leading down to the lake shore.

How wonderful to be back! She might even find the energy to do her laps in the pool, which was housed half indoors, half outdoors, an arrangement that made observing the changing light underwater endlessly interesting.

After a light lunch on the grand patio facing the lake, and a short nap, Megan did indeed obtain goggles and a swimming suit at the hotel gift shop and swam her thirty minutes of laps, undisturbed at that time of day by other serious swimmers.

Asta Holm-Dtlevsen's driver was not due to pick her up until seven that evening, so she still had plenty of time to unpack her few belongings and make more notes for her Krimi manuscript. Finishing that, she caught up on email and let Claire, Tina, and Renata know that she had arrived safely in Ascona. By return e-mail Claire gently advised: "Don't overextend yourself, dear, and remember to be on your guard. Don't forget there may be some connection between Jayne's death and what you told me happened at the Moderne."

Megan was waiting at the front entrance of the Castello when Paul Czermack pulled up promptly at seven. To her surprise Asta Holm-Ditlevsen was in the back seat of the car.

"I couldn't wait to meet you," confessed Asta charmingly, as Megan slipped inside. She liked this straight-forward woman. There was another congenial passenger in the car as well: Asta's dog Minne. Megan could not believe her eyes, the dog looked so much like her Button. And Asta could hardly believe that Megan too owned a Maltese dog. Soon Megan was showing iPhone pictures of her Button boy to an admiring Asta and Minne.

The car drove down Ascona's main street fronting the lake and turned into the hillside driveway of a large two-story house set back one block from the lakefront promenade with its beckoning cafes. Its second floor overlooked the lively scene on land and water.

A happily yapping Minne led the way to Asta's office/den where the Strindberg canvases graced the walls. Megan was left to admire them while her hostess saw to the concoction of sangria which was served with tasty-looking hors d'oeuvres.

"And how was your flight? Not too tiresome, I hope?" inquired Asta.

"Oh, no, I got a good night's sleep, thanks to your generous first class reservation, and my seat companions were quite interesting." Megan added: "I always sleep to music, so I was all wrapped up comfortably with my earphones and iPod."

"Oh, and what music did you select to listen to as you changed continents?" asked Asta in amusement.

"It was a toss up between Bach and Brahms, and I chose Brahms," answered Megan happily.

"Ah! Brahms! He is my favorite, favorite composer," breathed Asta fervently. "Look here, on my desk I have this new book of his correspondence." Megan picked up the book with interest. It was one she had not seen and in it were two of the several photographs taken of the composer's Vienna lodgings at Karlsgasse No. 4 shortly after his death in 1897. "Oh!" she exclaimed with pleasure. "I've written an entire article on the photographs of Brahms' rooms."

"But why do I not know about this article?" Asta asked almost petulantly. "I thought I had copies of all your books and catalogue essays."

"I published it back in nineteen seventy-nine and it wasn't in a catalogue, but rather an American journal called *Arts Magazine*.

"What is the title of this article? I must have it!" demanded Asta, reaching for a notebook and pen.

"I titled it 'The Visual Brahms: Idols and Images' and, let's see, if you really want to know, I've written similar iconographical ones, lectures actually, on Vivaldi, Mozart, Beethoven, Schubert, Bruckner, Mahler—both Gustav and Alma—Johann Strauss, Jr., and Poulenc. I call doing this musical iconography. And don't worry about trying to find a back issue of *Arts Magazine*. I'll Xerox and send you a copy of the article when I'm back in America."

"So, calling it 'Idols and Images,' what exactly did you mean by that?" Asta persevered.

"Well, Brahms lived the last twenty-five years of his life in those three rented rooms off Vienna's Karlsplatz, and on the walls he had images of what you could call his idols, the persons he most venerated. For example on the wall behind his piano a plaster bust of Beethoven was prominently displayed upon a wall bracket, a prized image he'd brought with him from his parents' home in Hamburg. And two more effigies, one in the music room and one in his bedroom, attested to the two greatest 'B's in the composer's life. Can you guess who they were?"

"I haven't yet studied the photographs in my Brahms book, but perhaps Bach? I know that Brahms was a collector of Bach holographs."

"You are quite correct, Asta." The Maltese connection had already put them on a first name basis. "A portrait of Bach hung over Brahms' bed. But can you guess the second 'B'? And it's not Beethoven." Asta looked perplexed and shrugged her shoulders in inquiring defeat. Megan picked up Asta's book.

"Look at this photo of Brahms' piano room, to the left of the Beethoven bust and lower down on the wall, see? Brahms had hung a laurel-wreathed bronze profile of Bismarck!"

"Ah! I see," exclaimed Asta. "As a North German, Brahms would of course have admired the man who pulled the German Empire together."

"Yes, just think of it! Bismarck and Bach! The Iron Chancellor of Germany and the master contrapuntist of the German baroque. So representative of Brahms, a man of the world who took a keen interest in politics. Did you know that his reading matter on trips always included a volume of Bismarck's speeches? And as a composer whose formal roots lay indisputably in Bach, as you well know, he usually had music by J.S. open on his piano."

The two women smiled at each other and sipped their sangrias. How nice to have so much in common, from Maltese dogs to Brahms, in addition to Strindberg and women painters. Asta tried to recall the last time she, the recluse, had entertained company in her home. When she did meet with people it was always at her husband's office at the other side of town.

"Dinner is served," announced Asta's butler discreetly. Asta, preceded by an eager Minne, led the way into her large dining room with its white-framed artworks on all four walls.

"Oh, my goodness! You don't really expect me to be able to *eat* in the presence of all these wonderful painters, do you?" gasped Megan appreciatively. Asta laughed. "You'll have plenty of time to look, not to worry."

A delicious dinner featured roast pork and red cabbage, followed by lemon mousse. After due regard to the potent painters on the walls as well as to Minne, who was patiently awaiting handouts from the table, they discussed the various Gustav Klimt exhibitions presently being held in Vienna at various museums with large Klimt holdings.

This major event included the Albertina Museum, the new Leopold Museum, which had a spectacular exhibit of Klimt, "Up Close and Personal, and the Wien Museum. Megan still stubbornly thought of the Wien Museum by its former name, the Historisches Museum der Stadt Wien, since her apartment on the Karlsgasse during her student years was so close to it that it became a second home.

"It was most generous of you to lend the Aarhus Museum all three of the Klimt University panels," said Megan.

"Oh, and have you been to Aarhus?" asked Asta, leading the conversation slightly away from Klimt, Megan thought. She decided to take a Danish tack.

"Yes. A dear friend of my youth is Danish and from Aarhus, so I visited her and her parents there several times. I used to be a folk singer and even composed a song in Danish, which they helped me with. Would you like to hear it?"

"Indeed!" exclaimed Asta.

After swallowing the last bite of her lemon mousse Megan commenced:

Jeg har kendt så mange byer,
men kun en med sommerskyer,
København, København,
min bedste ven.

Stockholm var stilig,
Paris var fransk,
London var livlig,
men ingen var dansk

hvad skal jeg gøre?
hvor skal jeg tage hen?
hjem til dig igen!
København, København,
min bedste ven.

I have known so many cities,
But only one with summer skies,
Copenhagen, Copenhagen,
My best friend.

Stockholm was stylish,
Paris was French,
London was lively,
But none were Danish.

What shall I do?
Where shall I go?
Home to you again!
Copenhagen, Copenhagen,
My best friend.

"Oh, but that is just lovely, so sweet!" cried Asta, clapping her hands in delight. "And your Danish pronunciation is excellent."

"Thank you. I have my Danish friend Lili Jensen to thank for that," answered Megan modestly.

"Shall we have our coffee with Strindberg back in my office?" Asta invited, nodding to the butler. Taken as she was by Megan, Asta had nevertheless not yet decided whether to share the Klimt panel in the living room with her guest. The two women returned to the office and there was more talk of Brahms.

"How did you, Megan, as an art historian, ever come to the idea of studying what you call 'the visual Brahms' and all those other musicians you have examined from an iconographical perspective?"

"Well, Asta, as you may have observed by now, music is actually my first love, even over art history, and so it seemed to me perfectly reasonable to apply the methods of my discipline to images of composers. It just occurred to me that if we scholars were to profit from the biographical clues provided in the portraits and self-portraits of painters, certainly we could apply a similar principle of 'image and icon' to musicians.

"For instance, especially in the case of my Beethoven book, what were the likenesses that composers themselves cultivated and sanctioned? What did that desire to control say about them? Beethoven was a perfect example of someone who self-consciously attempted to influence the contemporary images of him. Some he loved, others he hated with a passion."

Asta reached for her notebook and pen again. "What is the title of your Beethoven book? I must order it."

"It's called *The Changing Image of Beethoven: A Study in Mythmaking*, and it came out quite a while ago, back in nineteen eighty-seven, but recently a new paperback version has been printed with a long new preface that was lots of fun to write," Megan answered.

"It seems that without knowing it back in the nineteen eighties, I was doing what is called *Rezeptionsgeschichte*, reception history. That is, how the composer's image (and music of course) was received, conceived, tweaked, and altered to suit later ages and various nationalities."

Asta smiled encouragingly and begged her guest to continue.

"Well, my book began with contemporaneous portraits of Beethoven—paintings, drawings, sculptured busts. But soon I realized that the book was becoming a cultural history of the times and of how later musicians saw the composer. Take Wagner and Berlioz, for example. So the book continues through the nineteenth century and climaxes with the nineteen-two Vienna Secession exhibition of the sculptor Max Klinger's life-size, marble statue of Beethoven in thought on a bronze throne that was cast in Paris. The Empyrean eagle is at his feet. Quite an ensemble!"

"Ah, yes, Megan," responded Asta. I've seen the Klinger *Gesamtkunstwerk* in Leipzig at the Gewandhaus. Too bad it has now been removed to the new Museum there, as the installation at the Gewandhaus was far more compelling."

"I couldn't agree with you more, but at least Leipzig has embraced its hero again after consigning the statue to a basement during Communist times. It was actually the conductor Kurt Masur who was responsible for reclaiming the Klinger Beethoven out of the basement where it had been stored during World War II. He had it installed in the Gewandhaus. During the nineteen seventies, when I used to speak for his biannual symposia on musicians, he wore a bolo tie as silent protest against the Communist way of life. Did you know that?"

"I did not, but I am not surprised. One feels the thrill of freedom and being supremely in charge of the destiny of the music just in the way he conducts," declared Asta.

"By the way, from afar, Klinger so admired your Brahms, that in the year eighteen ninety-four he mailed him an extraordinary homage, a series of forty-one etchings and lithographs entitled 'A Brahms Phantasy.' Every note of the composer's *Schicksalslied* had been meticulously engraved on the copper plates that bore Klinger's fantastic pictorial response to Brahms' setting of Hölderlin's fatalistic poem on human destiny.

"You can see one of the framed prints on the wall in that photograph of Brahms' music room in your book here," Megan said, eagerly opening again Asta's book of the composer's correspondence and handing her the pertinent page.

"Ah, why did I not make the connection before?" Asta asked herself incredulously. "I have of course seen Klinger's marble memorial to Brahms in the Hamburg Musikhalle."

"Yes, and perhaps you knew of Brahms' elegant response to the extraordinary *Sendung* from Klinger?"

"No, what?"

"Well, when Brahms published his penultimate work in the summer of eighteen ninety-six, the *Four Serious Songs*, he prefaced it with a dedication to Klinger. So we've come full circle."

Asta had also come full circle. She yearned to share the Klimt panel with a like soul and now she believed she had found one in her dinner guest.

Could she take her into her confidence? If she swore her to secrecy, would this enthusiastic scholar from Texas keep her oath? She decided to take a chance. Clearing her throat, she broached the subject obliquely. "Megan, surely there are artworks by Schiele which only you have seen in private collections and about the existence of which you have had to remain silent?"

"Quite so," agreed Megan. "While his sisters were alive I was requested by them not to discuss which works by their brother they owned. And more recently, when I visited a private collection in California that included an important Schiele oil thought to be lost, I was sworn to secrecy. I have kept that oath, if reluctantly, because my friend Rudolf Leopold, founder of the Leopold Museum in Vienna, had searched for this particular canvas all his life."

"In that case, I too should like you to take an oath of secrecy for *me*. There is something I want to show you, but I do not want, under any circumstances, to have the art world, especially art dealers and collectors, know that I am in actual possession of the work. Many people suspect I have it, but no one has been able to prove it. And I? I neither confirm nor deny it. Do you think you could keep my secret if I shared it with you?"

Megan thought this over in silence for a full minute, realizing that if she swore an oath of secrecy to Asta, and the artwork turned out to be Klimt's *Theology*, she would never be able to confirm its presence in Holm-Ditlevsen's collection. And this was the very Klimt panel that Janette Killar, Helene Blumenstock, Renata Teuer, Lyonel Retter, and others firmly believed was there in Ascona.

What to do?

She decided to take the leap and emulate Asta's personal recourse of neither confirming nor denying its presence in her Ascona collection.

Anyhow, she was dying to see the Klimt panel, if that is what it was, with her own eyes. It had never been photographed while in the artist's basement. None of Klimt's contemporaries had seen it, except possibly for Schiele, who once commented on the "thousands" of drawings he had seen at Klimt's studio. He had never made mention of a Klimt panel. It was only hearsay, after all, that the artist had redone Matsch's *Theology*.

Solemnly Megan turned to Asta and, ceremoniously raising her right hand, pronounced: "I promise not to talk or write about what you might now show me."

Asta's pale blue eyes lit up with pleasure and confidence and she bade Megan follow her to the living room, once again with Minne joyously leading the way.

35

In Alaska, Günther Winter was not at all happy with the report Eddie had given him over the telephone from New York concerning the Crespi woman. He had actually lost track of her overnight and had no idea where she might be, since she had not returned to the Moderne Galerie the next day.

"Her sister und friends are still here at zee hotel, Günther had told Eddie, "und zey, as vell as I, vanted to keep tabs on her. You had better return here und resume your security duties."

In fact Günther had run across the trio at breakfast that morning, faking interest in their day's excursion plans and making a few suggestions of things for them to do before their plane left the next afternoon. Good riddance, he had thought to himself. But ever the elegant host, he had a basket of fruit sent to their suite that afternoon.

Should he telephone Crespi's university and see if any information as to her whereabouts was forthcoming? Better yet, since she had left for New York on the same flight as Eddie, how about contacting the Galerie St. Sebastian and asking whether or not they knew where Crespi was—New York still, or perhaps back in Dallas? This was the question he put to Helene Blumenstock when she answered his call. "Oh, no," she had replied readily, "she's already in Switzerland. But she'll be returning for a board meeting at the Moderne Galerie next weekend."

In Switzerland? There was only one place concerned with Klimt that curious Crespi could be visiting. Ascona.

Would that old hermit woman Asta Holm-Ditlevsen open the doors of her private collection to a relentlessly nosy scholar like Crespi? *Um Gottes Willen!* That Crespi woman should have retired from scouting works of art years ago. Why did she still concern herself with art history? Hadn't she just been honored for a life-long career in the discipline? It was time to stop. Damn her curiosity!

Well, at least in Switzerland she would learn nothing about his big *Sendung* to Alaska. True, Crespi might be able to confirm what the art world has long suspected, that Klimt's *Theology* panel was indeed in the crazy Danish woman's collection.

But, Gott sei Dank, such a confirmation could in no way lead to the majestic panel he had so recently installed in the basement stronghold of his Alpenglow annex.

36

There was still daylight filtering through the tall windows of Asta Holm-Ditlevsen's two-story living room overlooking Ascona's water front, and the four ceiling spots completed the beautiful illumination of Klimt's *Theology* panel that took up the entire back wall of the capacious room.

"I can't *believe* it!" cried Megan. She felt her heart pounding and began blinking her eyes, in case the vision proved to be just that, a vision. But the painting was there, robust in coloring with sapphire blues above and cerise to crimson reds below. Small stained ivory statues of Krishna, Buddha, Christ, and Mohammed occupied the lowest crimson part of the panel. Their expressions were grave and enigmatic. Above them were knots of intertwined figures. Women, men, and beasts of all kinds floated upward toward the sapphire blue sphere against a shower of silver, skeletons, and skulls, then gold rivulets and birds. A few of the figures, again both humans and beasts, reached the pale blue top register of the panel.

"It is simply overwhelming, is it not?" inquired Asta after several minutes of silence. "Why would Klimt have redone Matsch's *Theology* in such a pessimistic manner? What was he trying to say?"

Megan continued looking at the panel in silence, slowly shaking her head now and then. She put a hand lightly on Asta's arm to signify that she had heard her but that she was still thinking. Finally she spoke.

"I think that, although the panel is full of haunting and haunted specters, with skeletons, humans and animals vying for space, this is not so much a message of pessimism, but rather of theology in the thrall of, or perverted to, *another cause.*"

"What do you mean?" asked Asta, vastly surprised by Megan's words.

"I mean, Asta, that Klimt seems to have painted an exposition of what, in the popular thought of the Vienna of his time, has come to be called social Darwinism. Look at the features of some of the men and women who have made it to the top of the panel, to the realm of cerulean blue. Their features are unmistakably Semitic, especially the women, some of whom look astonishingly like the Jewish society matrons Klimt painted."

Asta was listening attentively.

"Remember, this was the time of exponential aftermath to Wilhelm Marr's startling book on Judaism versus Germanism, making Jews 'outsiders' not because of their religion but because of their race. Now why, in an increasingly prejudiced Vienna, would Klimt position recognizable Jews as having attained celestial heights? What could this have meant in a city that had a popular unashamedly anti-Semitic mayor in Karl Luegar? And what could Klimt's *Theology* ceiling panel have meant in particular for the university auditorium of Vienna, where gentile students had recently formed a union to protest the increasing percentage of Jewish students and professors in their ranks?

"Think about it, Asta! Some of Klimt's most important patrons were Jewish. They were assimilated, educated, wealthy barons of industry and commerce. They were just the opposite of the poor orthodox Jews flooding the city from the empire's rural provinces in the east, the hated 'Ost-Juden' with their black clothes, long beards and ear locks. If you look at Klimt's middle plane in which the struggle to survive takes place you can see a few almost caricatures of what was commonly associated with a Jewish face— hawk noses, dark complexions."

"For heaven's sake, Megan. I understand what you are saying, but was Klimt, like society, condemning the Eastern Jews while literally elevating the assimilated ones above other factions of society?"

"No. I think that in a panel supposedly dedicated to Theology, Klimt was indulging in a supreme irony. He was condemning what had become a new religion, the survival of the fittest. What he felt was a 'religion' that was pushing theology out of the way. In other words, he was condemning a social Darwinism that had no place for the weaker elements of society. Remember Klimt came from humble beginnings himself."

Both women remained silent for some time, staring at the spellbinding panel.

"I am convinced by what you say, Megan," said Asta at last. "No wonder Vienna also produced a Theodor Herzl and that he in turn introduced Zionism and the idea of a new homeland in Palestine to world Jewry."

"Yes, no wonder."

"Could we have some more of your sangria, Asta?" asked Megan suddenly. "I think I need a drink and I definitely need to sit down."

"I do too," Asta responded with alacrity. "You have revealed to me what I was always searching for in this great, enigmatic panel of strife and ossified religions. I am happy that I shared my Klimt with you. I did the right thing. Thank you."

31

Rita Herring was right. Her brother Thad had barely spoken to her since they both returned to Vienna from the States, she with a mission-accomplished record, he with two embarrassing failures to live down. Their father was still furious with Thad, accusing him almost daily of being a bumbling, good for nothing and assigning him menial tasks about the house. Since Frau Herring had died some ten years ago, the family had come together in Jeremy's two-story house on the Bastiennegasse, out in Vienna's wooded eighteenth district. Ostensibly, Rita and Thad had moved back home to take care of Jeremy, but in fact as it turned out, it was their father who was taking care of them. It was he who had tasks and employment for them. Still an active art dealer, Jeremy had numerous delivery and pickup assignments for Thad, both in and out of the country, and until recently, Rita had taken care of all his business correspondence.

Earlier this morning Günther Winter had telephoned him from Alaska in what could only be called an imperious panic. That meddling art historian Megan Crespi was in Switzerland, very probably visiting the collector Asta Holm-Ditlevsen in Ascona. Her movements were to be followed and reported to him at once. Also the Holm-Ditlevsen home was to be searched for any single large-size work of art.

Winter was only one of his clients, but certainly the wealthiest and the most demanding. And the most unscrupulous, a good match for Jeremy and his astute if not always legitimate dealings in the art world. Getting the Hundertwasser estate and the artist's Vienna apartment for Günther some years ago had been a tour de force, taking the Austrians and the Austrian government by surprise before anyone could suggest that it be preserved as a national museum. How often had he visited Günther holding court on the roof of the Ankerhaus, sitting regally in the outdoor bathtub and ordering his visitors to admire the view of the Stefansdom.

More often than he liked, Jeremy sighed. It had been damn foolish of him to allow Thad to become Günther's murderous errand boy. The traffic "accident" in Geneva had been successful, but the mess up in Santa Fe, then Girdwood, was a double whammy The kid simply wasn't up to complex planning. The Moderne Galerie spray-paint errand he had given Rita had gone off like a charm.

The nine-word *Kurrentschrift* message had been successfully delivered. Jeremy had painstakingly written it out in the old cursive hand in order to deflect any suspicion that might fall upon him as an international art dealer. In his own good time he would follow through on the provocative message Rita had left at his instigation: "Want to trade your Klimt whore for the Secretum?" Günther, as always, was too impatient. There was a tempo and a time for everything and right now inaction was the best action.

In the meantime, Rita's new job at the Nebehay Antiquariat was proving to be a gold mine of information for him. Dr. Hanskarl Klug was entrusting more and more of the daily record keeping to her, and she was transferring important confidential client information to Jeremy on a regular basis.

Soon he would discover, he hoped, the identity of the Nebehay client who was selling to Dr. Klug, piece by piece, what appeared to be an endless trove of previously unknown Klimt drawings. Rita reported that they were all preparatory sketches for the first Adele Bloch-Bauer portrait. It had been a long, drawn out process in which Klimt had been engaged for five years, from 1903, when her husband had commissioned an oil portrait of his wife, to 1907.

Like so many others, Jeremy wondered what had taken Klimt, the known and admitted womanizer, so long to complete the golden portrait. Why so many manila paper pencil studies of the slim, sinuous Adele in various seated poses, her abundant black hair piled on her head, her dark eyes steadily answering the artist's stare? What had happened during her many visits to the artist's cat-infested (Klimt would have said "populated") garden studio in the Josefstädter Strasse, and what had occurred during his visits to her at her husband's grand apartment on the Schwindgasse near the Karlskirche?

Ferdinand Bloch-Bauer's intelligent young wife was restless. She was eighteen when, by family arrangement, she married her thirty-five-year-old sugar baron husband. After two miscarriages and the death of a son two days after his birth, her potential career as a mother was over.

Being a society hostess came in fits and starts. She had moods, was an avid reader in several languages, had declared herself a socialist, and was a chain smoker with tobacco-stained teeth. It was probably in the company of Alma Schindler-not-yet-Mahler, that she had first met the virile Klimt, in 1900. There must have been a certain electricity. The artist's first sketch of her dated from that year.

A year later Klimt painted in short order, unusual for him, the first version of a theme that was to haunt him: the Apocrypha's *Judith and Holofernes*. It constituted a painted ode to Eros every bit as thrilling as Beethoven's musical ode *To Joy*. In spite of Klimt's specially designed frame which identified the picture in large letters as "Judith und Holofernes," his contemporaries simply could not or would not believe the artist had intended a portrayal of the pious Jewish widow. Earlier depictions of her had never actually conveyed *delight* in her dreadful, heaven-directed mission to decapitate the plundering commander of the Assyrian army. Surely Klimt had meant Salome, who asked for and received the bloody severed head of the man who had scorned her, John the Baptist.

But no, Klimt had transferred the thwarted lust of the historic Holofernes into the sexuality of a modern day woman: a literal femme fatale. It was Judith, personal slayer of lust, with half-closed eyes and parted lips, who was for him, more than any dancing Salome, the spell-binding representative of Eros. There was no mistaking the climax in this coupling of death and sexuality. Sigmund Freud take note. But what made Judith so evil in her orgasm was the hideous conditions under which it was achieved, the death of her partner.

Klimt suggested the phenomenon of mutilation, castration Freud would say, on three levels: the decapitated head of bearded Holofernes held triumphantly in Judith's right hand at the viewer's bottom right of the canvas, the wide bejeweled gold collar cleaving of Judith's own head from her body, and finally the vertical bisecting of Judith's own torso through diaphanous drapery placement.

Jeremy had also discerned how Klimt painted, with an archaeological slyness most others had not noticed, a specific biblical site reference right into the Judith canvas. The cone-shaped mountain symbols, fig trees, and grapevines behind Judith's head were all direct quotations from the ancient Assyrian palace relief of Sennacherib at Nineveh in northern Iraq.

But what intrigued Jeremy the most about this painting, the first of two Judiths Klimt would paint, what fascinated him the most was what contemporaries of the artist, both friends and enemies, had gossiped about. And this was the striking similarity of the earlier Judith, with her long face, abundant black hair and dark eyes, to society hostess Adele Bloch-Bauer.

Fortunately the scandal caused by Klimt's first University panel *Philosophy* immediately shifted public attention away from the Judith/Adele gossip. Both works were in the same 1901 Secession exhibition. For lovers of art Klimt's unfathomable panel was not populated by famous philosophers of the past, as they had imagined it would be, but by despairing naked figures, both male and female, adrift in existential space. The "shameful eroticism" of Klimt's pessimistic allegory was considered "outrageous" by the public and by critics.

And there was something else.

Klimt's *Judith* had a partly concealed right hand. Only three curved fingers were shown holding the head of Holofernes—the little finger, the ring finger, and a partially concealed middle finger. Adele Bloch-Bauer, who as a child had endured an injury to the middle finger of her right hand, was known to resort to all sorts of gestural artifices in order to conceal the deformity, whether in society or in photographs.

Jeremy was well acquainted with all of Adele's photographs and portraits. And he knew that, unique to his oeuvre, Klimt would paint the same woman twice, with a second "white" portrait of Adele in 1912. It was a standing portrait in which attention is drawn away from the bent and somewhat obscured fingers of the right hand to the left hand, as thumb and forefinger form a circle, sensuously feeling the grey trim of the subject's white, fur-lined full-length mantel. In this later portrait, bedecked with blooming flowers and motifs from Japanese art, Klimt again suggested the "choker" motif of the first Adele portrait and his first *Judith* icon by painting in detail the high-necked white dress collar. In 1909 he had reprised the biblical theme in a second *Judith and Holofernes* painting.

As far as Jeremy was concerned each of the Adele portraits referred back to both Judith representations. It would be the high point of his life in art if he, through the somewhat naïve and willing medium of his billionaire client Günther Winter, were to bring back the golden Adele to Austria. Of course he would never present this possibility to Günther, who only wanted Adele for his private collection. That covetous man must never know the real reason why he, Jeremy, was urging him to trade his newly acquired Klimt treasure, for the Moderne Galerie's golden Adele.

It would be a cerebral chess game in which Jeremy, not Günther, made the next move. In the meantime he had instructed his hired pawn in Geneva to pay a visit to Ascona *immédiatement*.

38

One other object of importance stood out in the spacious living room of Asta Holm-Ditlevsen. This was the beautiful concert grand Steinway to the far right of Klimt's *Theology* panel. As the women sat sipping a new supply of sangria, commenting on the odd fact that Klimt had never painted a self-portrait, Megan suddenly became aware of the piano and gasped with pleasure. "Oh, Asta, so you play the piano?"

"Indeed I do. It is one of my great comforts in life. I am working my way again back through the Busoni edition of Bach's *Klavierwerke*. I have all of Bach's piano works. Do you play piano as well, Megan?"

Megan looked sheepish and blushingly modest: "I do, but only by ear, only in the key of C or C minor, and only the French, Italian, and Spanish songs that I used to play as a child with my father on violin." Uncharacteristically, she did not offer to demonstrate for Asta. Instead she asked: "Have you ever played the Bach flute sonatas with someone?"

Asta looked nonplussed. "That's how my husband and I met! We were both at the conservatory and he was a flutist looking for a pianist. We played the Bach sonatas often."

"Well, this is too much!" exclaimed Megan. "I too am a flutist, and the Bach B minor Sonata is my favorite piece of music. Too bad I don't have my flute and the music with me here."

"That is simply solved," murmured Asta, half to herself. "I think I still have Rikard's old Haynes flute with the gold embouchure. And I know I have the music. Let us look for it."

Minne and Megan followed Asta back to the office and watched her open up a wall cabinet. After a few minutes of searching, she turned around with a slim black flute case in her hands. "Success!"

"Why don't you warm up, Megan, while I find the music?"

Overjoyed, Megan complied, noting the nice acoustics of the room as she moved slowly through the major and minor scales. In the highest register she began her favorite warm-up exercise: playing the descending figures of the beginning of Edward Elgar's cello concerto, which took her through all the registers in a most satisfying manner. Asta returned with the music in hand and a music stand. The two women set up and within minutes had begun the delicious sonata. When they got to the presto in 12/16 time with 32nd notes, they collapsed in laughter when Megan flubbed her part, not maintaining the off beat holds long enough. Far better flutists than she had had problems with this presto, so she was not discouraged, just embarrassed.

After their music session the two women returned to contemplating the Klimt. Asta proposed they take a boat tour the next day around the lake to the Italian town of Luino, where a fascinating weekly market was held on weekdays. Megan agreed readily. She had once photographed the imposing statue of Garibaldi there, the first monument in all of Italy to be dedicated to the Italian freedom fighter. But she asked if they might avail themselves of the chauffeur in the morning to visit the cemetery where Erich Maria Remarque and Paulette Goddard were buried side by side in nearby Ronco.

Asta's eyes sparkled with delight. "Imagine that you know about that remote cemetery and its distinguished inhabitants," she declared. "Of course. We will have Paul drive us tomorrow after breakfast. It's been ages since I was last there."

Late that evening, back at the Castello hotel, Megan called Claire, her sister, then Renata, and finally Janette, communicating to all three that her visit with Asta Holm-Ditlevsen had gone extremely well, but that she had nothing to report so far as anything regarding Klimt was concerned. Fortunately, only persevering Janette asked if she was sure Klimt's *Theology* panel wasn't there in Ascona.

Megan was able to answer truthfully: "I can neither say yes nor no." Janette seemed to accept that, remarking only on how secretive so many private collectors were. Having been assured that her little Button was thriving in the company of her sister's dogs, and with images of Garibaldi fighting Austrians in her head, Megan fell into a deep and contented sleep.

* * *

The next morning, after a delicious cereal, fruit, and tea breakfast on the sunny terrace of her hotel, Megan joined Asta in the back seat of the Lancia and Paul Czermack headed beyond the Ascona lake front to the southwest.

Arriving at the small port town of Brissago, the car took a climbing road up above it to the village of Ronco sopra Ascona with its magnificent view of the islands of Brissago and their lush botanical gardens. Parked at the church of San Martino with its Mediterranean mimosas and agave plants, the two women left Paul with the car and started walking up to the Ronco cemetery.

Suddenly, out of nowhere, a black helmeted man on a black Vespa zoomed by, almost running them down. "They all drive so recklessly nowadays!" exploded Asta.

Within minutes, since Megan remembered the way, she and her hostess were standing at the two gravestones: those of Remarque and his wife Paulette Goddard, who died in 1990, twenty years after her husband.

"How old were you when you first read *Im Westen nichts Neues?* asked Asta, sentimentally.

"*All Quiet on the Western Front?* Quite young, perhaps eighteen. When I was teaching I used to assign it to my class on twentieth-century art, and was thanked by many a student for having done so. I also used to end my lecture on Käthe Kollwitz with her plea, *'Never again war!'* It's good to bring in a pacifist message whenever possible, I think."

"I couldn't agree with you more, Megan, even if it hasn't seemed to have helped world history," sighed Asta, throwing an affectionate glance at the new friend with whom she seemed to share so much. "Shall we return to Ascona via Monte Verità?"

"Fantastic idea, Asta. Yes. Have you ever read Daphne du Maurier's fictionalized story about the strange vegetarian/nudist colony there?"

"No. I didn't realize she had taken up the subject, That would be interesting."

"What I love about Monte Verità is that it attracted Isadora Duncan *and* Mary Wigman, in addition to all the names we usually think about from Jung to Klee," said Megan, immediately assuming an angular, Wig-manesque pose.

"Yes," responded Asta, "and Rudolf von Laban set up a summer dance school there to teach his *Ausdruckstanz*, dance expression, before the outbreak of World War I. That's why Wigman was there. When I studied dance as a child our teacher used the Laban notation system to record our chorographical ideas."

"Well, that's one more thing we have in common, Asta," responded Megan with a laugh. "I too studied ballet as a girl and one summer Alexandra Danilova gave a guest class at our school. In *Dallas*, think of it! She had a devoted English secretary with her who tended to all of 'Shura' Danilova's needs."

Paul drove the women up to the top of Monte Verità and past the Casa Selma, where the nudists used to sun bathe, and on to the Japanese teahouse, where the three shared an iron pot of delicious white tea. The trio then returned to Ascona's water front in time for the two women to board a local vessel that made stops along the Lago Maggiore south coast, crossing the border with Italy to pick up and discharge passengers at Luino.

The black Vespa that had been following the Lancia since they left for Ronco that morning quietly drew up to the wharf as the ship left shore. The driver removed his hot helmet and sat motionless with crossed arms while watching the busy lake front scene for some ten minutes. From his position he had a good view of Asta Holm-Ditlevsen's empty house overlooking Ascona.

"You do have your passport with you, don't you, Megan?" asked Asta on board the small, sparklingly clean ship which was making steady progress toward the next Swiss port.

"Yes, thank you. I'm never without it," Megan assured her hostess.

After an hour's journey and several picturesque stops amid verdant vegetation that grew right down to the water line, they disembarked at Luino's modern wharf and walked across the Via della Vittoria to admire the dramatic Garibaldi monument showing the patriot with raised sword in hand. Megan told Asta that she had once gone all the way to Sardinia merely to get to the small island of Caprera and photograph the white farm house where Garibaldi had retired after his tempestuous military career on two continents.

"Why would you care about that so much?"

"It wasn't so much the farm house or Garibaldi's grave that I was eager to see, as it was to repeat the voyage of the plucky German sculptor Elisabet Ney. She conquered Giuseppe's heart by sailing all the way from Italy to Caprera, where he was living in self-imposed exile. She had come, she announced, to sculpt his image. He obliged in quick order. She had just done the same thing with that woman-hater Arthur Schopenhauer. He also could not resist her charms.

"By the way, Ney ended up in Austin, Texas, and she is one of the extraordinary women artists about whom I have taught, lectured and written for years. Excuse me for going on and on about this, but as an art historian I believe in always going to the locales involved with one's subject."

"On no, I love hearing about your art history travels. Do continue."

"Well, I once went to Elba, simply because of Napoleon's exile there, but I'm afraid I'm now too fond of creature comforts to sail all the way to the miniature island of Saint Helena way out in the South Atlantic Ocean. I used to challenge my students to go, but so far no one has taken me up on the dare."

Just then Asta's cell phone buzzed and, drawing it from her slim purse, she answered. A frown immediately crossed her features.

Turning to Megan a few seconds later she announced: "There has been an attempted break-in at my house!"

39

Günther Winter looked searchingly at Eddie as he reported in after his return from New York. "Und you really did not spot zee *verdammte* Crespi voman taking a cab to zee airport?"

"No, sir, I didn't catch sight of her again after loosing her the night before." Eddie again wondered why Herr Winter cared so much about the whereabouts of the nice Crespi lady. And he had really liked her jesting sister Tina and her droll friend Ellie when they were at the hotel. He was sorry they had already returned to Texas by the time he got back to Alaska.

"You'd better get back to your post," Günther abruptly dismissed Eddie, turning from the hotel's front desk and heading for the annex. *Perhaps Jeremy Herring has now learned something specific about what Crespi is up to in Switzerland,* he thought. *I'll give him a call.* Relaxing in his swivel desk chair in the inner sanctum of his annex, Günther placed a Skype call. He wanted to see the man's features when he talked to him. Jeremy beamed up almost immediately.

"Yes, Günther, what's up?"

"You tell me. Do you know vhere zee Crespi voman ist right now?"

"Certainly! At the moment she's making the rounds of Laggo Maggiore ports with Holm-Ditlevsen. They boarded a noon ship and have been gone for several hours."

"My god, zis voman ist all over zee map! She vas supposed to be in New York after she left here so suddenly. In fact, I flew my man Eddie over zere to keep tabs on her. But she eluded him."

"The Swiss rendezvous must have been arranged at the last minute. I sent an agent to stake out the Danish woman's house to try to find out what was going on. In all probability Crespi is being shown the Klimt *Theology* panel. I'm absolutely certain Holm-Ditlevsen has it."

"*Ja*, dat's zee Klimt you should have sold to *me*," pouted Günther.

"Don't be ridiculous. I didn't even *know* you when the panel became available," chided Jeremy. "Anyway, how old were you in nineteen seventy— fourteen?"

"Let me know what your agent finds out," Günther changed the subject, slightly mollified.

A shadow crossed Jeremy's features, one that Günther immediately noticed. "Will do," concluded Jeremy, abruptly hanging up the Skype connection.

"Damn that greedy Günther!" he exclaimed to the sympathetic shade that was once his wife.

Megan and Asta hurried back to the Luino pier and boarded the next vessel bound for Ascona. By four-thirty the boat had docked at the wharf just a few steps from Asta's house. A worried Paul Czermack was waiting for the women at the dock and, as they briskly walked up the incline to the house, he related what he knew.

Both the maid and the butler had been out on errands most of the morning. When the maid came back in the early afternoon she noticed that the servants quarters' bathroom had its casement window strangely ajar a few inches. It was always kept closed. She mentioned this to the butler when he returned and he set about checking the back of the house. He immediately discovered that attempts had been made to jimmy open not one but three of the resistant old casement windows. No actual entry had occurred, but the evidence of an attempt to do so was there for the police to examine, and in fact a detective was still there asking questions and making notes when the women arrived.

No, there had been no disgruntled or recently let-go employees. All of Signora Holm-Ditlevsen's servants had been with her for years, and loyally so.

"I suppose I should have a better alarm system with surveillance cameras installed," conceded Asta morosely after the detective had gone. "But here in halcyon Ascona? To have to be on one's perpetual guard like that? I've always felt safe enough with all my personnel here."

Megan sympathized, privately wondering in alarm whether, as with the Santa Fe killing, the attempted entry could have anything to do with her pursuit of Klimt's secret panel. There had been no Klimt in Santa Fe when Jayne Box was murdered, but certainly there was one in Ascona. And what about the mysterious Alpenglow occurrence when that young man had catapulted over the barrier, almost running into her? Could all these events be tied together? Unwillingly, she was beginning to see a connecting thread.

"You know what?" Asta said, suddenly interrupting Megan's gloomy train of thought. "I'd like to get out of here for a few days. How would you like to fly to Helsinki with me to see the retrospective of Helena Schjerf-beck that just opened? It's the largest exhibition ever of her works. As a matter of fact, some of my best Schjerfbecks are in the exhibition."

"Oh, Asta, I would *love* to," answered Megan instantly.

She, too, was all of a sudden overcome by a feeling of wanting to get away. She needed some air between her and Klimt matters. She was already in Europe, and she wasn't due in New York until the end of next week. Why not? She hadn't been to Finland for perhaps a dozen years.

"We'll take my private jet. I keep it at the Lugano airport. Could you be ready for us to pick you up by nine tomorrow morning?"

"Absolutely," answered Megan with enthusiasm.

Bidding Asta goodbye, she joined Paul in the limousine and he headed across the lake front to her hotel. "See you in the morning then," she said in farewell to Paul as he pulled up to the Castello del Sole. Minutes later Megan started to insert her key into the door of her hotel room.

The door swung open. It was unlocked.

41

It was not obvious to Megan that any of her things had been gone through. Nothing had been taken, as far as she could ascertain, but on the bed table the photograph of her dog Button she had placed on top of her laptop was facing outwards rather than inwards toward her bed. It could have been picked up and admired by the chamber maid, the same one who had carelessly neglected to close the door completely, she reasoned. But she also had a nagging awareness that there could be other explanations. She must stay on guard, remembering Claire's cautionary words.

But let's hope it was just the maid's negligence she told herself, turning her mind to packing for the morning and a new country. Wait a minute. Why not *two* countries?

She was not going to miss a chance, while she was still in Europe, to visit her dear friend in Paris, Henri-Claude de La Granger. He was her primary source for "The Mahler Murders" mystery she was writing.

She telephoned him right away and he was delighted with the idea. With a tantalizing laugh Henri-Claude informed her that he had just met someone with a small but most "unusual" Klimt collection. Teasingly he refused to go into details over the phone. Making a second phone call, Megan changed her return flight for New York to depart from Paris.

So this would still be a business trip, Megan assured herself, thinking of her vigilant CPA, Perry Harkens, who never let her take chances on her income-tax declarations. Perry always insisted on going down to the IRS office without her to handle her occasional audits. "I can feign benign ignorance much better than you," he had informed her early on in their long friendship.

Not wishing to take advantage of Asta's jet hospitality, Megan also made a commercial flight reservation for two days hence from Helsinki to Paris. That would give them time to take in the Schjerfbeck exhibition and see museum curator friends. They could also visit Sibelius's home, Ainola, just twenty-three miles outside Helsinki on Lake Tuusula. Strains of *Finlandia* seemed to follow one about the house. Asta confessed she had never been there nor to the Akseli Gallen-Kallela house and studio just north of Helsinki.

"Shame on you," Megan had chided Asta. "Gallen-Kallela was Finland's greatest *male* painter at the turn of the last century," she said, poking gentle fun at her own feminism and Asta's loyalties to Scandinavian women artists. The duo agreed, they would try to incorporate some of those cultural gems into a two-day sojourn, during which thoughts of attempted break-ins would be strictly banished.

42

Jeremy's Swiss agent, Pierre Balis, was reporting in from Ascona again, after having admitted to him yesterday that his attempt to enter the Holm-Ditlevsen house while the women and staff were away had been unsuccessful. This time the news was good and bad, Pierre informed his employer.

"Tell me the bad, first," barked Jeremy pessimistically.

"This morning I followed the Danish woman's car to the hotel where Crespi is staying. The chauffeur drove them to the Lugano airport, where they boarded a private jet. I have no idea where they were headed."

"That is strange. I can see why Crespi would be leaving Ascona, but I wonder why her hostess would have gone with her."

"Don't have a clue, but we may have one shortly," continued Pierre.

"What do you mean?"

"The good news I have for you is that, while in Crespi's hotel room, I managed to hack into her laptop and now copies of all her outgoing and incoming email will automatically be transferred to my computer."

"Excellent! Ah, just excellent!" Jeremy congratulated himself on having hired an impecunious but gung ho techie, rather than once again entrusting a delicate mission to his bungling son Thad. "Keep me informed as soon as you get any definite information."

"Right-O." Pierre rang off. He checked out of his room at the Castello del Sole, courtesy Jeremy Herring, and headed out to his Vespa in the front parking lot. It would be a good six hours drive back to Geneva, but he loved the thrill of cycling with the wind against his body, music playing through the earphones under his helmet.

* * *

On Asta's jet, a 1999 Gulfstream Ivsp, the talk returned to Klimt's *Theology*. "The more I consider what you pointed out, Megan, the more I think your idea of an ironical reading of social Darwinism makes sense. Is it known for sure that Klimt was a philo-Semitic?"

"I've never encountered any information to the contrary. Nor have I heard that an anti-Semitic remark ever escaped his lips. Quite the opposite of the high society woman whom he never painted, but once vigorously pursued, Alma Schindler Mahler."

"What do you mean? I know about Klimt's thwarted seduction attempt when she was a young girl traveling in Italy with her family, but not about what you're implying as far as Alma's being anti-Semitic. After all, she was married to not one but two Jews, Gustav Mahler *and* Franz Werfel."

"That's the amazing point. Not only her diaries but also her conversation was full of eye-popping Jewish slurs while she appreciated her healthy 'Aryan superiority' even over her own half-Jewish daughter Anna Mahler.

"Imagine that she could write about Jews as an 'alien species' and speculate, à la Wilhelm Marr, about the 'incredible' differences between races and ways of thinking. She was right in line with Vienna's Natural History Museum when, in nineteen thirty-eight, it held an exhibition composed of plaster casts on 'The Physical and Spiritual Appearance of Jews.'"

"But, wait a minute," Asta stopped her, "go back to Alma. As the wife of Werfel, didn't she have to flee Austria at the time of the *Anschluss*?"

"Oh, yes, she left right after the annexation of Austria by the German Reich, in nineteen thirty-eight. She was in danger of being 'Jewish by kinship,' a fine irony and one she richly deserved, if you ask me."

Just then the plane began to bank and the women admired the scenery below as the lively harbor of Helsinki came into view.

"Look, right there, you can see where we'll be staying," said Asta, pointing out the Hotel Kämp. "It's an old-fashioned hotel, but I love the place. It is within walking distance of everything and it overlooks the Esplanade. Also, it's not far from the Ateneum Museum where the Schjerfbeck show is on view."

Discreetly rubbing her fallen arches—too much ballet training in her early teen years—Megan wondered what "walking distance" and "not far" meant to her energetic octogenarian friend who had already forged ahead of her at both the Ronco cemetery and in Luino.

"I'm thrilled we'll be staying at the Kämp Hotel. I love being right on the Esplanade, and even more important for me, is the fact that Gustav Mahler stayed there during his brief visit to Finland in nineteen-seven. That was when he and Jean Sibelius had their famously discordant discussion about music."

"Oh? What was that?"

"We have the Finnish composer's version of the event. Seems they were talking about the symphonic medium and Sibelius fervently said how he admired the 'profound logic' that created an inner connection between all the motifs. But Mahler disagreed: *"Nein, die Symphonie müss sein wie die Welt. Sie müss alles umfassen* ("No, the symphony must be like the world. It must embrace everything.")."

"How do you know all this?" asked Asta, again intrigued that an art historian would have so many musicological facts at hand.

"Because a few years ago I lectured on Mahler's experiences in Finland for the London Existential Psychotherapy Group's inner circle seminar. That's when I got to report on Gallen-Kallela's 'kidnapping' of Mahler."

"Kidnapping? What was that?" asked Asta, intrigued.

"He took him from the Helsinki harbor in his motor boat out to the arts and crafts house, Hvittrask, which was the studio home of the architect Eliel Saarinen and his two partners. It was there, in the cozy living room of Hvittrask, that Gallen-Kallela seized the opportunity to paint a portrait of his famous acquaintance.

"He seated him in a chair before the mighty fireplace, so that his face was illuminated by the rosy glow of burning logs. Although the fireplace is nowadays roped off, I have actually sneaked past the ropes in order to turn one of the great chairs around to face the fire, the way it was when Mahler sat and patiently posed there. And of course I quickly photographed the site before returning the chair to its regular position."

"I'm beginning to understand your photographic devotion," smiled Asta as the plane approached the Helsinki International Airport. "I'm only sorry that I could not allow you to photograph my...," she lowered her voice, "Klimt."

Megan did not tell Asta that, as soon as she had returned to her Castello room that first night in Ascona, and even before making phone calls home, she had made a careful sketch from memory of the various realms and swirling subjects of the *Theology* panel. She made color notations as well and even tentatively labeled a few of the recognizable faces in the lower and upper registers.

In her mind's eye, she had marveled at how Klimt's redoing of *Theology* matched and carried out the overwhelmingly pessimistic message of the other three University ceiling panels—*Philosophy, Medicine,* and *Jurisprudence*—with their spiraling nude figures set against a cosmic void. "Outrageous!" local critics had opined. All three panels were inhabited by female figures who were blatantly naked rather than heroically nude. A storm of public protest was unleashed and eighty-seven professors signed a petition demanding Klimt's pictures be rejected as unfit to adorn their university building.

What, Megan contemplated, would they have thought had they seen Klimt's fourth allegory, *Theology*, with its message not of religion but, apparently, of race, in a specific condemnation of the social Darwinism to which society seemed increasingly drawn.

Megan was suddenly brought back to the present by the gentle jolt of Asta's jet landing at the Helsinki airport. Thirty minutes later, and by mutual agreement, the two women were unpacking and taking a brief lie-down in their adjoining rooms at the stately old Hotel Kämp. Megan reached for her laptop and sent off a group message cheerfully announcing her safe arrival and whereabouts in Helsinki.

* * *

That evening, after arriving back in Geneva, Pierre Balis opened up his computer and and hacked into Megan Crespi's email. Instantly he telephoned Jeremy Herring. "Contact has been made," he reported triumphantly. "Both persons of interest are in Helsinki at the Hotel Kämp, planning to take in the sights for a couple of days, starting with the Ateneum."

44

Günther Winter, dressed in his blue caftan fashioned after the one Klimt was famous for wearing, leaned back in his leather armchair with a sigh of contentment. He was in the secluded basement of his Alpenglow annex, a large glass of Scotch in his left hand. He stared appreciatively at the Klimt paintings he and a trusted workman had painstakingly installed so recently.

The two large oils from Switzerland glimmered in front of him. One of them measured four-by-four feet when taken out of its original panel. It matched in size a Klimt image already in Günter's basement. The second oil measured six-by-eight feet. They, along with the third Klimt image, had been set into a large horizontal panel—a sixteen-foot-wide by eight-foot-high stretch of exquisite mahogany board that Günther had procured previous to the arrival of the two Swiss Klimts.

Rising to the height of eight feet, the continuous dark panel with its three glowing insets filled the entire west wall of the brightly illuminated basement room. Ceiling spots were aimed directly at the riveting images. Klimt's secret panel—the Secretum—had originally housed two individual paintings, and now they had been reinstalled for Günther's private viewing, completing the *kolossal* trio of Klimts in Alaska.

Mesmerized, Günter's glance moved from the commanding center painting to the image on the left, then back again to the center work. And finally to the image he had long owned on the right. *Unglaublich!* Unbelievable!

The story of this acquisition was an extremely convoluted one, involving Schiele, the Leatherer family, a bold burglary, and Klimt's nephew and grandnephew.

Günther Winter could not know that originally Egon Schiele had been aware of the existence in Klimt's basement of two artworks embedded into a great square panel. Klimt referred to these as his "Secretum."

Immediately after Schiele had made sketches of Klimt on his deathbed in February of 1918, he had contacted the one person among their shared patrons whom he thought would know what to do about the revelatory basement panel Klimt had once shown him, swearing him to secrecy.

Now that Klimt was dead, the secret had to be maintained since living persons in Vienna were involved and great damage could be done, not only to them but to Klimt's name and legacy.

Schiele had turned to Otto Leatherer's younger brother Fritz, who lived near him in Vienna's Hietzing district and who had the money and the discretion to do what must be done. Fritz immediately arranged for two men to break into Klimt's studio.

After stealing a few Japanese objects from the artist's substantial collection in order to blindside authorities, they entered the artist's basement and set about sawing the great square wooden panel there in two. They left the two imbedded paintings intact. One was square in shape, the other rectangular.

Later, securely crated, the two works had gone straight to Switzerland where Fritz kept them in their unopened crates in the basement of his summer house outside Geneva.

His older brother Otto died in 1985. Fritz had no direct descendants and so after his death in 1990, the house outside Geneva with its basement contents went to the same grandniece who had inherited Otto Leatherer's collection—Klara Hubner, the retired flight attendant.

Not being interested enough to open the two crates marked *Kunst* in her greatuncle Fritz's crowded basement trove, Klara simply had them removed to the same downtown Geneva bank vault where Otto Leatherer's possessions were stored. And there they had stayed briefly until the amazing offer from Jeremy Herring had come proposing to buy all the art contents of the combined Leatherer trove, sight unseen.

Unbeknownst to Günther Winter until his recent talk with Megan Crespi in Vienna, one other person had obviously come to know of the panel's existence. This was Klimt's grandnephew, Hans Ernst Klimt. It was he who on his deathbed had blabbered to Megan Crespi about the secret panel, the Secretum.

One other person had known about the Secretum—the dying man's father, Friedrich. Friedrich had been the son of Klimt's deceased brother Ernst and, as a boy of fifteen, he had been shown the Secretum panel by Klimt himself. This was the artist's laconic way of providing the boy guidance in worldly and sexual matters when his widowed sister-in-law had implored "Uncle Gustav" to give the boy some instruction.

Klimt's nephew Friedrich loyally kept to himself knowledge of the Secretum almost to the end of his life. Only a week before his death, in 1944, had Friedrich imparted this shameful secret to his son, Hans Ernst Klimt, who in turn had confessed it to Megan as he lay dying.

Günther stood up, his Klimt kaftan flowing, and placed a CD into his player system, turning up the volume. He sat down, savoring his drink and picturing his new acquisitions with pleasure. The fourth movement to Beethoven's Ninth Symphony sounded mightily through his Bose speakers.

Klimt, painter of the Beethoven Frieze, would definitely have approved, he easily persuaded himself without the slightest tinge of conscience. He also had no misgivings about never having married or fathering children. His time was totally devoted to business, art, and the acquisition of art.

The latter was, without his realizing it, becoming an obsession.

45

So, Pierre Balis has traced Megan Crespi and the old Danish hag to Finland!

Jeremy Herring, sitting in his crowded home office at the Bastiengasse house and watching a light rain fall outside his window, considered the situation. Three days in Helsinki. Nice and remote. But whom could he send to dispatch the elusive Crespi? Certainly not his blundering son. Nor his daughter, who any day now could come up with the name of that anonymous seller of Klimt drawings to the Antiquariat Nebehay. Pierre Balis was a geek unburdened by morals, but nothing more. This time he needed a professional operative. And he knew just the one.

Checking his online address book, he located the phone number for Hedwega Schreck. She was a former hospital nurse turned policewoman. She had resigned her police post during the furor that arose when she refused to reveal by what means she had obtained the damning evidence that convicted a serial rapist. The sadistic sex offender had held the city of Vienna under siege for months several years ago.

Truth was, Hedwega had, on her own, followed the suspect to his apartment. He was with a young girl whom she believed was his intended new prey. When she broke in impulsively, she came upon the suspect preparing to torture the terrified girl he had gagged and tied down on the kitchen table. Hedwega had, literally, turned the tables after incapacitating him with a Taser X26 shot to the crotch.

She had strapped the wretched writhing man down on his own table, then given the Taser to the dazed young woman to wield at her revengeful pleasure. After only one electroshock dose from the girl the man was more than willing to write out and sign a document confessing to multiple rapes and murders.

At the trial he tried to recant, but there on the document acknowledging his crimes that had been presented as evidence were the signatures of Hedwega and his intended victim. The jury convicted him on the basis of the document.

Fellow officers suspected violence had been involved, knowing Hedwega's purposeful personality and resourceful nature, but, loyally, not a single one had voiced an opinion. Nevertheless, the newspapers and talk shows had a field day arguing both sides of the case, with public sympathy puzzlingly in favor of the criminal, who may have been coerced by the policewoman and who therefore may have had his rights violated.

Violated? Hedwega had finally resigned in protest over the investigation of her that public opinion had forced her superiors to instigate. The investigation had come up empty handed.

But now the tall, athletic brunette with the piercing amber eyes and no-nonsense demeanor was in business for herself. Proven criminals ought to be stopped. Those with clever, high-priced lawyers, who escaped punishment time and again, leaving their victims without recourse to the law courts. And business had proved to be plentiful.

When Jeremy's call came through, Hedwega had just finished a tasty, crisp Wienerschnitzel, its golden crust plentifully flavored with fresh lemons grown in her own garden. Jeremy had two missions for her. She listened with interest to his description of the woman, Megan Crespi, who needed to be put out of the way. What was her offence, she wondered. But she was a professional, her fee was extravagantly high, and she did not ask why, only when and where.

Her eyes opened wide to the "where" answer: Helsinki. But she was game. After that Jeremy had a task for her in New York. The deal was concluded dependent upon Hedwega's being able to catch a flight the next day at such short notice. Going online she found she could book an 8:15 am flight on Finnair for the following day. It would arrive in Helsinki at 11:40 am. As a precaution and to give herself a greater edge, she followed Jeremy's recommendation. She reserved a single room at the Hotel Kämp, facing the Esplanade, if you please.

46

Megan and Asta had spent the late afternoon at the Helsinki Art Museum in the Tennis Palace, where of all things, a Georgia O'Keeffe exhibition was being installed. Megan's young colleague, John Gilbert von Galen, the director, had immediately welcomed them and led them through the behind-scenes hanging of canvases. That evening the two women were invited to John's house to share an impromptu family meal and to meet John's wife Margo and their three young children.

Megan and Asta had wisely decided to save their best energies for the much anticipated Helene Schjerfbeck retrospective. They planned to devote tomorrow to an all-day stint at the Ateneum Museum where, in addition to the Scherfbeck show, there was also an exhibition of artists who, like Gallen-Kallela, had worked in Taos in the 1920s. The New Mexico connection just keeps cropping up, thought Megan in wonderment. But at least this time, she assured herself happily, it will be under pleasanter circumstances.

The next morning after a delicious buffet breakfast that could have fed an occupying army, Megan and Asta walked the several blocks over from the Esplanade toward Railway Square and the Ateneum Museum. The curator of the exhibition, Lisa Moorehead-Printz, met them at the front entrance and led them straight to the exhibition which occupied both the ground and second floors of the grand old Ateneum building.

It was stunning to be able to compare Schjerfbeck's hopeful self-portraits as a young woman with those spectral ones of herself done in later years. In her senior years she had been in poor health but at least she had been relieved of the burden of caring for her demanding mother, who cared not a whit for her obvious talent.

Megan and Asta took a break for a long and lively coffee with their hostess in the museum café and then continued their tour while Megan made notes and took photographs from time to time. Asta had lent fourteen of her some thirty paintings by Schjerfbeck to the exhibition and they had been hung splendidly, in meaningful rapport with their neighboring canvases.

As they prepared to take a look at the Taos paintings on view, Lisa excused herself and returned to her office for a meeting with her docents. The Taos tour did not take long and was, with the exception of Gallen-Kallela, a bit repetitive. Asta asked if they could return to the café for a late lunch and a bit of a rest. It was, after all, past three o'clock.

As the two women sat sipping their drinks, another woman, probably in her mid-forties, was gazing discreetly at the pair from her table by the café entrance. From there she commanded not only a good view of the café's clientele but also of the main exhibition hall entry and exit. Megan said something that made Asta laugh in the middle of a bite into the apple pie, *omenapiirakka*, dessert she had ordered. She choked, gulped, then began gasping for breath, coughing and clawing the air in helpless panic. Megan immediately began thumping her back, but to no avail.

"Here, let me help," commanded Hedwega authoritatively, responding by instinct to the crisis, and placing herself behind the jerking figure of Asta. Expertly, she wrapped her arms around the chocking woman and began administrating abdominal thrusts, using the thumb of her balled right fist to exert pressure upward on Asta's diaphragm. After the third thrust the morsel of pie that had lodged in her trachea was expelled and Asta was able to cough it out. Her esophageal moment, as she later called it, had passed.

Drenched in perspiration, Asta fanned herself while making embarrassed thanks to the helpful stranger. Megan added her fervent thanks and begged her to sit with them while her friend continued recovering. They introduced themselves in English and learned that the woman was Viennese—Monika Straus, "with *one* s," she said.

The fact that she was from Vienna ignited Megan, who soon was chatting away about Klimt and Schiele, giving her Danish companion more time to pull herself together.

"Well, of course I've heard of the Schiele museums in Tulln and Neulengbach," countered Hedwega, amused as well as impressed by the American's enthusiasm for her subject.

Asta, now fully recovered, thanked her good Samaritan once again and then spontaneously invited her to join them for dinner that evening. "We're staying at the Hotel Kämp."

"Now that's a strange coincidence. So am I," Hedwega/Monika responded.

Delighted, Asta and Megan took their leave and, at Megan's insistence, went back by taxi to the hotel for a long lie-down before dinner at eight. Hedwega also returned to the hotel, after walking slowly eastward along the Esplanade Park toward the city's market square and the sea beyond. Gazing out over the water, Hedwega thought to herself that the Helsinki assignment had begun exceedingly well.

47

Promptly at eight o'clock Hedwega joined Megan and Asta, who were already comfortably seated at a corner table on the terrace of the Brasserie Kämp. Hedwega had taken the sauna and was feeling extraordinarily fit. And curious. It was not often, if ever, that an intended victim had invited her to partake of a meal. Who was Megan Crespi really, she wondered, and just what had she done to deserve being on Jeremy Herring's hit list? He had briefly muttered something to her about Crespi's being a dangerous "hindrance" to art dealers worldwide, but that was all.

Now as she sat listening to Megan's spirited tales of art research in remote places, she began to wonder how this woman from Dallas, Texas, could possibly be a threat to the art world. Hadn't she done what no Austrian had done? Actually sought out the village, the building, and the basement cell where Egon Schiele had been incarcerated? And now, one hundred years later, that building was a respected museum, bringing a new tourist trade to the otherwise unprepossessing town of Neulengbach.

Nevertheless, as she watched Crespi carefully lay out her after-dinner pills, washing them down with generous gulps of water, she realized she was already thinking of how to slip some thallium sulfate into the mix.

Tasteless, colorless, and water-soluble, her pill of choice was excellent for such a dispatch job. After being consumed by the target, it took several days before symptoms such as sudden hair loss, stomach cramps and nausea began to appear, and usually death was attributed to ailments dubbed as mysterious. Still available in some countries as a rat poison, there had been a big scandal in Japan a few years back when a young daughter had murdered her mother by lacing her tea with thallium.

"So, would you like to accompany us, then?" repeated Asta.

Hedwega was suddenly jerked back to the present by Asta's question. "Sorry, would you repeat that? I'm a little hard of hearing," Hedwega lied.

"Megan and I were just saying that we'll be going to visit Sibelius's house at Lake Tuusula tomorrow. It's about a thirty-minute trip north from Helsinki. Would you like to come with us, was the question."

Hedwega could scarcely believe her luck, and her enthusiasm showed in her immediate answer, "But of course. That was one of my reasons for vacationing here in Finland, to see Sibelius's home." Another lie.

After exchanging a few amusing stories about the two hundred-and-fiftieth anniversary celebration of Mozart's birth that had taken place in Vienna in 2006, contaminating its streets and shops with a swarm of tasteless Mozart souvenirs, the women adjourned for the evening, promising to meet for breakfast at eight the next morning.

Yes, thought Hedwega to herself as she prepared for bed. One of my thallium pills in Crespi's morning coffee or water glass should do the trick. And I'll be safely back in Vienna before she begins to feel any of the deadly effects.

* * *

But things did not work out as Hedwega had envisioned. Yes, they had all met for breakfast as planned, but, swearing in irritation as she petulantly announced it, Crespi declared that she had forgotten to bring her morning pills down to breakfast with her. She did not touch her water and drank only a single cup of mint tea. Hedwega had had absolutely no opportunity to doctor the drink. She would simply have to wait for another chance, perhaps after they had been to the Sibelius house that morning.

Asta had hired a chauffeur to drive them out to the isolated Sibelius house, set in a deep pine forest that looked out onto Lake Tuusula just outside the market town of Järvenpää. The composer had built and named the two-story timber house Ainola in honor of his wife Aino. He had lived there with her and their six daughters from 1903 until his death in 1957, at the age of ninety-one.

The moment the three women entered the house they were transported back a century. Sibelius's grand piano was the first thing they saw. All the furnishings and paintings on the wall were original and the cozy atmosphere of the large living room was charming with its view of the lake. Megan nostalgically and meticulously took detailed digital shots of some of the paintings she had lovingly photographed decades ago with her beloved Rolleiflex 2.8F camera.

Later, they walked outside along a steep and treacherous path overgrown with pine roots to the graves of Jean and Aino (hers was smaller, Megan pointed out), then down to the water and Sibelius's sauna.

Despite the chilly weather, several men were swimming in the lake. They exchanged a few jovial remarks with the women, inviting them into the water. Not a good place to dump Crespi, thought Hedwega. Too many people. Somehow I've got to get them to that outdoor café back up by the house.

Eventually, as it was very slow going for Asta, who was beginning to walk with a limp, they took welcome refuge in the café, just as Hedwega had hoped. This might be her last chance, as far as non-violence was concerned. The women ordered drinks and the cake that was touted on the menu as being Sibelius's favorite. Megan had asked for hot apple cider—perfect. But how to slip the pill into the glass unobserved? And there were other customers at nearby tables. Irritating.

Suddenly a tall woman entered the café with a small white dog on a leash. It was a Maltese! Asta and Megan both turned in their chairs, straining to follow the dog's trotting progress across the terrace. "Isn't it *darling?*" cooed Asta. All eyes were on the mutt. Hedwega made a quick, inconspicuous pass over Megan's cider.

The deed was done.

48

Günther Winter decided to continue his Klimt dalliance in Alaska. He could handle any pressing business from Girdwood just as well as from Vienna. He really wanted more time to look at and digest the newly installed Klimt panel. He had carefully photographed the two new images in their elegant mahogany setting the day before. And at Jeremy's specific request he had emailed to him in Vienna a high-quality color photograph of the center painting. After a last loving look at the golden trove, he checked out the basement security system yet once again, then went upstairs to his office.

Günther caught up on email, then phoned Jeremy Herring for news of Crespi. Jeremy was optimistic. She had been tracked to Helsinki and then was planning to continue on to Paris. The situation was being covered. In fact he had just heard from his Vienna operative, Hedwega, that the multi-city mission was about to produce the desired results. Final confirmation would not be forthcoming for a few days, because this time, Jeremy emphasized pointedly, "we are not dealing with an accident. Instead we have a slow-acting but highly effective poisoning."

"*Gut*! Finally. Und ven do vee move to phase two of zee Moderne Galerie operation?" asked Günther.

"We have given the museum people a chance to cogitate about the break-in and we'll move to phase two at the end of the coming week, when their board meeting takes place."

"Do you tink it vill vork?"

"Renata Teuer and Lyonel Retter have had more than a week to ponder the meaning of the *Kurrentschrift* note left on her desk. They will have to share it with the board. That is when things should begin to happen, you'll see."

"Vell, I certainly hope so. Vee haf a lot hanging on zis."

"You let me do the worrying, Günther. That's what you're paying me for."

"It's not zee money, it's zee art exchange I am tinking about. You know vat it means to me."

"And to *me*," replied Jeremy with unusual fervor.

"How could zey resist such an extraordinary trade?"

"We'll know in a few days, Günther. In the meantime send Eddie Hoch back over to New York. Hedwega is going to need him when she gets there."

49

It was a fond farewell that Megan and Asta exchanged the next morning before Megan's flight to Paris. They had hoped to encounter Monika Straus again at breakfast but, as they learned when checking out, Madame Straus had left very early that morning. Asta planned to return to the Schjerfbeck exhibition that afternoon, but promised Megan she would fit in a visit to the Gallen-Kallela house and studio before returning to Ascona.

"And you must come back to play more Bach and, please, bring your dog with you, Megan, so Minne can meet Button," Asta cajoled.

"And you consider yourself and Minne as being invited to far off Texas," enjoined Megan. "It's really not as cowboyish as you might imagine. There are museums galore in the area and Dallas is green, very green. A perfect place to live, except in the summer."

"You ought to come live in Ascona. We have ideal summer temperatures."

Megan's taxi pulled up and the two women embraced. "Till next time!" called Asta as the car drove off.

Passing through airport security, Megan was singled out to walk through one of the millimeter-wave scanners, and as she obligingly did so she felt as though she were walking on hot coals. Startled, she asked the security guard if the floor of the booth were heated, but he just looked at her as though she were a crazy old lady and waved her through.

Well, I suppose I *am* a bit crazy, thought Megan—all this sudden international travel, and leaving little Button behind for days without his Mama. As she put her shoes back on she noticed that the hot-coals-feeling persisted, and cursed under her breath the state of a world in which travel was now so complicated. Hurriedly, before boarding, she sent a group email to her sister and friends that she was on her way to Paris.

Earlier that morning Hedwega Schreck, wearing the blonde wig and horn-rimmed glasses she always used for travel, had also passed through one of Helsinki's security scanners. She boarded her flight back to Vienna and, mission accomplished, settled into the Krimi Roman she had begun reading on her flight out.

Megan's flight was uneventful, no interesting seat partners this time, and she was just as glad, as she was feeling a tad under the weather. She found a taxi, after waiting in an exceptionally long line, to take her to the eighth arrondissement where her host lived on the upper floors of a spacious building devoted to Gustav Mahler books and recordings, the Médiathèque

Musicale Mahler. Megan remembered the password for entering the court-yard and rode the elevator up after ringing the bell of Henri-Claude de La Granger's private quarters.

A beaming Henri-Claude greeted her at the elevator door. "At last we see each other again, after so many years," he said, reaching for her roller bag. "Your usual bedroom upstairs awaits you, and lunch will be served after you've had a chance to clean up." Megan smiled and nodded at her friend's grinning butler, Hassan, who took great pride in the food he served.

"Let me bring your bag upstairs," commanded her host.

Happy to be back "home," Megan trotted up the stairs to the guest room, with Henri-Claude close behind. Just as she entered the room a large German Shepherd appeared from the far side of the double bed, growling. In another instant it lunged at Megan, barking and nipping her on the arm.

"*Bas!* Vito, down! Ah, Megan, I'm so sorry," shouted Henri-Claude, grabbing the dog, who immediately stopped barking and lay down docilely at his master's feet.

"You see, Lucien Duval—you remember him, don't you?—was stay-ing up here for a week until just this morning, so you must have startled Vito. Are you hurt?"

I, startle the *dog?* I think it was the other way around, thought a disbelieving Megan to herself, as she daubed with her sleeve at the drops of blood dripping from her upper left arm.

"Ah, but I see you are bleeding. You *are* hurt. Can I help?"

Megan noticed that she was beginning to shake from the aftershock.

"Let me just sit down for a minute, Henri-Claude," she said, lowering herself to the bed and continuing to dab at the blood. Her host brought a towel from the bathroom and soon the bleeding stopped.

"But we must get this looked at, right away," declared Henri-Claude. Megan would have rejected the suggestion out of hand except for the fact that, in addition to now shaking uncontrollably, the soles of her feet seemed to be on fire.

After resting a few more minutes on the bed and reassuring a very concerned Henri-Claude that she would be all right, Megan obediently followed him down to his car and he drove her to a neighborhood walk-in clinic. An older doctor took charge of the case, reassuringly cleaning and dressing the wound.

Megan was still shaking and her stomach had begun to hurt. She brushed her hand lightly against her hair to smooth it and out came half a handful of hair! At the same time she could feel urine leaking into her panties, causing her to jump up and ask for a bathroom. The attending physician looked at her keenly and indicated the way to the toilet.

When Megan returned to the examination room he asked her: "Has your hair ever come out like that before?"

"No. Never."

"You say you just flew in to Paris from Helsinki. Did you eat anything in particular on the plane?"

"A croissant, strawberries, and some tea is all I had."

"I see. What have you eaten in Finland the past few days? Could you have been in a restaurant where there was rat poison in use?"

"What do you mean? I've just been bitten by a large dog. That's why I'm here. Not because of a stomach upset. Anyway, I vomited while in the bathroom, so I feel better now."

"Do your feet feel hot?"

"How could you know *that*? Yes, they have had a burning sensation since this morning when I went through Helsinki airport security. I thought that was the problem."

"Your heartbeat is highly irregular," commented the doctor, listening intently through his stethoscope.

"I am going to ask you to see a specialist right away. You are exhibiting symptoms of having ingested poison, very likely thallium sulfate."

Megan and Henri-Claude were nonplussed. The doctor made a call and sent them on their way to the nearest hospital, the Clinique Madeleine on boulevard Malesherbres (appropriately named, Megan thought, tweaking the name to fit her black mood). The doctor's specialist colleague was just about to make rounds but had agreed to meet them.

A youngish French Moroccan nurse took blood and urine samples and had them analyzed immediately. The physician made an appearance soon afterward, looked at the test results, and said: "You have thallium sulfate in your system. It is a very dangerous poison that is given to rats and, in Saddam Hussein's day, to his political enemies. We must put you on hemodialysis immediately. This will help remove the toxic substance from your blood."

"Hemodialysis? Good lord! How long does that procedure take?" asked Megan in alarm.

"About four hours. Monsieur de La Granger, you might as well go home for now. But we can do it in our outpatient dialysis facility and you can pick up Madame Crespi late this afternoon. You may or may not need another hemodialysis tomorrow, depending on how you feel. I am also going to give you the antidote, Prussian blue, which you can take by mouth. It will reduce the retention of thallium in your system. But you must take this exactly as I prescribe, five hundred milligrams by mouth a day, no less, no more. It is extremely lucky that you went to an emergency clinic for a dog bite, believe me."

It was a very subdued and sobered Megan who returned at last with Henri-Claude to the Mahler haven. More hair had fallen from her scalp and her host was now beside himself with worry. Hassan fixed Megan an omelet, which she found soothing. She wondered whether or not Asta might also have been exposed to the rat poison, possibly at the Hotel Kämp? She would give her a call just as soon as she woke up from what she told Henri-Claude she hoped would be a very long and restorative nap, *sans chien*!

* * *

Megan did awake feeling much better a few hours later, if still weak and now a bit nauseous. She realized that she had not contacted friends or family concerning this latest site and eventful chapter in her life, so, reaching for her laptop at the side of the bed, she began a group email to Tina, Claire, Renata, and Janette, adding her brother Giangiorgio as well.

"Last week at this time I was in Alaska, then New York, then Switzerland, then Finland. And as of now I'm no longer in Helsinki but in Paris..." she began. Then she went into detail about the rat poisoning she had been a victim of and its bizarre, uncomfortable symptoms.

"Good thing I usually wear a hat, since my scalp shows through at the back of my head," she concluded her newsletter, even taking a selfie surrounded by the tripartite mirror gracing her dressing table. Then she decided to telephone Asta.

"You won't believe where I am," exclaimed Asta after she checked the caller ID while answering the phone. "I'm inside Gallen-Kallela's house. It's marvelous."

"And you won't believe what's happened to me since I left you," replied Megan. She filled in her friend on the details, including the four hours of hemodialysis, then asked: "But how about *you*, Asta? Have you had any of the symptoms I just described?"

"No, none. I've felt fine. But how terrible that you have endured this. We all three partook of the Sibelius cake, so it could not have been that. Unless, I wonder if Monika was affected as well? But she did not give us her contact information, so we'll never know. I had certainly better inform the Hotel Kämp, don't you think? Oh, how awful about that huge dog mauling you! Yet another reason to own small dogs, the way we both do." Conversation switched to Minne and Button and Megan promised to send Asta a photo of her pooch.

Henri-Claude looked in on Megan and was pleased to see her looking more perky and even sitting up in bed. To take her mind off things, he proposed that, when she felt better, they pay a visit to the Klimt collector he had told her about. "It is probably the smallest Klimt collection in the world, but it is, I promise you, unique."

No amount of guessing on Megan's part could induce Henri-Claude to disclose what the collection consisted of, or whether Monsieur Jacques LePingre had any Schieles as well. "His collection must remain a mystery until you see it. This will motivate you to take your daily dose of Prussian blue and get well soon, I hope."

"Taking Prussian blue makes me feel close to Monet," Megan quipped, feigning better spirits than she actually felt. That evening she was well enough to come downstairs for dinner and Mahler talk, although her appetite was non-existent.

"You must keep your strength up! How about some chicken broth followed by your favorite crème brûlée that Hassan has just made?"

"That sounds wonderful, Henri-Claude. I'm sorry to be such a bother."

"Bother, nothing. I am just so relieved you're beginning to feel better. And so is Hassan." Hassan was especially fond of Megan because on previous visits she had trotted out her bag of magic tricks, causing the dear, childlike man the greatest amusement. The crème brûlée proved to be too rich for Megan, however, and she reluctantly pushed it away after the first bite, as she had begun to feel nauseous again.

"Don't rush things, Megan," Henri-Claude advised. "I recommend we postpone our talk about your Mahler murder mystery until tomorrow."

"Thank you," said Megan gratefully. Taking leave of Hassan and her host, she slowly climbed upstairs and went right to bed, exhausted but hopeful. When she had more energy she really must start thinking about the strange set of circumstances that had imperiled her life more than once: the man who almost knocked into her at the Girdwood aerial tram station, and now the exposure to rat poison. Were these both coincidences? And what about the burglary at Santa Fe? Could the murder have been meant for her?

This thought made her sit up in bed. She decided to give Claire a call. She was so much more perceptive about people and events than she was. Her old friend was, it turned out, extremely worried about her safety and her tendency to be naïve in trusting others.

"You are generous and well-meaning to a fault," she chided Megan. "Please be on your guard. Don't take people at face value. That Monika Straus, for example. Just please, please don't take any more chances!"

Sobered by Claire's admonitions, Megan promised to be super careful. She had trouble falling to sleep, haunted now by the three recent inexplicable events that now seemed to be intertwined.

50

Earlier that evening in Geneva, Pierre Balis had found Megan's email from Paris to "Dear All" on his computer. He immediately sent it to Jeremy Herring in Vienna.

"Damn it to hell!" was Jeremy's furious reaction when he read the missive. "Do I have to knock off Crespi myself? At my age? At eighty-five? Why are there only incompetents around?" Angrily he telephoned Hedwega Schreck, who had returned to Vienna, having reported the success of her operation.

"You'll get no fee from me," he declared adamantly. "Megan Crespi is alive and in Paris. Seems she was bitten by a dog on arrival at her host's house, rushed to the doctor and diagnosed with rat poison in her system. She is slowly recovering."

"I can't believe it," exclaimed a deeply chagrined Hedwega. "I gave her a full dosage of thallium sulfate. And I saw her drink it down. That woman must have an iron constitution."

"Never mind what sort of constitution she has. The fact is you have failed in your mission."

"I can only ask that you give me another chance. I could get to Paris by tomorrow afternoon."

"I will for sure give you another chance, not because I want to but because I goddamn *have* to. I want you to come out to the house right away. I have a packet for you to hand deliver to the Moderne Galerie Museum in New York next Saturday morning. You'll fly directly to New York from Paris, understood? As far as Paris is concerned, we have the address where Crespi is staying. You know what she looks like now, and you can track her movements until a chance comes up for you to follow through. Use force this time. And remember, she will now be on her guard."

* * *

Henri-Claude was concerned. Megan had not made as rapid a recovery as they had both envisioned. They had had many good talks, including a detailed tweaking of ideas for her Mahler murder mystery, but Megan was still feeling weak and nauseous. By phone and by email she kept her sister and friends advised of her seeming lack of progress and the fact that she had not left her host's house for any outside activities.

Two days later, early in the morning, and with her reluctant acquiescence, Henri-Claude drove Megan back to the outpatient unit of the Clinique Madeleine for another hemodialysis session. That afternoon, for the first time, she felt better and said so emphatically. "Let's see if we can visit your Jacques LePingre tomorrow," she urged. "What did you say he does? Oh, yes, you said he's a poet. I hope we don't have to listen to a recitation."

"Ah ha! You do feel better. He doesn't live in Paris, however, he lives in Thomery-By, out near Fontainebleau forest. He's a very secretive character. But do you think you would really be up to the drive?"

"Well, it's sitting down both ways, isn't it?" Megan responded cheerily. "And anyhow, if we go all the way out to By, let's also drop by Rosa Bonheur's house and studio. I know, male chauvinist pig that you are, that you have never taken the trouble to see it."

"You really *are* better, Megan," cried Henri-Claude, happy to see his old friend back in her teasing mode. And it would be interesting to visit the famous painter's studio, something in fact he truly had never taken the time to do.

A number of years ago, he had been in Megan's company visiting the Musée d'Orsay where Bonheur's 1849 *Plowing in Nevers* had been put on display. It was on the ground floor of the recently opened museum. And it was there partly in response to the persistent complaints she and her colleague Eleanor Tufts had made in the early 1980s over its being stored in neglected splendor in the basement of the royal Château at Fontainebleau, along with some half dozen other works by Bonheur.

Henri-Claude and his excited guide had gazed long and lovingly at the large work showing two teams of straining oxen plowing up the autumn earth, their human tenders miniscule beside them. It was a dedicated *animalière's* hymn of praise to the simple agricultural life of the country over the corrupt life of the industrialized city. When a group of Japanese tourists walked right past the large canvas without looking at it, Megan had chased after them, imploring them to return to admire the rare work of a *woman* artist. They did.

Another time Henri-Claude and Megan had been in New York's Metropolitan Museum together and Megan had dragged him to see Bonheur's giant canvas *The Horse Fair*, pointing out the painter's sly inclusion of herself as one of the center horse riders and the pre-Seurat-like right bank of dappled yellow green grass.

There would obviously be no denial of Megan's keen wish to show him the artist's château-cum-atelier, now that she was feeling better.

They decided to go to By the next morning and see the Bonheur house first, after making an appointment to visit the Klimt collection at two in the afternoon. Much cheered by the upturn in her health, Megan emailed her "crew" the latest news: she was still on the Prussian blue medication but it looked as though she would definitely not need another hemodialysis. And she felt well enough to visit By the next day.

Claire emailed back concernedly: "Don't try too much too soon." And Tina also sent a note of caution, knowing in advance that her admonition probably would not be adhered to by her stubborn older sister.

The next day Megan and Henri-Claude departed for By well before noon and reached the château an hour later. The artist's work had brought her early financial independence and she had bought and lived with her childhood friend in the stately château, surrounded by a high wall, for the last forty years of her life. Wrought-iron decorations forming the monogram "RB" decorated the house and studio gates.

Inside the studio, where the artist's last canvas, paints, and palette were, Megan showed Henri-Claude Bonheur's plaster cast of Beethoven's life mask, mistakenly displayed as his death mask. This was an error to be seen in many homes after the composer's death, including the residences of Gabriele D'Annunzio and August Strindberg.

Megan and Henri-Claude also examined Bonheur's small darkroom, in which she developed her photographs of the animals she kept, animals that ranged from gazelles and monkeys to a tame lion. Stacks of wood-framed glass negatives lay on one side of the darkroom. What a wonderful research topic for some future Bonheur scholar, Megan enthusiastically told her host.

After a light lunch in town, they pulled up in front of the small L-shaped house owned by Jacques LePingre. He was on the doorstep to meet them at exactly two o'clock. A small, dapper man with a wide smile, and a bald head, he talked nonstop, leading them through the dark house and out onto the enclosed back patio. There they sat down and imbibed the tea placed before them. A strange place to look at Klimt, Megan thought somewhat impatiently, blinking in the strong sunlight.

The conversation centered upon, of all things, Klimt's illegitimate son, the handsome bisexual Gustav Ucicky, for whom a young LePingre had worked as a cameraman in Austria during the 1950s and early 1960s. He had helped to film Ucicky's postwar hit, *Die Hexe* ("The Witch"). Some of his father's paintings that Ucicky had acquired from Jewish families after the Anschluss had, in a complicated business maneuver, been willed to complicitous Austrian museums. But there was one Klimt he had kept for himself. Before his death from a heart attack in 1961 he had given it to LePingre.

"Would Madame Crespi care to see it now?" asked her loquacious host.

Megan nodded an eager assent. She was consumed with curiosity as to what the Klimt work could be, even though it looked as though the showing would take place outdoors in bright sunlight, which seemed horribly unwise,

Almost skipping with pleasure, Jacques disappeared inside the house for a few minutes, then returned to the patio bearing a small black leather box which he ceremoniously handed to Megan. Henri-Claude looked on with a knowing smile. When Megan opened the box, which was partitioned into two sections, she saw two thick locks of black hair, both streaked with silver.

Yes, Jacques explained, that lock on the right was one of Gustav Ucicky's own luxurious curls of hair, cut by Jacques himself. The one on the left was Gustav Klimt's hair, cut from his head while he was in the hospital dying of pneumonia after his stroke. Klimt's model, Maria Ucicky, mother of their illegitimate son Gustav Ucicky, had visited him there and come away with the precious souvenir.

And hirsute souvenir was all that it was. Megan was terribly disappointed but managed to convey the proper surprised admiration. "Have you had DNA testing done on them?" she asked, trying to think of something relevant to say.

"I will someday, should I ever decide to sell the pair. But for now they are my own cherished keepsakes. After Gustav Ucicky's wife left him, taking their infant son Peter with her, Gustav and I became very close, lovers in fact, and before he died he wanted to give me something precious. This was it."

That was only a partial truth. In fact, Ucicky had given Jacques something of far greater value and significance.

The conversation moved awkwardly to other famous locks of hair—Beethoven's, Napoleon's, Mary Shelley's, Jane Austen's, John Lennon's, Bob Marley's. All of a sudden Jacques said excitedly: "There is *one* item I would trade Klimt's lock of hair for." Megan's ears perked up. *A trade? As in trade for the Secretum?*

"What might that be?" she questioned sharply.

"You yourself have reproduced it in your Klimt book, the *Self-Portrait as Genitalia*. It is such a deliciously naughty little thing." Jacques LePingre looked meaningfully at Megan.

"Well, I last saw that little self-parody in Otto Leatherer's collection in Geneva and that was decades ago. I have no idea where it is now," said Megan, knowing that whoever the mystery dealer had been who had recently bought up the entire art contents of the Leatherer bank vault, must also have acquired this little self-portrait, unique in Klimt's oeuvre.

After some more forced small talk, Megan and Henri-Claude took their leave. "Remember, if ever you should come across that little Klimt self-caricature, I would be willing to swap my Klimt/Ucicky hair locks for it," enjoined LePingre as they walked back through the house to the front door.

Just at that moment the door was thrust open from the outside and a slender young black man in very tight faded blue jeans eyed them with surprise. "Oh, *chou chou*, I thought your guests had already left!" Quick introductions were made. Jean-Jean Jolie was identified as Jacques' partner, and the extended leave-taking came to an amiable end.

"Did you show them those old drawings you're always messing around with?" Jean-Jean asked Jacques after Henri-Claude and Megan drove off.

"Shhh!" cautioned Jacques. "You're talking about our livelihood. Of course not!"

In Henri-Claude's Renault an exasperated Megan fumed all the way back to Paris. "Why, Henri-Claude, did you ever think that a lock of Klimt's *hair* would seriously interest me? It's the location of Klimt's missing *artworks* that compels me, not an alleged lock of hair. Just imagine, LePingre hasn't even legitimized his precious souvenir with a DNA test!"

"Perhaps Ucicky had already done so," theorized a slightly chagrined Henri-Claude. "He loved touting that he was Klimt's son in the high circles of Hitler's Vienna henchmen within which he so freely moved. In fact that's why his wife left him."

"Well, whatever the story, thank goodness we combined a visit to Bonheur's atelier with this silly trip to LePingre," Megan pouted, irritated at herself for having expended her newly returned energy on such an otherwise thankless trip.

There was no reason Megan could know that Klimt's lock of hair would soon play a role in the lives of those killing for Klimt.

51

Hedwega Schreck had a rented car waiting for her at Orly upon her arrival in Paris and she drove directly to 11 Bis, rue Vézelay where Megan's host lived. She checked in at a modest hotel on a nearby cross street. Two days later, after practically living in her car, parked discreetly further down rue Vézelay, she followed them on what turned out to be an out-of-town expedition to Thomery-By. Wearing her blonde wig and horn-rimmed glasses, Hedwega felt confident that she would not be recognized, not even in such a small village. She followed them to LePingre's house and waited a safe distance down the street.

So far, Megan's host Henri-Claude de La Granger was solicitously accompanying her everywhere. Annoying as the delay in eliminating her target would be for Jeremy, Hedwega was savvy enough to know that, once Megan had fully recovered, it would be far easier to catch her alone on one of the busy streets of Paris. Far better to follow her on foot than in a car. Eagerly she monitored her email for an update from Jeremy on Megan's cyber communications.

It came soon enough.

In a self-congratulatory email to Claire and Tina the afternoon after the By trip, Megan described how she had been given a clean bill of health by her doctor, who had taken fresh blood and urine samples. The only restrictions were to continue taking the Prussian blue for one more week, to keep on drinking as much liquid as possible, and to get plenty of rest. That Megan could do on the flight back to New York the next day. The board meeting at the Moderne Galerie that weekend would most probably take all morning and much of the afternoon.

Thanks to Jeremy's rerouting of that email, Hedwega now knew of Megan's exact travel plans. She hastily made a flight reservation on Air France to the States for the next morning. Keeping an eye on Moderne Galerie's comings and goings would be child's play compared to trying to come upon Crespi alone on the streets of Paris, where her solicitous host never left her side. Just let Crespi take one New York subway ride after the Saturday board meeting and the rest would be easy. Anticipating exactly such a close encounter, she carefully repacked the blonde stalking wig and clear, horn-rimmed eyeglasses.

Later that evening Jeremy called Hedwega. Günter Winter had contacted him. Plans had changed significantly, he informed her.

Now it was important that Megan be kept alive!

He would explain later, but from now on Hedwega's job was simply to follow to the letter the orders he would be texting or Skyping her once she touched down in the States. And she was still tasked with the job of delivering the packet to the Moderne Galerie on Saturday morning.

Early the next evening, Friday, on separate planes from Paris, both Megan Crespi and Hedwega Schreck arrived in the States; Megan at Kennedy, Hedwega at Newark. Thanks to Crespi's re-routed emails, Hedwega knew the specific hotel where she would be staying while in New York, the Hotel Wales on Madison Avenue. Having changed in the Newark airport ladies room to her wig and glasses, she took a taxi across the Hudson to Manhattan and was able to book a room at Hotel Wales. She had to pay an outrageous sum for a junior suite, the only lodgings available at such short notice. But no matter. Things were looking up.

52

"What a terrible ordeal you've been through dear," pronounced a worried Renata Teuer, when Megan appeared at the Moderne Galerie early Saturday morning prior to the ten o'clock board meeting. They had talked on the telephone the night before and Renata had been brought up to date on the German Shepherd attack, the rat poisoning ordeal, and the disappointing visit to the Klimt "collector" Jacques LePingre. They had about an hour before the meeting began and the two friends spent it catching up on the state of things concerning the break-in of the Galerie and the vandalizing of the Adele portrait.

"So far the police have come up with nothing concrete," complained Renata. "A couple of contacts in the criminal world have pointed to a local gang that recently infiltrated the Museum of Modern Art cloak room, making off with checked briefcases and other personal items, but nothing parallel to what happened at the Moderne."

"When did you reopen the second floor?"

"Oh, several days ago, after we installed a makeshift exhibition of Emilie Flöge's designs and fabrics that turned out to be pretty impressive. It's gotten good reviews in the press, and no one is the wiser concerning the spray-paint attack on Adele. The protective glass cleaned up easily and we have now added a five-inch glass frame around the protective glass panel overlay. If there is a next time, god forbid, no paint could possibly overlap or drip onto the actual painting. For all intents and purposes, the portrait is now sealed in invisible glass."

"Has Erich Knadel come up with anything more?"

"Only to suggest, or have I told you this already, that the writer of the *Kurrentschrift* note left on my desk was probably not written by an Austrian or a German. Something about too many loops, I think he said."

"Well, that might or might not be a helpful lead. Time will tell, I suppose. What is the plan for the board meeting? Are you going to tell them about the break-in?"

"Oh, yes, we are going to have to do that, swearing everyone to, ahem, secrecy, if such a thing is possible. But we can't suppress knowledge of the event from the board any longer. There was already too much speculation in the news media when we temporarily closed off the second floor to visitors last week. We'll have to tell them about the *Kurrentschrift* note as well and its peculiar proposal of trading Adele for the Secretum."

"Who knows, perhaps one of the knowledgeable board members will come up with some ideas or even answers," consoled Megan.

"That is our hope," replied Renata ruefully.

An hour later the board meeting was in full progress. In addition to Lyonel, Renata, and Megan, a group of nine members sat around the large conference table on the fourth floor of the Moderne Galerie. Lyonel had given the bare facts about the break-in and spray painting of the glass protecting golden Adele, and now he was circulating Xerox copies of the *Kurrentschrift* note.

Elderly Paul Pfeffer, a longtime former curator at the Museum of Modern Art, spoke up: "This business about trading for the Secretum. Could it be referring to the University panels that are now in Aarhus, as well as what we suspect is Klimt's redo of the *Theology* panel, very likely in the possession of Asta Holm-Ditlevsen?"

"That is exactly what we had first suspected," answered Renata. "In fact Megan is just back from having visited her. Fortuitously this Asta woman had invited Megan to visit her Scandinavian artists collection in Ascona just when we were about to contact her."

"Ah! And does she indeed have the Klimt *Theology* panel?" asked Pfeffer eagerly, turning to Megan.

"Unfortunately, I can neither confirm nor deny that she does. We actually left Ascona for Helsinki pretty quickly to see the Helena Schjerfbeck retrospective at the Ateneum," answered Megan.

"And how was *that* exhibition?" Pfeffer inquired with keen interest.

"Overwhelming. As I've written somewhere, her old age portraits are every bit as searing as Picasso's. And Asta has some of the best of them."

"It's too bad we cannot give her a showing here at the Moderne," volunteered Lyonel, "but we are, after all, a museum dedicated to German and Austrian art, so we have to stay on message. I got grief enough from certain purist critics when we exhibited some of my medieval armor collection along with selections from my mother's private German and Austrian holdings."

"So that means the Moderne Galerie could some day have an exhibition of Paula Modersohn-Becker, of Gabriele Münter, and of Käthe Kollwitz, in a *Women Artists of German Expressionism* show?" asked Megan aggressively for the umpteenth time. Renata and Lyonel exchanged knowing, martyr-like glances. They had been through this several strenuous times and the board had always voted no. But Megan never gave up hope.

"To get back to the matter at hand," said Renata, "if the *Kurrentschrift* note had been placed by an agent for Asta Holm-Ditlevsen, surely she would have shown her hand by now. And Megan's recent personal contact with her apparently revealed nothing suspicious. Isn't that right, Megan?"

"True," confirmed Megan.

Suddenly there was a knock at the conference room door and Renata's personal assistant Christina entered the room with a large flat packet that had just been hand delivered. It was addressed: "To the Moderne Galerie Board Meeting Now in Progress." Christina had thought it important enough to interrupt the meeting.

"Let us see what on earth this has to do with us and the board," said Lyonel, tapping his fingers apprehensively on the thick mailing folder. It contained a nine-by-twelve-inch sealed envelope and a single sheet of fine paper upon which a message had been printed.

Lyonel unfolded the paper and read the message out loud:

You have the unique opportunity to trade your Klimt whore for the Secretum. If you think we are not serious, consider what happened to Megan Crespi. Communicate with us at the cyber address below: it will only be active until six o'clock this evening.

Lyonel looked pale. "Exactly what happened to you, Megan?"

"Oh," replied Renata before Megan had time to answer. "I haven't had a chance to tell you that Megan was seriously ill in Paris. She somehow imbibed a substance used for rat poisoning and had to undergo two hemodialysis treatments. She could have died."

"Yes," Megan affirmed, "the substance was analyzed as thallium sulfate and somehow I was exposed to it, probably when I was in Helsinki earlier in the week. If I hadn't been attacked and bitten by my host's dog in Paris and rushed to an emergency clinic, the poison might not have been detected until it was too late for an antidote."

Now, alarmingly, pieces of the invisible puzzle were irrefutably coming together for Megan, who had been in deep denial.

She continued, addressing the entire group earnestly: "I hadn't put this all together until now," she admitted. "But when I was in Vienna last month, I learned about the existence of a previously unknown panel by Klimt, one that was described by his own great nephew as 'shameful' and 'secret.' I let this slip to that fanatic Hundertwasser collector, Günther Winter, and he in turn announced with great pride that something 'colossal' had just been shipped to him for his art collection in Alaska."

Megan took a deep breath. "Since then, bizarre things have been happening. There was a senseless killing at my hostess's summer home in

Santa Fe just before we made our arrival, which had been delayed by a few days. The neighbor who watered her plants once a week when the house was empty was found murdered there. She was felled by a single blow to the head. I now think it may have been a case of mistaken identity—that I must have been the intended victim."

Everyone in the room gasped. "I further think," continued Megan, "that the instigator of this killing gone awry could have been Günther Winter. Just two days after the murder in Santa Fe I received a call from him inviting me to visit him in Girdwood to see his Hundertwasser collection. I went there with my Santa Fe hostess, my sister, and one of her friends. While we were at the aerial tram station on top of Mount Alyeska, a man suddenly lunged toward the guard rail where I was leaning. He missed me only because I happened to straighten up as he passed by. He himself went over the railing and fell down onto the slope, where he was attacked by a bear defending her cub. She mauled him badly. Medics got to the man and took him to the local emergency clinic in town."

"Well, didn't the police *question* him?" queried one of the board members.

"No, because at the time we all thought it was just a crazy tourist accident. A man rushing to photograph the 'Beware of Bears' sign. And then, shortly after that crisis, Renata called urging me to come here immediately to confer about the vandalism that had just happened to Adele. Lionel, Renata, and I wondered whether Asta Holm-Ditlevsen might have had anything to do with all this. After all, her three Klimt University panels are in the Aarhus Museum."

"Oh, yes," interjected another member of the board, "doesn't she in fact own all *four* of the University panels?"

"That still has to be determined," Megan replied evenly, remaining true to her promise to Asta. "What I *can* tell you is that I was able to visit her..."

Renata interrupted: "Holm-Ditlevsen actually called and invited Megan to visit her in Ascona, just as we were getting ready to make contact with her for that very reason. We suspected it might be she who had the Secretum in her possession. But apparently not, since she did not respond to that key phrase when Megan was able to interject it casually into the conversation. Isn't that right, Megan?"

"Yes, that seemed to settle that," continued Megan. "I was able to see her Scandinavian collection in both Ascona and Helsinki, where we went together after a break-in attempt at her Ascona home. Now why would there be an attempted break-in at her house, after all her years in Switzerland, just when I was in town? And then it was in Helsinki, at the airport security on the way to Paris, that I first felt the symptoms of my system's having been poisoned. My feet were burning hot, as though I were walking on coals."

"Yes, that is one of the definite symptoms of thallium sulfate poisoning," declared the physician on the board.

"But are you saying that you think the Danish woman, what's her name, could have attempted to poison you?" asked another member of the board.

"No, no. But a third unusual thing happened while she and I were in Helsinki. In the museum café Asta suddenly had a terrible choking fit, and a very competent woman immediately came to the rescue, applying the Heimlich maneuver just in time. Her name was Monika Straus. We of course invited her to join us for dinner that evening out of gratitude. She just happened to be staying at our hotel. Now isn't that an odd coincidence? So the next morning we had breakfast with her as well. She even went with us, at our invitation, to see Sibelius's home, and we had a late lunch in the café there. But the next morning, when we checked out of the hotel, she had already left."

"That makes three different occasions when that woman could have doctored your food or drink," mused Renata.

"And the symptoms wouldn't have manifested until a day or two later," supplied the physician.

"All right. Let's pull this together as best we can," Lyonel said brusquely, glancing at his watch and thinking of the deadline mentioned in the printed note.

"We have had possibly three attempts on Megan's life in the last three weeks. Attempts most probably instigated either by the Danish owner of

Klimt works, or by the crazy Austrian Hundertwasser collector, Günther Winter. Does he own any Klimts at all, Renata? Megan? Do you know?"

"Yes." answered Megan while Renata vigorously nodded in agreement. "Up in Girdwood, Alaska, of all places. He has what could be called a secondary collection, with excellent drawings not only by Klimt, but also Schiele. He showed them to me after I viewed what he'd termed his 'colossal' *Sendung*, his sending."

"And what was that?" asked Lyonel, surprised.

"Well, since I haven't been sworn to secrecy and I wouldn't keep an oath to that fanatic collector anyway, I can tell you that it was a Hundertwasser triptych, one totally unknown to the art world. It was interesting enough, but I have to tell you that I noticed dust on the frame edges, hardly likely if the triptych had just been installed, as Winter claimed."

"Hm. Then my money is on this Winter fellow," declared Lyonel. "Why else would he have suddenly invited you to Alaska to see his collection if not to find out whether you were on the trail of the 'shameful secret' Klimt panel, the one you yourself had told him and us you'd heard about? Could that in fact have been the 'colossal' thing he'd just had shipped to himself?"

"Why don't we open this and possibly find out?" urged Renata, pointing to the as yet unopened envelope Lyonel had drawn out of the packet.

"Quite right!" Lyonel agreed, tearing open the envelope at once. It contained a dozen color prints of the same photograph. The copies were quickly distributed among the board. All were labeled "Secretum."

The photographs were of the center image of Günther Winter's mahogany panel. What Megan, Renata, Lyonel, and the board saw was a new and shocking version of Klimt's famous "Kiss" motif. Unlike the original oil, the famous *Kiss*, begun in the same year, 1907, as the Adele portrait's completion, this new *Kiss* showed a standing pair of ecstatic lovers.

They were locked in a naked embrace.

Klimt had once before shown two nude lovers embracing. It was the "kiss for the whole world" of his great 1902 Beethoven frieze. As preamble, it accompanied the Vienna Secession's exhibition of the Leipzig sculptor

Max Klinger's *Beethoven Enthroned* monument. In Klimt's frieze the features of the embracing nude couple had been obscured.

In this new version, however, the naked couple floated against a churning cosmos peopled with showers of small figures. The faces of the lovers—shown in three-quarter view with eyes closed—were instantly and unmistakably recognizable.

They were the faces of the forty-five-year-old Gustav Klimt and the twenty-six-year-old Adele Bloch-Bauer.

53

The conference room had gone numb with shock.

After some minutes of silence, one of the board members asked, looking at her copy of the photograph labeled Secretum, "Who are these miniature men and women in a silver mist, floating around the kissing couple?"

"My god!" cried Megan as, at the same time, Renata gasped in sudden recognition. "These floating figures are quotations, writ small, straight out of Klimt's University panels. Look! Here on the upper left, wrapped in the arms of a giant octopus, is the elderly 'condemned' male nude of *Jurisprudence*. And down below on the left, here, is the enigmatic female head with the immense swirling hairdo that anchors *Philosophy*. And look at the upper right. That is the figure of Hygeia with her serpent from Klimt's *Medicine* panel."

"And here, on the lower right, facing up toward the kissing pair, is a miniature ivory statue of Christ, presumably from *Theology*," added Renata excitedly.

Megan refrained from confirming her colleague's astute guess, but was equally excited by this display of key quotations from all four University ceiling panels.

"So this is what our unknown perpetrator wants to trade for our Adele?" asked Lyonel in awe but indignantly. "How *dare* this jerk threaten us?"

"Perhaps what he's really after is the sale of the painting to the Moderne Galerie," said Paul Pfeffer discerningly. "The whole world knows what you paid for the Adele portrait. Maybe he thinks he can get beaucoup more for this grand naked kiss?"

"Certainly acquiring a picture that solves the great riddle of whether or not Klimt and Adele had an affair would be worth a lot in the art world," mused a board member, looking at Lyonel questioningly.

"I'll be damned if I am going to trade the Moderne Galerie's Adele for this Kiss, no mater how much light it sheds on their relationship!" exclaimed Lyonel.

"Anyway," Megan said soothingly, "this *Kiss* doesn't necessarily *prove* that they had an affair. The Secretum could have been Klimt's own private fantasy. He could have been creating in paint something he, the louche womanizer, might never have obtained in the flesh."

"But even Adele's family and descendants pretty much thought there had been an affair between her and Klimt," Renata rejoined. "No, I think the painting definitely clinches the fact. By placing this compelling union of a man and a woman in the middle of quotations from his University panels, Klimt was reconfirming, indeed fortifying, his view of an Eros-driven universe. He was telling us that the compulsion to mate is the strongest of all human urges. Remember, Klimt dragged out the painting of Adele's first portrait for five long years."

A heavy silence reigned in the room for a few minutes.

"Well," said one of the board members, "I think we should test this bizarre situation by offering to buy the *Kiss* painting. Surely that is what the sender of the photographs is really after?"

"I would be willing, more than willing, to acquire it for the Moderne," said Lyonel slowly, "but we would have to verify its authenticity first. And I do not like the threat contained in the note or the spray-paint attack.

"I will not be coerced. Our Adele is going nowhere. She is the Mona Lisa of our time and will remain at the Moderne. That is my final word."

"We could offer not to trade, but to purchase this nude *Kiss* painting.

And only on condition that you, Megan, are allowed to see and study it in person," suggested another board member.

"But that could be extremely dangerous." said someone quickly. "If there has already been an attempt to poison Megan, then why put her in danger again?"

"I doubt that she is still in danger," Renata said thoughtfully. "The perpetrator knew that Megan was hot on the trail of this panel and wanted to get her out of the way before she discovered just what exactly it was. But now he, or she, has revealed the 'shameful secret' to us all, in an insane scheme to persuade us to make a swap."

"Let's go forward with a proposal to consider their request," said Lyonel, looking at his watch again. "We don't have all that much time before the cyber address they gave us is deactivated."

"And if we do nothing?" asked Pfeffer.

"If we do nothing? God! What might they try next? Another spray-painting spree in the Moderne, this time for real? Who knows? No, I don't want to take a chance," Lyonel declared firmly.

After more consultation, an answer was cautiously composed. It read:

YOU HAVE OUR ATTENTION.
UPON VERIFICATION IN PERSON OF KLIMT'S
PUTATIVE WORK, THE MODERNE GALERIE WOULD
CONSIDER MAKING YOU AN OFFER.

"Nice and neutral," approved Renata. "This way they won't know whether or not you are referring to the trade they want, or an offer to purchase."

"That is my intention," said Lyonel, clicking the Send on Renata's board-room Mac.

54

Asta Holm-Ditlevsen had trouble falling asleep her first few days back home in Ascona. Minne was not well. She had been coughing incessantly and was at the vet's for observation. And then images of what poor Megan had been through kept passing before her mind's eye. What had started as a rewarding visit to Helsinki to see art, had become tainted by Megan's medical catastrophe brought on by ingestion somehow of rat poison.

For the hundredth time she asked herself how that could possibly have happened. One of the breakfasts at the hotel, possibly? But then why only Megan and not she as well? They had eaten the exact same food. Danger was afoot everywhere, it seemed, even to the attempted break-in of her own home. Tomorrow, she promised herself, she would take steps to install a security system. With that comforting thought, she finally fell into a deep sleep for the first time. All was quiet in Ascona.

At three in the morning a large grey van soundlessly pulled up to the front of Asta's isolated house. Two men with black face masks emerged, opened up the back of the van, then swiftly approached the front door. One of the men expertly applied a variety of keys and within seconds the heavy front door swung silently open. In another few seconds, they entered the bedroom of the owner's house, as they had been instructed to do by Günther Winter. Their petite prey was sound asleep, breathing regularly and snoring quietly. One of the men expertly slipped a garrote wire around the sleeping woman's throat then pulled it tight. The snoring stopped immediately. A single gasp for air was the only sound.

Making for the living room now, the men sized up the painted panel that took up the back wall of the two-storied room. It matched the measurements they had been given. One man measured the sliding glass doors and nodded affirmatively to the other man, who was already engaged in removing the panel from its moorings. Together they maneuvered the painting away from the wall and over to the sliding doors that faced the lake. With a few more motions the panel was thrust through the doors and carried slowly downhill to the parked van, the back wide open and ready to receive its treasured cargo. In another few minutes, with the panel firmly strapped in place, the van silently drove off toward the nearby Italian border.

The entire operation took fewer than fifteen minutes.

55

Jeremy Herring watched Lyonel Retter's email response come in on Günther Winter's computer. They were both seated in front of the large screen on Günther's conference table in his downtown office facing the Stefansdom in Vienna. Winter had briefly returned to Austria the previous day. They were speaking in German, unusual for Jeremy.

"All right. The Moderne has taken the bait," cooed Jeremy.

"What's so good about that?" questioned Günther, "They want to *see* it before they'll deal."

"I had anticipated this. That's why I told you to get it, the Secretum, out of Switzerland and install it at your Girdwood annex. Far easier to deal with the Moderne Galerie in the U.S. rather than in Europe."

"So we get Crespi to Girdwood. Then what? Now they know the location of the work. So what's to prevent them from calling in the police?"

"On what charge?"

"Well, on suspicion of being behind the spray painting of Adele, for one thing. The *Kurrentschrift* note definitely links that with our proposal of trading for the Girdwood panel."

"I plan for us to have insurance against just such a move on their part," answered Jeremy. "Accompanied by Hedwega Schreck, we will have Eddie Hoch limousine Crespi out to Kennedy, with the express warning that if she is followed the deal falls through instantly. Once at the airport on the general aviation ramp near where your fleet is kept, we fly her in one of your Gulfstream 650s to Anchorage."

"How do you know about my jet fleet?" asked Günther.

"Never mind that. Your many asserts are hardly a secret, Günther, and I have my ways. The point is to swap, if necessary, Crespi for Adele, and to have the Moderne Galerie duo—Lyonel Retter and Renata Teuer—where we can manage them in the Lower 48, and where they can manage the shipping of Adele."

Jeremy did not tell Günther that the idea of bringing Megan to Girdwood was specifically to *force* the return of Adele to Austria, once she had verified Klimt's workmanship on the *Kiss* panel.

Jeremy's deceased wife Rachel had come up with this bold plan during her last visitation to him. In no uncertain terms, as redemption for a life of crime, Rachel had urgently told Jeremy that he must return the iconic painting to Vienna's Belvedere Gallery.

The painting had been on exhibition there for decades before that damn restitution case was won by Bloch-Bauer's grandniece, Marjorie Niederman. Wouldn't you know that it was another Jew, composer Arnold Schönberg's grandson, Rupert, who had successfully won the case. What a debacle for Austria, he mused.

"I am not comfortable with your idea," said Günther suddenly. "Our identity will be revealed and we could be brought up on kidnapping charges."

"Not if we have Crespi sign a waiver that she is taking the trip voluntarily. You must have one of your agents waiting at your private hangar at JFK to manage the plane boarding."

"What about the police tracking Crespi's whereabouts, if she is reported as missing?"

"She will be relieved of cell phones, computers, and any other form of communication before we get her on board your plane."

"All right," Günther slowly agreed. Then, turning abruptly to Jeremy, he said in a loud and authoritative voice, "And now you'd better get out. You have business to attend to and so do I. I am returning to Anchorage this evening.

As soon as Jeremy left, Günther checked his email. He scrolled to the message that was waiting for him. "All gone as planned," the curt text read. "Desiderata now in Italy awaiting your further instructions."

"*Ja-Ha! Endlich, endlich!*" Günther shouted, hitting the air with outspread fingers. He had Klimt's *Theology* at last. No matter that the holdout Danish witch had to be done away with. Now, finally, Klimt's magnum opus would be joining its fellow masterpieces in the Girdwood temple where proper adulation and privacy could be afforded.

He emailed Jeremy to take care of the shipping arrangements immediately, and with that had his chauffeur drive him out to the Vienna airport for an evening flight to Anchorage aboard his gorgeous two-engine Gulfstream G650. It was prepared and waiting for him. My other jet should be flying Megan Crespi to Alaska tomorrow evening, he thought contentedly. What a pleasure it will be to see her face when I show her the Secretum *and Theology.*

56

Klimt's grandson, Peter Ucicky, son of the artist's illegitimate son Gustav Ucicky, was having a heated discussion with his wife Lena as they sat on the narrow balcony of their modest apartment overlooking the Spanish Steps in Rome. They lived not far from where Giorgio De Chirico had spent his last years and directly across from the two-room apartment where John Keats had died.

"Yes, I *know* we have huge debts, Lena, but you can't blame me for not having *tried* to get the money. Our last lawsuit has wiped out my savings." The miserable man looked uncannily like Klimt, with the same stocky build and large eyes."

"You haven't tried hard enough. You missed your chance to sue the Leatherer estate for ownership of its Klimts."

"Listen. I tried really hard to reach the last Leatherer heir to find out what Klimts she had inherited. But then I learned she had died in a traffic accident in Geneva right after the collection was sold. Don't you remember?"

"Of course I do," Lena allowed, still angry at her naïve husband. "It's just such a pity you didn't get to her sooner after we learned Fritz Leatherer had died. That you could have done, at least. It doesn't matter that you can't stand the things your grandfather painted. It's the fact that you are his *grandson* and probably have a right to any works that have a suspicious ownership history."

Peter looked miserable. His scolding wife had started to press him once again about laying claim to Klimts that had been seized during the war. A number of drawings had been showing up on the art market lately, and they were mostly, as always, drawings of naked women doing, well, embarrassing things.

"And you couldn't get a word out of that American art dealer who lives in Vienna, could you?"

"Only that he had been unable to notify me about his acquisition of the Leatherer collection because it had instantly been bought by a client of great wealth and influence. Although I have asked several times, he refuses to tell me who it was. But I have my definite suspicions," he added, hoping to mollify his wife.

"Who do you think it was?"

"Probably that billionaire Viennese collector Günther Winter. It's not just Hundertwasser works that he covets, I know that for a fact. He has bought many drawings by Klimt, as well as ones by Schiele."

"So, have you made contact with him?"

"Not yet, cara. It's hard to pin down his whereabouts. He spends his life on airplanes. Travels all over the world. His office in Vienna won't answer my requests asking where to reach him."

"You'd think that he would be really interested in talking to Klimt's *grandson*."

"On the contrary. I believe my being Klimt's grandson is the reason why he does *not* wish to see me. After all, as Klimt's grandson, even though my father was born out of wedlock, I believe I should have the right of ownership to any work by my grandfather that does not have a squeaky clean sales history.

"And that is why you were suspicious when Jeremy Herring sold the collection so quickly? It was then that you decided it must have been to Günther Winter?"

"Right. This is exactly why I want to find out what Winter has. One way or another, I'm going to confront that slippery man, however hard he may try to avoid me."

"Don't worry, cara," soothed Peter, "somehow I will get us the money we need to pay our debts. And you'll be able to take all the trips you've ever wanted to."

51

Although the board meeting had been over for quite some time after the unanimous approval of a three-year plan for future exhibitions, Megan, Renata, and Lyonel continued to sit in the conference room talking over the events of the day. They were still huddled together when the awaited email response came in for Renata. She read the contents out loud: "Prepare for Crespi to be picked up by limousine on the southeast corner of 86th Street and Fifth Avenue in exactly thirty minutes."

"Talk about pinpointing. That's right at our own corner here," exclaimed Renata as Lyonel and Megan both frowned. "They must be keeping the *Kiss* panel somewhere in New York or maybe New Jersey. Only a half hour from now? Precious little time to organize any backup plan."

"I'll call Joe immediately," said Lyonel, referring to Joe Seguire, his longtime private bodyguard. And I will lend you, Megan, my GPS track stick," he said, handing what looked like a miniature thumb drive over to her. "I'll tell Joe to keep an eye on your movements, just in case of any dirty business. And, Megan, keep your cell phone on at all times."

"What does a 'GPS track stick' do?" asked Megan in genuine ignorance.

Lyonel explained, not mentioning that he always wore an extra one built into the heel of his left shoe, "It can follow your movements by satellite anywhere in Manhattan or around the globe."

Properly impressed, Megan started to put it into her big shoulder bag, but Lyonel stopped her. "Keep it close to you, not in a bag. Place it on your person somewhere, ok?"

"Right," Megan answered, tucking it down firmly into her blouse. She checked that her iPhone was on and also that she had a supply of Prussian blue and pills with her; she did. Plenty of the little monsters.

Renata, worried over the length of their business at the Moderne, phoned a friend and arranged for him to feed her dog Tilly at home. Then they took the elevator downstairs, briefly stopping by mutual consent at the second floor and going into the Adele room to gaze at the enigmatic woman in gold once more.

"I promise you, Adele," declared Lyonel solemnly, "you shall never leave the Moderne."

* * *

Hedwega Schreck had been busy. As instructed, she hand delivered Jeremy Herring's packet to the obliging door guard at the Moderne Galerie, disappearing immediately back in the direction of Madison Avenue. Following the old art dealer's terse orders, she then summoned Eddie Hoch to pick her up in Winter's New York limousine at four o'clock in front of the Hotel Wales.

Keeping her blonde wig and glasses on, she entered the black Lincoln Town Car when it pulled up. She directed Eddie to wait on the next side street until further word arrived from Vienna. It came an hour and a half later. Jeremy had texted:

Pick up Crespi at Fifth Avenue and 86th Street, southeast corner, thirty minutes from now. Drive north by way of Central Park so as not to alarm her, then head for JFK and the general aviation ramp where you'll see Günther Winter's private hangar.

* * *

Exactly half an hour later a black limousine pulled up at the Moderne Galerie. Megan, Renata, and Lyonel were waiting on the front steps. "Get the license plate," Lyonel hissed to Renata.

The chauffeur, whose broad cap brim covered most of his long, lean face, did not lower his window nor leave his seat at the steering wheel to open the door for his passenger. He merely signaled with one thumb pointing vigorously backward that Megan was to enter the limousine. With her indispensible black bag on her shoulder, she slid into the leather backseat and turned to give Renata and Lyonel a courageous, affirmative smile.

Without a word the driver sped off up Madison, entering Central Park at 96th Street. In the limo a small liquor bar faced Megan, and on the other side of the driver's compartment glass a black curtain was drawn. After a silent six-minute drive, they reached the Lenox Avenue exit and headed uptown. A woman's voice with a noticeable Austrian accent said over the speaker system: "Welcome, Megan Crespi. You will be at your destination in twenty minutes. Please to sign the paper on the bar counter attesting to the fact you are coming of your own free will."

What? thought Megan. This is beginning to sound ridiculous. After all, I *am* here of my own free will. How else? And why does that woman's voice sound familiar?

Just then the limo came to a full stop. Several road construction signs blocked traffic north on Lenox Avenue and eastward on 116th Street. They had no choice but to turn west on the latter.

When Megan saw that they were headed west on 116th Street, pleasant memories filled her head. This is the street that cuts right through Columbia University's campus, she recalled. It was a campus she knew intimately after having earned her B. A. at Barnard right next door and a Ph. D. at Columbia. At least I'm in my old neighborhood, she thought to herself, still fretting about the mysterious request to sign what looked like a very legal and unnecessary document.

Eighth Avenue and Columbus Avenue were also beset with street-repair signs, so Eddie was only able to head north when he got to Amsterdam

Avenue for the commuter traffic trek up to 125th Street and, finally, the Triborough Bridge to JFK.

Damn it, Eddie cursed to himself, we should have headed directly over to the FDR Drive rather than go tooling through Central Park.

When they stopped for a particularly long traffic light at 116th Street and Amsterdam, the woman's stern, accented voice sounded again over the speaker. "You will have to sign that document and hand it over *now*, Miss Crespi."

"You know what?" replied Megan with an unexpected outburst of anger. "I don't think I *have* to do anything." Furtively, she reached for the door handle, determined to get out of the limo. It was locked. *Good Lord, what have I got myself into?* she chastised herself, feeling panic for the first time.

The woman's voice started to reply, but at that same moment there was the sound of a car crunching into the back of the stopped limo, pushing the long car forward into the intersection and blocking traffic. Cars honked on all sides. The chauffeur jumped out, automatically releasing the door locks, and so did Megan. She began to run toward the Columbia campus, ignoring Eddie's, and then Hedwega's urgent commands to stop. While Eddie dealt distractedly with the apologizing man who had bumped into him, Hedwega began to run frantically after Megan.

58

Rita Herring had interesting news to report to her father. She could hardly wait for Hanskarl Klug to close up Nebehay's Antiquariat in downtown Vienna so that she could hurry home. "Dad, Dad! I have news!" she shouted as she entered the two-story house out on Bastiennegasse.

Jeremy Herring was sitting at the dining room table reading aloud to someone. As Rita swung around the corner, Jeremy put his book down and reproached his daughter quietly: "Say hello to your mother first, Rita."

"Oh, yes, hallo Mutti," obliged Rita, nodding to the empty chair her mother used to sit in when she was alive.

"That's a good girl," said Jeremy approvingly. Then turning from Rachel, whose ghost visited him almost every night around dinnertime, he said, "All right, tell me your news." His children were perfectly bilingual because their father always spoke to them in English. Their late Vienna-born mother, Rachel, had used only German.

"Listen. I think I have a definite lead as to who the mysterious seller might be of Klimt drawings to Hanskarl Klug at Nebehay's."

"Yes? Yes? Go on."

"Today another package arrived. We had already had some dozen mailings over the past year, but this time there was a stamped notice *in French* on the back saying "heavy." Of course, as usual, there was no return address on the packet. And as you know, we always mail payment to a P. O. Box on Spain's island of Ibiza. So it could be that the seller of these Klimt drawings actually lives in France or on Ibiza somewhere."

Jeremy's wrinkled old face flushed with excitement. "Ah! That must be why the Crespi woman flew to Paris from Helsinki." Eagerly he continued: "Why else would she include France in her itinerary? She must have known or been on the track of the owner of the drawings that Nebehay's has been buying. Was the one received today also a study of Adele Bloch-Bauer?"

"Oh, yes, and each pencil drawing we've received—this makes thirteen of them now—has been in a different pose, no repeats. The whole series comes across as *intimate*, if I can use that word."

"How do you mean? Erotic?"

"No, just intimate, you know, head studies with different expressions—smiling, quizzical, impatient, commanding—like that."

"Oh," scowled Jeremy, somewhat disappointed. "But all of excellent quality?"

"Absolutely, Dad. Dr. Klug thinks each one of them could fetch well over fifty thousand Euros if offered to the right collector. Say a Japanese or North Korean."

"So what does Hanskarl pay the anonymous seller?"

"The seller seems to have little idea as to their worth, because so far he, or she, has accepted the net sum of 30,000 Euros for each drawing.

"All right, all right, *danke*, Ritachen. You've given me a lot to think about."

After pondering things over dinner, Jeremy telephoned Günther Winter in Alaska with the news. Günther agreed with Jeremy that the identity of the anonymous seller had been significantly narrowed down, if you counted all of France as being within the parameter. But a P. O. Box in Ibiza might yield some results.

"I shall contact Hedwega Schreck in the morning to see if, when she was shadowing Crespi in Paris, there were any other places she went to besides the clinic and the hospital. We may have a whole new source to shake some Klimts out of."

"All right, Jeremy," said Günter. Perhaps I can find out someting as vell. I'm returning to Wien tomorrow afternoon und shall visit Nebehay's myself. Perhaps I can vrangle information out of Dr. Klug."

* * *

"What do you *mean* we can't take a Caribbean cruise this month?" demanded an angry Jean-Jean Jolie. Jacques LePingre tried to soothe his adorable but spoiled rotten partner.

"Look, *chou chou*, you don't have a *clue* as to how much money our constant traveling costs me, and I don't want you ever to worry your pretty little head about such things. But occasionally I must tend to business on behalf of our posh lifestyle."

"So does that mean we have to go back to Ibiza again?" pouted Jean-Jean.

"Yes, that's about the size of it. I'll have some funds to pick up at my P. O. Box, and while I'm doing that you can lounge on your favorite beach. And the Arctic Monkeys are playing at the Anfora dance palace again. Come on, *mon chér*, please don't be angry," Jacques cooed.

"Allllll right, Jacques," allowed a mollified Jean-Jean. "But let's not leave until next week. *Bien?* I've got tons of errands to run in Paris, and I need to have the annual service on my Jaguar, *d'acord?*"

"We'll see."

59

Megan glanced back as she ran up the steps toward the bronze statue of Columbia's *Alma Mater*, into the lap of which she had once as a student dared to climb. A tall woman with blonde hair and dark rimmed glasses was running after her—about thirty yards back. *Oh, no!* Megan ran up the steps past *Alma Mater* to the entrance of Low Library and dashed inside. The short sprint had left her breathless, and she knew she would not be able to elude her pursuer for any length of time. Panting loudly, she looked around, assessing the situation.

There was no one inside the spacious lobby at this hour, close to five o'clock. Ah! Good. No one would see her take the unpretentious door to the far right that led to the subterranean system of corridors that extended from one end of campus to the other. Megan had discovered them when she was a Barnard student. And she had used them to great avail during the Columbia student riots of 1968, when she was teaching there.

It only took a few seconds to run across the lobby to the door. *Please, please don't let it be locked!* Megan grasped the old door handle. It turned. As she slipped inside, carefully pushing the door closed behind her, she heard what had to be the pursuing woman's footsteps on the lobby floor. Then she heard her shout to someone: "She's in *here*."

"Wait for me!" commanded an out-of-breath male voice.

Yikes! The chauffeur has joined in the chase, Megan realized. Let me get over to St. Paul's chapel fast. It was an underground route she had taken several times before as a member of the choir during her years at Barnard. What fun it had been to amaze her fellow choir members and their beloved choir master, Searle Wright, by suddenly appearing in the basement where rehearsals were held during lock-down hours, when anyone who was late could not enter the chapel.

Now that knowledge could be life saving, Megan thought as she made her way up into the rehearsal room. But this was not lock-down time and her pursuers might find this room merely by getting inside the chapel from the campus entry. She knew exactly what to do next. No one could see or find her if she were hidden in the great dome.

Quickly she ran upstairs to the chapel level with its mighty Aeolian-Skinner pipe organ and red brick Catalan vaulting. Racing past the organ and choir stalls, she headed for the front doors of the chapel. There, on the inside to the left, she climbed up the narrow circular staircase that led past the clerestory level to the dome.

Her footsteps echoed eerily in the empty chapel. Assuming a position from which, if she bent over the dome's railing, she could see anyone entering the chapel from far below, she gave herself the luxury of panting out loud, and sitting on the floor as she fought to bring her breathing back to normal.

* * *

Hedwega was furious with Eddie. If he hadn't taken excessive time to reassure the driver who ran into them that he would take care of the negligible damage to the limo, he could have stopped Crespi from running away. Now, after they checked every room in Low Library, including closets and bathrooms, they would have to search every building on campus, if Crespi were even still on campus. Who knows, she might have doubled back out a side door of the building, caught the 116th Street Broadway subway and gone in any direction.

"Let's concentrate on the nearby buildings," directed a furious Hedwega as they returned to the *Alma Mater* steps outside Low Library. The closest building to Amsterdam Avenue where the limo was now parked, was a small one named Buell. Quickly they checked it out. Few people were around, certainly not Crespi, although they asked several persons if they had seen a lady in black slacks and jacket with a large black shoulder bag come in. Negative answers.

The next closest building was an imposing chapel with a four-columned entrance and the words "Pro Ecclesia Dei" above. They entered quickly, their footsteps echoing in the nave. Silently they checked the apse, behind the altar, and side aisles. Nothing. They discovered the stairs leading down to the rehearsal room underneath the altar. No one. Back upstairs Hedwega and Eddie headed slowly for the chapel entrance, took a last look around and nodded to each other in mutual assent that Megan was not in the building.

"*Vedammtes Chorgestühl!*" cried Hedwega as, her eyes on the stained glass windows above, she ran head on into the last row of prayer stalls, falling to her knees. Her blonde wig was knocked off, her glasses fell to the floor.

Up in the dome, Megan, who had been listening intently to the sound of footsteps echoing below, slowly inched across the sturdy balcony railing to see who had suddenly shouted in German. Leaning way over she was just able to see a very tall man helping a woman up.

Oh my god, it's Eddie and Monika Straus! Just then, as she leaned an inch further to confirm what she saw, the track stick she had thrust down her blouse fell out and hurtled directly onto the altar pavement, bouncing several times with loud metallic sounds.

"*There she is!*" shouted Monika triumphantly.

🝮🝮

"Did you get the license plate number?" Lyonel asked Renata in consternation as they watched the Lincoln limousine move down 86th Street and make a left turn on Madison heading north.

"Yes, yes, I got it—here, it's typed into my iPhone. And I also got a photo of the limo."

"Good. I'll have Joe Seguire do the logistics and we should have some information soon. Let's go up to your office, Renata. I have some Klimt drawings I want to show you."

"Oh, I didn't see you bring anything in this morning."

"I didn't. These are all images on my BlackBerry," said Lyonel, nodding affably to the Moderne's watchful entry guard. They took the elevator up to the fourth floor and sat down in Renata's office. Lyonel handed his smartphone to her and sat back to savor her rapt reactions as she swiped through thirteen different Klimt pencil studies for the museum's Adele portrait.

"Colossal! Where do these come from? Have you bought them?"

"Yes, I've purchased them all over the past year or so. Every month in Vienna, Nebehay's acquires another one and gives me first choice to buy. As you can see, they are unknown, until now, studies of Adele, not so much for Klimt's portrait of her, but individual moods that he caught with his pencil."

"Look at this one," Lyonel said, taking his BlackBerry from Renata and swiping back to the second image. "Here she is *smiling*, showing her teeth. This is unique in images of her because she was so concerned about her tobacco-stained front teeth."

"They're all quite remarkable drawings, but you're right, this one is like a photograph of her, caught unawares."

"The point is, they would make an interesting exhibition in the same room as our Adele, don't you think? That is, if this inexplicable, wonderful supply doesn't run dry."

"Great idea! But are you going to have to wait another year to assemble a dozen more?"

"That's the mystery," Lyonel mused. "I think you should include Vienna on your next business trip for the museum and do a little investigating. What say?"

"You know I never turn down a chance to visit the city where I was born," Renata responded with excitement.

"It's a deal then. How soon could you leave?"

"How would later this week be?"

"Excellent! But this time perhaps not take Tilly with you, as you may be making trips elsewhere should you manage to track the source of these superb Klimt drawings."

"Sorry, but Tilly goes with me," said Renata firmly.

"As you wish," conceded Lyonel, knowing when he was beaten. That miniature Schnauzer had certainly accrued a lot of air miles.

* * *

After an uneventful ten-hour flight from Vienna to Anchorage in one of his Gulfstream jets, Günther had immediately telephoned Jeremy for a report on Megan Crespi's movements. "I haven't been able to get into contact with either Hedwega *or* Eddie," a distraught Jeremy admitted.

"You mean to say zat zere is no confirmation of getting Megan on my plane yet?" Vat zee hell is going on?"

"I'm using all available means to find out, believe me, Günther. It is probably just a communication problem. The land and wireless lines in New York had a brief disruption in service a few hours ago and suddenly I'm receiving hordes of emails that were originally sent to me months ago. It must be something like that."

"Okay, but let me know as soon as you know. I'll be in my Girdwood annex," Günther said, abruptly hanging up.

God, I didn't even have time to tell him that the Klimt *Theology* panel is temporarily stalled at Milan's Malpenza Airport, realized Jeremy too late. UPS Worldwide Express had called him to say the ten-foot tall crate had to be preauthorized. Jeremy had managed to fax the desired papers to Malpenza immediately, but still the crate would have to wait for the next UPS flight out to Montreal, where it would be transferred to a flight to Anchorage.

Problems, only problems, fretted Jeremy. I'm getting too old for all this, he silently complained to the sympathetic shade who had once been his wife.

61

There's no way down, and they're coming up for me!

Megan watched Hedwega and Eddie search for the circular stairway up to the dome where she stood, temporarily immobilized.

A scene from childhood flashed through her mind: she and her brother Giangiorgio were playing alongside a creek that had trailing vines hanging down, touching the water. Giangiorgio dared her to do a Tarzan swing on one of the vines. Could she swing across the creek to the other side? Without a second thought, Megan had grasped the nearest vine and pushed off from the bank. But she hadn't pushed hard enough and the vine did not quite reach the opposite side. It swung back but not far enough to reach her brother as he stood watching helplessly. The slowing pendulum left her no choice but to drop down into the cold creek water.

That seemed to be the same situation now. But where was the vine? She felt something cold next to her and looked down. It was the wire cable securing one of the dome window latches. How long was it? She didn't care. In that moment, as she heard Eddie running toward her on the catwalk opposite, she grabbed for the cable. And then stopped dead.

Good god she was seventy-seven, and if she tried to swing down to the chapel floor on that slicing cable wire with her whole body weight on her hands, even if she *could* hold on, she might never play the piano or the flute again. To say nothing of broken bones. Words, not actions were required here.

"*Why the hell are you chasing me, young man?*" she asked imperiously. Suddenly recognizing him she added: "And aren't you Eddie from the Alpenglow Hotel?"

"Uh, yes Ma'am, it's Eddie all right, but I need to get you back into the limo right away," he said, panting from the chase.

"You're damn right you need to get back to the car," chimed in Hedwega, who had just reached the dome catwalk. "*You have a plane to catch!*"

62

Jean-Jean was pissed. Nothing had gone right on their Ibiza trip. Jacques had obstinately booked their flight for the very next day, right after the visit from Henri-Claude and his Klimt-expert friend. He hadn't even had time to run his errands in Paris, much less leave his Jaguar to be serviced. Jacques could be so pig-headed sometimes. And their favorite suite at Gay Hotel Marigna was already taken. Plus the Arctic Monkeys had canceled their run at Anfora's. At eight in the morning they decided to have breakfast in town, but what a debacle. There were just too many straight tourists on the streets and the sidewalk cafes were crowded and noisy.

And now Jacques was upset and in a bad mood because there was nothing waiting for him yesterday in his P. O. Box. They were supposed to fly back to Paris late this afternoon, but now they had to delay until Jacques got his dough. Maybe it would arrive today and maybe not. They sat down at a café inside, where it was quieter and less crowded, and ordered breakfast.

"I still don't see why you have to go through this ridiculously intricate setup just to receive payment for one of those old drawings you keep selling," he complained.

"The one who's *ridiculous* is *you*," snapped Jacques, tired of his partner's continuous complaints. He hadn't had much sleep, since the sweaty dance scene at the Anfora hadn't really started until after one o'clock in the morning, so he was more edgy than usual.

"Well if *that's* how you feel, Mr. Senior Citizen, you can damn well have breakfast by yourself!" Jean-Jean pushed his breakfast aside, stood up and turned to leave, with the acid injunction: "I'll see you at the post office at noon. Maybe you'll be in a better mood by then." With that he strode out of the café, peeled off his T-shirt, and trotted toward the beach to the admiration of several onlookers.

Jacques was actually happy to have some time to himself. Feeding Jean-Jean's appetite for a luxurious and active lifestyle was not only expensive, it was exhausting. He was, after all, forty-seven, eighteen years older than Jean-Jean, the physical fitness fanatic. He didn't see how he could continue this way without exhausting his trove of, still, some ninety-nine drawings by Klimt. They were all images of that Jewish society lady whom he'd obviously bedded down. Ever since the Moderne Galerie in New York had acquired the *painted* version of Adele Bloch-Bauer, Klimt's pencil studies of her had increased in value.

Was Nebehay's cheating him? He'd just come across an auction catalogue. Some of the auctioned drawings, very similar to those he owned, had asking prices in the Euro 50,000s, not the Euro 30,000 he received each time from Nebehay's.

Have I been taken for a *fool*? There's one way to find out. I'll simply visit Nebehay's in the flesh. I haven't been to Vienne in ages. And a vacation from Jean-Jean might be just what the doctor ordered. Yes. Let Jean-Jean see what it's like to fend for himself for a while. *Alors!*

Jacques LePingre's mood lifted. Finishing his and Jean-Jeans's breakfast he walked back to the hotel softly singing his favorite Charles Trénet song:

Ménilmontant, mais oui madame,
C'est là que j'ai laisser mon coeur,
C'est là que je viens retrouver mon âme,
Toute ma flamme, tout mon Bonheur.

Ménilmontant, but yes madame,
That is where I've left my heart,
That is where I go to find my soul again,
All my flames, all my happiness.

***

At some ten minutes after twelve o'clock Jean-Jean showed up at the Ibiza post office. His T-shirt was on, but he knew the admiring looks cast his way were for him. Now where was Jacques? Come and gone? He waited ten more minutes, then walked back to their hotel mildly puzzled. When he entered their suite he found a note on the bed. It read "Payment received, hotel bill is paid, meet me at the airport for the five forty-five pm flight."

No signature, no word of love. *Bien!* If that's how he wants it, that's how he'll get it. *Je ne m'en fous!* He quickly stuffed his backpack and went down to sit by the hotel pool. Soon a bevy of boisterous boys his age had gathered around him and he was happy again.

In fact he lost track of time and only got to the airport at the last minute. Jacques would be fuming. But no, when they caught sight of each other, all was as though nothing had happened, they were so happy to see each other. They held hands on the flight back to Paris and not a word was spoken about the spat they'd had that morning.

But back in Thomery-By when Jacques announced he had to go to Vienne and go alone, Jean-Jean did pout a bit, but only for a bit. He did treasure his older companion and respected how he conducted his affairs. That night they went to bed at a decent hour, but lay awake reviewing the events of the day.

Jean-Jean is so young, Jacques thought. I really must make allowances for that and take care of him.

Jacques is so fragile, thought Jean-Jean. I do need to take better care of him.

Simultaneously the two turned toward one another, sighed with contentment, and fell asleep in each other's arms.

63

As they walked down the steps of Low Library, an exhausted Megan was flanked by two watchful but relieved companions. They had their target back in hand. Eddie was concerned about the parking place he had improvised on the west side of Amsterdam and 116th Street, and Hedwega was busy informing Megan of the fact that she was not Monika Straus, but Hedwega Schrek, policewoman now turned private investigator.

"But why would I need to be investigated, much less kidnapped?"

Megan asked heatedly, pretending not to know that Günther had to be behind the bizarre set of circumstances.

"This is exactly why you were given that paper to sign, so you would agree that you were not being kidnapped. It was merely a simple legal procedure."

"But why would all this be necessary if I'm only on my way to see a work of art?" Megan was pushing it now. It was obvious that Hedwega and Eddie knew she was aware of who was behind this farce. She considered interrogating Monika/Hedwega about their Helsinki encounter, if it were chance or planned. And had she too experienced the effects of "rat poisoning"?

Or had she in fact been the one to administer it in the form of thallium sulfate?

It was too much to take in all at once. Megan pushed the dark thoughts away.

"*Oh, no!*" shouted Eddie suddenly, running ahead of them to Amsterdam. "They've booted the limo!" A police truck was just leaving the scene and Eddie used his long legs to chase it to a halt. He seemed to be making headway in getting the police to relent.

Hedwega and Megan had almost reached the limo when the quiet purr of a motorcycle cruising down the campus walkway toward Amsterdam caused them both to turn around.

"*Professor Crespi!*" shouted the slender man on the Harley-Davidson Thunderbird in disbelief.

"*Horst!*" exclaimed Megan. "Horst Uhr. Of all people."

He had been Megan's favorite graduate student when she was still teaching at Columbia. In fact she was the sponsor of his brilliant dissertation on the German Expressionist artist Lovis Corinth. For the formal defense of his dissertation she had assembled an all-woman committee of professors. This was a first in Columbia University's sexist history at that time, back in the mid-1970s.

"How *wonderful* to see you, dear!" Megan cried in disbelief and joy. She felt a spring of hope. "What are you doing now and where are you going on your beautiful H-D?"

"Actually what I'm doing these days is where I'm going. To a show on Corinth's self-portraits that I curated for Mannheim's in Soho."

"How wonderful!"

"Hey, what are you doing right now, Megan? Could you possibly ride with me down to the show?"

Never had Megan accepted an invitation so instantly. As Hedwega watched, immobile and open-mouthed, Megan quickly climbed onto the back of the motorbike, wrapping her arms around Horst's chest.

"Let's go!" she commanded.

"Sure. But what about your friend?"

"Forget my friend, just get us out of here. Take Broadway."

Hedwega, helpless, stood shouting curses after the disappearing motorcycle and its two passengers.

* * *

"Pull over," commanded Megan urgently, after they had reached 110th Street. Horst had turned right, heading for Riverside Drive. "Let's stop and talk a minute. I need to tell you something."

"Sure thing. Here, this is a good place to stop. Hold on!" Horst parked his cycle on the sidewalk next to a bench. They dismounted and sat down.

"Horst, I really, really want to see your show, but I can't right now. I said yes back there at Columbia because I needed to get out of a tight situation. Can't sketch it out for you now because, somehow, I've got to get down to the Moderne Galerie immediately. Shall I take a cab, or would you be willing to drop me off on your way down to Soho?"

"Sure thing. I'd be happy to take you there. But I must say, you've got me mystified, big time."

"Sorry, really," apologized Megan.

They stood up, remounted the cycle and Horst took off with a re-sounding roar, weaving in and out of heavy traffic and slow busses. Some twelve minutes later, with an effusion of thanks and promises to explain later, Megan was running down the stairs to the staff entrance of the Moderne.

* * *

Renata had worked late at the museum that evening and was still there when the guard on duty phoned up to announce Dr. Crespi.

"Of course. Send her right up."

Two minutes later the women were seated in Renata's office with the door closed. Megan related what had happened and how she had gotten away.

"This is getting *sinister*, Megan, and I'm afraid you may be in real danger."

"Oh, I don't think so. I just panicked when they wanted me to sign that legal document with its confusing mumbo jumbo."

"But the fact that they began searching the Columbia campus for you..."

"Yes, but it was merely to get me back inside the limo. I don't believe they actually intended to harm me. In fact Eddie, the super tall fellow I told you about whom my sister and I met in Alaska, well, actually Eddie was quite polite when they caught up with me in the chapel dome. Almost apologetic."

Renata looked unconvinced.

Megan continued: "The point is, we are certain that it's Günther Winter who is behind this whole farce—from the vandalizing of Adele to the note asking if we wanted the Secretum. And they must know that by now *we* know."

"Right. So why don't we just go ahead with the plan if they contact us again. In other words, your going to whatever destination it is to confirm that the artwork is actually by Klimt. I still think it must be nearby"

"Oh no," Megan remonstrated. "I haven't told you what they said after they caught up with me in St. Paul's chapel. Hedwega said most specifically that I had a *plane* to catch."

The two women looked at each other silently for a full minute.

"Let's check our email," Renata finally suggested. "Perhaps there is some sort of message from them."

Both glanced at their latest emails. Nada.

The jarring sound of Renata's office phone made both women jump. It was Lyonel Retter.

"Renata, I've gotten another hand-delivered message from our unknown friend. Though I don't know how the hell he found out where I live.

The doorman just brought it up. Let me read it to you."

"Okay, I'll put you on speaker phone, since Megan is also here with me in the office."

"You mean she's back from seeing the Secretum?"

"No, that got sidetracked; we'll explain later. Go ahead, read the message."

"All right. Here it is, *quote*:

THIS IS YOUR LAST CHANCE.
HAVE MEGAN CRESPI STAND IN FRONT OF THE
GUGGENHEIM MUSEUM SIDE ENTRANCE AT PRECISELY
EIGHT AM DAY AFTER TOMORROW. SHE MUST BRING
HER PASSPORT. SHE WILL BE PICKED UP ONLY IF SHE IS
ALONE AND NO ONE ATTEMPTS TO FOLLOW HER.
THE FATE OF ADELE WEIGHS IN THE BALANCE.

"That's nice and blunt," Renata said. "Megan, are you up to a repeat round?"

Lyonel chimed in over the speaker phone: "Only if you think you are not in any eminent danger."

"Of course I'm willing to do it. As I said to Renata, they need me alive, not dead. And how intriguing that they want me to bring my passport. Maybe I'm being flown to Vienna!"

Lyonel thanked her, with an admonition to keep the GPS track stick on her person at all times.

"Golly! I forgot to tell you both that I lost it during the chase. It fell from the dome of St. Paul's chapel right down to the floor. No opportunity to retrieve it. Sorry."

"All right, I'll supply you with another one right away," said Lyonel, digging the track stick out of the heel of his left shoe. Have the guard alerted and I'll get hold of Joe Seguire, who has you still at that chapel up at Columbia. He'll bring it to Renata's office right away so you'll have it tomorrow.

Lyonel hung up and the two women looked at each other.

"Listen, you must be hungry," Renata said. "I'd just ordered a huge sandwich, chips, and dessert from the local deli before you came. Wouldn't you like to share with me?"

"You bet I would." Megan had not realized how famished she was.

As they sat eating, they reviewed the portentous events of the day, and again Renata urged Megan to be careful. Lyonel's track stick arrived, brought up to the office by the night security guard, and Megan made doubly careful that it was secured in her bra. "If I didn't have to go to the bathroom so often, I'd store it in an even safer cavity," she joked with Renata.

"If we have to wait two more days before you're being picked up, you'd better stay with me at my place," offered Renata. "I don't think it is a good idea to rebook your Wales Hotel room now."

"I'd appreciate that very much. Your new condo is terrific and so close to the Moderne. I remember how much fun we had when my sister and I stayed with you last year upstate at your barn."

Megan sat up with a start. "Speaking of my sister, I'd better give her a call."

"Yes, listen, Megan, why don't you go into the conference room and make all the calls you need. I'll finish up here and we can walk to my place together afterwards."

Megan returned to the cozy room in which the board meeting had taken place just a few hours earlier. It seemed a century ago. She had long talks with both Tina and Claire, who were most relieved to hear from her and to learn that she was all right. Megan spared them the details of her mouse and cat experience with Hedwega, Megan being the mouse, but she did tell them about seeing Mr. Tall again, Eddie Hoch.

"What fun. I hope you gave him my greetings," Tina said enthusiastically. Not quite, thought Megan sarcastically. She remained silent on the subject.

Megan also gave Janette Killar and Helene Blumenstock a call at the Galerie St. Sebastian, bringing them up to date on the recent events. They, too, were worried about her safety, and cautioned their impetuous colleague to proceed carefully and slowly.

"I need to get home to Tilly," called Renata from the other room.

With a cautious look around once they got outside the building, the two friends walked down toward Renata's condo, which had a glorious, unobstructed view of Central Park and the ragged silhouette of the tall buildings that framed it on the far side. Exhausted, they soon said good night to each other, retiring for what they both hoped would be a good night's sleep.

64

Günther Winter had changed his mind.

No, it would not be a good idea to fly Megan Crespi to Girdwood to see his Klimt panel. Better that she not know about his cellar haven dedicated solely to the artist. Let her continue to think that Hundertwasser's altar piece was the star of his collection.

Better to show her Klimt's single panel elsewhere than Alaska, just in case anything unforeseen should happen.

Once he made up his mind as to the efficacy of his new plan, he contacted his secretary in Montreal to call off the rerouting of *Theology*, which had just arrived there. While he waited for the call to go through, he scratched his upper left arm vigorously. It had itched like this before but he had paid no attention. At last the phone call was answered.

"Hildegard? I've just air freighted from Milan to the Montreal airport a crated picture panel. I want you pick it up and unpack it yourself. Place it in the conference room there on the back wall, away from but facing the windows. A prospective buyer will be flying in to examine it. She is under the impression that the panel is in an unnamed private collection, and I want to keep it that way. Understood?"

"Yes sir," responded Hildegard quickly. She was used to receiving sudden chores from her boss and this seemed of no greater urgency than other assignments. Probably the panel would be yet another one of his multicolored Hundertwassers.

The city of Montreal was one of the hubs of Winter's far-flung pharmacology business, as well as the center for his banking negotiations, the latter under an assumed name. Megan Crespi could not possibly associate him with the city or the country.

Although she would eventually have to be done away with, it was good that things had worked out the way they had. He liked the woman. She was, with all her snooping faults, a fine-arts zealot like himself.

She would return to the Moderne Galerie with a positive authentication, and Lyonel Retter would jump at the chance to trade the Adele for his own sensational Secretum. Klimt's startling nude *Kiss* was both admission and confirmation of his affair with Adele Bloch-Bauer.

Yes, Günther was pleased with his new plan.

* * *

After a refreshing night's sleep at Renata's, Megan arranged to meet her ninety-four-year-old former publisher, the legendary George Braziller. He had brought out her books on Klimt and Schiele in the 1970s, and had commissioned her memoir *In Passionate Pursuit* soon after 9/11.

She remembered vividly the first time she had met George. He came up to her after a lecture she had delivered at the Guggenheim, back in 1965, and introduced himself, referring to her in his salutation as "Miss Crespi." Instantly Megan had corrected him: "Ms. Crespi, if you please." He acquiesced and had never forgotten the reprimand which they now both remembered as inordinately hilarious.

They met at the Met in front of Rosa Bonheur's giant, galloping canvas, *The Horse Fair*. Braziller his hair now white, was an intelligent man with an energetic face and merry, penetrating eyes that had not faded over time.

"What shall we talk about this time, now that we have paid our customary homage to Bonheur," asked George, smiling at his Texas protégé who seemed unusually excited.

"Oh, George, I can never hide anything from you," exclaimed Megan, lightly jabbing him with her elbow.

"So, what is it this time?"

"This time I'm back with our Gustav. I am chasing down a painted panel by him that had been lost for decades, but now seems to have made a reappearance, possibly on *this* continent."

"That sounds like a difficult task."

"It has turned out that way so far, George. And it has required a bit of travel as well."

"Megan, you've never minded that."

"But now, dear George, tell me what have *you* been up to?"

"As you know, Megan, I'm only publishing two books a year now, and this time both of them are poetry volumes. One is by a Cuban *woman*, you'll be pleased to know—Ofelia Casas. The other is a Frenchman. Now, this should interest you, Megan. His poems are sonnets dedicated to the subject of various Klimt drawings, and he describes them beautifully in verse."

"*What?*" Megan burst out. "Tell me, George, does he illustrate his sonnets with reproductions of the drawings?"

"Oh, yes. And they demonstrate the artist's evocative way with the pencil, that's for sure."

"Hm. I need to write down the French poet's name. What is it, George?"

"LePingre, Jacques LePingre. But I thought you'd be more interested in the female poet."

Megan did not acknowledge Braziller's second sentence, so fixated was she on the male poet's name she had just heard from the lips of her publisher.

Jacques LePingre?

The man she and Henri-Claude had visited just a few days ago in Thomory-By?

"Ordinarily, yes, George," she finally responded, "I would be more interested in the woman poet, but right now, because of my Klimt chase, I'm more interested in the male one. Any chance of obtaining a copy of this book?"

"Well, well, well, Megan," smiled Braziller engagingly, "I somehow happened to have brought you *both* books, printed just last month." He pulled them out of the lightweight Gristedes cloth sack he had taken to carrying instead of his heavy leather briefcase and handed them to an elated Megan.

"Oh, *thank you* so much, George." Ignoring the Cuban woman's volume, Megan examined the French poet's book, skipping the sonnets and concentrating on the reproductions of Klimt drawings. They were all portrait studies. Portrait studies of a single person—Adele Bloch-Bauer. And none of them had been reproduced or noted in the definitive oeuvre catalogue on Klimt recently published by Janette Killar.

"This is a far, far greater gift than you can possibly imagine," Megan said, quietly.

* * *

Over lunch by herself at her favorite Jackson Hole restaurant, near both the Moderne and the Guggenheim, Megan mulled over the fortuitous find Braziller's book gift had brought her.

Accompanying a dozen sonnets, all dedicated à la femme enchanteresse, oh, dame mystérieuse, were twelve reproductions of the poetically addressed Klimt drawings, each one responding to a changing mood of Adele.

The sonnets themselves were rather ordinary, forced rhapsodies really, but the *drawings*. Never had Megan seen such concentration, such searching portrayals by Klimt. His laconic line brought out aspects of Adele she had never seen before—bored, questioning, fearful, imperious, seductive.

Megan must find out how a man living in Bonheur's tiny village of By could have come by a dozen superb Klimt drawings. She sent off an email to Henri-Claude asking him to fill her in on everything he knew about the author of the sonnets. And on his connection to Klimt, other than the lock of hair.

Henri-Claude happened to be online at the same time, so his answer came almost immediately.

"As I told you, Jacques is a very secretive fellow and a poet of sorts. He informed me recently that he might be having a book published at long last in America rather than in France, where he's tried to get something published for years. His young partner Jean-Jean couldn't be less interested in the arts. It's a strange relationship, really, built more on sex than on mutual interests. But it has lasted for some four years, and that's a record for Jacques. The only connection with Klimt that I know of is that lock of hair he proudly showed us. That's all I know. Why are you asking, *ma chère?*"

Megan hedged: "Oh, I had some thoughts about authenticating Klimt's lock of hair, that's all."

After she finished her tuna salad, Megan took the subway down to see Horst Uhr's Corinth show at the Mannheim gallery in Soho. She missed him by only five minutes, the receptionist told her, just as Megan's iPhone began softly sounding Massenet's *Méditation.* Thanking the receptionist and stepping outdoors quickly, she answered a number with caller ID blocked, and found herself talking to a worried Joe Seguire.

"Dr. Crespi? Are you all right? We have you down in Soho."

"Yes, thank you Joe. I forgot that I was wearing the track stick. You've found me. And all is well. I'm just gallery hopping."

"Okay then. But do you have any other plans to leave midtown Manhattan?"

"It's possible, but thank you so much for checking on me, Joe."

After visiting two other nearby galleries she hurried back to the Moderne Galerie for dinner at Candle 79 again with Renata and Lyonel. She was getting a wee bit tired of vegan food. They discussed plans for the day after tomorrow, focusing on what might be the possible location for Megan's expertise if a plane flight and passport were involved.

Lyonel suggested: "If Günther Winter is behind this, as we think he is, then it might be as far away as his remote hotel in Alaska."

"Yes, but then why did the second note specifically instruct Megan to take her passport with her?" asked Renata.

"It really could be as far as Vienna," chimed in Megan. "God knows he has the wherewithal to do such a thing. Just use one of the planes from his own fleet of jets."

"Do remember to keep that track stick on you at all times," cautioned Lyonel, "and for Christ's sake, *don't lean over!*" They all burst into laughter.

At Renata's condo that evening Megan caught up with calls to her sister and Claire, both of whom had conscientiously checked the front of Megan's house for any mail that was too large for her mail slot. Button was still at Tina's and loved playing with the doggies there. All was well in Dallas. When was she coming back, did she know?

"Totally unknown," responded Megan quite truthfully. "I am prepared, as well as I can be, for anything."

* * *

It was Megan's second full day in New York. Since she actually had some time on her hands, rare for her, she decided to try to hook up with her musicologist buddy Will Meridian, the Beethoven expert who lived up in Riverdale. He answered the phone right away when she called and enthusiastically bade her to come right out. The timing was perfect. He had just returned last night from the Beethoven House in Bonn.

"Do, do come," he implored. "I'll have lunch set out on the patio for us."

Remembering this time to alert Joe Seguire that she was going out of midtown Manhattan range via bus to Riverdale, Megan set off happily to meet her old friend. She had some thoughts on Klimt's legendary *Beethoven Frieze* of 1902 and its possible relation to the Secretum panel she was about to see in person.

Lunch was a delicious array of spring rolls and mint tea, and afterward the two settled down with Will's personal copy of Janette Killar's weighty catalogue raisonné of Klimt's work. They turned to the illustrations of the *Beethoven Frieze* which had been shown in its entirety at the fourteenth Vienna Secession exhibition. Now restored after World War II, it was on permanent display in the Secession Museum's basement gallery.

To accompany the Leipzig sculptor Max Klinger's marble life-size statue of Beethoven enthroned, Klimt had created a seven-paneled pictorial voyage through infernal and celestial regions as a symbolic paraphrase of Beethoven's Ninth Symphony. The frieze climaxed with joy, as did Schiller's ode and Beethoven's music.

The hero enters into a "kingdom not of this world," but a kingdom of pure joy. A look-alike choir of angels intones a line from Schiller's ode, *To Joy,* as with *diesen Kuss der ganzen Welt* ("this kiss for the whole world"), pure love finds itself. The tall hero, his muscular back to the beholder, is a heroic, powerful *nude*. He embraces the nude female figure of "pure" love in the purest of kisses, shielding most of her body with his own.

The bodies in this kiss were identical to those in the Secretum photograph that had been sent to the Moderne Galerie.

The noble motivation of Klimt's Beethoven kiss, Megan reminded Will, was not appreciated by the public as "pure." Incensed by the portrayal of a naked couple kissing, critics condemned the frieze as an allegory of venereal disease. It was painted pornography, "fit only for a Krafft-Ebing temple." Due partly to the city's rabid anti-Semitism, some critics also condemned the hero/knight of the opening panel, only too identifiable as the controversial director of the Vienna opera, Gustav Mahler.

Megan looked fondly at her old friend. Will was reliable. Megan told him about most of the events that had occurred during the past two weeks in Santa Fe, Europe, and New York City. He, like Tina and Claire, was immediately concerned for her safety. Megan did not mention what she would be doing at eight o'clock the next morning.

"Speaking of Klimt," said Will, "do you know about the Austrian Euro one hundred coin that was minted in two thousand four, Megan?"

"Oh, yes, the 'Secession coin.' I know it's coveted by collectors. Three figures from the *Beethoven Frieze* are on it, including the Mahler knight, right? But I've never seen one in the gold flesh, have you?"

Will's blue eyes twinkled as he leaned back and pulled out of his right trouser pocket a Secession coin. Sure enough the verso sported the figures of the knight and two women from Klimt's frieze.

"How many of these do you have?" exclaimed Megan.

"That's the only one, I'm afraid. They were mostly all gobbled up the day after they came out."

The two friends happily continued to talk shop about Beethoven, Mahler, and Klimt until Megan glanced at her watch. It was already five o'clock.

"We still have time to trade folk songs again," Will said, walking over to a wall lined with mandolins, five-string banjos, and guitars, including a twelve string guitar. Taking down the latter he said: "I have finally mastered Big Bill Broonzy's *Worried Man Blues*, commencing to strum and sing lustily, beginning and ending with the refrain:

> Well, it takes a worried man to sing a worried song
> Yes, it takes a worried man to sing a worried song
> It takes a worried man to sing a worried song
> I'm worried now but I won't be worried long

Megan listened with fascination. Will became a different person when he imitated Big Bill. What fun to hear him. Who would guess that it was a world-renowned Beethoven scholar performing the blues?

"Now it's your turn, Megan," Will said, handing her a regular guitar. "Sing me one of your Neapolitan songs. How about *Core 'Ngrato*?"

"Oh, dear, I haven't played the guitar in a long time, Will, but I'll give it a try," Megan said gamely. Putting her left leg on the low footstool Will had used, she plucked a short melodic intro, then began:

> *Catari, Catari, pecche me dice sti parole amare,*
> *pecche me parle e 'o core me turmiente, Catari?*
> *Nun te scurda ca t'aggio date 'o core, Catari,*
> *nun te scurda!*
> *Catari, Catari, che vene a dicere stu parla ca me da spaseme?*
> *Tu nun'nce pienze a stu dulore mio,*
> *tu nun'nce pienze, tu nun te ne cure.*
> *Core, core, 'ngrato,*
> *t'aie pigliato 'a vita mia,*
> *tutt'e passato e*
> *nun'nce pienze chiu!*

> Cateri, Cateri, why do you say those bitter words to me?
> Why do you speak to me and torment my heart, Cateri?
> Don't you forget, that I've given you my heart, Cateri, don't you forget.

Cateri, Cateri, why do you come and say those words that hurt me so much?
You do not think about my pain,
you don't think, you, you don't care.
Heart, heart, oh ungrateful
You have stolen my life.
Everything is over and
You don't care anymore!

Megan finished with a flourish and Will clapped loudly.

"Do stay longer," he urged, insisting that Megan go out to dinner with him. And she did so gladly. Over a delicious dinner at a nearby Italian restaurant she asked, thinking of the Klimt lock of hair she had recently been shown: "When you had the Beethoven Center's lock of the composer's hair subjected to DNA testing, was it possible to determine from the eight strands whether or not the huge amount of lead in Beethoven's system contributed to his deafness?"

"So far no," Will answered. "But tests are continuing to be made."

"Do you think a DNA test could be made on, say, a lock of Klimt's hair to determine whether or not it is genuine?"

"I suppose so, if they dug up his body and got its genetic code for a match."

"Yikes!" Megan let the topic drop and instead asked if her friend knew Michael Jackson's twelve single hairs went for almost two million dollars. It was Will's turn to say "Yikes!"

At long last, with a rush of thanks and a hard embrace, Megan took leave of her treasured colleague and hailed a cab to Renata's condo. Renata was already asleep.

Before she retired for the night Megan used her pocket knife to chisel out a miniscule rectangular trench in the interior heel of her left sneaker. No bra spills this time. She laid her track stick securely in place and covered it with a thin bit of Velcro from her cosmetic kit. Then she packed up supplies in her beloved shoulder bag, making sure she had her furry scarf, her defense against airplane air conditioning. What new Klimt hell would tomorrow bring? Soon, with the aid of a sleeping pill, she fell asleep.

In the early morning she and Renata had a quick breakfast together. In fact Renata left the condo before Megan. After a final check of the items in her shoulder bag, including her iPad Mini, she laid Renata's extra set of keys on the breakfast room table, closed the door firmly to the apartment, and began the short walk down Fifth Avenue to the side door of the Guggenheim on 89th Street. She arrived there at precisely eight o'clock.

A black Lincoln Town Car with a dented back fender was already parked at the curb.

65

"Asta Holm-Ditlevsen has been found murdered in her bed."

Renata telephoned the grim news to a horrified Lyonel that morning at eight-thirty. She had just gotten off the phone talking with her Swiss grandmother, who read the news out loud to her from the *Neue Züricher Zeitung*.

"Terrible! Do they know who did it? And why?"

"No, but it may have been a burglary gone wrong, because a large work of art was missing from the house."

"Don't tell me! That sounds like the Klimt *Theology* panel we've suspected she owned all along. What else could it have been?"

"Too bad we can't confirm this with Megan. She certainly would be able to tell us what was in the living room, since she was just there."

Lyonel jumped at the idea. "It's eight thirty. Megan should be on her way to some airport by now. Let's see if we can possibly get through to her on her smartphone."

Renata dialed Megan's number, hoping against hope that Megan's phone was turned on. It wasn't.

* * *

As she approached the black limo Megan saw Eddie at the wheel, this time without the pretense of a chauffeur's cap. He actually half-smiled at her as she entered the back seat. There were no smiles from Hedwega.

As soon as Megan was settled with her safety belt on, Hedwega turned to her and commanded: "I am going to have to ask you to entrust your smart phone and any computers you might have in your bag to me for the duration of your trip. They will be returned to you when you get back to New York."

"What? No legal paper for me to sign this time, just depriving me of any means of communication with the outside world?" Megan shot back.

"This is absolutely necessary. We cannot disclose the location of the panel you will be seeing today. The private collector has forbidden that. But you will be back in New York by this evening."

"Depriving me of my iPhone and computer seems totally exaggerated," said Megan bitterly. "This is the sort of thing that made me jump ship last time I was in this limo." She had turned her iPhone off before getting in the limo, hoping not to draw attention to it. In vain.

"You may certainly jump out if you wish," sarcastically replied an exasperated Hedwega, as they drove up the East River Drive toward the Triborough bridge. "But just remember what happened to the Moderne Galerie's Adele."

Ah, so she knows about *that*! Megan thought triumphantly. Eager to put more pieces of the convoluted Klimt puzzle together, she decided, with great misgivings, to acquiesce to Hedwega's demands. A pity that she would be out of telephonic contact, she thought, as she handed over her beloved iPhone and MacBook Air. At least she had the track stick on her.

Megan did not jump out of the limo this time, calmed by the certainty that her movements were being monitored by Joe Seguire, who in turn would report to Lyonel Retter. A comforting thought to hang on to in this bizarre Klimtonian adventure. Also in her shoulder bag she had another trick up her sleeve.

They zoomed past La Guardia and in another ten minutes they were traversing the general aviation ramp at JFK. Direct-ramp access with its bare bones check in, Megan gratefully realized, would mean that she would not have to remove her shoes and pass through a scanner. A few seconds later they pulled up to the side of a slim, twin-engine Gulfstream G650.

"Do you have anything else? I'll have to look through your bag," Hedwega stated firmly as they got out of the limo. Megan shrugged. *Hell's bells* she thought in exasperation knowing that they would find her new iPad Mini at the bottom of the bag.

Hedwega found it instantly and drew it out of the bag with a scowl on her face.

"I see being truthful is not one of your assets," she commented. "Any other communication items we should know about?" asked Hedwiga as she frisked Megan up and down.

"No," lied Megan evenly.

The lie worked. Boarding the elegant gray jet a minute later, Megan felt a huge sense of relief as she settled down in the large and comfortable cabin. How right Lyonel had been to insist that she carry his track stick on her person. She pushed the heel of her left sneaker down hard and felt, very slightly, a reassuring small flat object. All was well. Megan sat back to see where on earth this jet with its roaring engines was taking her. Hedwega and Eddie sat opposite her, their faces without expression. The plane headed north.

❦❦

In Vienna, Jeremy Herring was holding a family conference. In her last visitation, the shade of Rachel had been insistent that he move to thwart Günther Winter in his gluttonous attempt to procure the Adele from the Moderne Galerie for himself. As Jeremy communicated this to his offspring, he noticed they were squirming in their seats.

"What is the matter with you two?"

"Look, Dad, we know you—and Mutti—care very, very much about restoring Adele to the Belvedere. But how can you possibly thwart Günther Winter, with all his billionaire resources?" asked Thad.

"It doesn't take money, it takes *ingenuity*."

"Do you have a plan, Dad?" Rita asked, rolling her eyes at Thad.

"Yes, of course I do."

Jeremy opened the drawer of the coffee table in front of him and withdrew a color photograph of Max Klinger's *Beethoven Enthroned*.

"This, *this*, is what will bring Adele to Wien!" he exclaimed triumphantly. Thad and Rita stared at the photograph uncomprehendingly. It was clear to see that the sculptor had deified the composer who sat on a bronze throne, his torso bare, his legs crossed, and his hands clenched into fists in front of him. The blank staring eyes of the face were fixated upon the world of ideas. Presentation and pose had conspired to promote the tone hero from Promethean striver to Zeus-like creator. This was Beethoven, the enthroned, cogitating genius. That much Jeremy's children understood.

Staring at the color image further they studied the empyrean eagle, attribute and companion of the king of the gods, who alone can ascend to Olympian heights. The amber-eyed eagle seemed scarcely to dare land on the cloud-piercing cliff that supported the throne of ideas upon which such a godlike creator sat.

A celestial accompaniment of five ivory cherubs' heads embedded in the throne above Beethoven's back greeted the spectacle with approving glances. The angel to the right pointed to the creative deity. Removed from the world, Beethoven was occupied in the divine work of creative thought. This too, after their father explained what the eagle was, Thad and Rita comprehended.

"But still, how does this statue have anything to do with getting Klimt's Adele back to Wien?" they asked practically in unison.

Their father wagged a finger at them and said "Patience, *meine Kinder*, patience.

"Look carefully at the cherub heads. See the one on the far right and how its single finger points at Beethoven?"

"Um hum, yes.?"

"Now follow the exact line extending from that finger. See what the finger is pointing to?"

Silence.

"Well, I don't know," hesitated Thad. "If it's not Beethoven himself, then what could it be?"

"Oh! I see," exclaimed Rita. "The finger is actually pointing across to Beethoven's two fists!"

"Correct, dear," Jeremy confirmed with satisfaction. It was always his daughter rather than his son who caught on to things.

"Now draw another imaginary line from the point of view of the eagle's amber eye. What do you get?"

"It also seems to lead directly to Beethoven's clenched fists?" Thad hazarded.

"Right! So the fists are very important, not just compositionally but also in themselves. What do you think that might mean?"

"That Beethoven was *holding* something in his fists?" guessed Rita.

"That's an idea, but it would be pretty hard to squeeze anything into that marble as the fists are fused together, one on top of the other. Instead just follow the line straight down from the fists. Where do you end up?"

"His feet?" asked Thad, perplexed.

"You're on the mark, Thad. His *feet*. Now notice the small crevice, just visible, between the upper and the lower foot."

"Dad, what are you getting at?" Rita asked, getting bored with the guessing game.

"Okay, kids. You know that when I was a G. I. at the end of the war I was assigned to an art restitution unit that brought me first to Germany and to Leipzig, and then later on to Vienna, where I met your wonderful mother and stayed.

"During my second month in Leipzig I was assigned to inventory the works stored in the basement of the old Leipzig Museum of Fine Arts. The museum proper had been destroyed by allied bombing in December of nineteen forty-three. Among other works safely stored in the basement was the Klinger monument *Beethoven Enthroned.* There were no working lights in the basement at that time and so I had to work with a heavy, battery-powered flashlight lantern, taking inventory on my clipboard.

"When I came across, actually stumbled against, the Klinger statue I was stunned. What a fabulous sculptural ensemble! A placard at its feet said that Klinger had worked on it for over fifteen years. I ran my lantern over every inch of the work—the cliff, the eagle, the feet, the drapery over the legs, the gold throne arms, the marble hands, arms, chest, blank eyes, and head of Beethoven.

"By flashlight I examined the throne as it rose behind him and looked carefully at each cherub head, five in all, carefully set into a blue mosaic band of opals and antique glass fragments that held the black-studded butterfly wings of agate and jasper with gold leaf underlay.

"Do you follow me?" Jeremy interrupted his description abruptly and looked at his son, whose facial expression had begun to go vacant.

"Sure, Dad, sure. Go on."

"Yes, go on." urged Rita.

"The flashlight beam not only picked up the gold leaf and gleaming opals, it also illuminated a narrow dark crevice between Beethoven's feet. I wondered if there were anything inside it. I poked deep inside the hole with a knife and made contact with something. Slowly, I eased out what seemed like a small leather cylinder of sorts. When I pulled it out and rolled it open, I saw a handwritten document in *Kurrentschrift* bearing three signatures. The first, was that of the writer of the one-page sheet, and the other two, those of witnesses to the document. I was at least able to figure out that much. Of the signatory and two witnesses, one of the three names meant something to me immediately."

Jeremy took a deep breath. "Nowadays that name is known not only to me but to the whole art world. The signatory was Adele Bloch-Bauer. The two witnesses were a certain Reinhold Blitz and Rudolf Schnell. The date was twenty-three May nineteen-two."

Thad and Rita gasped.

"What did the document say?"

"I couldn't read *Kurrentschrift* at that time, so I just quickly photo-graphed it by the light of my lantern. I replaced the leather roll with the document inside and continued my inventory work."

"Well, now you *can* read *Kurrentschrift*, and fluently," cried Rita. "What did the document *say*?"

"The single sheet of paper was a statement of intent: it said that the writer of the document, Adele Bloch-Bauer, obligated herself, in the event of the death of Gustav Klimt, to ensure that any oil portraits which he made of her would eventually go—*für alle Zeiten* ("for all time") —into the imperial collection of modern art. The collection was being formed at that very time by the art historian Franz Haberditzl. Haberditzl, as you both know, was painted by Schiele.

"Just at that same time, the Vienna Secession had been urging that the rooms in the Upper Belvedere be committed to *modern* art, both Austrian and foreign. So the Modern Gallery, as it was called, opened with that purpose in May of nineteen-three, a year to the month after Adele's document had been signed and witnessed."

"So, that means," said Thad, trying to comprehend the ramifications of this discovery, "that it was Adele Bloch-Bauer's intention and desire that whatever oil portraits Klimt might paint of her in the future would eventually go for all time into the state's collection. I remember Klimt worked on that first nineteen-seven portrait of her for seven years."

Rita spoke up excitedly. "If this had been known back in the nineteen nineties and early two thousands, wouldn't that have strengthened the Austrian state's claim to the Adele portrait? I know that Adele had asked her husband Ferdinand eventually to contribute all their Klimt works to the Austrian state. She died of meningitis in nineteen twenty-five, and when Ferdinand fled Nazi Austria for Switzerland, he left the paintings with the Belvedere. Thus it would seem that Klimt's golden portrait of her did belong, uncontestably, to Austria."

"You're damn right it should have," answered Jeremy heatedly.

"So why didn't you speak up?" Thad asked.

"A mere photograph would not have constituted acceptable evidence in a court, and I no longer had access to the document itself. By the nineteen eighties, Klinger's Beethoven had been removed from the museum basement and, thanks to the Leipzig Symphony's conductor Kurt Masur, was set up in the small foyer of the Gewandhaus. There it greeted music lovers for some twenty years before it was reinstated in the new Leipzig Museum of Fine Arts. Unfortunately, it was not in a setting dedicated to it and it alone, as had been the case in the Gewandhaus."

Rita looked thoughtful. "Dad, are you saying that if you had the original document right now, you could hand it over to the Austrian government and they could contest the judgment that awarded Adele to Marjorie Niederman in America?"

"Exactly."

"So how do we get hold of it?" Thad asked eagerly, sensing that his father might be giving him a new and exciting assignment.

"You, Thad, go to Leipzig, to the museum, and you ascertain if, after all these years, the leather roll with the document inside is still in its hiding place in the crevice of the Beethoven statue.

"It is a distinct possibility," he continued, "because although a museum restorer may well have cleaned the marble to its former purity, there would have been no reason to investigate more than casually the insignificant concave slit between the statue's legs. And if the leather roll is still there, you grab it."

"Dad!" cried his son, "what an *ace* you are holding. If this works out, if I find the document in Leipzig, why you could enable the Austrian state to act *legally* to prevent the Adele portrait from remaining in the States."

"Yes, I know. And that is exactly what I intend to do. That is what your mother wants," he said, smiling at the approving shade only he could see.

"And Rita, I need you here, or I'd send you along with your brother."

Thad and Rita beamed at their clever old father with a mixture of admiration and excitement, tolerantly ignoring his dementia concerning their mother.

"So get cracking, Thad," commanded Jeremy. "Tomorrow you leave for Leipzig."

61

The 23rd of May 1902 was a warm day in Klimt's atelier on the Josef-städter Strasse in Vienna's seventh district. The artist had been working on his present commission, an oil portrait of Frau Adele Bloch-Bauer, for well over a year now. He hoped that he could spin the work out for yet another year or so. Frau Bloch-Bauer's presence in his studio, as she sat for portrait sketch after portrait sketch, was inspiring. As inspiring as her conversation was stimulating. Her husband Ferdinand, a sugar industrialist, was seldom in Wien, and Adele, who had married her husband when he was thirty-five and she nineteen, was lonely. Her salon circle included Gustav and Alma Mahler, Richard Strauss, Stefan Zweig, and the socialist Karl Renner. But those salons in her drawing room, though precious, were rare and far between.

She had come to enjoy the portrait sitting sessions more than she dared confess to herself. Klimt's eyes seemed to bore into the very depths of her soul. And then one day he put his pencil down, walked over to her in his flowing blue caftan—under which, it was said, he wore nothing—and pulled her face to his in a prolonged kiss. She knew she wanted more, wanted him to give himself to her as she was ready to give herself to him. And so they became lovers, a secret known only to themselves, and perhaps to the sheets of studies Gustav continued to make of her in ever-changing moods and positions.

On that early May evening, Gustav invited Adele to go with him to the Secession building downtown off the Ringstrasse. Yes, the building was closed now, but he knew the affable night watchmen, and it was his burning desire to walk through the Beethoven exhibition with Adele, to explain his great frieze to her in every detail. And so they went into town and to the Secession. All was dark. But Reinhold Blitz and Rudolf Schnell recognized the artist and willingly let them in a side entrance. They spent a full two hours walking through the great exhibit, also admiring the Max Klinger monument to Beethoven in the center room. They returned again and again to Gustav's seven-part frieze in the side room, while he explained the different figures in the panels.

As they started to leave, Gustav said he would like to emulate the Kiss of the frieze, in front of it, in real life, in present time with Adele. The lovers kissed. Adele looked at the great unfolding frieze of the striving of the human spirit, then looked back again at Gustav.

We must protect your immortal work, Gustl, she said. Give me a page from your sketchbook. I want to write out a document here and now that says whatever portraits you may do of me should be inherited not by my family, as I have no children, but by our mother country, our beloved Austria.

In a few minutes the simple document was written out in Adele's beautiful Kurrentschrift. The cooperative night watchmen were drafted to cosign the document as witnesses. After the guards had left again, the lovers decided to store the document for temporary safekeeping inside the Beethoven statue where they had detected an almost invisible crevice between the statue's feet. Neither of them felt right about having such a document in their respective homes.

It came to pass that neither Gustav nor Adele ever got back to the Beethoven exhibition before it closed and the statue shipped back to Leipzig. They had forgotten about its existence as life and love unfolded before them in rich daily portions.

Completion of the gold portrait of Adele extended for another five years.

68

Megan was surprised to see that they had only been in the air for a little over an hour before the plane began making its descent. Looking out the window she saw a cultivated expanse of trees and greenery, what looked like botanical gardens, and then an urban area with skyscrapers and a number of church steeples. The city was set on a long harbor bordering the bend of a broad river. This was a skyline she had not seen before.

"Where are we?" There had been no conversation during the uneventful flight.

"That is of no consequence to you," answered Hedwega primly. "We will stay on the plane until our transportation arrives."

They set down smoothly on a far runway of a largish airport and soon a black limousine pulled up to the plane. Gad! Günther must have a whole fleet of these things, a wary Megan thought to herself.

"Now we go down," Hedwega instructed grimly. Eddie stayed on board while the two women descended and entered the limo. They were driven to a seemingly abandoned harbor section of the unnamed city, full of warehouses and a few bars. The limo drove up to a bland looking eight-story warehouse opposite an active construction site.

As they stepped outside the limo Megan heard some of the construction workers shouting to each other. They were communicating in French. Ah, ha! We must either be in Quebec or Montreal, and I'd hazard Montreal from the size of this harbor. She wondered whether the track stick in her left shoe was transmitting back to Joe Seguire in New York. Just pressing her heel over the amazing thing made her feel better.

Briskly, Hedwega led the way to the back of the building and into a large ground floor office. Hildegard was expecting them and, without so much as a word of greeting, immediately showed them into a large, well-appointed conference room, the back windows of which looked out upon the St. Lawrence River. On the opposite wall, with a large sheet over it, stood a tall panel about eight feet in height.

"All right. Take the sheet down," barked Hedwega. Hildegard quickly obliged and one moment later Megan was staring at the Secretum.

"This is *amazing!*" Megan could not help exclaiming out loud. The other two women apparently did not share her enthusiasm. Silently they sat down in straight-backed chairs opposite the artwork and on either side of the entry door, keeping a watchful eye on Megan.

Megan looked at length, standing far back from the canvas, then going up very close to it, observing the hardly visible, smooth dabs brush work, then stepping back for a view of the entire painting.

At length she asked if she could look at the back of the panel.

Hildegard hesitantly answered yes. She had not foreseen such a question. Since the artwork was leaning against the wall, Megan could only see the lower half of the canvas, and the light was poor. But she could discern what looked like the broadly sketched outlines of two seated figures. Expertly she ran her fingers over the canvas, ascertaining that it was indeed an old one.

"Ok to use my flashlight?" Megan asked, delving into her shoulder bag.

"*Stop!*" shouted Hedwega, jumping up and running toward her.

"For goodness sake! It's only a *flashlight*," countered Megan. Hedwega grabbed it from her and unscrewed the flashlight, tumbling two batteries into the palm of her hand. Looking long and hard at them she finally returned the batteries to the flashlight chamber and screwed the top back on. Reluctantly she handed the flashlight back to the damned woman who kept doing suspicious things.

Megan beamed her ray of light across the verso of the canvas. There was nothing in the upper register, but in the lower plane the silhouettes of two seated figures could be seen, both in elegant Secession-style chairs and facing each other.

That was all, but it was enough for Megan. She realized that Klimt had used the canvas back to sketch out the placement and sizing of two life-size profile portraits. There were no descriptive fills and it was difficult even to ascertain the sex of the two people, whose clothing had not been defined. But the figure on the right looked as though it might be related to Klimt's first portrait of Adele Bloch-Bauer. The figure's hands were clasped tightly together in front. That would date the panel recto as having been painted around 1907, the date of the gold Adele. She could not tell anything about the other portrait, so sketchily had it been drawn, the chair seemingly more important than the figure.

Megan turned her attention anew to the front of the panel, stepping back again to fathom the full effect of the dark cosmos of stars and small floating figures that swirled around the two naked kissers. She observed that the figures in the upper realm were all quotations from Klimt's three, actually four University panels, counting Asta's panel. The life-size nude kissing couple below, was the actual reverse of the artist's *Beethoven Frieze* kiss, in which the naked male faced away from the beholder, covering the female's body and face with his own. Here the lovers faced blatantly outward, their features in three-quarter view unmistakably depicted. The photographs sent to the Moderne Galerie board of directors had not lied. This was the kiss of Gustav Klimt and Adele Bloch-Bauer, enunciated for eternity.

As for authenticating the *hand* of the artist, there was no mistaking Klimt's unique pressure and slanting of the brush as evidenced in strokes applied evenly in downward turning motions. Nor was there was any mistaking the artist's palette of colors, ranging from, in addition to gold, onyx black through the color spectrum to ivory white. Yes, this panel was definitely by Klimt. And yes, this painting was totally unknown to the art world.

Knowing the answer would probably be no, Megan asked anyway. "Might I make a few color notations?" Hedwega and Hildegard exchanged urgent glances.

"Is that absolutely necessary?" demanded Hedwega, scowling.

"It is if I am to authenticate this painting properly," Megan answered authoritatively, finding new courage in the presence of Klimt.

"Go ahead, then," Hedwega snarled in unwilling acquiescence.

Megan pulled out a small notepad from her jacket pocket. Fastening the notepad cover was a small pen. Pulling out the pen caused the pad to open up smartly with a loud snap. Hedwega lunged at Megan and was on top of her in an instant. Her weight forced the two of them to the floor. From that vantage point the former policewoman examined the note pad and pen. Finding them in order, she allowed Megan to crawl out from underneath her.

"*Don't do anything stupid like that again,*" she chastised Megan who was struggling to get herself and her shoulder bag up.

Furious, Megan silently began making notes on the panel's colors. The mere enumeration of them took her mind off the bizarre situation she found herself in. There were earthy brown blacks, mysterious purple blacks, little wedges of silver and gold, and deep cerise reds chasing vaporous sapphire blues. Crimson orange and pink films revolved within a whirling gray white vortex that tossed small nude figures out into a dark blue, star-speckled sky. It was breathtaking, and it was one hundred percent Klimt.

Some fifteen minutes later, satisfied that she had completed her task to the best of her abilities and still smarting from the floor pounding she had taken, Megan turned to her charming companions and announced that she was finished.

Murmuring that she was "breaking in a new receptionist," Hildegard abruptly returned to her office. Megan's minder walked her to the front door of the warehouse. The limo awaited them and the drive back to the airport took place in silence.

Eddie was still in the cabin when they reboarded and, out of Hedwega's line of sight, he managed the smallest of smiles Megan's way.

It was one o'clock. Once the plane was under way back to New York he opened the cooler next to him and handed out bagels with cream cheese, capers, and Canadian salmon as well as bottles of Canada Dry. Of course, what else? Megan sighed.

After they finished and all had used the restroom, Hedwega seated herself opposite Megan. She handed her a pen and a yellow legal tablet and said: "And now you will please to write out your authentication of the artwork you have examined."

"*Not on your life,*" hissed an emboldened Megan. "That is not how we American art historians do business. They can authenticate in Europe to their hearts' content, but over here we do not write willy-nilly certificates attesting to the authenticity of works of art. We confer with other experts in the field and we communicate with the owners of the artworks in person. I must know with whom I am dealing before I authenticate the putative Klimt work you have dragged me off to see. I must know the source from which it was acquired. I must ascertain its whole provenance and location history from the time that the artist painted the work to now."

No amount of verbal persuasion on Hedwega's part could change Megan's mind. Eddie stayed out of the fray. Inclined, in fact eager, to use force on this stubborn woman, Hedwega decided to go up to the pilot's cabin and confer with Jeremy Herring by phone. Jeremy told her she should report her problem directly to Günther Winter. He gave her his boss's private number.

Winter was not surprised by what Jeremy's agent reported. He fully understood that Megan would want to consult with the owner of the Klimt in order to procure the provenance of the panel. Now, for him it was enough that Megan simply return to the Moderne Galerie with her first-hand report to Lyonel Ritter and Renata Teuer.

He calmed down Hedwega and instructed her to drop Megan off where they had picked her up, at the side entrance of the Guggenheim. She could damn well walk the few blocks down to the Moderne. How he would like to be a fly on the wall when Megan reported having seen the Secretum in the flesh. Hanging up, he then called Hildegard and instructed her to fly the panel back to Anchorage.

Hedwega did as she was told, regretfully so, as she would really have liked to sock that old biddy in the face. Soon the New York skyline came into view. The jet came to a stop on Kennedy's far tarmac and the omnipresent black limo was already there for Eddie to convey them into Manhattan. Just as the limo pulled up at 89th Street and Fifth Avenue, Hedwega abruptly and unceremoniously returned Megan's mini iPad, MacBook Air and iPhone. With the spring of a much younger woman, Megan quit the car and began walking down Fifth Avenue to the Moderne Galerie, her welcome home away from home.

Their job done, and with Günther Winter's approval, Hedwega and Eddie made their way back to their homes in Vienna and Girdwood, respectively. Long flights for both.

"She's back in Manhattan! She's within two blocks of you right now," Seguire reported to Lyonel Retter, minutes before Megan reached the Moderne on foot. Joe had kept Lyonel and Renata apprised of Megan's whereabouts, tracking her movements from Kennedy to Trudeau airports and her specific warehouse location in Montreal. Earlier he had reported that Megan was on a plane heading south toward New York, and then that she had landed and was on her way down the FDR Drive. And now she was crossing on 96th Street toward the Galerie.

Both Renata and Lyonel hurried downstairs to greet Megan at the museum door. She looked and sounded intact, but seemed very tired. They escorted her up to the conference room, waited while she went to the rest-room, then gathered in Renata's office, eager for Megan's news.

"The Secretum is *without doubt* the work of Klimt. And, in the flesh, it is absolutely stunning. The colors haven't faded at all and Klimt's full palette was dedicated to the canvas.

"Here, I have notations on the colors," she said, withdrawing her notepad from her shoulder bag and handing it over. The color photographs sent to the board members were on the table already, and Lyonel and Renata were able to equate various parts of the canvas with the colors of Megan's annotations.

"This is fascinating," admitted Lyonel.

"Do you think we could offer to *buy* it?" Renata asked with a spark of hope.

"That is the only thing we can offer. As I have said, *Adele stays at the Moderne*." Renata and Megan nodded in vigorous agreement.

"When we hear from Winter again, and I am convinced that it is Winter we are dealing with, I shall make our counteroffer to purchase the panel. Until then we must sit tight. Good work, Megan."

"Thank you. It was a weird journey, I can tell you that."

"You were very courageous to take it on, especially at your age, Megan," responded Lyonel.

Megan was not too tired to chastise Lyonel once again for the offence of ageism, but she did it in a gentle way and they both grinned.

"Megan," said Renata gently, "I don't know whether I should tell you now or later, seeing as you must be exhausted from the trip, but I do have some sad news to give you before you read or hear about it yourself. Shall I tell you now?"

"Yes, by all means. Another blow can hardly hurt me now."

"I'm sorry to tell you that Asta Holm-Ditlevsen is dead."

"*Oh, no!*" cried Megan, totally shaken by the shocking news.

"Yes, and unfortunately there is more. She was found murdered in her bed by thieves who then removed a large art panel from her house. Her body wasn't discovered until the morning, when her maid brought in breakfast."

"Do they know who did this? Have they caught the murderers?"

"No, the Swiss police are working on it, but there are just no leads. The murder and theft must have taken place early in the morning hours, before Asta's maid was up. It's just ghastly, Megan. She was garroted."

"Garroted! Oh, how terrible!" she moaned.

She was visibly upset that Asta, with whom she had spent wonderful times just days ago, had met such a horrible end. For a few long minutes Megan sat in silence as she absorbed the grizzly news and fought to regain her composure. The sinister happenings of the past two weeks flashed before her—the murders and the attempted murders. She realized with revulsion that Asta's violent death was *another killing for Klimt*!

Fighting to pull herself together, Megan tried to find a commonsense way to help her deal with the tragedy. Through her grief she realized now that her oath to Asta was no longer valid and she could admit to her two friends exactly what was stolen from the Danish woman's Ascona home.

"All right," she said haltingly. "Now I can tell you. Lionel, Renata, you were both correct when you theorized that Klimt's *Theology* panel belonged to Asta and was in her Ascona home."

"Why didn't you tell us this before?" asked Lyonel, obviously per-turbed by Megan's previous unwillingness either to confirm or deny his theory that *Theology* was in Switzerland.

"Because I took an *oath* not to reveal what I'd seen at Asta's home.

"Does, uh, did she have relatives, or anyone who knows what the disposition of her estate might be, with all those Scandinavian artworks?" Renata wondered.

"All I know," replied Megan, "is that the one child she had, a son, died quite some time ago in a car accident. And of course she's been a widow for several decades."

"I guess her staff has reported the robbery, but don't you think we should contact the Swiss police and inform them as to what was stolen? After all, it's a major, major artwork by Klimt!" said Lyonel heatedly.

"Think I'll make the call myself and right now," he decided abruptly, getting up from his chair and leaving Renata's office for the conference room.

Renata turned in her chair. "Megan, you must be absolutely exhausted. Why don't you go over to my place and get some rest? I haven't changed the sheets on your bed yet."

"Thank you, honey. I think I'll take you up on that. Yes, suddenly I am very, very tired and very sad." The two friends stood up, embraced, and Renata walked Megan to the elevator. "See you for dinner then?"

"Yes, of course. I'll fill you in on all the events of the day."

"And oh, by the way," Megan paused, digging down into the heel of her left sneaker, "give this back to Lyonel with my cramped thanks."

10

When it came time for his actual departure, Jacques LePingre could not bear to visit Vienne without his adorable Jean-Jean. They both felt bad about the falling out they had had in Ibiza. Jacques was able to get a second reservation for Jean-Jean and that morning they drove into Orly, parking the Jaguar in the nearest pay lot possible. Jacques's duffle bag was so heavy that Jean-Jean had to carry it to the airport entrance for him. Then Jacques took it over and passed through airport security easily.

Jacques LePingre was carrying an extremely valuable parcel in his huge duffle bag. The outside pocket contained what he had described to Jean-Jean as "a back up item." More importantly, the duffle bag contained the complete set of eighty-seven Klimt drawings of Adele still in his possession. To Jean-Jean they were still just "old drawings," but to Jacques they constituted the fortune he now hoped to acquire by selling them, not one at a time, but all together.

Surely he could get more money for the entire collection than he could for single images. He had tried that for a year and, although the income had been decent, he was increasingly suspicious that Nebehay's was not being honest with him about the value of the Klimt drawings he had sent them. Yes, he would declare exactly who he was—reveal his identity as the seller of the Klimt drawings—to Nebehay's director, Dr. Hanskarl Klug. But he would also gallery shop around a bit. In fact he might even approach the Albertina Museum. It already had a fine collection of Klimt drawings, but *qui sait*, perhaps they would covet having even more.

After a smooth flight, the two men took a taxi to town and checked into to their favorite downtown hotel, the Pension Suzanne at Walfischgasse 4, just two blocks over from Nebehay's on the Annagasse, and within a stone's throw from the Opera House. And also nearby at the Künstlerhaus, wonder of wonders, something was taking place each evening that would interest them both: a rock opera entitled *Klimt, Das Musical*.

But first to business. Although it was past four o'clock, they walked over to the Nebehay shop, presuming it was open until six in the evenings. It was indeed still open and they entered the shop with their precious parcel. Rita Herring greeted them and called Herr Dr. Klug to come to the front of the shop. He wore a dark blue smock over his street clothes, just as old Christian Nebehay had done during business hours. Jean-Jean nudged Jacques lightly to convey his amusement at the old-fashioned air of the place.

"How can I help you, *meine Herren*?"

"Monsieur, I am Jacques LePingre, the person who has been sending you one Klimt drawing a month for over a year now.

"*Ach, ja!*" responded Klug, attentively eyeing the large parcel in LePingre's arms with keen interest. "Delighted to make your acquaintance in person. Won't you and your friend have a seat in my inner office?" No further introductions were made.

Rita scurried ahead in front of them, discreetly retiring behind a rear door that she closed, almost.

Seated at a table that looked like a pool table, with its green felt covering, Jacques made his initial move.

"I am in possession of a large number of Klimt drawings—eighty-seven in all—very like, but also very different from the thirteen drawings I have sent to you before."

"Are any of them portrayals of Adele Bloch-Bauer, as before?"

"They are *all* of her, and they present a series of different views and moods, as well as some intimate ones."

Intimate ones? Klug carefully played his response move: "I should not have to tell you that so many drawings of just one person would glut the market. I doubt that any single collector would go for the whole package. Is that what you are contemplating, putting the whole batch up for sale?"

LePingre countered. "Yes, I had that in mind. Selling them as a whole. What do you think the lot might bring?"

"That is extremely hard to predict. First I would have to examine the drawings one by one, have them authenticated as genuine Klimts by experts. Only then could I approach, very confidentially for your sake, different wealthy clients I have, also one by one. This could be a very long procedure."

"*Oui, oui, oui.* I understand. But, tell me, why would you approach them one by one rather than just send out word to all your clients?"

"Because this is the way it is done here in Wien. *This is not a department store.* Things are extremely complicated already, providing provenance, authenticating each drawing, and so on." Jacques' face fell.

"And if I offered them simultaneously to a number of clients," continued Klug, "that would start what could be an acrimonious bidding war. This, if noticed by the Austrian government, would block any drawing from being sold to customers who are not in Austria."

"But a bidding war is exactly what I should like to have happen!" exclaimed Jacques, loosing his cool and his advantage.

"*Ach*, well, if you would like to go over the drawings with me, or leave them here for a day or two, I can give you a better idea as to what sort of client I could approach on your behalf."

"No, I do not care to leave the drawings with you this evening, Herr Klug, but I would be happy to go over them, sheet by sheet, with you day after tomorrow," Jacques replied, glancing over at a very bored Jean-Jean. He wanted time to try some other galleries.

"So," Jacques continued, loosing his knight to Klug's bishop, "you cannot tell me right now what you think all the Klimt drawings would fetch? Not even an estimate?"

"No, not even a guess," said Klug mendaciously, spreading his hands in a gesture of futility.

"All right then. I shall return in two days and we can go through the drawings. What time shall I come? We're staying at the Pension Suzanne, right near you."

"*Ach*, good. How about right after lunch?"

"That is fine; shall we say one o'clock?"

"One o'clock. *Dreizehn Uhr.*"

This would give Klug time to mass market the news that he would soon have a significant batch of Klimt drawings to offer. The first person he would contact, however, before putting the word out to other collectors, would be his best client: America's Lyonel Retter. He had already bought thirteen of the set, and how appropriate it would be to own *all* of them for his Moderne Galerie.

The two Frenchmen took their leave and stepped out on to the Annagasse. "When can we eat?" Jean-Jean wanted to know.

"Right now," allowed a very hyper Jacques. "Let me treat you to a real Viennese meal. Look! There is a Wienerwald restaurant right across the street. Let's go there. The chain is very atmospheric and you will love having a Wienerschnitzel with plenty of lemon on it." The two men disappeared happily into the restaurant.

Much later, at two in the morning Vienna time, Hanskarl Klug made a telephone call to Lyonel Retter in New York, catching his favorite and most reliable client in an exceptionally receptive mood at eight in the morning.

* * *

Rita Herring closed up shop for Dr. Klug shortly after the departure of the Jacques LePingre visit. Stepping out into the street and looking around to be sure she was not overheard, she called her father.

"Dad? I have *sensational* news. A client has come in with a package of eighty-seven Klimt drawings of Bloch-Bauer to sell. This is the same anonymous client who has been selling us, month by month, those gorgeous Klimt studies of her I've been telling you about. At last the veil has been lifted and I know *who* the supplier is. It's a certain Jacques LePingre, a Frenchman. He will be back day after tomorrow after lunch with the drawings for Dr. Klug to see."

Jeremy Herring was all ears. He did not want Günther Winter to get wind of this. He especially did not want Günther to acquire any more artworks having to do with Adele for his already bulging Klimt collection, whether here in Wien or off in godforsaken Alaska. He knew he would be able to motivate the Austrian government anew in an attempt to recall the Adele oil portrait. All he needed was to get his hands on the document in the Beethoven statue cache. It would be a cultural disaster if these new drawings were to leave the country. *He knew what Rachel would say.*

At last his positioning of Rita at Nebehay's had paid off. She could keep a sharp eye on things. Whoever was offering this Klimt trove would have to be sidetracked, kidnapped, perhaps eliminated if the drawings could not be pried loose from them.

"Keep me informed of what happens at the shop day after tomorrow, Rita, and congrats on a job well done."

As soon as he had hung up, Jeremy Herring telephoned Hedwega Schreck. He had another assignment for her.

* * *

Megan and Renata had finished a delicious meal at the Toon Thai restaurant over on Park Avenue. They had barely entered Renata's apartment when the land line rang. It was Lyonel, his usually calm voice sounding uncharacteristically animated.

"Renata? I would like you to speed up your departure for Vienna to tomorrow. And if possible talk Megan into going with you. We'll foot the bill. I've just been advised that a trove of close to a hundred Klimt sketches of Adele Bloch-Bauer is going to be put up for sale at Nebehay's. Naturally Klug called me first. And even though it seems impossible that such a large number of Klimt drawings could be unknown, I want you two to examine them and pass judgment on whether they are authentic. If so, I will make Klug an offer he can't turn down. Just think what an exhibition *this* would make for our Moderne."

Renata had turned on the speaker phone the instant Megan's name was mentioned and so Megan was able to nod an enthusiastic yes to Lyonel's proposal that they leave for Wien tomorrow.

"All right," said Renata, "I'll see if I can make reservations on tomorrow's afternoon flight. It will get us to Wien by eight-thirty in the morning the next day."

"Excellent!" Lyonel paused, then said: "And both of you...be *careful.*"

Renata got through to Austrian Airlines immediately and there were still two business class seats available. She grabbed them, smiling victoriously at Megan.

"I don't have to keep Tilly in her carrier when I travel business class," she announced with visible satisfaction. Going to Tilly's closet she pulled out a hand-sewn, pebbled calf-skin leather dog carrier she had had custom made in Wien. It was a deep chocolate brown, matching some of Tilly's fur.

Megan felt a stab of jealousy. Dear little Button would have to wait for her a bit longer in Dallas. She phoned Tina and broke the news. Always a good sport, her sister told her not to worry. Button was doing just fine with four other dogs to play with.

After a reassured Megan hung up Renata asked, "Do you think we should borrow Lyonel's track stick?"

"If you don't mind being the one to carry it this time. My left heel went numb wearing it to and from Montreal yesterday," bargained Megan.

"Done." Renata replied with gusto. She turned to her little dog who had been eyeing her questioningly.

"*Tilly baby, morgen fliegen wir nach Wien!*"

11

The next evening, at precisely six o'clock, as Jacques and Jean-Jean were partaking of Italian fare at Annagasse's Sole restaurant, a tall, full-figured woman with blonde hair and horn-rimmed glasses checked in at the Pension Suzanne. She sized up the modest ground-floor room where breakfast would be served the next morning, then climbed the stairs to her room and settled down with a *Krimi Roman* for the next few hours. In her mind she calculated the impressive revenue this latest rush assignment would net her.

Just before she went to bed she inspected her Beretta Tomcat with its threaded barrel and the nine millimeter suppressor attached to it. The whole ensemble fit neatly through her belt down her right side and beneath her loose jacket. She had also brought along a sizeable but lightweight aluminum suitcase. It was empty.

The next morning, with her suitcase at her side, she lingered over an early breakfast until two men speaking in French entered the room and served themselves at the simple bar counter. Hedwega slipped out unnoticed and set up watch behind a low partition in the narrow lobby. After finishing breakfast the men suddenly began arguing with each other. They went back upstairs to their room and stayed there for several hours. Hedwega had a long wait, but she couldn't take chances.

At noon the Frenchmen reappeared and she followed them to the Café Mozart, opposite the Albertina, where they had a light lunch. Keeping her eye on them, Hedwega ordered coffee. When the two men returned to the Pension Suzanne, Hedwega resumed her watch in the lobby, her suitcase beside her. She was startled by the quick reappearance of her targets who, it seemed, had returned to the hotel simply to pick up a large duffle bag. And then they were out on the street again.

Only a few steps behind, she followed the pair to the Krugerstrasse, knowing they must be headed for Nebehay's. But before the men got to the end of the street they noticed on the left a set back entryway to the Hotel

Römischer Kaiser, a back entry that was a shortcut to the Annagasse. The hotel's main entrance would obviously lead out to that street. Eager to get to Nebehay's on time, the two men turned into the entryway.

Hedwega Schreck was right behind them.

Protected momentarily from passersby and traffic, she pulled out her handgun with silencer attached and in rapid sequence shot each man in the back of the head. In both cases the shots shattered the brain and death was instantaneous.

As they fell to the ground the duffle bag also tumbled down. Hedwega grabbed it and instantly ran inside the Römischer Kaiser, pointing and shouting "Help, help! People have been shot!"

The alarmed hotel staff ran out the back entrance the screaming woman had entered, and a small group of people began gathering around the two blood-spattered corpses. Cars began stopping, curious as to the growing crowd. Finally a police car, its siren blaring, tore down the street, scattering pedestrians.

In the deserted hotel lobby Hedwega quickly transferred the duffle bag to her metal suitcase. Then she walked calmly and slowly out the main hotel entrance onto the Annagasse, up to the Kärtnerstrasse, and, blending in with the crowd, turned right in the direction of the Graben.

Mission accomplished.

* * *

Delivering her suitcase to Jeremy at his house on Bastiennegasse, Hedwega told him he owed her big time and he agreed. No drawn out intimidation or precarious public kidnapping had been necessary. Just simple executions, clean and neat. No evidence left behind at the murder scene, and a clean getaway with the desired goods undamaged.

She wondered what could possibly be in the suitcase to be of such value, but she had learned years ago to be circumspect when it came to dealing with Jeremy. He was obviously pleased, and she was more than satisfied with her remuneration. Perhaps she could retire now, she thought. She envisioned the little cottage she had recently bought for herself out at Purkersdorf in the Sandstein-Wienerwald. How wonderful it would be to live permanently in the Vienna Woods. Jeremy had paid her handsomely: one hundred thousand Euros. A double fee for a double murder.

12

Leipzig was really a cool city, Thad thought, as he ambled around the great Thomaskirche, hoping eagerly to hear some Bach at JS's own church. But the organ was not being played that day and reluctantly he gave up. Directly across the street and facing a larger-than-life statue of the composer in all his flowing Baroque splendor, including a truncated pipe organ behind him, was a restaurant that featured a "Bach Menu." Sitting down at an outdoor table and facing the bronze Bach effigy, he happily devoured food and drink. God only knew when he might eat again.

After his hearty Bach bacchanal, and laughing at his own pun, Thad walked rapidly toward the central railroad station, turning onto the Katherinestrasse where the new five-story Museum der Bildenden Künste proudly stood, resplendent in its surrounding glass cube. Hm, a little too much transparency, Thad thought apprehensively. What will it be like in the Beethoven room? Not facing directly out onto the damn giant cube, I hope. He was to find out soon enough.

Unsuccessfully arguing that he was still a student, he grudgingly paid the adult fee for entry into the museum and studied a floor plan of the building outside the gift shop. The *Beethoven-Plastique* was on the first floor. Bolting up the stairs Thad entered several rooms hung with old Dutch paintings—how boring.

Moving in a different direction, he suddenly turned into what was the Beethoven chamber. In addition to the *Beethoven Enthroned* it was empty of art objects, except for one other statue by Klinger. It was a half-torso portrait of *Die neue Salome* from 1893. Two severed male heads stared out blankly from among the folds of a very contemporary Salome's loose garment. Like the Beethoven monument, this sculpture had benefitted from the newly discovered fact that the ancient Greeks did not produce all their statues in pristine white marble. They actually used polychromy in many of their works. The same was true of early Etruscan and Roman sculptures.

Yes, Thad had found his marmorean prey, but now a new problem presented itself. With only one other sculpture in the whole room, which was pretty large, how was he going to find cover when he probed the statue? The Beethoven monument was set in the center of the otherwise empty space. Thad looked up at the ceiling. Hot damn! It was all totally sky lighted. Light literally poured into the room. Pretty hard to grope old Ludwig surreptitiously. And the four white walls of the room were all completely bare. Absolutely no chance for any paintings on a wall to distract museum visitors. As they entered the room people would of necessity be focused on the central point, Beethoven. The Salome statue definitely took a back seat, placed behind the Beethoven in the far right corner of the room, almost as though an afterthought. And then there was the female guard standing at the entrance to the room, another hindrance.

Thad exited, depressed at the logistical hurdles before him. On the exterior wall by the Beethoven room he read a wall placard that gave a short didactic on the two statues. It also noted that 105 works by Klinger, mostly graphics and paintings, were acquired by the City of Leipzig in 1939 from the collection of the renowned publisher, Gustav Kirstein, after his wife committed suicide rather than face deportation under the Nazis. Recently, after pressure from local restitution adherents, a number of Klinger's works had been returned to heirs of the Kirsteins.

Suddenly Thad remembered his father had told him that a similar but even worse fate had befallen Leipzig's multi-figured monument to Mendelssohn, which had stood on the east side of the old Gewandhaus. During the Nazi regime the bronze sculptural group was removed and melted down. Not until 2008 had a reconstruction of that monument to the composer been created. The town, well the whole damn country, had been tough on Jews during the 1930s, Thad reflected.

But now he must get to work if he could hope to return on the train to Wien that evening. He would have to create a diversion. He felt in his pocket for the tool he had made at home and had brought with him. It was a simple fuse trick: a firecracker that exploded when its dangling string was ignited.

He waited for his moment, some five, then ten minutes. There were damn few visitors to the museum now. No one to attract the scrutiny of the guard. He himself had had to amble on, pretending to read other wall plaques in the area. Finally—oh, saints be praised—a large group of eager, American tourists was entering the room next to the Beethoven room. The guard immediately turned and entered the chamber which was devoted to Klinger's large-scale painted works. Not a soul was in the Beethoven room.

Oh, perfect. Thad positioned himself at the corner where the two rooms met, quickly lit the firecracker lead with his cigarette lighter, and rolled it long and low into the roomful of tourists. BAM! The homemade cracker made a noisy ruckus and visitors began screaming in the now smoky room. The guard ran to the center of the explosion, desperately trying to find the source.

Thad made his move. He darted to the Beethoven statue and knelt before the narrow crevice that was cut under the composer's legs, just as his dad had described. Thad had brought an ice pick with him and he quickly worked it into the crevice, then pulled. Nothing. The pandemonium in the next room began to lessen. Desperately Thad inserted the ice pick again and this time he felt something. Out came the ice pick slowly *and* a flattened old leather roll. He did not stop to open it. Instead he thrust it inside his jacket pocket.

Stumbling into the Klinger painting room, he shouted, along with a dozen others, "*Was ist geschehen?*" "What has happened?" He rubbed his eyes and pretended to look terrified. The female guard, now joined by several other guards, tried to calm the group. Properly calmed down, Thad took a staircase to the ground floor and exited the museum.

He had the Klimt scroll!

13

Called back to Vienna on an urgent business matter, Günther Winter was making one of his rare visits to the gallery he owned on the Annagasse opposite Nebehay's Antiquariat. All seemed well at the *Kunst Vienna: Damals und Heute* establishment. Several medium-sized Hundertwasser limited edition prints in attractive thin black frames hung in the front window, and inside visitors were milling around the latest exhibition.

The show featured Diane Radice, a modern-day Frieda Kahlo. The artist addressed herself to green topics in an impassioned protest against climate warming. Not that her paintings were all forest green. The color blue played quite a role in her depictions of polar bears stranded on melting islands of ice. One work showed a pregnant woman, nude except for a beaded amber necklace. Behind her was a dense cluster of black, burnt trees—stark angular skeletons in a landscape where green had no home. The paintings were selling nicely, Günther's gallery clerk whispered to him.

Suddenly the sound of a siren penetrated the premises. Something was happening outside on the Annagasse. Günther stepped outdoors. No, it was happening on the next street over, the Krugerstrasse. Taking a shortcut through the lobby of the Hotel Römischer Kaiser, Günther exited onto a gruesome scene: two men, lying in their own pooling blood, and police questioning potential witnesses.

He noticed that Rita Herring was among the spectators and made his way through the crowd to her side.

"What is going on?" he questioned her in German.

"It is terrible! These two men from France were in our store just two days ago. And they were on their way back to see us again today. They had a sheath of drawings they wanted to sell to Dr. Klug."

"Oh, and did they?"

"No. Dr. Klug was going to have to authenticate the works."

"Hm. Who were the works by?"

"Well, supposedly they were by Klimt. A lot of them, a *whole lot of them*."

"By *Klimt*?"

Günther could barely suppress his raging curiosity. But silence had its results as well. Unexpectedly Rita proffered additional information.

"Yes. And some of the drawings were described as 'intimate.'"

"That is nothing new for Klimt. Just think of his portfolio of drawings for Lucian's *Dialogues of the Courtesans*. The artist often drew women masturbating and thrusting their genitals at the viewer."

"Ah, but these 'intimate' drawings were all of one recognizable woman."

"Whom?"

"Adele Bloch-Bauer."

14

Megan, Renata, and Tilly had had a comfortable flight across the Atlantic. Tilly was quite accustomed to long plane rides and all she asked was to be out of her container and in her mama's lap. Every now and then she signaled that she wanted to be walked briskly up and down the aisle, or go to the ladies' room (yes, she was even trained to pee into the toilet bowl), but that was her only demand.

Easily passing through customs, as they had nothing to declare, they hailed a cab from the taxi line and drove in the bright morning sunshine straight to Renata's small but cozy apartment on the Linke Wienzeile, across the street from the Naschmarkt, not far from the Ringstrasse. Tilly was the first out of the cab, already recognizing "her" territory. Later in the day Megan would check into her regular hotel, the Römischer Kaiser, where she had been able to book her favorite room overlooking an inside courtyard, rather than facing the noisy Annagasse.

After plopping their bags down and setting out water for Tilly, they walked over to the popular Rote Bar at the Hotel Sacher. They ordered an unusual but delicious "breakfast": *Backhendl* with fried parsley, which they both savored slowly.

Thus fortified, they headed back to Renata's apartment for Tilly and then back toward the Annagasse. By eleven o'clock they were walking through the door of Nebehay's Antiquariat. No one was in sight.

"Hanskarl?" Renata called out.

"Hey, Hanskarl," Megan chimed in.

Tilly joined in with a single bark.

A voice sang out: "I'd know that bark anywhere."

Parting the curtains to his inner office, Hanskarl Klug appeared, his face creased in a welcoming smile.

Tilly! Renata! Megan! What are you all doing in Wien?"

He ushered them into his office and they sat around the green "pool" table. He offered them coffee, which they both declined with thanks.

"We're here on a mission from Lyonel to take a look at the Klimt drawings you telephoned him about. He couldn't wait to have our input, as well as your expert opinion."

The genial expression on Klug's face changed noticeably.

"I'm afraid you have come in vain," Klug said emotionally. The French client who wanted to sell them to me was one of two men murdered yesterday afternoon on the Krugerstrasse. They were shot in plain daylight and yet there were no witnesses to the killing."

"Incredible! On the peaceful Krugerstrasse?" Renata exclaimed.

"You said *French* client? Was his name possibly LePingre?" Megan asked tensely, alarm bells going off in her head. LePingre was the man Henri-Claude had introduced her to in Thomery-By last week. Too many coincidences here. And the second murdered man could have been his partner.

"Yes, it was LePingre," confirmed Klug, wondering how Megan could have guessed that. "How did you know?"

Ignoring his question, Megan asked: "Was either of them able to tell the police anything before they died?"

"No, no, they were both shot close up in the back of the head within five seconds of each other. They died instantly."

"Oh, how *awful*," said Renata, automatically reaching down for Tilly who, sensitive to the agitated sound of the conversation, wanted onto her lap.

"Did they have the Klimt drawings *with* them?" Megan wanted to know.

"Nothing was found on or near the bodies. So this means I have no Klimts to show you, and our dear friend Lyonel is out a tremendous acquisition, at least from the brief look I got at the drawings day before yesterday."

"You *saw* them?" both women cried in unintentional chorus.

"Yes, I did see some of them. There were supposedly some eighty-seven in all, and I believed LePingre. He was the Frenchman with whom I'd had the business dealings that netted Lyonel the dozen Klimt drawings he bought from me over the past year. Recently he sold me a thirteenth Klimt, which I then also sold to Lyonel..."

"Oh yes. Lyonel showed me a photo of it just a few days ago," interrupted Renata.

"Yes, well then you observed that this latest drawing seemed to be more of the same sort as the previous ones: poses of Adele looking left, looking right, looking unblinkingly out at Klimt. All of them of the same high quality."

Renata and Megan sighed at the thought of the lost treasure.

"The really interesting thing though," continued Hanskarl, "is that LePingre said, seemingly just in passing, something that stopped me cold."

"What?" again the women chimed in chorus.

"He said that some of the drawings were *intimate*."

For a third time the women voiced the same word. "*Intimate?*"

"Why don't we put our heads together over drinks this evening, Hanskarl," offered Renata, "and see if we can figure things out. Especially who it could be that would *kill* for works by Klimt?"

Hanskarl gladly took up the offer and they agreed to meet at a real pub, Zu den Drei Hacken, at the end of Singerstrasse around six-thirty that evening. By then they would all be ready for something alcoholic. Even Megan.

A customer entered the shop's front room and Tilly rushed out to defend her humans. As they got up to leave, Megan gave Hanskarl a supportive arm squeeze. And then they were out on the street, gazing at the gallery opposite which featured several Hundertwasser prints in its windows.

"What shall we do first?" Megan looked inquiringly at her museum director friend, knowing there were always dozens of things Renata tried to fit in on her Vienna trips.

"Let's see if the Albertina Museum's Manfred Hubner can shed some light on this Klimt business. Perhaps the Frenchman approached him as well, hoping to sell his drawings to them." She dialed the museum on her smart phone and within seconds was setting up coffee with Manfred at the museum in a half hour.

"Renata, why don't you tackle Manfred, since I don't know him as well as you do, while I go over to Im Kinsky, my favorite auction house ever since it sold Schiele's *Procession* for over four million, and see if they've had any offers?"

"Good plan. Tilly and I will meet you at Trzeniewski's around one thirty and we'll have a real *Brötchen*."

The two friends walked off in different directions filled with hope that with their combined efforts they could turn up some clues as to where the missing Klimt drawings might be.

* * *

"Günther?"

"Megan! Vhat are you doing *here*?"

They had almost collided in front of the Kinsky Palais, where she had been conferring with Peter Staub concerning any Klimts that might have come in yesterday or today. The visit yielded nothing, and Megan had just emerged from the Palais, shielding her eyes from the sun. She could not believe that she had almost bumped into Günther Winter here in Wien. The last time she had seen him was at his Alaska hotel when he showed her the extraordinary Hundertwasser triptych, the centerpiece of his collection. And yet why shouldn't she come across him in Vienna? It was after all his hometown when he wasn't flying around the world. Or flying *others* to and fro, she thought, looking at him accusingly.

Yes, Lyonel was right to suspect Winter of being behind the Secretum trade proposal. It had to be he. Who else was such a fanatic about Klimt?

She decided to be frank. "I'm here tracking down a trove of Klimt drawings that was briefly offered to a gallery here."

"*Ach, ja.* I know about zat incident. Had any luck?"

"I have a few leads," she lied instantly, not understanding why she did so.

"Und by any chance are you performing zis little detective job for our mutual friend Lyonel Retter?"

You're no friend of Lyonel's, Megan thought loyally. She decided to take another tack.

"Did you hear about the murder and robbery of Asta Holm-Ditlevsen?"

"*Ja, ja,* awful, isn't it? Vhat do you tink vas taken? One of her Scandinavian women painter's vorks?"

"Come on, Günther, you know exactly what was taken. Klimt's *Theology* panel."

"*Ach,* so you know for sure zat vas in her possession?"

"Yes, I saw it with my own eyes when I visited her in Ascona last week. And now it has disappeared off the face of the earth—*apparently.* She looked Günther straight in the eyes.

Winter did not blink. He mustered up a look of concern and muttered something about its being a sad day when burglars would actually kill for a Klimt. He asked Megan if she would like to have dinner with him that evening, an invitation she could truthfully decline due to a previous commitment.

"What about zee next night?" he pressed, not giving up on the chance to grill her about what she knew of happenings at the Moderne Galerie after she had confirmed the authenticity of the Klimt panel she'd examined in Montreal. He had, as yet, heard nothing from the museum director or from Lyonel Retter. Perhaps another board meeting had been called. What else could explain the silence? Except that here was Megan in his, in Klimt's own city, looking for clues. Surely Lyonel had sent her.

"No can do," replied Megan. "I'll be on my way back to the States by then."

Günther sighed resignedly and stretched out his hand in farewell. God, I'm shaking hands with a probable thief and a possible killer, Megan thought to herself, shuddering slightly. As she walked on to meet Renata at

Trzeniewski's she felt a cold chill coming over her. It had been a genuinely spooky encounter.

And to think, she had once liked this man. Even danced with him. Could it be, that with his billions and his shady associates, like the art dealer Jeremy Herring, he not only already had Klimt's *Theology* but also the French trove of the artist's drawings of Adele?

15

Thad Herring's cheeks were flushed with joy. Not only was his dad hugely pleased with the success of his Leipzig trip, he had actually said he was *proud* of him. And this in front of his domineering sister Rita, who, with a morose expression on her features, looked definitely sulky.

But Rita was not sulking, she was worried. Worried that Jeremy would find out about her unwise blurting out to Günther Winter about the aborted sale of Klimt drawings to Dr. Klug. Worried he would find out that some of the sketches of Adele Bloch-Bauer had been described as intimate. She knew he would have done anything to get his hands on such a treasure.

She need not have worried. Without telling his children yet, Jeremy had indeed done everything to acquire the Klimt drawings. *Just as Rachel, in yet another vision, had urged him to do.*

After praising Thad once again, Jeremy said good night to his children and went into his study. He closed and locked the door. Then he turned his attention to an aluminum suitcase. He opened it. Inside was a large duffle bag. He pulled it out, grunting under its weight, and laid it on the far end of a table with good overhead lighting.

Slowly, with mounting tension, Jeremy unzipped the bag. On top was a small wooden box. He opened it. There in a double compartment were two locks of hair. One was labeled Gustav Ucicky and the other was labeled

Gustav Klimt. Well, Jeremy thought, that's an appropriate coupling. Who knows what I might be able to get on the open market for such a trophy.

Putting the box carefully aside, he then undid the heavy package's outer wrapping.

Yes! There it was, the thick roll of Klimt drawings, bound with wide bands of velvet. He cut the bands and rolled out the drawings. Putting on white museum gloves, he counted the drawings quickly. There were eighty-seven of them. The top sheet was an almost finished study for the Adele portrait of 1907. So was the second drawing, in which the artist's pencil emphasized the background fill in her dress: Egyptian eyes encased in elongated triangles. What a find! This was delicious.

With mounting awe Jeremy carefully went through the next four drawings. They were all frontal studies of Adele's face with its dark eyebrows, large eyes meeting those of the artist, long aristocratic nose, and slightly parted luscious lips.

The next four drawings were studies for the placement of Adele's hands, both bent inward at the wrist. Slightly above chest level, the long fingers of Adele's right hand encased and partially covered the fingers of the left hand. The little finger stretched across the fingers of the right hand. Ah yes, Jeremy reminded himself, that was to hide the deformity of one of her fingers.

Eagerly he lifted the eleventh drawing up to the light. Something was unusual about it. Hadn't he already just seen it? How could that be? He went back to the earlier group and leafed through them again: the drawing was a very slight, but noticeable, copy of the first head study. It was an excellent variation but it was not in the hand of Klimt!

With mounting trepidation Jeremy began looking at the remaining drawings. They were *all expert forgeries!* The first ten drawings had served as models for the remaining ones, resulting in ten, sometimes twelve, sometimes even fifteen variations on the original sketches. Only an expert would have been able to tell that the drawings were not by Klimt. And Jeremy was an expert.

"This is impossible," he said out loud angrily. *Rachel's shade suddenly appeared at his side.* She tried to console him. The main thing, she told him, was that he had the Bloch-Bauer/Klimt legal document, signed by two witnesses in 1902. That is all he needed to get Adele back to her homeland. The others, the authentic Klimt drawings, could only add to his already considerable wealth.

Jeremy calmed down but he had only half listened to his wife. His mind was already calculating which dealers in Japan and South Korea he would entrust to sell the Klimt forgeries to greedy and gullible collectors there. As for the legitimate drawings, he would place a call early next morning to his most avaricious Austrian client, Günter Winter.

* * *

Günther Winter was furious that Jeremy Herring had not informed him that Nebehay's had just been offered a trove of almost a hundred Klimt drawings.

He decided to call Jeremy's agent Hedwega Schreck. Her *Detektiv Büro* and phone number showed up immediately on his smart phone. He dialed her number, and Hedwega herself answered the phone.

His business commission for her was simple. A troublesome American art dealer who lived in Wien's eighteenth district, Währing, was about to inundate the market with a batch of a certain artist's drawings. The artist's name was unimportant, he assured her.

Winter wanted the man, who was elderly and lived with two grown children, put permanently out of commission. In other words, *eliminated*. It could look like a heart attack.

It should be possible to follow him on his regular Thursday visits to the Zentralfriedhof to lay flowers at the grave of his wife. The manner of putting him down would be up to Hedwega. The name of her target was Jeremy Herring.

Jeremy Herring! Even though her thoughts wandered more and more in the direction of early retirement, Hedwega could not resist this last assignment. Nor the no-nonsense tone of her caller, Günter Winter.

The sum offered Hedwega for successful completion of their business arrangement was twice what Herring had just paid her. A pity that it was Jeremy whom Winter wanted dead, but Jeremy was old and probably didn't have that much longer to live anyway. She accepted the assignment without a twinge of regret.

16

Their last full day in Vienna became a packed one for Megan and Renata after they had met for lunch. Megan went off to meet with the singer Renata Fledgling concerning a DVD she wanted to put out on Viennese songs at the turn of the last century. In the meantime, Renata Teuer—yes, the two women knew each other and were amused at the correspondence of their first names—would make a quick trip to the Photoinstitut Bonartes on the Seilergasse to see their latest exhibition. Afterward, always on the lookout for unusual jewelry for the Moderne's gift shop, she paid a call on the Wiener Silbermanufactur, placing several orders for some of their Wiener Werkstätte design brooches. And then she met with the architects at the Coop Himmelblau to discuss a possible design collaboration.

Back in New York, Joe Seguire was following Renata's movements around Vienna, thanks to the track stick she was wearing.

Megan's consultation with the engaging Renata Fledgling had taken up more of the afternoon than she expected. The lyric soprano had wanted to re-create one of the Vienna salons at the turn of the century. Megan suggested that they emulate the famous Dumba salon where Klimt's most Austrian of Austrian works, the *Schubert at the Piano*, had been on display, along with his allegory of music as personified by a fuzzy, fair-haired, definitely Viennese lyre-strumming coquette.

For musical numbers Megan had suggested Franz Lehár's *Vilja Song* and Alma Mahler's atmospheric *Die Stille Stadt*. She also proposed Schönberg's String Quartet No. 2, with its tortured vocal line in the last two movements. Fledgling had accepted all her suggestions with charming enthusiasm.

Reaching the door of Zu den Drei Hacken at almost the same time, Megan and Renata spotted Hanskarl Klug, already seated at a corner table. They quickly joined him, glad to be off duty, so to speak.

As it turned out they did talk business, reporting sadly on their lack of success in determining to where the Klimt collection of drawings could have vanished.

Renata and Hanskarl each began with a small beer, pfiff, then graduated to dark ale, while Megan nursed a Baileys Irish Cream filled with ice.

The dinner discussion turned to whether or not Hundertwasser's work was worthy of inclusion in the Moderne Galerie. So far nothing by the avid environmentalist artist was to be seen there. Megan turned the conversation to Kollwitz, whose compelling work also seemed to have no place in the Moderne.

"You can scold Lyonel when we get back," ventured an amused Renata.

The talk returned to the two murdered Frenchmen and their missing trove of Klimt drawings. But the sweet libation sipped by Megan was beginning to take effect.

"Let's all go out to the Heurigen," she suggested with gusto. At first surprised by this suggestion from a seventy-seven-year-old usually teetotaler professor, Renata and Hanskarl soon agreed that a visit to one of Vienna's outlying outdoor wine taverns with live Schrammelmusik would be just the thing. It could lift their spirits and take their minds off the depressing killings for Klimt. And after all, this was Megan and Renata's last night in Wien.

Which of the many Heurigen locals should they go to? Again an increasingly tipsy Megan voted her preference before her friends could speak.

"Oh, by all means let's go to Mayer's on the Pfarrplatz, where Beethoven used to go."

"But first we really have to pick up Tilly," Renata announced urgently. A taxi was just pulling up in front of the Drei Hacken and they grabbed it, giving her Linke Wienzeile address.

A half hour later found a happy dog lapping up water from a bowl, while her three humans, seated under a vine bower outdoors, were sipping *Gespritzers,* young white wine blended with soda water. They were listening to the accordion and double guitar of the Schrammel musicians as they sang old and modern songs in delicious Viennese dialect.

One of them was truly hilarious if spooky: it celebrated the "jolly" population of Vienna's Central Cemetery: *Es lebe der Zentralfriedhof* ("Long live the Central Cemetery"). In Viennese dialect the words ran:

Es lebe der Zentralfriedhof, und olle seine Toten
Der Eintritt is für Lebende heit ausnahmslos verboten.
Weü da Tod a Fest heit gibt die gonze lange Nocht.
Und von die Gäst ka anziger a Eintrittskort'n braucht
Wann's Nocht wird über Simmering, kummt Leben in die Toten
Und drüb'n beim Krematorium tan's Knochenmork ohbrot'n
Dort hinten bei der Marmorgruft, durt stengan zwa Skelette
Die stess'n mit zwa Urnen on und saufen um die Wette.

Long live the Zentralfriedhof, and all its dead
Today, entry for the living is prohibited without exception.
That's because Death presents a feast the whole night long.
And the guests don't have to have a single entry card
When night breaks over Simmering, the dead come to life
And over there at the crematorium they are roasting bone marrow
While back by the marble crypt stand two skeletons
Who lift two urns in a toast, trying to outdrink each other.

The listeners to this raucous, preternatural ditty could hardly know that the Zentralfriedhof would be the site of a killing for Klimt the very next day.

After the bone-chilling number, Renata, to lift their mood, sentimentally requested *Wien, Wien, Nur Du Allein*. The musicians surrounded their table and they all three joined in the chorus:

Wien, Wien, nur du allein
sollst stets die Stadt meiner Träume sein!
Dort, wo die alten Häuser stehn,
dort, wo die lieblichen Mädchen gehn!
Wien, Wien, nur du allein
sollst stets die Stadt meiner Träume sein!
Dort, wo ich glücklich und selig bin,
ist Wien, ist Wien, mein Wien!

Vienna, Vienna, only you alone
shall always be the city of my dreams!
There where the old houses stand,
There where the lovely girls go!
Vienna, Vienna, only you alone
shall always be the city of my dreams!
There where I'm happy and blessed,
is Vienna, Vienna, my Vienna!

"What a grand conclusion to our last night in Wien," said Megan happily. Renata and Hanskarl agreed. All thoughts of the Klimt killings had faded, at least temporarily.

"*Zahlen, bitte!*" called out Hanskarl to a passing waiter, waving a one hundred Euro note. The waiter turned, smiled, and reached across the table for it. Tilly made a sudden lunge for the waiter's hand and gave it a light nip.

"*Böse Hündin!*" scolded Renata, retrieving Tilly and spanking her ever so lightly. The good-natured waiter readily forgave Tilly, resulting in an over generous tip from Hanskarl.

A taxi took the three passengers to their multiple destinations under a warm May night sky that twinkled with stars. *Wien, Wien, Nur Du Allein!*

* * *

Under that same sparkling night sky, in his Ankerhaus penthouse that once belonged to Hundertwasser, Günther rubbed his aching back. It had begun as stomach cramps in his lower abdomen—something he ate?—but was now centered in his lower back. Also his skin itch seemed to be worse, probably because he had been scratching too much. Oh, well. The hot water bottle he had put behind his back in his computer chair already seemed to be easing the pain.

He was most eager to hear from Hedwega Schreck. Tomorrow would be Thursday, the traditional day of the week that Jeremy Herring made his visit to the Zentralfriedhof and his wife's grave.

* * *

It was ten o'clock in the evening. The Moderne Galerie was closed for the night. Other than the night guard observing the various galleries on his computer screen, only one other person was in the museum at that late hour.

Lyonel Retter was standing deep in thought before Klimt's golden Adele. Her inscrutable steady stare held him captive, as it had so many times before. She *was* the Mona Lisa of New York. How could a character like Günther Winter think, even for a moment, that he would ever trade this masterpiece for a panel constituting the Secretum, a work that compromised both Klimt and Adele?

Yes, for scholars it was an open secret, the extended affair between Adele and Gustav, but the general public did not have a clue, nor should they, he thought. Once again he experienced a protective feeling of wanting to shield his Adele from notoriety.

Had she not, in life, experienced enough when her Vienna coevals salaciously pointed out the similarity of her exquisite features to those of Klimt's terrifying representation of Judith?

Lyonel thought of Richard Strauss's bloodthirsty opera *Electra* premiered two years after Klimt's painting. It was an uncanny stage counterpart to the artist's chilling Judith of *Judith and Holofernes*. And contemporaries had noted the similarity between Vienna's Anna Bahr-Milddenburg's petrifying stage portrayal of *Electra's* Clytemnestra to the Judith in Klimt's portrayal, and hence to the Adele portrait. Gossip had never been at a loss for topics in the Vienna of the 1900s.

Lyonel yanked himself back to the troubled present. He had sent Renata and Megan off to Vienna on an urgent mission, one which netted no results. The mystery of the why and whereabouts of the unknown Klimt collection of drawings that had ever so briefly been put up for sale was unsolved.

Still demanding action, he reminded himself, was the response he, in the name of the Moderne Galerie, should give concerning the authentication by Megan Crespi of the Klimt panel she had seen in Montreal. It had been a cyber chess game: each player waiting to see what might come next. It was his move, however, and he would have to act very soon now. He would wait until Renata and Megan returned to New York. Tomorrow, with its fresh hell, would come soon enough.

17

Hedwega, dressed in black slacks and a matching loose black jacket, had waited in her dependable old Porsche Carrera convertible at the far end of Bastiengasse since seven o'clock that Thursday morning. The adjacent green Wienerwald opened up beckoningly to her. But her eyes were fixed upon the only two-story house on that block. For the tenth time she checked the Taser X26 in her right jacket pocket.

Her long wait was rewarded at ten o'clock. She watched the bent figure of Jeremy Herring issue forth from the front door and enter a white Mercedes-Benz wagon. Tenderly, he placed a bouquet of roses in the back seat on his side and sat with his engine idling.

What's he waiting for, fretted Hedwega. *Verdammt!* His kids were walking out of the house now. They got into the car, seemingly in animated conversation with their father. Obviously they had not wanted to accompany him. Hedwega could hear the sounds of an argument. But finally Jeremy, with his two passengers in tow, backed out of the driveway and headed off in the direction of Vienna's huge Central Cemetery far across town, in the outer district of Simmering.

Knowing exactly where the Herring family was going, Hedwega took an alternate, faster route, parked by the trolley car stop, and entered the main gate of the interdenominational Zentralfriedhof long before Jeremy arrived. She watched the frail man with his two adult children walk up the central avenue toward the Karl-Lueger-Gedächtniskirche and then head through the section devoted to Vienna's musicians—Salieri, Beethoven, Schubert, Brahms, and Johann Straus, Jr.

Getting closer to the Karl Lueger church, the Herrings stopped momentarily to look at the large marble cube, tilted on end, that marked Arnold Schönberg's grave. It had an ironic juxtaposition vis á vis the anti-Semitic *"schöner* Karl," who had been mayor of Vienna from 1897 until 1910. Then the group veered off to the far right, heading slowly back in the direction of the cemetery's main entrance.

Hell! Where are they headed now, thought Hedwega, angry that she might have to target not one but three people, unless the grown brats got bored and wandered off. It was a long, hot walk. This is a *huge* cemetery, thought Hedwega. She remembered what the Viennese were fond of saying about their monster burial site where some three million inhabitants could be found: *Halb so groß wie Zürich,aber doppelt so lustig* ("half as big as Zurich, but double the fun").

Now where were they going? The trio had quickened their pace. Can it be? They were entering the segregated *Jewish* section? She remembered that there had been a vandalizing of some forty graves there just a few weeks ago. *So, the Herrings were Jewish? Ach,* who'd have known? Jeremy seemed to be so anti-Semitic, always dropping crude remarks about the Jewish take-over of the art world. Oh, well, it was another case of Otto Weininger's self-hatred. So Rachel's grave was here? The confirmation came as the Herrings suddenly stopped at a row of regularly spaced graves with small headstones. Jeremy stooped over and carefully laid his bouquet of roses down in front of one of them while Rita and Thad watched somewhat impatiently.

It was now or never. Hedwega quickly looked around. No other visitors were visible. Pulling the Taser from her pocket, she shouted out Jeremy's name. They all three turned around, straining to see who was calling so loudly.

Hedwega's Taser fired silently three times in quick succession, first Jeremy, then Thad, then Rita.

Hedwega ran forward and beamed them again directly in the chest while they were writhing on the ground. Cardiac arrest occurred almost immediately for all three. Thad took the longest to die. But not taking a chance, Hedwega directed the powerful current through all three bodies one last time. Then she strode quickly back to the cemetery entrance on Simmeringer Hauptstraße and her parked car. In her black mourner's outfit she went unnoticed.

Hedwega did not wait until she got home to contact Günther Winter. Shaking with the tension of it all and nonplussed by the ease with which she had carried off the assignment, she telephoned him immediately from the car with the good news.

"Herr Winter? I can verify that your assignment has been carried out successfully. In fact, because all three targets were on hand, I can report that all of the Herrings have been eliminated."

"*Prima!*" shouted Günther, half in admiration, half in disbelief. "I will wire your bank payment this afternoon, and I will *triple* it because you have taken care of multiple problems for me."

* * *

Hedwega Schreck never had a chance to pick up her funds or retire to her little cottage in Purkersdorf. As she was deftly maneuvering her Porsche past oncoming traffic onto the Simmeringer Hauptstraße, she was hit broadside by an approaching streetcar—"der 71er." An ambulance rushed her to the hospital.

Death was not instantaneous. Paralyzed from the neck down and with multiple head wounds, she lived three weeks in great pain, in spite of the morphine drip, before dying,

No one claimed her mangled body.

18

Günther Winter should have been in a celebratory mood. The female agent he had hired to get rid of Jeremy Herring had reaped nothing but success. But somehow he felt depressed. Certainly not from a guilty conscience. He was emotionally incapable of feeling empathy. That had been one of the keys to his success in his empire building.

But nevertheless he felt no joy, no real feeling of relief or accomplishment. Also his skin hadn't stopped itching for hours now and his back still hurt. He was actually feeling a bit nauseous. Perhaps he should see a doctor. Yes, he would consult his internist in the morning. He dialed up for an appointment immediately.

And now he had other more important things to tend to. Turning on his bedroom laptop, he briefly searched for messages, but there were none of the sort that interested him. Then, consulting his old Rolodex, he telephoned Herring's hacker genius in Geneva, Pierre Balis, who had worked for him before. He connected immediately and told the courteous geek what he wanted: another email address that would self-destruct within eight hours of using it. Balis asked when he wanted to make it go live. "Immediately," answered Winter.

After a few minutes Günther was gazing at his new email address. First writing out the short message by hand, he then typed it into the body of the email. The addressee was lretter@modernegalerie.org. It read:

YOUR TIME IS UP AND SO IS ADELE'S.
RESPOND WITHIN EIGHT HOURS.

* * *

"Welcome back, ladies." Lyonel Retter greeted Renata and Megan after they had dismissed the cab that brought them, their luggage, and Tilly directly to the Moderne. Their nine-hour Austrian Airlines flight had landed on time at two o'clock on Friday afternoon.

They had texted Lyonel upon arriving at JFK, and he had immediately texted back, urging them to come straight to the Moderne. He had urgent news. Joe Seguire had already informed him of their whereabouts, thanks to Lyonel's track stick.

"You all three look very tired, " sympathized Lyonel, looking at Tilly, who had already curled up in her special basket in Renata's office.

"What's the news?" Megan asked, fearing the worst.

"We've heard from our Adele admirer," said Lyonel grimly, handing them both printouts of the email he had received.

"What do we do?" Renata cried out in frustration. "Wait for another spray paint job on Adele? Double our security?"

"No. We pretend to take the offer of a trade, but we insist upon seeing the Secretum *in situ* before we make the trade. We want to inspect it for any possible damage."

"And if there isn't any damage? I mean, what are you getting at?" asked Megan, baffled by Lyonel's words.

"All three of us fly to Montreal, if that's still where the panel is. We'll take my cargo plane and bring with us an empty crate that is the right size for a panel of, say, one of Klimt's University panels. In other words, we pretend we've come to ship back the Secretum, and we announce that the Moderne's Adele is in a second, smaller crate, ready to be exchanged. I will give the order to our museum carpenter to create both immediately, one for the Secretum panel, and one for Adele. Actually both crates will be empty."

"But," Renata wanted to know, "what if Winter, and we are still presuming that it is he, what if Winter insists on uncrating the Adele before showing us his panel?"

"We'll have to play that by ear. I think I can be insistent enough to have our way first," said Lyonel, drawing himself up to his full ambassadorial height.

"So do we send back our answer now or wait?" Megan wanted to know.

"We wait till the final hour.

Let him sweat!"

* * *

Günther Winter was indeed perspiring. He was in the downtown office of his Viennese internist and she had bad news for him. They were speaking in German.

"Herr Winter, you have what seems like sudden onset diabetes, but there is more, I'm afraid."

"What more is there? Won't I just have to cut out sugar in my diet?"

"I'm afraid the diabetes is just a side symptom of what you may have. Now let me ask you a few questions."

"Yes," Günther agreed, feeling his depression coming on again.

"Do you experience abdominal pain after you've eaten dinner and have gone to bed for the night?"

"Why, yes, Dr. Wissenfort, I have been feeling pain recently, but only very recently. It may be that I'm eating too much meat. I gave up being a vegan a few weeks ago."

"With these stomach aches do you also experience nausea or vomiting?"

"That too has been happening in the past couple of weeks. How did you know this?"

"I'll tell you presently. What is the color of your stool; have you noticed any changes?"

Günther was aghast. He never bothered to glance down at his stool. He was too busy. "I have no idea," he answered, feeling like a schoolboy who has not done his homework.

"Does your lower back ache during the bouts of stomach pain?"

"Yes," Günther answered unwillingly.

"Have you noticed that the skin under your nails is yellow?"

"Not really, no." He held up his fingers to check. The skin really was yellow looking.

"I'd like to take a closer look at your eyes," Dr. Wissenfort commanded, bending close to him and looking at each one through her ophthalmoscope.

"What do you see?"

"I see that the whites of your eyes are not white. They have a yellowish tinge."

"Well, I suppose that my eyes have been looking tired lately, but then I've been busier than usual."

"Has your skin felt as though it were itching in the past few weeks?"

"Actually, it has. I've been scratching like mad."

Dr. Wissenfort went over to her desk and sat down facing him and fingering a file.

"Herr Winter, I have looked at your chart from the last time you saw me, and I notice that you have lost a considerable amount of weight."

"Don't you think that could have been because of my having been excessively vegan in my choice of food? That is why I decided to get off it."

"I will tell you what I think, and then you will have to decide if you want to see a specialist."

"Could it be *zat* bad?"

"Yes, I am afraid it is. Herr Winter. From all the symptoms that you present, I must deduce that you have Stage Four pancreatic cancer."

"Is that *treatable*?" Günther's voice broke.

"I'm afraid not. You probably have ten days at the most, a week more likely.

"In other words, Herr Winter, *you are actively dying.*"

* * *

At the Vienna Medical School Günther had immediately consulted with the city's leading cancer specialist, who, considering Herr Winter's stature in the business and art world, had instructed his receptionist to squeeze him in between his regular appointments. His diagnosis was the same as that of Dr. Wissenfort, although couched in less clinical a manner.

Günther returned home to his Ankerhaus penthouse a broken man. He dismissed the servants and went out on the roof to his Hundertwasser tub. Running the bathwater as hot as he could bear it, he stripped off his clothes and stepped in. Looking at his reflection in the water he was horrified. Even in that tap water he could see that his skin had a yellowish tint. Why hadn't he noticed this before? Well then, how often did he spend time gazing at himself in a mirror? He held up his fingers and examined his nails. Yes, it was so. The skin under the nails did look yellow.

"*It is true! It is true!*

"*I do have pancreatic cancer.*"

And according to the specialist, he had even less time than Dr. Wissenfort had given him: at the most a week. What had he done to deserve this? God, he was only fifty-six! Raising his eyes to look at his beloved Stefansdom with its tiled roof, and then on to the hills beyond, he knew what he had to do. The word contrition was not in his vocabulary. What he had in mind was far more permanent and far vaster in scope.

* * *

Peter Ucicky was ecstatic. He had been successful in tracking down the elusive Winter. As usual, he had no luck calling Vienna. Winter was always either "out of the country" or "away from the office." But a call to several of the Austrian generic pharmaceutical firms had finally yielded results. The new receptionist at Winter's base in Canada, Montreal, had been inadvertently helpful when he telephoned, pretending to be the CEO of a certain Chemico Innovations Company.

"No sir," she had said in reply to his query asking to speak to Monsieur Günther Winter. "He is not in Montreal. We rarely see him here. But you could try reaching him at his Alpenglow Hotel in Alaska, if you haven't been able to contact him in Vienna."

That was all the grandson of Klimt needed. Booking the next flight out of Vienna, he called out to his wife in triumph. He would confront Winter in Alaska!

* * *

Dressed in his beloved Klimt caftan and back down in his study, which was hung with small, fanciful Hundertwasser oils, Günther consulted his Cartier watch.

One more hour until the deadline he had sent the Moderne Galerie. He stared at the in-mail on his large desktop computer screen. There were many messages but not from the Moderne Galerie. What were they thinking there in New York? He had not really thought out the alternative, should they not accept his terms. And now how could he possibly find the time or the means to set things in motion again. Jeremy, Rita, and Thad Herring, all his right hands, were dead. And so was Hedwega Schreck. Hildegard was in Canada. The only trustworthy agent he had in America was young Eddie Hoch at the Alpenglow Hotel.

Ach! Alpenglow! That was it! He, Günther Winter, would arrange the ultimate Klimt exhibition and invite his enemies, the holders of *his* Adele, to see the *entire* panel that held his three Klimts. But they would have to bring along the price of admission. And that was the Moderne Galerie's Adele. Yes, that would rectify everything. He would rescue Adele and restore her to her rightful place, *his* collection. Retter, Teuer, and Crespi would be the helpless witnesses to this last grand choreography of his life, of his death.

The advent of a new email dinged on his computer. He looked up and saw it was from lretter@modernegalerie.org. Holding his breath as he opened it, he read the terse message Lyonel had sent:

"Your bargain accepted under these following terms: upon disclosure of the present location of your Secretum panel, we shall bring a crated Adele Bloch-Bauer with us. We are prepared to exchange it for the Secretum, for which we shall also bring a crate. This transaction is dependent upon our examination to determine that the Secretum is in no way damaged or compromised."

For once in his life Günther lost his cool. He emailed back immediately, forgetting that he was using his personal account. "Meeting point is Girdwood, Alaska, Hotel Alpenglow. Inform me of your arrival time at Anchorage. There will be a large moving van on the private tarmac. It will be driven by a member of my staff.

"Imperative you come immediately."

80

It was four o'clock in the afternoon. Lyonel had his track stick back in the heel of his left shoe. It had not been detected by JFK's minimal security at the private ramp. Now he, Megan, and Renata were walking toward his cargo plane where the "Adele crate" had already been loaded. Renata had regretfully but sensibly left Tilly at home.

They took their seats in the pressurized upper cabin of Lyonel's 747 and watched the Manhattan skyline disappear. Settling in for the ten-hour flight before them, they animatedly discussed what Renata and Megan had done in Vienna. Then they each opened up laptops and began reading their respective EBooks. Both Megan and Renata were snoozing within ten minutes. They were already jet-lagged from the Vienna/New York trip of the night before. Only Lyonel stayed awake during the whole flight. He was eager to see the authenticated Klimt Secretum panel and even more eager to meet his nemesis in person. He hoped he could refrain from socking the man in the face.

Ten hours later, at two in the morning, the plane landed at Anchorage. The women waited in the cold night air as Lyonel supervised the unloading of the crates and reloading of them in the van parked by the plane. The van's driver had walked up to watch the proceedings.

"*Eddie*?" Megan asked incredulously. She had last seen him in New York as the chauffeur of Winter's limousine.

"Yes, Dr. Crespi, it's me," Eddie admitted somewhat shamefacedly. "I am here to take you and your cargo to the Alpenglow. How is your sister?"

"Fine, thank you."

"All right, girls, let's go," commanded Lyonel as he climbed up into the van.

"Did you just call us *girls*?" said Megan jokingly.

Lyonel ignored her question, focusing on the tricky business ahead of them. And even Renata gave her a disapproving look as they followed Lyonel into the van.

Fifty minutes later they pulled up to the brightly lit lobby of the Alpenglow Hotel. The night clerk came out to meet them.

"My employer has booked three rooms for you for the rest of the night," he said politely. "Feel free to order breakfast sent to your room when you wake up. You will be contacted at ten tomorrow morning."

The three visitors from New York headed straight to their respective rooms and were asleep within minutes.

* * *

Another guest had checked into the Hotel Alpenglow earlier that evening. He was suffering extreme jet lag, but otherwise he was ready for a confrontation with the man who had more than his rightful share of his grandfather's works. Peter Ucicky telephoned his wife Lena in Rome to assure her that he had arrived safe and sound in Alaska.

After depositing his three passengers, Eddie moved the van around the corner of the hotel to Günther Winter's annex and, with the help of the night clerk, began unloading the precious cargo. After the crates had been safely carted down into the basement and the night clerk had returned to his post, Günther eagerly commanded Eddie to open the smaller one immediately.

It was only then, by the bright light of the overhead cellar lamps, that they discovered the Adele crate was fastened with three enormous padlocks. Eddie tried various keys and he tried force, but to no avail. The locks remained locked.

"I don't have the tools to open these padlocks," apologized a frustrated Eddie.

"*Scheisse*! All right, ve'll just have to vait for zem to give us zee keys to zee *verdammte* padlocks tomorrow."

"Yes, sir. Good night, sir."

A furious Winter did not bother to acknowledge Eddie's silent withdrawal. He glared long at the padlocks as though he could *will* them open.

But suddenly he felt nauseous and rushed to the bathroom sink, making it just in time. He retched and retched again, feeling weak, tired, and nauseous afterward.

High time I went to bed, he advised himself grimly.

* * *

The next morning at eight-thirty, three alarm clocks went off in three adjoining rooms. The trio gathered in one room and ordered strong coffee and breakfast. At ten o'clock the telephone rang in Lyonel's room where they were seated around a table with a gorgeous view of Mount Alyeska.

"This is the hotel concierge. My employer asks that you meet our security agent downstairs in the lobby."

"We'll be right down," answered Lyonel, putting on his shoes with the hidden track stick. Megan and Renata disappeared briefly into their respective rooms and soon met Lyonel at the bank of elevators. Megan once again eyed the gold-and-silver doors she had so admired on her first stay in the hotel.

Moments later they were being greeted by Eddie in the lobby. "Please follow me," he murmured, leading them to the back door of the spacious lobby and out into the courtyard facing a building that looked like a large bunker, almost windowless. It was Günther Winter's annex.

And it was Günther Winter, dressed in a blue caftan, who greeted them at the heavily barred door, his jaundiced face expressionless.

"Enter," he commanded. They followed their unsmiling host into the main room. Without any formalities Winter announced that their Adele and Secretum crates were in the basement. "Follow me," he commanded, heading for the cellar.

* * *

In New York, Joe Seguire was tracking Lyonel Retter's movements since he boarded the cargo plane at JFK. Some ten hours later his computer screen showed the plane set down at the Anchorage airport. The slow movement of the sensor mapped Retter's progression south, then pinned down "Girdwood" as the sensor came to a rest. Utilizing the web, Joe pulled up a detailed overhead view of the small town of Girdwood. He spotted where the track stick had stopped: it had come to rest upon a very large, four-winged building labeled "Alpenglow Hotel." The next morning the sensor was still at the same spot.

Joe immediately placed calls to two of his retired police buddies. Then he called Günther Winter's personal pilot, who had been waiting instructions in the hangar of Winter's 35A Lear Jet, and told him that he was coming out with two other men. He should be prepared for immediate takeoff for Anchorage, Alaska. The sensor had not moved in the last eleven hours and Joe was taking no chances.

* * *

Günther Winter, sick and wan, eyed what he considered his three hostages warily. Crespi he knew. Now he did not smile at her.

He turned to his other two "guests."

"You, zen, are Renata Teuer and you are zee infamous Lyonel Retter," he identified his apprehensive guests.

"*Infamous*, certainly not, but yes we are," Lyonel affirmed with no change of facial expression.

Günther's body language—crossed arms hugging his chest—broadcast to Megan that the man was extremely agitated.

"We want to see your Secretum panel as quickly as possible," iterated Lyonel slowly in a quiet but imperious voice.

"*Ja, ja, ja,*" you shall see it und soon. But first I vant to verify zat it is Adele in zee crate."

"No," answered Lyonel evenly. It shall be the other way around, Herr Winter," emphasizing that he knew exactly with whom he was dealing.

"Vill you be content with seeing Klimt's *Teology*?"

Not betraying his surprise, Lyonel barked "No. You can show us *Theology* if you wish, but we came here to assess the physical state of your Secretum."

Megan had trouble hiding *her* anger. So that was the fate of poor Asta's Klimt panel. To be buried here in this dank cellar, prisoner of this madman!

"But I *vant* you to see *Teology*," Winter almost whined.

"Yes," Renata nudged Lyonel, "let us see the famous *Theology*."

At that moment Günther's body language changed dramatically. In what looked like a convulsion he raised his right hand to his lips, just in time to receive the vomit that issued from his mouth.

"Excuse me," he coughed weakly. "I shall haf to leave you for zee moment. Please to return to your hotel rooms. I vill call you ven to come back."

Eddie, looking surprised and concerned for his unpredictable boss, ushered them out and saw them back to the hotel.

* * *

"What do we do now?" Renata wanted to know. Back in their Alpenglow rooms each of them had immediately tended to texting, email, and phone calls. Renata had called about Tilly and Megan had called Tina, who reported that Button was well and happily playing with her four Japanese Spaniels.

"But he misses *you*," she assured her older sister.

"Well, I can't thank you enough for taking care of him. Did you remember to administer his first-of-the-month's pills?" she added.

"Gave them to him when I did my own dogs," Tina assured her.

The women then gathered back in Lyonel's suite, which was the largest of the rooms assigned them.

Renata asked: "Shouldn't we discuss our strategy and any back-up plans?"

Lyonel looked up at the ceiling and walls. "I don't think so. Our rooms could be bugged."

Renata put her finger to her lips and pointed to Lyonel's left shoe. Megan nodded her comprehension that they were not truly alone, that their every move was being tracked by Seguire and his men.

Realizing that they must stay in their rooms to await Winter's command-performance call, they each resumed reading their EBooks. Renata was reading a cookbook, Megan a biography of Ernest Shackleton, and Lyonel, *The Economist*. Finally the call came. But it was not from Winter, it was from Eddie Hoch.

"Mr. Winter sends his apologies. He will not be able to continue his meeting with you until tomorrow. He hopes you will take advantage of the aerial tram that commences from the hotel, and enjoy the view from atop Mount Alyeska. Please be assured that your lodgings and meals are being taken care of by your host."

"Thank you, Eddie," said Megan, who had been the first to reach the phone."

"Dr. Crespi?"

"Yes?"

"I am just so sorry."

"Why thank you, Eddie. Thank you very much."

They hung up at the same time.

"Well!" cried Megan, rubbing her extended fingers together as she relayed the latest news. "Now we have a chance to be *outdoors* in this gorgeous place. See, there's still lots of snow," cried the woman who lived in hot Texas, looking out the window to Mount Alyeska as it towered above the hotel. It was so distant, yet so available, if they took their "host's" suggestion. They stepped out into the hall in case their rooms were actually being bugged.

Megan urged her companions to take the aerial tram with her. It was so convenient, and the mountain in its snowbound majesty so beckoning.

"And what if the cable is rigged and we are left hanging upside down in the tram car, or worse?" asked Lyonel, always on guard.

Renata, a great outdoors woman, countered thoughtfully, "I do not think Winter is out to get us *before* we see his precious Secretum, and certainly not until we have made the so-called swap of artworks."

Reluctantly persuaded, Lyonel agreed to Megan's fervent suggestion. Donning their heavy jackets they took the elevator down to the lobby, then traversed the long corridor flanked by gift and clothing shops.

"Wait a minute!" cried Renata. "That pendant would be *perfect* for the Moderne's gift shop!" They entered the store, Lyonel rolling his eyes heavenward. The women examined a number of pendants and Renata ended up buying several, asking for the business card of the local silversmith who had fashioned them.

Then they proceeded again down the corridor to the aerial tram. Without further interruption they reached the tram platform. A car filled with excited tourists was just about to ascend, and they quickly climbed on board, reaching the melting snow line in about four minutes.

Arriving at the top they followed other tourists out onto the viewer platform. Megan could see that the broken railing had been repaired. This was the spot where just weeks ago that man, probably her *attacker*, had fallen.

"This is as good as the Austrian Alps," admitted Renata, as they gazed out over the mountain range and down at their hotel, which now seemed minuscule in the snow. They spent the greater part of an hour walking around the marked trail paths, Megan lagging behind her athletic companions. And then they had a long hot coffee in the warm café. They did not take the aerial tram down until six pm.

After a brief lie-down they met again for dinner in the smaller of the hotel's two dining rooms. Lyonel and Renata had to admit that the cuisine and the wine (Megan abstained) were first class. They moved into the cocktail lounge to talk where, they reasoned, no listening devices might overhear them. Megan ordered a Baileys Irish Cream "with plenty of ice, and in a flat-bottomed glass."

That night, thinking of the unfathomable day ahead of them, they slept fitfully.

* * *

Günther Winter did not sleep well either. Immediately after his vomiting attack and after he had gotten rid of his hostages, he called the hotel physician to come to the annex immediately. Dr. Stanley Harris appeared within minutes. Pensively he examined his formerly vigorous, fit employer, asking him the same questions he had been asked in Vienna.

"*Ja, ja, ja,*" answered Günther impatiently. "But how long do you calculate I can hang on?"

"You should be in the hospital this very minute, Mr. Winter, sir. There is not a moment to lose."

"*Nein!* I am not leaving zees bunker. Just tell me how long you tink I have?"

"As I said, you really should be receiving hospital care. I cannot give you a time table, but you are in crisis mode, believe me. We've got to get you to a respirator, among other things."

"I may need a respirator but *vere* I have it ist my choice.

Dr. Harris gave up. He made an urgent call to the hospital's ER and after a few minutes was assured that oxygen, intravenous tubing, and a heart monitor were on their way, along with two medics.

By mid-morning Günther was in stable condition, although his jaundice had become more prominent. Dismissing the medical personnel, he once again put on his blue caftan and went down to his Klimt basement to rest and meditate in front of the three artworks set side by side in the mahogany panel that took up the length of one long wall. *Theology* was hung on the opposite wall.

Feeling calmer, and with the new strength gained from being on oxygen overnight and from being with his Klimts, he went upstairs and called Eddie to contact his three guests with a new invitation to come right over. Eddie did so.

As the trio followed Eddie to the annex they looked at each other apprehensively. What was the fanatic up to now?

* * *

Peter Ucicky had checked every floor of the Hotel Alpenglow, including its conference rooms. There was no place for a Klimt collection. He walked slowly around the exterior of the hotel, scrutinizing the four wings with their towers. One of the wings at the rear of the hotel ended just a few feet from what looked like an auxiliary building, a two-story annex of sorts. With windows only on the top floor, it gave the impression of a bunker. Ah! A perfect place to store his grandfather's ill-gotten art.

Working himself up to a perfect fit of righteous indignation, he moved toward the annex, past a large Alpenglow van, then slipped behind a tree at the sound of hotel guests walking his way.

* * *

They were surprised by the relative enthusiasm with which they were received this time by Winter. He was clad, to their silent shock and wonder, in his blue Klimtian caftan. Winter/Klimt led the way down to the basement and showed them, along with Eddie, into the large room where the Klimt artworks were. Both long walls had floor-to-ceiling curtains drawn across them. Günther drew their attention to the right side wall of the room and drew open the curtains.

There, gratifyingly present to the three Klimt lovers, was the great University panel *Theology*. No damage, Megan noted. It looked just as it had looked at Asta's home in Ascona. Winter gave them time to take it in then announced: "Vhat you are about to see surpasses even zis vork."

They turned around and faced the opposite curtained wall. Günther pressed the remote control in his hand and the curtains parted in the middle. The Secretum was revealed.

Renata and Lyonel gasped. Unlike Megan, they had not seen it in the original, only in those color photographs Winter had sent to the Moderne Galerie. They could only marvel at the execution, content, and scale of the colorful allegorical work with its corporeal kiss. The features of Adele and Gustav were easily recognizable and seemed to defy the beholders.

Lyonel admitted to himself that it was indeed a spectacular conception, linking attributes from all four of the University panels below, around, and above the kissing nude couple. And certainly it confirmed all rumors that there had been a love relationship between the painter and his model. But *he*, Lyonel Retter, had the model, and his Adele far exceeded, at least for him, any revelatory confession in Winter's panel.

Some five minutes elapsed without a spoken word. Suddenly Günther pressed the remote in his hand again and the curtain on the right pulled back completely to reveal a canvas and white frame exactly the same as the Moderne's Adele. The person portrayed was Adele. Adele in exactly the same pose, dress, and chair as in Lyonel's Adele. Even the gold background was the same.

But it was executed in gouache, not oil.

"Zis ist my ersatz Adele," Winter fervently admitted. "She has lived vit me a long time." His tone became more urgent: "But now I vill und must have zee real ting."

No one spoke. A poignant silence prevailed.

"Und now I shall show you vhy zee real Adele belongs only here."

Günther touched his remote again. The left curtain drew back to reveal an unbelievable sight.

It was a Self-Portrait by Klimt!

* * *

Joe Seguire and his two police companions had landed in Anchorage an hour earlier. They rented a car and fifty minutes later pulled up to the Alpenglow parking lot in front of the hotel.

"Now the scanner is showing that Retter is not in the hotel proper but in a building right behind it to the left," Joe reported, studying the screen of his iPad.

"Do you think we should barnstorm the place?" asked one of his friends.

"Let me watch for movement a bit more and then we'll make our decision. In the meantime let's drive around to the back and park as close as possible to the building. It seems to be an annex of some sort."

"Fuck!" said the other policeman, ogling the heavy, double-door entrance to the annex as they drove up. "That's going to take some heavy metal to get in there."

"Well, that's just what I have," replied Joe, who hated the word "fuck" everyone seemed to use in every sentence nowadays. He opened up his

backpack. Drawing out three fragmentation hand grenades he dangled
them in front of his approving friends.

"*These should blast through any door.*"

* * *

Seguire's actions had been observed by Peter Ucicky, who was still
hidden behind his tree. After previously watching one man and two women
enter the annex, he had started to make for the building, but at that moment
a car out of nowhere appeared around the corner of the hotel heading for
the annex, causing Ucicky to hurry back to his tree. If they blast that door
open, he thought to himself, I'll be right behind them. It would be great to
confront Winter in his own lair.

* * *

"But Klimt never *painted* a self-portrait!" remonstrated Megan in
total disbelief.

"He even *said* that there was no self-portrait of him. That he was
more interested in others, in *women*, than in himself," Renata confirmed
challengingly.

I simply cannot believe it!" Lyonel seemed frozen to the spot.

An expression of total bliss came over the features of the gaunt monk
in Klimtian caftan.

"Now you understand vhy Adele *must* live here und not in New York
or Wien.

The three hostages continued to stare at the painting, and painting it
was. One could see the oil pigment even from a distance. The astonishing
thing about this portrait, however, was how it constituted an exact mirror of
the Adele portrait. Gustav sat in an identical, sparsely rendered chair and
faced across the Secretum panel towards the Adele gouache. While Adele
stared out at the viewer, Klimt had depicted himself in profile view, holding
a cat and looking across the naked kiss of the center panel to Adele. He
was seated to the left of the canvas, balancing Adele who took up the right
half of her space. The same gold fill that permeated the void in the Adele
portrait was present in the Gustav canvas.

Even the gold saturation of Klimt's caftan, no longer blue but
gold, emulated the fill of Adele's dress. In both portraits the glimmering,

jewel-like intensity prevailed with its mosaic filling and Byzantine crowdedness. Emblems such as the repeated Egyptian eye-triangle and Mycenaean swirl were even foreshortened in articulation of the armchair definition. The taut contrast between the plasticity of the pale faces and the two-dimensionality of the ornamental surround owed its pungency to a tension between realism and microscopic detail. There was the same inclusion of a green carpet square at the end of the canvas, this time on the far right.

"It is a genuine Klimt, there is no doubt," whispered Megan to Lyonel and Renata.

"And it's worth well over two hundred million, I would guess," Lyonel whispered back.

They stepped back again to take in the whole. The three artworks glistened under the overhead light and the compositional statement made by the ensemble, with Gustav and Adele on either side anchoring down the allegorical image with its embracing nude kiss, was absolutely stunning.

"Stunning, ist it not?" asked Winter, as if reading their thoughts.

They could not help but agree. They dared not ask the question burning in their minds: from where and how did Winter come by such an unknown find?

But they were not to know the answer. Suddenly Winter wheeled toward them, closing the curtains again with his remote.

"*Now it ist your turn! Give me zee keys to zose padlocks on Adele.*"

* * *

"Okay, *now!*" Joe had commanded when he saw the scanner lose contact, after Lyonel and his visitors descended into the annex cellar. Silently the three men left the car and eased up to the double doors in front. They checked them out. The doors were closed and apparently barred on the inside. Cautiously, the men moved back six paces. Joe took the three hand grenades and gave one to each of the police officers, retaining one for himself.

"On the count of three," he whispered.

"*One, two,...*"

* * *

Günther Winter pulled out his just-oiled Springfield and repeated his demand: "Give me zee keys to Adele's padlocks."

"I'm afraid they're back at the hotel," Lyonel replied evenly.

"Zee hell zey are!" Günther shouted in exasperation. Pointing his pistol at Megan, he threatened: "I vill shoot Megan, zen I vill shoot Renata, if you do not produce zose keys!"

He cocked the hammer, and, aiming the pistol point blank at Megan, he began to count.

"*One, two,...*"

* * *

"*...three!*" shouted Joe Seguire as he and his men simultaneously threw their grenades at the annex doors, which blew apart. They rushed in, sighted the open basement door, and, revolvers drawn, bolted down the stairs.

"*...three!*" hissed Günther, firing his pistol at Megan just as the sound of an explosion reached their ears. But the bullet did not hit its target.

It rammed into Eddie, who at the last second had lunged forward to wrest the pistol from his obviously insane employer. The bullet meant for Megan hit him in the shoulder. He lay on the floor spasmodically jerking from his wound.

Megan rushed over to him, hoping the man who saved her life had not sacrificed his own. She cradled Eddie's head in her lap. Renata joined her, attempting to staunch the blood coming from the bullet hole in his shoulder. Too far from the madman to try to wrest the pistol away from him, Lyonel moved to shield the women and the wounded man on the floor.

The single gun shot was still echoing in the basement chamber as three men, led by Joe, burst into the room.

Günther turned toward them, aimed his pistol at them, then in one swift movement turned it upon himself, placing the gun directly at his heart. He died immediately, his lusterless eyes fixed on the Adele crate.

As the group stared in shock at Winter's bleeding body, the clatter of hurried footsteps sounded on the staircase. Turning around they saw a stocky man in his early sixties burst into the room.

"*Which one of you is Winter?*" he yelled, eyeing Lyonel accusingly. In silent answer Lyonel pointed to the corpse on the floor. Peter Ucicky glanced in disbelief from Winter's body to Lyonel and back. Next to the inert body was another man on the floor. He was writhing in pain while two woman tried to comfort him.

"What the *hell* is going on here?" Peter exclaimed.

"Who the hell are *you*?" challenged Lyonel.

"I am Peter Ucicky, *the grandson of Gustav Klimt!*"

"Why are you *here*?" Lyonel demanded.

Peter looked quickly around the room and saw four large artworks that had to be by Klimt. Three of the paintings were unknown to him. The fourth looked amazingly like the famous Adele Bloch-Bauer portrait of which he had seen so many reproductions.

"As Klimt's grandson, I am here to claim these artworks."

There was a moment of silence.

"Well this is a fine time to be doing that, considering all that's just happened here," said Megan, staring at the man in a mixture of disbelief and indignation.

"And how do we know you're Peter Ucicky?" quizzed Renata.

Ucicky pulled out his passport, opened it to his photograph, and waved it in Lyonel's face. Agitatedly, he declared that he had been on the track of Günther Winter and the Leatherer legacy for months. "And now I find him—*dead!*"

Joe Seguire and his men, with guns still raised, looked questioningly at Lyonel Retter, who gestured to them to stand down.

Soothingly, Lyonel said: "Your claim might get to court, Mr. Ucicky, if you truly are Klimt's grandson, *and* if you have the time and financial means to contest ownership of these works. But be prepared for years of litigation."

Lyonel was already calculating how much he would have to pay this desperado claimant to the Klimt *Self-Portrait*. Never mind about the Secretum, which out of respect for his Adele, he would never show in his museum.

Looking up from where she sat on the floor with Eddie, Megan observed that not only was the man's physique like Klimt's, but also his wide eyes and deeply furrowed forehead. Even his balding pate with the tuft of hair in front was like his grandfather's.

She was convinced that he was, as he claimed, Klimt's grandson. So were Renata and Lyonel.

Lyonel took the reins. "Your claim, Mr. Ucicky, of being the legitimate owner of these Klimt works is riddled with complications. The work to your right, *Theology*, belongs to the Holm-Ditlevsen estate and the work to your left, Secretum, was legally sold by the art dealer Jeremy Herring to Winter. The image of Adele next to it is only a copy in gouache. An excellent one, but nevertheless merely a copy. Mr. Ucicky, the only work that you, as a bloodline descendant of the artist might have clear title to, is this canvas," said Lyonel pointing to Klimt's *Self-Portrait*. And that would only be if any applicable statute of limitations has not expired *and* if a suspect provenance could be proved. But claiming it would likely be a very long, drawn-out legal affair."

Thinking of his already massive legal debts, Ucicky felt suddenly helpless. He fixed a pleading look at this American man who seemed to be so conversant with the law and with Klimt artworks.

Lyonel expanded upon the ownership complications to the eagerly listening group. Then, calmly turning to a distressed Peter Ucicky and speaking in a low voice audible only to the trembling man, he proposed: "There is a short cut. I paid one hundred thirty-five million for the Adele portrait. *I am prepared to pay double the sum to you for your grandfather's Self-Portrait.*"

It was an offer not even a Klimt grandson could turn down.

Lyonel immediately issued directions to Seguire and his two capable cohorts to remove the Klimt *Self-Portrait* and load it in the Alpenglow van, parked to the side of Winter's bunker. This done, he had Seguire telephone the Girdwood police to come to the crime scene.

While they waited, Peter Ucicky, perplexed by his grandfather's two large panels and their complex iconography, examined the artworks with exasperated incomprehension. Never mind. He would now be a wealthy man, thanks to Lyonel Retter.

"If I win my case," he announced to the group grandly, "I shall allow the Belvedere to buy the two panels, this one *Theology*, and," pointing to the

Secretum, "what should we call that one? A strip tease version of *The Kiss*, I guess."

After the police had taken their statements and an ambulance called for the wounded Eddie, the group was free to leave. Safely back in his Alpenglow hotel room Ucicky immediately telephoned his wife to tell her all their financial troubles were over. He had a signed trade transaction in hand and would be flying home just as soon as he could get reservations.

* * *

The flight back to New York on Lyonel's cargo jet contained five passengers: Lyonel, Renata, Megan, and Joe Seguire's two police friends. Joe himself had stayed behind to aid the Girdwood police in their investigation of Günther Winter's suicide. At Megan's urging the police had not preferred charges against Eddie. In the cargo bay was a single crate holding its precious cargo, Klimt's *Self-Portrait*.

* * *

Back in New York, Lyonel and Renata decided that they would hang the extraordinary image of the artist on the west wall adjoining and facing the Adele wall of the Moderne Galerie.

The newspaper accolades concerning the "new Klimt at the Moderne Galerie" were unanimous.

After lecturing for the museum on the "reunited" Klimt pair, Megan at last returned to Dallas. Tina and Claire were there at the airport to greet her. Claire held an ecstatic Button in her arms. Megan doubted that she would visit Vienna again any time soon. She would return to writing her *The Mahler Murders* mystery.

But life sometimes follows art.

The discovery and then theft of a completely orchestrated score to what seemed to be an eleventh symphony by Gustav Mahler soon called her back to the homicidal homeland of the two Gustavs.

Button would not be left behind this time.

Readers Guide

1. The Viennese artist Gustav Klimt (1862–1918) is considered Austria's greatest painter of Art Nouveau. His elegant society portraits were created for the upper crust of the city's nouveau riche and were in constant demand. And yet his enigmatic, nontraditional allegories *Philosophy*, *Medicine*, and *Jurisprudence*, painted for the University of Vienna's Great Hall ceiling, were attacked in the press as "pornography" and "perverted excess." Their aura of pessimism and the nakedness of their floating protagonists/victims incensed the University professors and the public alike. So much so that Klimt bought them back from the state. Were viewers of the panels right to be outraged? Was there a message in the allegories that signaled a new age? Did the growing conceit of Social Darwinism play a role? In May of 1945 all three paintings were set on fire by retreating Nazi forces. Or were they?

2. The opening paragraphs of *Killing for Klimt* introduce the book's main protagonist, Megan Crespi, still agile and engaged at seventy-seven. She is a professor of art history *emerita* and a world expert on Viennese art and music, especially Gustav Klimt and Gustav Mahler. Megan and her best friend, Claire Chandler, come upon the corpse of one of their neighbors as they arrive at the latter's summer house outside Santa Fe. Could the neighbor, who conscientiously waters the geraniums every week when Claire is away, have slipped and suffered a fatal fall? Or had the woman been murdered? Could the killing have been intended for Claire, the house owner, or perhaps even for Megan?

3. The scene changes to Megan's recent visit to Vienna, where she hears the deathbed ramblings of Klimt's grandnephew concerning a "secret and shameful" panel—the Secretum. It had been stolen from the artist's basement just one night after his death. Is Megan right to think the panel might have been the fourth University ceiling painting, *Theology*, initially begun by Klimt's colleague, but completed by him? Do we know yet what it represented? Could

it have been a portrait? Perhaps a nude portrait? Or an allegory? Will this be important to the plot?

4. We meet Jeremy Herring, the American art dealer who ever since the end of World War II has lived in Vienna conducting extremely shady business deals. His major client is an equally immoral character, the billionaire Günther Winter. He is a fanatical fan of the painter Friedrich Hundertwasser. But he is also a secret collector of Klimt, works by whom he has in his bunker-like annex to the Alpenglow hotel he owns in Girdwood, Alaska. Is Winter right to keep his passion for Klimt a secret? What are his business dealings with Jeremy Herring? We learn that Winter and Crespi became acquainted on a cruise to Antarctica which they both happened to take two years earlier. And they like each other. Can their friendship endure the barrage of riveting new discoveries in the Klimt world? Do they become competitors? Is it possible that Winter will become a threat to Megan?

5. Winter has invited Megan and Claire to visit him at his Alaska hotel. When they take the aerial tram to the top of Mount Alyeska a terrible accident occurs on the viewing platform where a man bumps into Megan and catapults over the railing. Was this an accident?

6. There has been a break-in and vandalism at New York's famous Moderne Galerie Museum for German and Austrian Art. The priceless (well, $135 m!) portrait of Adele Bloch-Bauer has been attacked. Do we have any suspicions concerning who the vandal might have been? Why is Megan brought in on the case and can she be of help? What is the meaning of the mysterious *Kurrentschrift* note left at the crime scene: "Want to trade your Klimt whore for the Secretum?" Do the museum director, Renata Teuer, and the museum cofounder, Lyonel Retter, have any light to shed on the subject? How do they proceed? What is their response to the *Kurrentschrift* note? Will they or won't they consider trading the Adele portrait for an unknown Secretum? Why is Megan being followed?

7. Several chapters find Megan at the Swiss home of the reclusive Danish collector Asta Holm-Ditlevsen. Does she have Klimt's reworking of *Theology*? How do the two women get along? What do they have in common? Might

their friendship be dangerous for both? Why do they travel to Helsinki together? And who is Monika Straus, the enigmatic woman who enters their lives in the café at the Ateneum Museum? What has she done to earn their gratitude and friendship? Are they right to trust her?

8. Megan flies to Paris to visit her dear friend, the Gustav Mahler expert, Henri-Claude de La Granger, where she is suddenly bitten by his dog. What happens when Megan is rushed to a nearby medical clinic? What are her symptoms? Do they suggest something other than a dog bite? How serious is Megan's condition? Should her suspicions be raised at this point in her Klimt pursuit? Has she been perhaps too naïve concerning the surprising things that have recently happened to her?

9. Many of the book's characters have German names. A few are French names, one is Italian. Is there a humorous Dickensian theme evidenced in these foreign monikers?

10. The gay couple Jacques LePingre and Jean-Jean Jolie are introduced into the story line as having something of interest pertaining to Klimt to show Megan. Is she shown everything by them? Does LePingre's effort to sell Klimt drawings in person to Dr. Klug of the Nebehay Antiquariat in Vienna backfire? In what portentous way?

11. Music plays a key role throughout the narrative, from classical to folk. Why is this so? How does it advance the plot? Who are the characters to whom music is so important? Why do the words of one Viennese Heurigen song have special significance?

12. The city of Leipzig is the key destination for one of the book's villains, Thad Herring, son of Jeremy Herring. Why is he sent there by his father and is his mission accomplished? How would this benefit Jeremy?

13. One of the recurring motifs in *Killing for Klimt* is Nazi confiscation and dispersion of art held by Jewish owners during and after World War II. How did Klimt's *Theology* panel allude to contemporary Jewish history in his own day and age?

14. Toward the end of the book Vienna's huge Central Cemetery is the setting for one particularly ghoulish scene. In what surprising section of the cemetery does it take place? Who is the perpetrator and who are the victims? Do they deserve what happens to them?

15. *Killing for Klimt's* final scenes take place in Girdwood, Alaska, at Winter's Alpenglow hotel annex. Why has he commanded Megan, Renata, and Lyonel to join him there? Why do they agree? When they are taken down to his annex cellar what is the amazing sight that greets their eyes? How does the character of Winter disintegrate before them? Is Peter Ucicky really the grandson of Klimt? What constitutes the denouement of the narrative? Is it a surprising and satisfying conclusion?

16. Is Megan likely to embark on another Viennese adventure? If so whom will it concern and will the topic engage the reader?

CPSIA information can be obtained
at www.ICGtesting.com
Printed in the USA
FFOW04n0937081214
9248FF